Throne of Dreams

The Faeven Saga
Book 2

Hillary Raymer

To Heather, for everything

Trigger Warnings

- Sexually explicit content
- Death
- PTSD induced panic & anxiety attacks
- Emotional trauma
- Graphic violence
- Attempted sexual assault
- Grief
- Sexual themes throughout
- Kidnapping
- Blood

*"In the before, there was light
No darkness, no night
But nothing is ever as it seems.
The faerie queen, she waits
In the dawn, with the fates
To reclaim her once throne of dreams."*

~Tiernan Velless, High King of the Summer Court

Chapter One

S oft sand squished between Maeve's toes as she stood alone on the beach.

Except she wasn't truly alone. She knew Lir, the fae warrior now sworn to protect her, stood within the shadows of the palm trees and towering palace walls. He was always there with her, watching and keeping a steady eye. She'd grown accustomed to his presence and sensed whenever he was near. His scent lingered; citrus and something woodsy. Even now, he stood far enough away from her so as not to intrude upon her privacy. He stood where the sparse seagrass met the rocky cliffside, where the play of sunlight and shadow kept him just out of view.

The summer breeze whipped through her long, unbound hair, tossing the golden pink strands. Her dress of simple lavender satin clung to her waist and hips, but billowed around her ankles while she slowly padded away from the shoreline, leaving damp footprints in her wake. To the west, the Lismore Marin spread out like a vast wash of turquoise watercolors, dotted with frothy white foam, sparkling like thousands of diamonds. The sea was calm this morning, much like the rest of Faeven. Yet a sense of restlessness, of unease, seemed to lurk just beneath the surface.

Three weeks had passed since Rowan died for her. Since Casimir betrayed her. The sting of both wounds to her heart still cut deep. Three weeks and she didn't know if Saoirse lived. She didn't know what had become of the Furies, the monstrous brothers she'd brought back from the dead. The last time she saw them, they were snapping the bodies of Carman's guards in half like they were bowing oak trees weighed down by the first heavy snow. Recalling the sounds of it sent a shudder down her spine.

And Carman, the sorceress who raised her, was dead. Maeve had fulfilled her vow to herself and killed her. When she closed her eyes, she could see the way Carman's crimson blood mixed with rainwater on the balustrade, forming a river of red. She shook away the memory, ignoring the haunting of her past.

She walked along the coast, her gaze darting around her. She was in Faeven now, in the Summer Court. There had been no dark fae attacks, no rumblings of unrest, and not a whisper of schemes or plotted assaults. But Maeve wasn't a fool.

War with Parisa was coming.

But for now, she would accept the small slice of peace she'd been granted. No matter how temporary.

Maeve continued to stroll down the vacant stretch of beach. This was often where Tiernan would bring her to train, where she could practice controlling the wild magic inside her. For her entire life, she'd been raised to hate the fae. They were the enemy. Always.

Now she was one of them. The reality of it left a fog of harbored doubt in the back of her mind. For years she'd worn silver cuffs crafted by Carman that smothered her magic, leaving her weak. With them removed, that same magic flowed freely inside of her, wild and unencumbered. Fire and smoke, both gifts from her true mother, High Queen Fianna, had come naturally to her. But her more innate power, that of the *anam ó Danua*, was proving more difficult to wield. Creation, or soul magic as others called it, had become nothing more than a thorn in her side. The intensity of it was overwhelming. Daunting.

Tiernan constantly pressured her to draw on her power, to dominate it. But knowing she had the ability to bestow magic, to create life, to create anything...the magnitude of it was enough to keep her locked inside her bedroom for a full day after calling upon it once.

Soul magic stole her breath. Filled her with life. Terrified her.

Whenever Tiernan tested her, she panicked. She didn't know what to create to protect herself. He didn't train her with a sword or bows and arrows. She was allowed to keep her Aurastone on her at all times. The blade wielded its own kind of power. But other than that, he instructed her to use nothing but her own magic as self-defense.

The High King of Summer was irritating in the worst way possible, but she was indebted to him. He covered her scars with shimmery, rose gold tattoos that glided over her skin like satin. He kept her safe within the walls of his Court, protecting her from those who wished her harm. Loathing him wasn't easy when he always ensured she remained alive.

She neared the end of the beach, where the large stone statue of a kneeling fae warrior protruded from the top of a rugged hill covered in overgrowth and bright wildflowers. She'd seen him from a distance when she first arrived in Niahvess, and up close, she realized he was truly colossal. Carved from quartz and granite, the fae warrior bowed in silent protection of the Summer Court, with his head bent over the hilt of his sword, an oath of never-ending allegiance. She wondered how long he'd been there if the statue predated even the High King himself.

For a moment, she considered calling out to Lir and asking, but a flicker of something caught the corner of her eye.

A faint sheen encased this area of the beach like someone had draped a gossamer blanket upon it, glimmering with deception. The moss covering the rocky hill looked too green, each wildflower too perfect. The vision before her seemed to shift with each blink, beckoning her closer.

Glamour.

The word reverberated inside of her, and she knew it to be true. Something was hidden beyond this conglomerate of rock and plants. Whatever it was, someone meant to keep it concealed within plain sight and kept away from prying eyes.

She approached the glamour and hesitated. It could be nothing. Or it could be everything. Goosebumps pebbled across her flesh. An unnatural energy charged the air. Relying only on her instinct, she placed one hand before her, braced for impact, and stepped through the glamour.

Magic caressed her skin, swept over her shoulders, and brushed her cheek with the touch of a practiced lover. Colors blended and swirled around her as she moved further in. Another step and she was free from the glamour, standing in what she could only describe as a lagoon.

Cavernous walls of reddish-brown rock climbed up on all sides, and an alcove overhead allowed brilliant rays of sunlight to pour in, washing the sandy beach before her in ribbons of gold. The sea kissed the shore in long, sweeping lengths, and tiny white flowers bloomed along the water's edge, where the tide reached its highest point. Moss hung from the arched ceiling in patterns of green lace. This beach was a glimpse of seclusion, of pure paradise.

No wonder someone wanted it kept a secret.

Maeve inched closer to where the ripples of water barely seemed to crest. This wasn't some roaring, terrifying ocean. The water was languid, calm, and decently shallow. Carefully, she lifted her dress over her head and laid it across a large, gray rock. Save for her Auras-tone, she wore nothing but the necklace Tiernan and his twin sister, Ceridwen, made for her. It was a decadent opal with a beautiful amethyst on top, all wrapped in gold. She supposed it was meant to give her some comfort, knowing they could sense her emotions and come to her if she was in trouble, but she considered it more of a tracking device than a gift. The old Maeve might've yanked it from her neck and tossed it off the cliffs, but she wasn't the same as she was three weeks ago.

She knew the dangers of Faeven firsthand, and though she may have been more reckless and ready to die when she first arrived in the fae realm, now she wasn't so sure. Shaking off the anxiety, Maeve waded into the gentle waters, naked and blessedly alone.

The sea was blissfully cool and a dazzling shade of teal. She went further until she reached the lagoon's deepest point, just below her belly, and the memory of the last time she'd stepped naked into a pool of water rushed over her. Images slammed into her mind, happening so quickly she was left gasping for air. She'd been alone with Rowan, deep within the Summer forest, and he'd brought her to a faerie pool where the sounds of a waterfall were musical, and the overhang of trees shaded them from the sun. It was there he'd helped her to fight through her fear of drowning. Now whenever she saw the ocean, whenever she faced the horizon where the sky met the sea, she thought of him.

Pain lanced its way through her at the memory.

She thought about the way he kissed her, about the way he touched her, vividly remembering the feel of his lips against her throat and the way his calloused palms slid over her thighs. She wouldn't mind if those were the types of dreams she had when she tried to sleep at night. But sweet, tempting memories evaded her when darkness fell. Instead, the look on his face as sword after sword punctured his body haunted her. Maeve still felt the wet grass on her back as she cowered against the faerie hill while he covered her body with his own. She still saw the glint of the swords in the moonlight as they pierced his chest and wings, brutalizing his body. She still smelled his blood permeating the air as the strength faded from his lavender eyes.

He'd known all along that he would die for her. He'd told her as much.

"You'll be the death of me."

She hadn't believed him.

Maeve held her breath and dunked herself beneath the water's shallow surface. Below, everything was muffled. Her thoughts. Her heartbeat. All of it yielded to the stillness of the lagoon and the vast and absolute nothingness of the sea. When she resurfaced, she stole one greedy, gulping breath, and eased onto her back to float. The water sifted around her and below her, lifting her like she was weightless. A feather among the waves.

She was safe here. These waters weren't the torrential ocean that pummeled her with fear. There were no angry waves threatening to swallow her, trying to drown her. No, this cove brought a kind of familiarity to her, reminding her of a place that was once her haven—the hidden lake in the Moors. Overhead, sunlight sprinkled in through the gaping opening of the cavern's ceiling, reflecting rainbows off the timeworn walls.

The beauty and simplicity of it gave Maeve an idea.

She stood and shoved her wet hair back from her face. Peering up at the alcove, she followed the stream of sunshine to where it cast the ripples of water around her in gold. She wanted to capture this moment, she wanted to hold the beauty of the sun against the water in her hands. Closing her eyes, she reached for her magic, for the power she knew flowed through her. It hummed in acknowledgment, a teasing response to her effort. It was right there, just below the surface. A well of magic, a pull of creation, waiting to be touched.

Focused on what she wanted to create, Maeve stretched out her hand so the beams of sunlight wove between her fingers. Trembling, she sucked in a breath and pulled on that power. Her magic sang, bold and reckless, as she molded the luminescence into a golden chain. Warmth exploded inside her and spread to the tips of her fingers. Another breath shuddered from the tight walls of her chest as the magic of creation continued to flow. The tattoos covering her body glowed and shimmered, and she basked in their beauty. Vibrations pulsed through her, so intense her hair lifted from her back and spread out around her like a fan. She bent the radiant light to her will—twisting and weaving, forming it into that of twin mountain peaks, with the sun rising behind them—the crest of the Summer Court.

"You're trying too hard." A rough baritone chilled the air around her and Maeve startled, almost dropping the necklace.

"Damn it, Tiernan." Aggravation barreled into her, and she stiffened. It was one thing to be caught practicing her magic. It was something else entirely to be caught *naked*. Maeve shoved the necklace behind her back and spun around to face the High King of the Summer Court.

ONE LOOK at Maeve and Tiernan almost died.

Fuck, he *wanted* to die.

He sensed the alarm for his ward around the cove had been triggered, but before he could even respond to it, Lir arrived in a panic, claiming Maeve had vanished from sight. One moment she'd been directly in front of him, then he blinked, and she was gone.

Obviously, she'd been the one to set off the alarm, but what Tiernan couldn't figure out was *how*. By all rights and rules of magic, she shouldn't have been able to see through the glamour he cast around the cove. And she definitely shouldn't have been able to walk right through it as though it didn't exist. Yet there she was, standing waist deep in the sea of his personal beach, looking like a fucking goddess.

Ribbons of wet, golden pink hair fell over her shoulders and almost completely covered her breasts. Almost. Between the damp curls, he could just see her nipples and the supple swells of her breasts. It took every ounce of his self-control to force himself to meet her gaze. He didn't want to be caught staring at the curve of her waist or the flare of her hips. Besides, he'd seen her naked before. Twice, actually. Once when he'd bathed her after she nearly died from being poisoned by a dark fae. And the second time...his blood caught fire just thinking about it. Maeve's body, once mutilated by Fearghal, the prick of a fae who'd tortured her in the dungeon of the Spring Court, was now covered in rose gold tattoos—tattoos she'd allowed him to paint on her to disguise the scarring left behind.

Tiernan swore under his breath.

The next chance he got, he'd kill the fucking bastard.

Now, Maeve faced him and those sea-swept eyes of hers were focused on his every move. She'd tucked her hands behind her back and probably thought he hadn't just seen her create a necklace in the shape of his Court's crest out of nothing more than sunlight and magic. But he'd stood among the shadows of the cave so as not to disturb her. He'd considered calling out and announcing his presence, but then her expression changed, and he knew she'd tapped into the soul magic of the goddess Danua. The power of creation. And he'd never seen anything more mesmerizing, more intoxicating, than *her*.

He strolled forward. Lackadaisical. Carefree. The same way he always did when he wanted to piss her off. "What'd you make?"

"Just a necklace." Her brows knitted together. She held it out to show him. The chain clinked together, twinkling between her fingers. The mountains and rising sun had never looked more beautiful than they did in her hands.

Tiernan nodded. "It's nice."

A sigh escaped her, and she rolled her eyes to where sunshine peeked in through the alcove of the cavern. She was pretty when she was angry. And right now, she was *furious*. She was mad he'd discovered her and annoyed that he'd found her naked. He kept his lips pressed firmly together to keep from grinning. He could hear her thoughts like they were his own, a whirlwind through his mind, and though he didn't dare point it out, she may as well have been screaming at him.

Maeve shook her head. "It's just a necklace."

She tossed it toward the shoreline. He snatched it out of the air, then carefully tucked it into the pocket of his pants while she stared at him, wary. Always wary. She never quite trusted him; he'd have to work on that.

Maeve's hands trailed through the water, back and forth. "It's useless. It won't help me defeat an army of dark fae. Or kill Parisa." She gestured to the space around them. "Or protect my home."

She paused and his heart thundered, but he kept his face neutral. His expression remained a cool mask of indifference. But she'd said the word *home*. She'd described the Summer Court, *his* Court, as home.

"Niahvess, that is." She refused to look at him.

Tiernan took her disregard in stride. "Perhaps not, but you're taking steps in the right direction. You can't learn how to save the world in a day." He smoothed down the front of his shirt with his hands and she stiffened. "You're not me."

Her eyes turned frosty. "Not yet."

He smirked, the same dismissive smile he knew irritated and riled her up more than anything else. "You are in control of your magic. It doesn't control you."

Maeve crossed her arms, and he ignored the way the movement lifted her cleavage into full view. Her chin lifted, just slightly. "I know that."

He mimicked her stance. "Then prove it."

Goddess above, her thoughts were *loud*. And all over the place. She was trying to call upon her magic like it was a pet, like she was begging it to do her bidding, instead of commanding it. Her mind raced with ideas, with possibilities, but she didn't know what she wanted. Her focus was lost. She whispered and pleaded, but the magic remained just out of her reach.

Tiernan shook his head and ran a hand through his dark hair. "You're thinking too much about creating something instead of just calling it to you."

"I know that, too." She scowled and her full lips turned downward into a pout. The necklace she wore radiated with vexation.

He rocked back onto his heels in the soft sand and grinned. "Then what are you going to do about it?"

"Practice," she bit the word off. "It's not like there's a book on the magic of creation."

"You could write one," he countered.

Her mouth fell open. A look passed over her face, one he'd never seen before. He'd never been witness to an actual smile or her laughter. No, he'd seen her worst. Her tears. Her death glares. Her fear. But this one, this look was one of wonder, and it nearly stole his breath straight from his chest.

She held his gaze for a moment longer, then finally looked away. It was a game they often played.

He always won.

"Maeve." She looked over at him, cautious. Good. "Catch."

Purple bolts exploded from the tips of his fingers and headed straight for her. Thunder cracked overhead, and the skies turned a menacing shade of gray. He threw his magic at her, slammed her with his power, and though she stood firm, she didn't fight back. Maeve ducked under the water to avoid him and surfaced seconds later, sputtering. Again, he struck out at her. Wind collided into both of them, howling through the curved walls of the cavern like a lone wolf. Small waves thrashed around her while another round of violet lightning streaked across the space between them.

This time he met his mark. And though the strength of his magic barely grazed her shoulder, she hissed in pain. Just knowing he hurt her was the rawest form of torture. Maeve, High Princess of the Autumn Court, was quite possibly the most stubborn female he had ever met.

"Attack me," Tiernan growled.

She shoved her wet hair out of her eyes and glared at him. "If you'd just give me a minute to think, then I could—"

"No." Tiernan fired again. Harder and faster. "Fight."

Maeve yelped as another bolt skimmed above her head. "I don't know what to do!"

Panic. Icy tendrils of dread froze him from the inside out. Except he wasn't the one on the brink of hysteria. It was Maeve. His gaze dipped to the necklace hanging between her breasts. Her nipples hardened beneath the heat of his gaze, and damn if his cock didn't jump in response. Fucking gods, she was infuriating.

Thunder shook the ground beneath his feet and violet bolts rained down upon her. "Stop thinking and start doing!"

He attacked once more and this time she blocked with fire. Flaming orbs pulsed through the air as they raced toward him. Glowing streaks of angry orange and fiery red singed his skin, burning past him to the walls beyond. The heat was so intense, his knees almost buckled. Beads of sweat slid from his forehead to his jaw. He blew out a breath and stared the Autumn beauty down. She was far more dangerous than she knew.

"Good," he called out, ready to bring his storm down upon her.

But Maeve threw her hands up on either side of her and a shimmering, pearlescent bubble-like shield surrounded her.

Tiernan bit the inside of his cheek to keep from smiling. "Cute."

She gave him the finger and every tense, tightly wound muscle in his body went on high alert. If she only knew. Goddess above, if she only *knew*. Intent on infuriating her even more, Tiernan yanked off his shirt and tossed it aside. Her gaze devoured him; it stole across his arms, chest, abdomen, and lower still. No doubt she could see the hard line of his cock straining against his pants. He unhooked the Astralstone, the twin to her Aurastone, and gently laid it upon the sand. Its twilight hues sparked with the brilliance of midsummer stars. Then, just because he loved to watch her squirm, he unbuckled his pants and kicked them to the side.

Her gasp was entirely too good for his ego.

"Something bothering you, Your Highness?" he asked and sauntered into the cool water.

A pretty blush stained her cheeks, but she refused to look away. In fact, when her eyes blatantly dropped to his erection, her brow quirked and her chin jutted out defiantly.

"Well, now I know what kind of effect I have on *you*."

Tiernan made a sort of tsking noise. "On the contrary, I find fighting to be extremely arousing."

"You would." She rolled her eyes but kept her arms out, ensuring her little bubble of protection held. He drifted closer and the shield wavered. "What are you doing?"

"Cooling off." He pointed to the scorch marks on the wall of the cavern behind him. "You almost set me on fire."

Deciding he'd had enough small talk, he dove under the water and relished in the way it calmed his raging desire to kiss that smart little mouth of hers. He moved through the lagoon with ease, bringing himself closer and closer to her. Without warning, Maeve's panic crawled along his skin again. It scraped against his mind and ripped through his thoughts. She thought he was going to drown. She was afraid for him, and her fear heightened with every second he remained underwater. For a female who loved nothing more than to antagonize him to the fullest extent possible, she was a riveting complexity when it came to her actual feelings toward him.

He popped up through the surface, just on the inside of her pearly bubble.

Maeve yelped.

Tiernan smiled.

And her magic fell away.

She wrapped her arms around herself, covering her beautiful body—the one tattooed by him. There was another shift, another boil of his blood. His jaw clenched at the sight of the rose gold markings concealing her scars, and he remembered the way he'd nearly succumbed to his rage when Lir appeared with her, bleeding and broken, in his arms. He would never forget when she'd called herself a monster after Fearghal had carved her up. He wouldn't forget the single tear he'd wiped from her cheek while he'd painted the image of a rose around her breast. No, he wouldn't forget any of it.

But he *would* kill Fearghal. He'd torture him slowly and with painstaking accuracy, just as the prick had done to Maeve.

She drifted away from him, and the movement snagged his attention, drawing him back to reality.

"Where are you going?" he asked.

"Nowhere." She continued to cover herself, like he hadn't already been privy to every inch of her. "I just..."

"Just what?" Tiernan moved his hands through the water, creating small, incandescent waves. "Do I make you nervous?"

"You know you do."

Yes. He knew all too well. Still, he asked, "Why?"

Her gaze cut him down. "Why don't you listen to my thoughts and find out?"

The slight hit home. He did make a habit of doing such things. But then he shrugged and rolled her concern off his shoulders. "That's cheating."

"Like that's ever stopped you before."

He had the perfect retort on the tip of his tongue, but then her expression shifted to one of despondency. Something was making her unhappy, and the thought of it bothered him far more than necessary. The faintest line creased her brow, and he realized she wasn't looking at him, but beyond him, to a far-off place. Somewhere he wasn't invited.

"What is it?" He kept his tone gentle. Ceridwen had told him he came across as too demanding and that was likely why Maeve refused to talk to him about anything. Why she kept herself closed off from him. He seemed to think there was another reason tied into that as well, but he'd taken his twin's advice and tried to show more compassion.

Maeve looked up at him, and when she did, when those endless eyes met his, he knew he would move mountains for her.

"Can you help me find a memory keeper?"

Tiernan froze. Tension speared him, and he released a slow breath. He searched the High Princess's face for any kind of tell.

"That's a dangerous thing you ask, my lady." He carefully waded closer to her. "Why?"

"There are things I don't want to think about anymore." A cloud passed in front of the sun, and the air took on a chill. It left her in the shadows, and Maeve shivered.

Tiernan closed the distance between them in two strides. She held her breath at his approach; he heard the distinctive catch. With slow, deliberate movements, he reached out and rubbed his palms up and down her arms to warm her. She didn't flinch, but she didn't relax either.

"No memory is worth forgetting if it means bargaining with a memory keeper. You don't always get to choose which memory they take, or how much of one is left behind. Such deals require extreme vigilance and care. Most Archfae wouldn't consider entering into an agreement with a memory keeper, even if their lives depended on it."

"I understand."

"But?" Tiernan prompted.

"But I don't sleep well at night."

He knew. He took up the room next to hers after Lir returned with her from the Spring Court. He heard her cries and sensed her restlessness. She faced her demons in her sleep, and nightmares from her past haunted her.

"There are some things I'd rather forget," she continued. When the tension finally eased from her body, Tiernan let his hands fall away from her.

"Such as?"

She rubbed her lips together and his gaze dropped to her mouth. "Like all the times I was thrown into the cage and tormented as a child. All the times I was afraid."

"Those memories shaped you into who you are today. They've made you stronger. You learned to fight because of them, Maeve." He reached through the waves and just barely allowed his knuckles to graze her fingers. She didn't seem to notice, or mind for that matter.

She shook her head and strands of hair clung to her cheeks. "No. I learned to fight because Casimir taught me. Because it was necessary."

At the mention of the Drakon's name, Tiernan captured her chin and tilted her face up to his. Even after the removal of her cuffs, the top of her head barely reached his collar bone. She was rather short for a female fae, but he preferred her that way. There was nothing about her he wanted to change, other than the desire for her to let him in, to have her realize he wasn't her villain.

"No. You were *born* a warrior. You were born the High Princess of Autumn, the daughter of a fearless king and a merciful queen. And you, Maeve Ruhdneah," he used her true name, her birthright, "will never fear again."

Her damp lashes fluttered, and she lifted her eyes to him. "What if you're wrong?"

The words came out as a whisper. Soft, like the petals of the first summer rose, and he ignored the tug in his chest.

"I'm never wrong."

In one swift movement, she pulled her chin from his grasp. "It's more than just the cage. And fear. It's other things, too."

"Fearghal?"

"No," she spat, and a delightful sort of vengeance gripped her lovely features. "I want to remember him. I want to recall every vile thing he did to me in that godsforsaken dungeon, so that when I kill him, I'll enjoy every second of it."

Tiernan couldn't help it. *"Good girl."* He slid the words into her mind in a low, rumbling growl.

Fire sparked from the tips of her fingers. The water sizzled for only a moment, but she didn't scold him for slipping into her thoughts. Defiance danced around her, fiery and wicked and wonderful. "It's Rowan."

Tiernan rocked back on his heels. The name of the fallen fae had been the last thing he'd expected her to say. "You don't want to remember Rowan?"

"I do, but there are some memories I would rather forget."

Intrigue got the best of him, as it often did when it came to her. "Such as?"

She pressed her lips together in a thin, mocking smile. "That's really none of your concern, my lord."

She was right. Whatever she wanted to forget about Rowan was none of his business. Yet just knowing the male fae had kissed her, touched her, was enough to make him rip through the realms, find the asshole, and kill him all over again. Fury simmered beneath the surface of his skin. The urge to wreck and ruin, to completely *destroy*, burned like fire in his soul, hotter and brighter than any flame Maeve could throw his way.

He took a slow, steadying breath and clenched his fists twice for good measure, forcing the overwhelming urge back down to the deepest and darkest part of him. He couldn't be too angry with Rowan. After all, he was the one who had saved Maeve's life, just as Ceridwen knew he would. The vision had come to his twin not long after Maeve's arrival in Niahvess, though it wasn't completely clear. It had been blurry and sudden, leaving his sister breathless. Knowing Rowan's fate was somehow entwined with Maeve's survival was the only reason Tiernan ever left her alone with him, even if it had caused him more torment than he cared to admit.

"If you truly want to forget, then I'll see what I can do about finding a memory keeper." Though he sincerely hoped she would change her mind.

Maeve ducked her head and her hair fell around her like a silken waterfall. "Thank you."

Tiernan smirked. Despite being fully fae, she still possessed so many adorable mortal qualities.

"You know," he drawled, determined to maintain his reputation as a cocky High King so she wouldn't get any ideas and he wouldn't feel inclined to indulge her, "you could erase all of your memories of him. And let me replace them with some new ones."

His offensive comment elicited the desired response.

"You'd like that, wouldn't you?" She was wildfire, and Tiernan was drawn to her, unable to stay away.

"Very much."

Maeve whipped around and moved through the lagoon back to the shore. Drops of water fell from her hair and glided down her bare back. With every step, her hips swayed, drawing his attention to the sweet curve of her ass. There, her skin was smooth and flawless. There were no scars. No tattoos. It was the one area of her body Fearghal had not touched with his nightshade-dipped blade, the only thing that could scar a fae.

She stood upon the sand of his shore, and instead of changing back into the dress she'd discarded upon a rock, she glamoured herself clothing—tight black leggings, a scarlet top covered in crushed rubies that was cropped right below her breasts, and shiny black boots that came up over her knees. Maeve shook out her hair and the curls dried instantly.

Impressive. She was improving greatly in terms of glamour.

She turned away from him and bent over at the waist, clearly pretending to adjust her boots. Intentionally putting her entire backside on full display for him. "I can feel you staring, my lord."

His cock jumped, but he tamed it and kept his desire for her in a tight grip, far from where it could cause harm. "My Court, my rules."

She stood abruptly and faced him, her face a mask. "My body, my rules."

"Oh, believe me, *astora*, you are in complete control of your body." Tiernan rose out of the water and enjoyed the way her gaze drank in every solid inch of him, lingering for the barest of seconds below his waist, where he no longer had an erection. "What you do not control, however, is how my body reacts to you."

It was a low blow, and he knew it. But it was necessary. For both of them.

Humiliation burned her cheeks, colored them a vibrant pink, and she muttered a few choice words before running off back through the glamour. Away from him.

Good.

It was far better for her to hate him than anything else. Because the High Princess of Autumn was his *sirra*. His soul answered to her alone. He'd known it from the first moment she landed on the shores of his Court, and once her cuffs were removed, her magic sang a melody, and he knew the words by heart. He would destroy worlds for her. Fall to his knees for her. But he could never tell her the truth of his devotion.

Because if he did, he would lose her forever.

Chapter Two

Maeve hated him. She could not *stand* the High King of Summer. He was arrogant and callous. Maddening and infuriating. He insulted her on purpose and got pleasure from seeing her shamed.

Mortification scalded her cheeks as she burst through the glamour surrounding the cove and raced back onto the long strand of beach. Her legs fired her faster over the pink sand, fueled by her own frustration. She wanted to run away, far from Tiernan and his smirks, from his flippant remarks and pointed jabs. If she could, she'd flee the Summer Court altogether. Except she had nowhere else to go and no way out.

She ran as fast as she could until her feet barely touched the ground. Until warmth bloomed from the center of her back and the cool breeze rushed past her at incredible speed. It was like flying.

A burst of color flashed, and she caught sight of it from the corner of her eye.

Wings.

She had *wings*. They carried her up, higher and higher, so she soared on the wind. Maeve threw her arms out in front of her, desperate for purchase. Warm air glided through her fingertips and her wings continued to beat, full and wide. It was exhilarating and petrifying all at once. Dread bubbled up in the back of her throat and she swallowed a scream.

She needed...

Tiernan was there before his name fell from her lips. Except he was on the ground, and she was not. His gaze shot to the sky and zeroed in on her. Those twilight eyes widened in shock and an emotion she couldn't place before he concealed it.

"You're flying," he called up to her.

"Yes, obviously." She hovered in the air, about the length of a palm tree above the stretch of beach where the sand met the sea. "Please get me down."

Lir and Ceridwen *faded* in a breath later and both of their gazes latched onto her."Shit." Lir ran his hand over the twists of dark brown hair on top of his head. "She has wings."

Ceridwen's ruby lips lifted at the corners, and she clamped a hand over her heart. "She's glorious."

"I want to come down." She didn't want to be admired like a rare piece of artwork. Already more fae were pouring onto the beach from the floating city of Niahvess and pointing up at her. Some gasped, some applauded and cheered. All of them stared. "Just tell me how to land!"

"Keep going, you're doing great." Lir ignored her pleas and crossed his arms like he was enjoying the spectacle. "It's actually quite impressive."

"But I don't know what I'm doing!" Maeve's heart pounded and her stomach flipped as she kept her arms outstretched for balance. The warmth at the center of her back spread and she realized it was coming from the two little scars shaped like crescent moons. The ones she assumed were from some lost memory from her abhorrent childhood. With every shift of the breeze, her wings coasted, sending her higher.

"You're doing wonderful." Tiernan's voice infiltrated her thoughts

as she bobbled in the air. The compliment startled her, and she stole a glance at her wingspan.

They *were* magnificent. Feathers of soft ivory stretched out on either side of her, and the tips were dusted with rosy gold. They were magical and real. And they were hers. She wondered if they looked like her mother's, if Fianna's wings had been just as stunning. A knot of emotion twisted inside her chest and the distinctive tingle of tears threatened to slide down her cheeks.

"What's wrong?"

No doubt Tiernan had sensed her emotion, and she appreciated his concern. She glanced down at him, now further away than before. *"Nothing. It's just...overwhelming."*

His winning smile stretched across his face. *"Just don't try any fancy moves up there."*

Maeve snorted. As if she could. She was practically a brand new fae, not some High King with hundreds of years of practice.

His deep, rumbling chuckle cruised down her spine and when the sound of it grazed the innermost part of her wings, the most wicked sensation hummed along her skin. She gasped, bewildered that such an insignificant touch could be so sensual. She tracked him on the beach below and found him watching, his brooding eyes locked onto her. He stood with his hands in the pockets of his pants, his face devoid of all emotion. But then she saw it. The faintest uptick of the corner of his mouth.

He knew exactly what he'd done.

"Stop that," Maeve warned.

"What?" he asked, all feigned innocence. *"This?"*

That same brush rushed across the sensitive section of her wings again, except this time it was more powerful, and her entire body vibrated with arousal, from the tips of her feathers to her toes. It left her aching, wanting, needing. She bit her lip to keep from moaning in pleasure and it was then the warmth in her back subsided. Her wings vanished. She tumbled from the sky, falling, just as she had when Garvan dropped her so many moons ago during the Autumn Ceilie.

Maeve's scream pierced the air, echoed by shouts and cries on the ground. She clawed through the sky, the memory of falling still too fresh, too real. A blur of bluish-purple flashed before her eyes as her body careened into a solid wall. Then she was in Tiernan's arms.

His wings were twice the size of hers. They were the deepest shade of blue but shifted to violet in the sun. He plucked her out of the sky like she was weightless. She stared up at him, at the clenched line of his jaw, dazed and gasping. But he wouldn't even look at her. He cradled her like a child, and she flinched when he set her down on the beach without even acknowledging her. His eyes were piercing and full of disdain. He'd been the one who caused her to fall, yet he was acting like she was somehow to blame.

The fucking fae.

Her knees quaked and she stumbled forward in the sand, grateful for Lir when his ironclad grip snared her by the elbow to keep her upright.

She glanced over at Tiernan once more, ready to spit fire, but he nodded sharply to Lir, then *faded* without a word.

"Are you okay?" Ceridwen wrapped a comforting arm around her and soothed away her anger and annoyance. She filled the space with love and warmth, with a soul-reckoning tranquility that smothered Maeve's agitation and reminded her to breathe.

"I think so." Maeve's voice shook. She straightened, then put on a brave face. Dozens of local Summer fae were watching her. Judging her. "Yes, I'm okay."

Ceridwen took her hand and squeezed. "I didn't know you had wings. I mean, I thought you might because of your parents and brothers, but..."

"But the cuffs," Maeve finished for her. "I didn't know either."

"You looked incredible up there, little bird." Lir's silver eyes shone bright with something that could've been pride. "Even if you had no idea what you were doing."

A few of the fae who'd watched her fly then fall from the sky gathered closer. Three were children and their eyes sparkled with curiosity and wonder. They were small, no taller than her waist, and they approached her with quiet trepidation. Besides the occasional conversations with some of the fae inside the palace walls, Maeve had very little interaction with any other faeries. She hadn't even been to Niahvess yet. She'd only ever seen the city that seemed to float upon winding canals from the balcony of her bedroom. Lir gave her a slight nod of encouragement as she stole a glance at him.

Ceridwen's lips curved into a reassuring smile.

The first fae child to approach her was a little female. She was so startlingly pretty Maeve tried not to stare. Her hair was piled on top of her head and jet-black curls sprung from the bun pinned in place with tiny crystals. Spidery lashes framed a set of rich amber eyes.

The beautiful fae child smiled up at her. "Can I see your wings?"

"Darina, you can't just go around asking if someone will show you their wings," a female adult chided. She must've been the girl's mother, for they shared the same midnight hair and gilded amber eyes.

The girl's face fell.

"No, it's okay," Maeve said quickly to save the tears welling in the corner of the child's eyes. Then without thinking, "I don't mind."

Maeve hesitated. She wouldn't mind displaying her wings again at all, except she didn't know how to bring them back. There *had* to be a way.

She recalled Tiernan's words to her. He reminded daily that she was in charge of her magic, it didn't control her.

They're my wings. I can summon them at will.

Maeve reached for the sensation in the middle of her back, where the marks of two crescent moons took shape. She called to the warmth, to the tingle that raced down her spine, to the thrill of flying. In a rush of magic, her wings burst free, and a roar of giggles and squeals exploded all around. More children seemed to appear and each one had a thousand questions.

"How did you learn to fly?"

"Was it scary when you fell?"

"What do they feel like?"

And then, "Can we touch them?"

Maeve blanked and sent Ceridwen a look that was nothing short of desperation.

Ceridwen took Maeve's hand and together they knelt in front of the group of small fae. "Yes. You can touch her wings. Faerie wings are strong but sensitive. If you touch right here," she ran one finger along the tip of Maeve's outer feathers, "then Maeve will only feel the barest of touches."

The same little girl looked up at her. "Is that your name?"

"Maeve," a boy fae whispered, like her name was a reverent prayer to the goddesses.

"Yes." Maeve smiled. "That's my name."

"It's lovely," another, older girl sighed.

The next thing Maeve knew, all the faerie children were introducing themselves and telling her all about life in Niahvess. She learned that every single one of them had a different type of magic. Some were learning to concoct healing potions while others crafted charmed jewelry. They went to school, but it was nothing like schools in the human lands. It was more of an apprenticeship, where they were taught how to hone the skills of their magic, though they did have classes on the histories of the realms. They were crafters, creators, tinkerers, and inventors. They liked to play games and eat candy. Most of them came fully into their magic by their fourteenth year. And their favorite holiday was Yuletide—which took place around the winter solstice—because of the gifts.

After hearing all about the Yuletide festivities, some parents tried to corral the children away. But Maeve found she didn't mind answering their questions. She actually enjoyed the sense of creating a friendship, establishing a bond.

One fae girl piped up from the back. "Is it true you're a High Princess?"

Lir's face remained neutral, but Ceridwen's smile was a little too bright.

Maeve sat cross-legged on the beach and propped her elbows on her knees, tucking in her wings. "What makes you think I'm a High Princess?"

The girl pointed to the crown on her head, the one she completely forgot she was wearing.

"It's beautiful," she said with a whimsical sigh.

Maeve grinned and lifted it off her head. "Then it's yours." She crafted another one easily, just as Tiernan had taught her. "I can always make more."

To her delight, the fae children squealed.

"I want one, please!"

"Me too!"

"You're a creator like us!"

"Can you make a sword?"

For the next hour, Maeve sat on the beach, creating faerie crowns and striking swords. She indulged the children and let them choose their own colors and designs, then created them from the wonders of imagination. Her soul magic came easier to her this time, like it was as simple as breathing. She liked to think it was because Tiernan wasn't attacking her and forcing her to react. She wanted to think it was because she enjoyed what she was doing. Setting to work, she added glitter and initials, engraved dragons and sirens. If this was what it felt like to be magical, to see so many darling, smiling faces gazing up at her, then she wanted all of it.

"You should sell these," a fae male, presumably a father, commented. "You'd make a fortune during Sunatalis."

Sunatalis. She hadn't heard of that before and looked up at Lir with questioning eyes.

"It's an annual celebration," he confirmed, his silver gaze kind.

"I could never." Maeve smiled up at the male, who was setting a crown of lilies and silvery swirls upon his daughter's head. "If it makes them happy, then I'm happy."

He chuckled. "You know, every fae child in Niahvess will be knocking on the High King's door asking for you."

25

"Then I'll be sure to answer."

She finished up the last two swords and when the local Summer fae finally dispersed and headed back into the city, Maeve stood and dusted the sand from her leggings.

She found Lir and Ceridwen staring at her and asked, "What is it?"

"I'm impressed, Your Highness." Lir toed the sand with his silver-studded boot.

"Why?"

He shifted, uneasy. "I didn't expect you to be so...I mean, that is... Niahvess isn't—"

Ceridwen gently placed a hand on his shoulder. "What Lir is trying to say is that he's in awe of your ability to make everyone feel like they're worthy of your time. You shine when you're happy, Maeve. You simply glow."

A flush bled into Maeve's cheeks.

"Exactly." Lir nodded and coughed. Once. "That's exactly what I was trying to say." His dark brows lifted in amusement. "So, you want to fly home?"

"Absolutely not," Maeve laughed. "I think I'll walk."

"You know," Ceridwen said as she linked her arm through Maeve's. "You'll have to learn how to *fade* eventually."

"One thing at a time, Your Highness," Maeve teased and together they walked back to the palace.

MAEVE DIDN'T KNOW he was watching her. She didn't know he was smiling, enjoying the way she seemed to fit in so seamlessly with his people.

Tiernan couldn't have prepared himself for that moment. Not when she started creating flower crowns and swords for all the fae children, and not when they gazed up at her like she was a queen. She looked so natural among his citizens, so perfect...

And when she damn near orgasmed in the sky because of the simplest of touches, he'd almost come undone. Never had he been more grateful for an interruption from Merrick.

His top scout had returned from the human lands with news of a great stirring. It seemed the Scathing was no longer a gaping chasm of disease and rot, but a portal of some kind. A gateway. It was imperative they investigate it at once, especially since Merrick had found Saoirse—the elite warrior who was also Maeve's best friend—was indeed still alive.

The Furies, however, had not yet been located, leaving Tiernan uneasy. The Furies were capable of great destruction, darkness, and death. They left Faeven in ruin, and the rebuild after their deaths had taken much time and effort. Knowing they were alive again and free to roam the realm was unsettling. If they did in fact answer to Maeve, then that eased his worries some. It meant there was a chance they could be swayed to fight Parisa on her behalf. Merrick just had to find them first.

After discussing the updated reports with Merrick, they'd been on their way back to the beach where he'd left Maeve. Only what he'd discovered had left him too stunned to speak.

She'd been kneeling on the sand with her wings spread out, a throng of fae children huddled before her, and her smile...

Gods, if she ever smiled like that at him, his heart would cease to beat.

Even Merrick had known well enough, and understood the depth of his silence, to walk away without another word.

Everything about her was so perfect. So *right*. Then she laughed. An actual laugh and the pain of knowing it wasn't for him was brutal. The sound of it was a song, one he'd commit to his memory for eternity.

He forced himself to turn around, to walk away and not look back.

Chapter Three

The nightshade-soaked blade sliced into her skin. Fire and wrath serrated her flesh, marred her with sweeping, angry red lines. The burn of it was like a thousand suns.

Her frenzied magic tried to heal and save her, but there was no erasing the pain. Blood spilled from her wounds, sliding down her arms and abdomen in sticky rivers of red. Another slice. Another wave of agony. Still, he continued to ruin and wreck her. To scar her. To mark her with his blade.

He laughed from the shadows, faded in front of her and then behind her so quickly she barely had time to focus on him. His sickening whispers, his promises of pain, crawled over her neck and bare shoulders like the pinpricks of spider legs.

A rush of nausea slammed into her, left her doubling over and gasping for air. Dizziness swept through her until her vision swam and stars danced in front of her eyes.

But Maeve refused to scream. She refused to give him the satisfaction.

His menacing laughter echoed through the dungeon. It slithered over her, snake-like, and she shivered in spite of herself.

He angled the tip of his blade beneath her chin and tilted her face up to look him in the eyes. They were the color of kohl. Empty and cold. Corded black veins bulged along his neck and bare chest. His horns stuck out from his mop of copper hair. He flashed her a grin and displayed a set of dagger-like teeth.

"You will scream for me," he purred, bringing his mouth close to hers. "You'll beg me to stop."

Maeve spat, a mixture of blood and saliva landed on the corner of his mouth. "I'll kill you."

He licked it off with his tongue. "Not if I kill you first."

She knew he meant it.

Darkness descended upon them and then there was nothing.

Chapter Four

T iernan jolted awake.

The city of Niahvess slumbered beneath a waning moon, yet his heart thundered as though he had a nightmare. A faint sheen of sweat slicked his forehead and his dark hair clung to the sides of his face. Shaking off the strange sensation, he climbed out of bed. He shoved his hair back, slowly pacing his room. He hadn't dreamt in years. The last bad dream he remembered having was watching his father scream for him, and his mother weep for him, while he was tortured by trooping fae in the all-encompassing Autumn forest.

He could still feel the sting of the blade. He could still hear his father's bellows of rage. He could still see his mother's silent tears, and when her tender heart broke, it splintered through him.

Tiernan paced the wooden floors of his chamber, determined to shrug off the rising sense of fear. But he wasn't the one who was afraid. It was...

Without thinking, he grabbed his sword from his shelving of armor and bolted into the adjoining bedroom.

Maeve was in her bed and her room was empty, but her sleep was fitful. She thrashed. She whimpered. Her body jerked and flailed as though some unseen force had complete control over her.

He stood silent in the shadows of her room, listening to her nightmare. Fearghal whispered into her ear as he butchered her. Maeve's voice, however, was louder. Her threats and promises were just as vile.

Cautiously, he stepped closer to the bed, and for the first time in a long time, he didn't know what to do.

He sensed his twin before he saw her. She *faded* into Maeve's room and stood next to him.

"I felt it." Ceridwen spoke softly into the stillness. His sister was terribly pale, as though she stared death in the face. "I felt her fear. Her terror."

"Yes." Tiernan didn't know what else to say. He'd never experienced this kind of helplessness before.

Ceridwen crossed her arms, pulling her delicate satin robe tighter around her. "He haunts her dreams."

Tiernan's blood simmered and the compulsion to destroy clawed to the surface. He ground out the words, "I know."

"She'll have her vengeance."

There was something odd about the way Ceridwen spoke; it was matter-of-fact. His head snapped her direction and she shrugged, all nonchalance.

"I've seen it."

He nodded, then looked back to where Maeve tossed over in her bed once more. "Can you help ease her fear? Can you help her sleep peacefully?"

Ceridwen's blonde brows arched in the low light. "Interested in her well-being now, are you?"

"So she can rest," he clarified. "We're going to train later today."

Ceridwen didn't believe him. Her knowing smile said as much. "Of course."

His sister's magic filled the room, and the balm of her presence gently settled over Maeve like a sweet lullaby. It was a comfort, a loving caress, and it blanketed her, easing her terror. Melting away her trauma. Gradually, she settled into a state of calm. Her breathing grew even and deep. She curled into herself, tucking both of her hands under her chin.

Tiernan's heart twisted.

Once she was sound asleep, Ceridwen asked, "How did she get into the cove today?"

An excellent question, and one he couldn't answer.

"Lir said she walked right through the glamour." It was still impossible. His wards were expertly crafted, his glamour was some of the strongest in the realm. But Maeve had simply paraded right through, as though he hadn't spent dozens of years perfecting his craft. The lagoon was sacred to him. It was the one of the places he could go and be alone with his thoughts. Just himself and the quiet beauty of his Court. Now, however, it seemed he would be sharing it with a certain High Princess from Autumn. "He said she vanished right before his eyes."

Ceridwen stared hard at Maeve's sleeping form and a slight frown wrinkled her brow. "Who in the seven hells is this girl?"

His *sirra*, that's who. The one to whom his soul was bound.

He knew Ceridwen watched him and he schooled his expression into one of neutrality.

She lightly bumped her shoulder against his. "Aran wants to see her tomorrow."

Tiernan ground his teeth. "I'm aware."

There was a weighted pause between them. "And?"

"And I'll allow it." He couldn't refuse Maeve the chance to see her only family, even if Aran had been the one to cost him most of his own.

Ceridwen drifted back toward the bedroom door. Her lips twisted to the side as she gave him a once-over, noting he stood clad in nothing but a pair of black shorts with a sword in his hand.

"You should get some rest, too. Especially if you're going to be *training* tomorrow." She threw her hands up at Tiernan's look. "But seriously, at least try. I know you haven't been sleeping well."

He nodded in silent consent. He hadn't slept soundly since Maeve's arrival in his Court.

"Thank you, Cer." He glanced pointedly at Maeve. "For helping her."

"Of course." His twin flashed her signature smile and slipped out the door, closing it behind her.

Tiernan knew he should go back to his own bedroom. It would be better for both of them to have that constant distance. Besides, Maeve was safe now. She slept, and he should, too. But he couldn't take that first step, he couldn't cross back over the threshold that divided their rooms. Instead, he settled down into the leather chair by her bedside and laid his sword across his lap.

He didn't sleep at all.

AT SOME POINT during the night, Maeve thought she might be delirious.

She knew she'd had a nightmare. The ones involving Fearghal made a habit of lingering, of drenching her in sweat, and were difficult to forget. But in the early predawn hours, before the glow of the sun filtered past her sheer curtains, she could've sworn Tiernan was in her room.

She'd rolled over in her bed and her eyes had fluttered open, lost somewhere between the state of dreaming and not quite being awake. Over by her balcony doors, she'd noticed a shadow. One brief, fleeting moment of panic had consumed her, and her fingers had curled around the Aurastone tucked beneath her pillow. But there was no mistaking the High King's silhouette. Broad shoulders. Trim, narrow waist. Sculpted muscles from head to toe. He was staring out into the night, with one elbow propped against the glass pane of the door leading to her balcony. He was glorious despite being a complete asshole, and something purely feminine stirred inside her. A flicker of heat.

Minutes ticked by and she realized she was staring at his back, at his rather perfectly sculpted ass clad in a pair of snug black shorts.

Without turning around, he whispered, "Go back to sleep."

Exhaustion easily dragged her back under and she gave in to the abyss. When she finally woke up, sunlight filtered into the room, basking her in the soft glow of dawn. She rolled over to face the balcony. The adjoining door to his bedroom was closed tight, as though he'd never been there at all.

Chapter Five

Maeve stood in front of the double glass doors leading to her balcony. It was the same place Tiernan had been standing last night. She knew because the tempting scent of him still lingered. She inhaled, taking it all in. The sun-drenched palm trees. Warm sandalwood. Plumeria. She wondered what he was thinking about, why he was even in her bedroom at all...

A foolish notion.

The last thing she needed to think about was whether or not *he* was thinking about her. Those types of thoughts only led to trouble. It didn't matter if she found him terribly attractive, he'd made his sentiments about her quite clear.

She pulled open the doors and a rush of summer warmth flooded into the room, cooled by the delicate breeze rolling in from the sea. The air shimmered, dense and powerful. The wards and charms Tiernan placed around her living quarters remained strong.

Her stomach gave a small gurgle.

She pulled on a pair of leather leggings and her boots and strapped her Aurastone to her thigh. Searching through the wardrobe, she shoved aside the elegant gowns and grabbed one of the bejeweled corsets that reminded her of the sun and the sea. Beads and jewels in shades of turquoise, pale blue, and gold were stitched onto the soft fabric like armor. Even the thin straps were studded with gems. She freshened up in the bathroom, ran a hand through her mess of waves, then yanked open the door to her bedroom in search of breakfast,

Maeve wasn't at all surprised to see Lir waiting for her in the hall. She smiled up at him.

"Good morning, Lir."

His eyes were kind, far gentler than she'd once assumed of his nature. No longer was he the silent, stoic brute.

"Good morning, Your Highness."

"You know you can just call me Maeve." She started down the hall and he fell in step behind her. "I feel like we're past the formalities now."

"Of course, Your Highness."

Maeve gave her head a light shake. Typical. Lir was fiercely loyal, and he was also a staunch rule-follower. He never called her Maeve. It was either "Your Highness" or "little bird," depending on his mood.

They walked around the corner, and the carved doors of the library came into view. She'd been meaning to put aside some time to read, to distract herself from everything. She should be studying Old Laic and the wars from before to see if there was any mention of the ways to kill an Archfae. Of course, she could just ask Casimir...if she could find him. He'd been the one to kill her mother, the High Queen of Autumn. The mere thought of it caused her gut to seize and she clenched her jaw. Her fingers grazed the inlaid pearl handle to the library. There were other things she wanted to learn about too, like her mother and father, who were lost to her. She didn't even hold a single memory.

"I can hear your stomach growling." Lir's hand fell upon her shoulder and gently steered her away from the past. "Keep walking."

"Fine." She grumbled her displeasure but there was no real anger behind it.

After she ate, she was going straight to the library to read. If she got there soon enough, Tiernan wouldn't be able to drag her to the beach for training, at least not right away. It would be easy enough to avoid him for a few hours, especially after what happened yesterday afternoon on the beach. She often got the sense he was avoiding her as well. He never joined them for breakfast anymore, probably because of her.

But when she walked out onto the terracotta balcony where she and the others met for breakfast every morning, there he was—only him, looking as decadent as ever. He wore a shirt of the color of the Lismore Marin, the collar stuck up, and the top two buttons undone. His pants were gray, like smoke, and his sword was at his hip. He wore a gold ring on his pinky finger and in the sun-shaped setting was a stone that reflected the colors of his eyes. Deep amethyst. Cobalt blue. Twilight. Around his neck, however, was the necklace she'd created yesterday. The one resembling the crest of the Summer Court.

He'd kept it.

She glanced around the patio area. Ceridwen was almost always seated at the table with Brynn. Sometimes Merrick would join them. But today, no one else was there.

Tiernan stood up from his seat upon her arrival and gestured to the empty chair beside him. Awkward friction sparked between them, leaving Maeve uncomfortable in her own skin. She slid onto the seat next to him and rubbed her hands over her leather leggings. The cropped top of beaded sunbursts she wore suddenly seemed a little too snug.

His gaze flicked to the door, and Lir nodded once, then left.

Maeve kept her hands folded in her lap and squeezed them together. It was never just the two of them together unless they were training. She wished, more than anything, that Ceridwen was there to douse her in a wash of deep breaths and serenity.

"Coffee?" Tiernan asked.

"Please."

37

He doctored it just the way she liked, with two cubes of sugar and no cream.

"Hungry?"

"Famished." Even if she lied just to spite him, he would hear her stomach's betrayal.

One snap of his fingers and a full, albeit smaller than usual, spread of food appeared before her. Warm biscuits with raspberry jam. Crispy bacon. This wonderful mix of potatoes, onions, cheese, and gravy. All of her favorites, she noted with rising suspicion.

He cleared his throat and casually stirred the cup of coffee in front of him. "I wanted to apologize for yesterday."

Ah. So, this was an apology breakfast.

"Oh?" Maeve spread some of the sweetened jam onto a biscuit. "Which part?"

Tiernan brought his cup to his lips and eyed her over the rim. "The part where I left you on the beach."

"Mm." She didn't bother to look at him as she coated another layer of jam onto her biscuit. "I thought maybe you intended to apologize for practically bringing me to orgasm in the sky in front of everyone."

He choked on his coffee, started coughing, and slammed his fist into his chest. Maeve dropped her head and let her curtain of curls hide the immense satisfaction of his embarrassment.

But the High King always recovered quickly. The corner of his mouth lifted in a cocky grin and his gaze swept over her, reflecting raw male hunger. And it had nothing to do with the food on the table in front of them. "Afraid not, *astora*. I'll never apologize for bringing you pleasure."

Astora. Pulse of my heart.

She hated to admit it, but she rather enjoyed it when he used that term to address her. It made her knees soften.

Maeve detoured the conversation back to its original objective. She tore off some of her biscuit, chewed quickly, then swallowed. "Well, why did you leave then?"

The High King's gaze drifted to her, and his voice was calm when he said, "Merrick returned."

Her heart pitched and she bolted forward, closer to him. She had the utmost faith in Merrick. He was Tiernan's top scout. A highly trained hunter who could track down anything and anyone. His magic was incomparable. He was clever and stealthy, and he was *very* good at his occupation.

She couldn't disguise the tremble in her voice. "And?"

His eyes held hers, refusing to let go. "Saoirse lives."

"That's...that's good." Words were useless. Maeve pressed her lips together, but it was futile. Tears slipped from the corner of her eyes, and she hastily wiped them away. Saoirse, *her* Saoirse, was alive. The guards in Kells hadn't killed her. The relief in her heart was immense and swelled with each breath like a welcomed reprieve. She sniffled and her nose burned, and when Tiernan offered her a tissue, she didn't refuse him.

"It is," he agreed. His steady, unwavering gaze roved over her face. He waited until she composed herself and then said, "There's more."

All the muscles in her body tightened. "Oh?"

"First, the Furies have not yet been located, and it would seem the Scathing isn't what we originally thought. The extent of rot and decay has stopped, but Merrick reported it has become some kind of portal." He took another drink of his coffee, slowly. "I don't know what that means for us. I've never heard of anything like this in all of my two hundred and seventy-eight years."

Now it was Maeve's turn to choke.

His dark brow quirked in amusement. "What? Did you think I was older?"

She shook her head. "No. Of course not. I mean, you look great for your age."

Tiernan grinned and her heart shattered. His smile, his *real* smile, was breathtaking. It carved its way into her soul, and she knew right then she'd commit it to her memory forever. Shadows stole into the High King's eyes, but he blinked them away just as quickly.

Heat coasted over her skin, and she took a keen interest in her breakfast, opting to pluck a piece of bacon from the tray in front of her instead of looking up at him.

"If what you're saying about the Scathing is true," she spoke offhandedly and didn't meet his eye, "then are we still certain Parisa's death will end it?"

"I think that depends."

Maeve stole a look at him. "On?"

"On the exact words the will o' wisp spoke to you."

"The exact words," Maeve repeated. She transported herself back to that night deep within the Autumn woods, when she was cold. Afraid. Alone. When the forest floor soothed her, cradled her like a babe, because it recognized her as its own. She recalled the dancing faerie lights, the explosion of stars created by Lianan. Glancing down, she looked at the Strand in the shape of a constellation that encircled her thumb. She could hear the will o' wisp's voice in her mind like a tinkling of bells.

"The only way to save your kingdom...is by destroying the magic source of the Scathing."

The magic source. She'd assumed Lianan meant Parisa was the magic source. It had been the only thing to make sense at the time. But now...

"Oh no." Maeve raked her hands through her curls. "I must've misinterpreted her. Parisa might not be the cause of the Scathing at all."

"No."

"It's something else completely."

Not a question, but Tiernan answered, "Yes."

She stared down at the plate of food in front of her. Her appetite had vanished. "How do we destroy it?"

"That's what we need to find out."

Maeve considered his words. She may not be human, maybe

never was, but Saoirse was still mortal, and she wouldn't allow her best friend to suffer. Or any other soul, for that matter, even if they now despised her because she was fae. If she could save even one life, she would.

"I have to go back. Not only to save Saoirse, but to destroy the Scathing once and for all. I can't sit idly by and let the human lands suffer. They won't stand a chance on their own."

"Well then, my lady." Tiernan stood from the table and offered her his hand. "I suggest we increase your training."

Maeve knew she'd probably regret it, but she took his hand. "I thought you might say that."

TIERNAN FADED them back to the strand of beach where they usually practiced. It was far enough away from Niahvess not to disturb the public, and close enough to the palace in case things got out of hand.

Unlikely, but necessary.

Tiernan took Maeve by the shoulders and made her face him.

"You can do this. You are the lifeblood of magic. Of creation." He squeezed her gently, enforcing his words. "Whatever you see in your mind's eye, take it and make it yours. Do not hesitate."

She nodded and he was acutely aware of her resistance. The necklace dangling between her breasts told him as much. She was nervous.

"Don't think, just do."

Another nod, this one sharper.

"Draw on your anger if you must. Your vengeance. Imagine I'm Fearghal."

At those words, fire burned bright in her eyes. "What if I hurt you?"

He patted her cheek. "Then I'll expect you to tend to my wounds."

She subjected him to an eye roll, and he turned around to walk away from her when a gust of icy wind barreled into him. Hands out, he caught himself before his face slammed into the sand.

"What the—"

Tiernan jumped up, kicking sand in his wake. He spun back around. What he saw stole his breath. Pierced him through his heart like a dagger.

There stood Maeve, calling upon Summer, upon his storm, using his own magic against him. Menacing clouds of black boiled, blocking out the sun. Frozen drops of rain pelted the once calm shore. The grit of sand stung his face, blasted his arms. He raised his hand, shielding his eyes from its onslaught. The waves roiled, the sky roared. With her arms locked down on either side of her, she called up the full fury of his wrath. Gusts of wind howled in challenge, whipping around her, lifting her hair from her shoulders. Magic pulsed in angry, beating throbs so the ground trembled and the rumble of thunder cracked overhead. She called the heavens down, for the seven circles of hell had met their match.

Tiernan shoved his hair back from his face. All he could do was stare at her.

She glowed with the strength of her power, with the pure, raw force of it. Her grayish-green eyes focused on him as the storm above them intensified. She was magic incarnate. She was illustrious. She was a fucking *queen*.

He stumbled back a step as the might of the wind assaulted them. It lashed out and sparked with the blaze of fire. Lightning splintered across the sky and took the shape of swords. They fell like rain.

"Fuck." Maybe she *could* hurt him.

He used his own power to blast the swords up and away from them, back to the clouds from which they'd fallen. Her eyes widened in shock. Frenzied wind swirled around her, creating a cyclone, and the momentum of it was enough to almost knock him off his feet. It howled, angry and vicious. White-capped waves slammed the shoreline, drenching them in swells of brine and salt. The sea lashed the shore in raging beatings. But she didn't sway. And she didn't yield.

Fear.

Her fear was a raging river and it threatened to drown her.

She cried out for him. "Tiernan!"

"Son of a bitch." He reached for her thoughts, for her mind, and tore into the storm ravaging her from the inside out. Her emotions were *everywhere*. She was at war with herself, lost in the assault of power, wonder, and terror. Held hostage by the memories of her past.

"TIERNAN!"

Her scream had him running, and he slammed into the wall of wind barricading her from him. It threw him back like he was nothing. Like he wasn't a powerful Archfae.

"Ceridwen." He reached out to his twin. *"Cer, I need you. I can't reach her. I need your help to calm her down."*

His sister's response was a shout in his mind. *"She's too strong! I can't get through! My magic...it's not enough!"*

He saw it then, the flash of rising darkness creeping in from off the coast. It grew like a beast of its own, turbulent and powerful. A rogue wave. It would swallow them if he didn't stop it. If he didn't stop her.

"Tier, please!" Maeve begged, her body shaking and trembling, unable to recall the magic bound to her. Tears slid down her cheeks as another gust of wind lifted her hair from her shoulders, hoisted her up so her feet barely touched the ground.

If he didn't move fast, he would lose her.

He summoned the magic he kept at bay, the power of absolute destruction, the ability to devastate with nothing more than a flick of his wrist. It swept through him like the darkest night and called upon the most eternal shadows. They encircled him, answered to him. The air crackled as his magic clashed with Maeve's. Creation and destruction clawed at one another, each rise of power desperate to overthrow the other. Harnessing all the darkness inside him, he ripped through the storm, tore through the winds, until they were face to face.

Her eyes were wild, pleading.

"Let go," he demanded.

Her bottom lip quivered. The rogue wave closed in, threatening to crash upon them. To pull them out to the sea.

"Let go, *now*."

Tiernan didn't waste another second. One arm snared around her waist, and he dragged her against him. Capturing her face with his free hand, her eyes widened in shock before he crushed his mouth to hers. Reckless power exploded between them as he claimed her.

This was not a kiss of lovers. It was not tender. It was not cautious. It was desperate and hungry. Ruthless and punishing. He swallowed her gasp as their tongues collided; she tasted of cinnamon and smoke. The combination was intoxicating, and every muscle, every nerve in his body craved more of her. Her hands roved up his arms to his biceps, where she squeezed and held onto him like he was the only one who could save her.

Greedy and wanting more, he let his teeth graze her lips and she tilted her head back, exposing the creamy length of her neck, offering herself up to him.

He trailed kisses along her throat and followed them up with a sweep of his tongue. The barest of whimpers escaped her and he almost snapped. His body was alive with the feel of her touch. He wanted to take her right there on the beach, in the midst of the turmoil. He wanted to rip off those godsforsaken leggings and drive himself into her, over and over, until she screamed his name. And only his name.

Maeve wove her arms around his neck, fused her mouth to his, and lifted her knee like she was trying to climb him. He cupped her bottom and hoisted her up, nestling the stiff length of his cock right between her legs, and she anchored herself to him. He knew she could feel him, *all* of him, and she wanted him. The delectable scent of her arousal was potent, and he couldn't get enough of it.

Slowly, the winds died. The sea calmed. The skies cleared.

But he wasn't done kissing her. Not yet.

He wanted to memorize every inch of her. The shape of her mouth. The feel of her flesh molded to him. The curve of her jaw.

When she opened her full and lush lips for him again, he devoured her.

Tiernan needed to stop. He knew he should stop. But her thoughts...fucking gods—she wanted him to fill her.

In an unexpected rush, the last wave of her soul magic fell away, and she collapsed in his arms.

He dropped to the sand, cradling her in his lap. She kept her arms around his neck, her legs straddling his own. Trembles wrecked her body and he held on tight to her, gently rocking her back and forth. Reminding himself to disconnect, he slowed the erratic beating of his heart. He kept his breathing even, the rise and fall of his chest steady while he tried to get her to breathe along with him.

"Now, Cer," he called to his sister. *"Now."*

Instantly, Ceridwen's magic flooded over them. Warm and comforting ripples of tranquility settled them, soothed them, lulled them until eventually Maeve relaxed into his arms.

Still, she continued to hold onto him.

"Your magic..." she whispered, her voice raw and shaken, *"that* magic..."

"Destruction," he finished for her.

Her face was nestled against his chest and if he wanted, he could easily rest his chin on top of her head. But he didn't. He couldn't. Instead, he sat unmoving and enjoyed the tickle of her breath against his skin.

"Yours is...the opposite of mine." She curled closer into him, and he lazily let one hand rub up and down her back in calm, easy movements.

It wasn't exactly a question, but he answered, "Yes."

She said nothing for a while and didn't attempt to leave, for which he was silently grateful.

Tiernan wasn't sure he would be strong enough to let her go.

Chapter Six

Maeve was undone.

Physically. Emotionally. Mentally.

She'd never experienced that kind of power before, that kind of intense magic. It had stolen her senses and left her blind to the world around her. The tremor of it still hummed beneath her skin, warming her blood, like it was delighted by itself for finally testing the magnitude of its strength. But there was more. She could do more. Be more. She could create *anything*.

But soul magic scared her. Fear sank into her, bone deep.

She'd spiraled, the threads of her control had unraveled, and she'd almost lost her grip completely. If it hadn't been for Tiernan, the way he tore through the wind and storm to reach her, the way his violent darkness unfurled around him, she would've been lost.

It thrilled her.

And his kiss...

Sweet goddess, that kiss was everything at once. Brutal. Delicious. Demanding. The way he had captured her mouth like he owned her caused her knees to buckle. Her skin heated beneath his touch, and she'd wanted him. Seven hells, she *still* wanted him. Every muscle, every nerve ending was alive and aching, desperately wanting more. Slickness pooled between her legs and the friction from her damned leggings was agony. The most interesting part, however, was his obvious lust for her. He could deny it to his grave, but she was sprawled across his lap with the length of him pressing into her, and it had nothing to do with battle arousal.

Her lips twitched.

Desire fueled him, whether he liked it or not. Pure desire for her.

"Are you alright?" His voice came from somewhere above her head, soft and warm.

Maeve swallowed the rising knot of tension and when she crawled off his lap, planting both hands in the sand, he didn't hold her back. "I think so. Maybe."

His answering laugh was short and slightly brittle.

She sank her teeth into her bottom lip, still swollen from his kisses, and watched him, waiting for his reaction. His eyes were a summer storm, cloudy and menacing, and it set her on edge.

"You kissed me."

Tiernan's face remained impassive. Cool and calm, as always. "A necessary distraction."

The insult stung and grated beneath her skin. He loved to inflict hurt, the jerk. He stood up abruptly, dusted the sand from his pants, and adjusted the collar of his shirt. She didn't miss the fact that his erection had not yet gone away.

Which made it all the more interesting when Lir *faded* into the space between them. He glanced at his High King, who didn't even look unruffled, and then his silver gaze slid to Maeve. She was on her rump in the sand, with her curls a disheveled mess, while the heat of longing flushed her cheeks.

Lir held out his hand, and she readily accepted, allowing him to pull her to her feet. "Her Highness said I should come collect..." he looked down at Maeve, "Her other Highness. Before things get out of hand."

"Too late for that," Tiernan muttered.

47

His complete disrespect, his utter disregard, lit the barely tempered fire inside her soul. She stalked over to him, infuriated by his disdain for her. By the way he *lied* so easily. She faced him, sand shifting beneath her feet, and shoved him. Hard. The asshole didn't even stumble.

"Don't you dare act like you didn't enjoy it." Tendrils of silvery smoke curled around her in her fury, cloaking them. "Like you didn't enjoy *me*."

He was a mask. His calm resolve was carefully crafted into place. He didn't even blink. "I never said I didn't enjoy it. I said it was necessary."

Necessary. Right.

Maeve wasn't going to let him win. No, she would play his vicious game. She curled into Lir's side, intentionally locking her hands around the male's muscled arm, and relished in the satisfaction of seeing Tiernan's jaw tick.

"Well, orders are orders. Let's return to the palace, Lir." She shot Tiernan a furious glare and sent sparks of fire toward his feet. He didn't even flinch. "We wouldn't want the High King to be caught with Rowan's leftovers, now would we?"

The storm was upon them without hesitation. Angry clouds filled the sky and thunder cracked like the sounds of boulders colliding into one another. She almost flinched. Almost.

"Fuck," Lir grumbled and *faded* away with her before Tiernan could release the full temper of Summer upon them both.

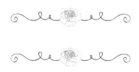

THE MINUTE they were back inside her room, Lir pointed an accusing finger in her direction.

"Are you trying to get us killed?" He pinched the bridge of his nose between his thumb and forefinger and squeezed his eyes shut.

Maeve crossed her arms and shifted her weight. Lir had never been mad at her before. "He started it."

Not her finest comeback, but it was all she had at the moment.

His eyes flew open, the silver of them ignited, then he lifted his gaze to the domed glass ceiling above their heads.

"Gods, my lady." His voice had calmed but held an edge. He pressed his lips into a thin line and took a staggering breath. "You cannot throw me into the middle of your quarrels with my High King."

When he looked at her again, his stunning face held a kind of earnestness. Almost like a plea. "I swore an oath to protect you with my life, remember?"

Maeve scoffed. "But surely that doesn't mean from the High King himself?"

The look he gave her stilled her heart, and he rolled the sleeve of his shirt, revealing a Strand of turquoise in the shape of ocean waves that curled around his arm, just above his elbow. "I pledged my loyalty to the Summer Court, to my High King. And to him, I vowed to fight for you until my death, to protect you from anyone and *everyone*, no matter the cost. This Strand, this magic, binds me to my word."

"Oh."

It was a weak response, but she hadn't realized the depth of Lir's promise.

"I'll be more cautious with my tone when you're around." Her gaze wandered to the open doors of her balcony, to where the sky remained an ominous shade of gray. "Besides, I'm pretty sure I can take him anyway."

It was a dangerous boast, but Lir laughed.

"Of that, I have no doubt." He shook his head. "I'd say the two of you are pretty squarely matched."

Matched, an interesting term, and one she all but forgot when Lir offered her his arm. "To the library, my lady?"

"You read my mind."

They passed by one of the many Summer courtyards where palms stretched out and shaded the crystalline pools lined with turquoise stones. Beneath the shade of one tree, lounging against the wall, she spied Merrick and Brynn.

"Your Highness." Brynn gave a wave and dropped into a curtsy.

Merrick flashed his dimples and bowed, his rush of hot pink hair falling across his brow.

"Merrick!" Maeve leapt over one of the sparkling pools and launched herself into his arms. He caught her mid-jump and stumbled backward.

"Hello to you, too, my lady."

"You're back." She knew he was, Tiernan told her as much, but seeing him alive and in the flesh made it real.

"I am." His smile faded as he watched her silently ask him for details, for any update on Saoirse. "She's alive." He casually draped one arm around her shoulders and squeezed gently. "She's living in what remains of Carman's fortress on the Cliffs of Morrigan."

"Oh, thank the goddess." Maeve's heart lurched. Just knowing Merrick had seen Saoirse in the flesh was enough to cause her nose to burn and her eyes to water. She sniffed, straightening her spine, adjusting the bodice she wore.

"Don't worry," he said, his voice soothing as his arm fell away. "She's just as fierce as ever and in perfect health."

A shift occurred. His bright blue eyes darkened for only a moment, but it was just enough for Maeve to take notice.

"What?" Maeve searched the soft planes of his face. "What is it?"

Merrick pressed his lips together and dropped his gaze to the petals that fell from the plumeria tree blooming nearby. "I asked if I could bring her back."

Maeve's heart sank. "She said no."

It wasn't a question and they both knew it.

"Saoirse said she couldn't leave Kells." Merrick ran a hand through his hair. "Not until the Scathing was no longer a threat."

Of course. Kells was still her home. She would stop at nothing to protect it, just as Maeve had done once before. Before everything she thought she knew ended up being a lie. Before everyone she cared for was taken from her.

"I have to go to her. She can't stay there. Not on her own." Maeve shook her head, blowing out a frustrated breath. "Especially since the Scathing is no longer just a chasm. If it's a portal, if something comes through it and attacks again, Kells will fall. I can't risk anything happening to her."

"She said you might say that." Merrick nudged their shoulders together. "And she warned me that if I let you get within a breath of Kells, she'd cut off my balls and feed them to the dark fae."

Brynn snorted with laughter, and even Lir cracked a half of a smile.

Merrick threw up both hands. "She was being serious."

Maeve's heart softened. "I know."

"Come on." Brynn draped one arm around Maeve's shoulders and the other around Merrick's. "Tell us about your journey over a drink."

IRRITATION RAVAGED Tiernan from the inside. It was infuriating the way Maeve had so easily tossed his own words back at him, the way she attached herself to Lir's arm, the way the tempting scent of her arousal lingered with every breath.

More than anything, he directed the rage at himself, for his treatment of her. He hated himself for it. Every time he disparaged her, every time he debased her, every time he was crude, ruthless, and vile...it was like taking a blade to his heart.

Hundreds of moons ago, in the depths of his despair, the greed for vengeance overtook him. He wanted to wreck those who had hurt him, destroy those who had ruined him and his family. He wanted their blood on his hands. He couldn't shake his mother's sobs from echoing in his mind. Nor could he forget the way the charmed rope had burned and sawed into his father's flesh as he tried desperately, endlessly, to reach Tiernan. To save him from being tortured.

He remembered it clearly.

Vividly.

They'd been called to the Autumn Court by Aran during the Evernight War to open negotiations for an alliance. But the Four Courts were more dangerous than ever, with the promise of treason and deception lurking in every backhanded compliment and passive-aggressive exchange. Dark fae had slithered their way into the once-trusted ranks of each Court, whispering their dealings and pledges of power to each king and queen. Some had been foolish enough to fall for such deceit. Others, like his parents, were not so easily manipu-lated. Tiernan refused to be sent away, but Ceridwen was another story. They *faded* her to another realm completely, where she remained until the end of the war.

After agreeing to meet on the outskirts of the Black Lake, close enough to Summer to escape if necessary, and far enough away from the heart of Autumn, Tiernan and his parents awaited the arrival of Aran. But the fae who ruled the reaping never showed up. Instead, Tiernan and his parents found trooping fae waiting for them.

They were Puca—shapeshifting fae who were neither inherently good nor evil, but who could be swayed to one side or the other if the deal was sweet enough. At first, Tiernan thought they were nothing more than a pack of wild foxes darting around the lake, until they shifted to their true forms, revealing themselves as grotesque beasts who looked as though they'd walked right out of a nightmare. They were towering monsters with curved horns sticking out on top of their heads. Covered in mangy black fur, they possessed both fangs and talons as sharp as any blade. When they attacked, they wielded both daggers and crossbows.

He was bound, gagged, and blindfolded—then forced to listen as the trooping fae tormented his mother and father. The Puca tied them to the trunks of trees with charmed rope that tightened with every struggle and burned the flesh with every twist. They carved

Tiernan up with blades of nightshade, just as Fearghal had done to Maeve, while his parents were forced to watch. The agonizing burn of the serrated edges digging into his skin was ingrained in his memory. He vowed then to never forget their faces. When they finished with him, leaving him to bleed out and die, they dragged his parents away to be murdered. But by that time, his mother was already dead.

She died of a broken heart. For him.

He knew the moment her heart had shattered. He could recall the exact second her soul cried out in despair for him. When his father followed his mother into death, it nearly broke him. That sensation, that utter torment of loss, was followed quickly by an eruption of magic. It filled him all the way to his soul, breathed new life into him. The power of a High King, passed down to him through his father's death, was the only thing that saved his life.

Alone by the lake, Tiernan gave in to the temptation of the dark. Wrath boiled beneath the surface of his skin, and he swore to the gods—any god that would listen—he would have his vengeance, that he would destroy all who harmed those he loved if given the power to do so. It was then, as he was wallowing in his grief and his mind was clouded by malevolence, that the god of death chose to answer him.

In his weakest of moments, Tiernan made a deal with Aed. Even now, the god of death's words whispered through his mind.

I will give you what you ask—the power of destruction. In exchange, when the time comes, I will take everything from you.

Shoving the memory of his mistake back into the darkest corner of his mind, Tiernan retreated from the beach where Lir had *faded* away with Maeve and returned to his own quarters. He knew she wasn't in the room next to his, but that she was somewhere in the walls of his palace. Laughing. Smiling. Bestowing the full extent of her fire, grace, and beauty upon everyone but him. She probably didn't even want him anymore, not after what he'd said to her. Not after he so casually dismissed her.

But fuck if his cock wasn't still *aching* for her.

He let his anger guide him into his bathroom, where he turned on the shower. Curls of steam filled the space and he inhaled, groaning when the scent of her—cinnamon woods, bonfires, and toasted vanilla—still lingered on his skin. He waited until the temperature was hot enough to melt the skin from his bones, then he ripped off his clothes and climbed in. Scalding water pelted his chest and torso, but it didn't matter, he was already aflame for her.

On the edge of agony, he grabbed his cock and pumped it over and over, picturing her furious little face. But it wasn't enough. He wanted *her* fucking him, not his own hand. He gripped himself again, harder and faster, all the while imagining Maeve's body beneath him. Skin like velvet. Rosy nipples. Flushed cheeks. Hair that fell around her like a damn waterfall of silk. He pictured her head thrown back in ecstasy, her body squirming and arching as he filled her, until the frustration of his own damned mistakes caused the orgasm to surge through him.

He splayed both hands on the shower wall.

Chest heaving, he opened his eyes.

The relief was fleeting. It wouldn't be enough. It would never be enough. Not so long as Maeve occupied every corner of his godsforsaken soul.

Chapter Seven

As much as Maeve wanted to go to the library, she wanted to hear what Merrick had to say first. The four of them walked onto the balcony where they usually dined, and Brynn waved her hand across a table. Bowls of fruit and little sandwiches appeared, along with a carafe of sparkling white wine.

Lir poured her a glass and Merrick downed his in three gulps.

"Kells is a shit show. I mean, Saoirse is holding everything together, but the city is in ruins." Merrick poured himself another glassful of the sparkling beverage. "The city center is gone. It's in ruins. The dock has fallen into the sea. The shops have been abandoned, the homes are crumbling and in disrepair. Everything is covered in overgrowth and rot."

Maeve swallowed. Paled.

"Mer." Brynn smacked him on his arm and jerked her head in Maeve's direction. "A little compassion, please."

"Shit. I'm sorry, Maeve." He reached out and gave her hand a reassuring squeeze. "I know that was your home once, too."

"It's fine. I'm fine." Maeve took a hasty sip of the bubbly liquid, and it burned down the back of her throat. She rolled the stem of the glass back and forth between her fingers. "Please continue."

"Anyway." He spared a glance at Brynn, whose eyes shifted from a sympathetic gold to a warning red and continued. "The damage to the city itself...I think it's irreparable. The Scathing reached as far as the Moors. Carman's fortress still stands on the Cliffs of Morrigan, but the servants cleared out long ago, so much of it is deteriorating. The entire city seemed barren."

Lir sat up straighter, then leaned forward and asked, "Is Saoirse there all by herself?"

Merrick shook his head. "No. Some of Carman's soldiers remained behind. At least the ones who thought their former queen was unhinged for wanting to bring her three sons back from the dead." His vivid eyes locked onto Maeve. "A few of them still think you should be queen."

"No." Maeve stared into the golden bubbles dancing in her glass. She could never.

Her allegiance to Kells died when she killed Carman, when the soldiers she trained alongside so easily turned on her. It made no difference to them if their queen was a wicked sorceress, and why would it? Kells was thriving on the outside, at least until the dark fae attacked. But the inside was rotten. Cruel and cold. So no, she would never rule Kells. If she did, she'd have a target on her back her entire life. She would know no rest.

"When I return to Kells, it will be to bring Saoirse back here and to get rid of the Scathing. So if the people want to return, they can, while being afforded the chance to rebuild."

Brynn kept her heart-shaped face impassive. "And who will rule them?"

"They can elect someone." Maeve rubbed her lips together and took another small drink. "Kells never belonged to Carman; it was the home of a human king first." The one Casimir killed. Along with her mother, Fianna. "She invaded and made it her own. Granted, it was prosperous beneath her rule for a while, but the people of the land should be the ones to choose who governs them."

"Another human monarch might invade," Merrick quipped.

Maeve lifted one shoulder, then let it fall. "They usually do."

Whatever happened to Kells after the Scathing would be for the mortals to decide. She was no longer one of them; they would never accept her. As long as Saoirse wasn't there to suffer the downfall, she told herself she didn't care if the human lands survived or not. It was a lie, but the people she once thought to rule would disown her. They feared the fae, thought them monsters, and would see her no differently, no matter how much it pained her.

Lir propped his elbows on the table and steepled his hands. "What of Tethra, Balor, and Dian?"

The Furies. The brothers she brought back from the dead. Her first *creation*. At the mere thought of it, frozen fingers of unease slid down her spine, and she shivered.

"Nothing yet." Merrick leaned back in his chair, tucking his hands behind his head. "There's a rumor they may have fled to the Moors. But no one has seen them since the night of Carman's death."

The Moors. Maeve had almost forgotten the Scathing had spread all the way to her favorite place. "How are the Moors?"

Merrick nodded. "They're failing. Parts remain alive, but much was lost to the Scathing. A pity really, it was a beautiful place. Did a bit of exploring while I was there." He sent her a pointed look. "Were you aware there's a hidden lake?"

"Yes." Maeve smiled, thinking of the lake that was once all hers. "That's where I found my Aurastone."

"Really?" Brynn's eyes widened, shading to a deep evergreen. "How interesting."

Maeve was going to let the comment slide, but then she saw the warning look Lir sent Brynn. "What do you mean, interesting?"

"Oh, um, it's nothing." Brynn waved off her question and took to inspecting one of her daggers, its blade glinting gold in the morning light. "I just thought it was an interesting way to find a dagger. You know, at the bottom of a lake. It's curious, is all."

"Is it?" Maeve knew whatever Brynn was going to say next was something she wasn't supposed to say. "How did the High King find the Astralstone?"

Lir cut in. "You'll have to ask him."

"Of course. I wouldn't expect anything less." Maeve wanted to roll her eyes but held back. She knew Lir was only trying to help, but it seemed any conversation of consequence should be had with Tiernan directly. At least whenever it came to her. She offered a small, apologetic smile, and he inclined his head.

Just then, Ceridwen appeared. She was decadent, as always. Dressed in a gown of magenta satin with her strap of jeweled daggers at her waist. Her golden hair spilled down her waist and ribbons of deep navy were woven in the gilded strands. She pouted when she saw the plates of snacks and the carafe of wine spread out on the table before them. "I wasn't invited to the party?"

Lir and Merrick were on their feet a second later, pulling out a chair for her and pouring a glass of wine.

"Apologies, my lady." Merrick filled her plate with berries and dusted sugar on top of them.

"I'm only teasing." Ceridwen popped a berry into her mouth. "What are we discussing?"

"Originally we were discussing when I would be able to travel to Kells." Maeve finished her drink. "The Scathing is still a threat, and unless I can destroy it, I stand no chance of convincing Saoirse to return home with me."

Home.

The word hung heavy between them, and Maeve became increasingly aware that every set of eyes on the patio was focused on her. She'd called Niahvess, their Court, her home.

"If it is a portal," she continued, "then perhaps I should seek out the will o' wisp for some clarity on the matter. She might provide some insight on something we've overlooked."

"No," Merrick slammed a fist on the table at the same time Lir said, "Absolutely not."

A delicate line formed across Ceridwen's brow. "Tiernan won't allow it."

Maeve's muscles grew taut, and she forced the words out between a clenched jaw. "Tiernan isn't my High King."

Silence descended upon them, and even the distant call of the sea seemed to die. Brynn frowned, Merrick refused to meet her gaze, and faint shadows clouded Ceridwen's eyes. She hadn't intended to sound so harsh. But it was true. She was fae now, and as one she could choose to whom she swore allegiance. She hadn't yet voiced her loyalty to any Court, and though Summer hosted her and protected her, Autumn was her soul. When she'd been afraid and alone running through the Autumn woods, fleeing Garvan and Shay, the Autumn Court had kept her safe. The woods shielded her from harm. It recognized her as one of its own. It sheltered her.

Lir shifted and stood, then came to stand behind her. He offered a silent kind of support.

"Her Highness makes a valid point, and we shouldn't judge her for it." He placed a strong, encouraging hand on her shoulder. "Maeve is Autumn. She is also Archfae. The choice will always be hers. Besides, we all know she despises being told what to do."

Easy laughter slowly erased the awkward tension between them.

Merrick glanced around the balcony, then tossed a look over his shoulder. "Where is our High King anyway?"

Maeve expelled a heavy sigh. "I pissed him off."

Brynn winked. "At least you admit it."

Merrick leaned across the table toward her and stole one more glance behind him. "Have you two fucked yet?" he whispered.

"Mer!" Ceridwen scolded, and Brynn rolled her eyes skyward.

"Sorry, my lady." Merrick ducked his head in shame, but his dimples were showing and she knew he wasn't sorry at all. "But did you?"

Any other time, Maeve might've been embarrassed. Or blushed.

59

But Tiernan had already insulted her enough for one day, so she schooled her expression into one of bored complacency when she said, "No. I'm sure Tiernan can get whoever he wants into his bed. But I will never be one of them."

Brynn crossed her arms, and a look of displeasure hardened her usually pretty features. "You really don't know him at all, do you?"

"I suppose not." Maeve would readily admit there was plenty she didn't know about the High King, but he hadn't put forth much of an effort either. "It's difficult to want to spend time with someone who enjoys humiliating you every day."

Ceridwen grabbed another berry. "He's not so bad."

"He is to me," Maeve countered, affronted by the fact that none of them seemed to have any clue how *awful* he truly was to her.

Ceridwen sighed. "You have to understand, his past—"

"Is no worse than mine," Maeve cut the High Princess off and met her gaze as she popped the berry into her mouth. "I have suffered just as much. He can at least mourn the loss of his family, whereas mine was stolen from me before I even knew them. But I don't let my past dictate my words. I don't insult you. Any of you. I don't embarrass you or shame you. I don't intentionally seek to hurt your feelings, and I never would." Maeve shoved back away from the table and stood up. "Not ever."

Ceridwen bit her lip and shared a glance with Lir. "I'll talk to him. It's just—"

"There's no need, my lady." Maeve dropped into a painfully formal curtsy, suddenly feeling far more human than fae due to the tidal wave of emotions rolling through her. "The High King has made his feelings for me quite clear, and except for training, I want nothing to do with him."

There was a tug in her chest. A distinctive pull, like a calling. A memory.

She shifted her gaze to the skies, and that was when she saw the space between the clouds and the sea glimmer and shift as though the worlds were peeling apart. The sparse clouds rolled back, revealing a magnificent, winged creature shrouded in a veil of silvery mist. It cut across the horizon and its glittering black scales sparkled like onyx dipped in iridescence.

Like calls to like.

Aran.

Her brother. He was back. Aran had come back, just as he promised. Excitement skittered along her skin, and she rushed to the railing of the outdoor balcony where they dined. He couldn't have come for her at a better time. She needed to get away from the Summer Court. Away from everyone who worshiped the ground Tiernan walked upon like he was a god. Away from the High King himself.

She spun around to find all four of the Summer fae watching her. But she focused on Merrick only. He stood, caught as though he didn't know if he should step toward her or stay put.

She gave him a small smile. "I'm glad you're back. Truly. Thank you for bringing news of Saoirse."

She knew she'd foolishly offered her gratitude again, but she didn't care. They should expect it from her by now.

Magic pulsed and coursed through her. She grabbed it, held onto it, and didn't let go. Heaving herself up onto the railing, she outstretched her arms and jumped off.

In the back of her mind, she was fairly certain Ceridwen screamed and Lir bellowed her name. But she was flying. Her wings burst from her back as she leapt off of the ledge. Warmth spread through her, full of life. They fluttered like feathered fans of ivory dipped in rose gold. She flapped them once. Twice. Not only were they stunning, but they were powerful. She was powerful. She soared toward Effie, the stunning winged *trechen* with her three eagle-like heads. Cutting through the sky, she flew to Aran, and was elated to seek the look of pure awe plastered to her oldest brother's face.

His jaw dropped as she coasted toward him.

"Well, well." His charming smile widened. "Look who finally got her wings."

She flew closer, hovered overhead, then called them in and dropped onto Effie's back, right behind Aran. Her arms flew around his waist, and she squeezed. His large hand covered both of hers and her head came to rest on his back.

"I missed you." She sighed against him.

"I missed you, too."

She didn't let go and he glanced over his shoulder at her. "Is everything okay?"

"Yes." No. But she wasn't ready to admit as much. Not yet. "Just happy to spend some time with you."

The wind rippled through Aran's rich auburn hair, and he swept it to the side for a better look at her. "We have a lot to catch up on."

"We do." Maeve nodded, but continued to lean against him, to lean into the easy comfort he brought her. "Can we go to the *Amshir?*"

She just wanted a reprieve. Some quality brother and sister time. An hour or two away from having to train, from having to practice, from having to learn to be someone she wasn't yet. A small break was all she wanted, nothing that would get either of them in trouble. But she needed to recuperate and compose herself after Tiernan kissed her stupid then told her it was just a means to an end. Like she was a problem, something he was either forced to deal with or fix.

Aran's emerald eyes darkened. "I don't think Tiernan will look too kindly upon me for removing you from the safety of his Court."

"Please, Aran?" She hugged him again. "He'll be able to find me. He always does. I need to get away. Even if only for an hour or two."

"Alright." He patted her hand. "But only because I love you."

Maeve's heart soared and unexpected tears sprung to her eyes. No one had ever told her that before. Not one soul had ever told her they loved her and meant it. Saoirse had often come close, describing her feelings with her poetic nature, but the word "love" wasn't in her vocabulary. Maeve supposed it was the warrior in her. The desire to never want to get too close to anyone, the understanding that death was only ever a breath away.

She leaned forward and wrapped her arms around him, resting her head on his back. "I love you, too."

Aran squeezed her hand once more and in a glow of mist, he directed Effie out to the open waters, to where the *Amshir* waited for them off the coast of Niahvess.

TIERNAN WAS LYING on his back on the leather couch in his room, one ankle kicked over the other, while mindlessly plucking at the strings of his guitar, when Ceridwen burst into his room.

Her face was flushed, and she radiated a kind of energy he hadn't seen from her in years. She was mad. A scowl lined her brow and her eyes darkened to that of an incoming summer storm. No, she was *pissed*.

She stomped up to him in a flurry of indignation with her fists planted squarely on her hips. "What is *wrong* with you?" Accusation lit her tone and if her words had been created by fire, he swore they would've scorched his skin.

"Me?" Tiernan asked, calmly sitting up and showing her the respect she deserved, while also quietly hoping she'd relax a little. He'd never seen her so worked up.

"Knock it off, Tiernan." She paced, stalking back and forth before his hearth in a whirlwind of tempered rage. She looked like she was trying to use her magic on herself, to soothe her mind and calm her thoughts, but she was failing miserably. Her face was flushed pink. Each time she blew out a shaking breath, she would squeeze her eyes shut. But whenever she opened them again, flames of frustration still ignited them. She condemned him by shoving a finger into his chest. "Would it kill you to just be nice to her every once in a while?"

He sat up, stretched out his legs, and set his guitar to the side. "I am nice."

"Oh, bullshit."

Tiernan laughed. Ceridwen never swore.

"It's not funny, Tier." She huffed out a breath. "War is coming. Parisa has been too quiet behind the borders of Spring, there's still the Scathing to deal with, and the Furies, and goddess above, if Garvan finds out about Maeve—"

The slim thread of control Tiernan held onto snapped. He shoved up from the couch, and the doors leading to his shared balcony with Maeve flew open, his fury evident.

"You think I don't know this?" Tiernan bellowed. "You think I don't know war is coming, that we have a shit ton of enemies to face? You think it's not on my mind every hour of every day?"

Ceridwen's eyes, a perfect match to his own, widened in shock. Her entire body had gone utterly still—he'd never taken that harsh of a tone with her.

Tiernan blew out a ragged breath and ran his hand through his hair. "I'm sorry, Ceridwen. I shouldn't have yelled at you."

He dropped back down onto the couch and propped his elbows on his knees, letting his head hang to relieve the weight of the realm from his shoulders. There was a gentle push of magic, a soothing sensation that coasted over him and eased the mounting stress from his bones. "Thanks, Cer."

She carefully lowered herself next to him and kept her hands folded neatly in her lap. Ever graceful. Ever elegant. Just like their mother had been before she was taken from them.

Ceridwen smoothed her gown, fiddling with a bit of lace on the hem. "There's something on your mind."

Everything was on his mind. He did not want to relive another Evernight War. He didn't want to watch his people suffer, he didn't want to lose good warriors, and he didn't want to watch the throes of war take innocent lives. He wouldn't be able to handle it if anything happened to Ceridwen, or Merrick, or Lir, or Brynn. And he would destroy the soul of anyone who dared to even look at Maeve the wrong way.

"I will die before I let our Court fall again. But Summer alone cannot stave off Parisa's so-called Dark Court. We need allies."

She nodded in solemn agreement. "We'll find them."

"There are too many unknowns. We don't know what lies within the depths of the Scathing. We don't know what Parisa is planning." Tiernan leaned back and let his head fall against the comfort of the cushions. "And the Furies haven't been seen since Carman's death."

Ceridwen tapped her nails together, and the rings on her fingers sparkled in every color of the rainbow. "Didn't you say the Furies answer to Maeve?"

"I did."

He expelled another deep and drawn sigh. It wasn't his finest moment, but he'd allowed himself to slip into Maeve's mind in those first few days after Lir returned with her from the Spring Court. He saw her memories of what happened in Kells and felt the distinct sting of betrayal she suffered when Casimir turned her over to Parisa. He watched as she brought Tethra, Balor, and Dian back from the dead, watched as they destroyed the soldiers who attempted to harm her.

"When the Furies were in Faeven before, it was under Carman's rule." Acid roiled in his stomach as he remembered the terror they'd left in their wake. It was almost unthinkable to ask for their help, but they were running out of options. "And since Maeve brought them back from the dead, asking them to aid us would be an asset."

He met his twin's gaze. Her face had gone deathly pale. She shook her head, and her golden hair tumbled down her back. "No, Tiernan."

He reached over and squeezed her hand. He needed her on his side for this, for everything they would face. "It might be our only choice."

Her bottom lip quivered. "But at what risk?"

"At the risk of losing everything."

She dropped her head onto his shoulder. "What of the Wild Hunt?"

"It's possible they'll answer to her as well. If she calls them back."

Gods, he didn't even want to think about having that conversation with Maeve. She'd likely rip his head off.

Beside him, Ceridwen shuddered. "It'll be dangerous."

"She won't have to do it alone." He wouldn't allow it. But if Maeve could use the magic of the *anam ó Danua* to bring back the Furies, then certainly she could call upon the Wild Hunt for assistance. Locating them would prove difficult. They were the eternal warriors, neither living nor dead. They moved with the storms, foretold of wars and strife, and existed within planes not of their own. "I'll help her, Cer. I promise I won't let her suffer alone."

Ceridwen stood and her gown rippled around her. "Well, you told me everything I already knew or suspected."

"But?" Tiernan asked, reaching for his guitar again.

"But you haven't told me what's bothering you *here*."

He glanced up to see his sister with her hand placed over her heart.

"What is it, Tiernan? What's wrong?"

His fingers moved over the strings, thrumming the chords of a painful melody. The one he wrote for a fierce faerie princess. The tune filled his room and the hauntingly beautiful notes lingered in the quiet.

"It's her," he murmured.

"Maeve?" Ceridwen's brow furrowed. "What about her?"

"It's *her*." Reluctantly, Tiernan met his twin's gaze. He let her see past his armor, past the shield he'd built to protect himself from his past mistakes, from his weakest, most unforgivable moment. He let her into his soul. Into his aura. So she could see firsthand this fresh hell he suffered. Unable to speak the word *sirra*, he whispered his torture in the form of a song.

"BORN OF FIRE, *smoke, and Autumn's last breath,*
    I thought to n'er see one so lovely as she,
    But in shadows, death he waits,

To trick the stars, and lure the fates,
And forever, all will be lost unto me."

CERIDWEN'S HANDS flew to her mouth. Crestfallen, tears slid from the corners of her eyes. "Oh, Tiernan. You have to tell her."

"I can't." He continued to strum his guitar mindlessly. "It's too dangerous. There's no way of knowing when the god of death will call in his end of our bargain. The more distance I keep between us, the better."

"That's not fair. To either of you," Ceridwen said. "If she's fated to you, she deserves to know."

"Trust me," he muttered. "I can assure you it's the last thing she wants to hear."

Being his soulmate was a death wish.

Beside him, Ceridwen shook her head in disagreement. Tiernan didn't want her sympathy, but the sound of his sister's heart breaking for him carved out a piece of his soul.

Chapter Eight

Onboard the *Amshir*, Maeve found herself once more inside Aran's map room. It was still as lovely as ever. She enjoyed the way the glass orbs in Autumn colors danced overhead, suspended by nothing but magic. On his desk were what looked to be bookmarks. Intricate designs were hand-painted upon the finely woven silk. They were long and tapered with beaded tassels. Displayed beneath a watercolor map of the realms, a number of little trinkets rested upon a wooden shelf. One in particular caught her eye.

It was a little black box and cushioned inside a tuft of crimson velvet was a marble. It was larger than most and filled her palm. But when she held it up to the light, her breath caught in the back of her throat. Captured inside the ball of glass was a perfect replica of the Autumn Court. She could see the snowy, white-barked trees with their leaves of crushed crimson, burnt gold, and flaming orange. If she shifted the marble in her hand, the Court inside moved with her, roving over the forest and showcasing the deep sparkle of the Black Lake. In the distance were the mountains rising to the east, barricading the palace and all of Kyol. For a split second, she thought she saw movement by the lake. But she blinked, and it was gone.

A petite fae wearing the colors of Autumn entered the map room carrying a platter of spiced pumpkin tarts and two bowls of stew. Maeve's mouth watered. She carefully set the marble back onto the velvet, but not before she noticed the engraved words on the underside of the box's lid.

"Aran?" She peered over at him as he nodded to the fae, who set down the tray and left without saying a word. "What is Belladonna's Atelier?"

"Belladonna's Atelier is a little shop I found during some of my travels." He moved toward the table where the fae deposited the food, gesturing for Maeve to sit. A smile played along his lips. "She's quite the...character."

Maeve's brows rose, intrigued. "She?"

He shook his head, then pulled out a chair for her. "It's nothing like that. Belladonna is only a friend. She just happens to own a mesmerizing shop filled with all kinds of magical things."

She smirked, grabbing a pumpkin tart from the tray. "If you say so."

"I do." His smirk mirrored her own. He brushed his auburn hair back from his face and his gaze focused on her. "So, tell me more about the Scathing."

Maeve paused, the tart halfway to her mouth. "What about it?"

Aran set one bowl of stew in front of her, then took the other for himself. "I'm Dorai, Maeve. One of the exiled. We see things. We hear things. Word travels fast on the seas."

She didn't doubt it. But the fact he confirmed as much gave her cause for concern. Word of her existence would spread. There would be no way to stop Garvan and Shay from finding out about her. Once they did, Parisa wouldn't be the only one she had to worry about. Maeve popped the rest of the tart into her mouth, swallowing hard.

"It's not so much a plague as a portal."

Aran nodded and a whisper of a shadow fell across his handsome features. "I've heard the same. Some sort of dark magic..."

She scooped up a spoonful of the stew and a medley of flavors—beef, onion, garlic, and spices danced across her tongue. "Yes. And I don't think it's caused by Parisa."

Aran's spine straightened. "You're certain?"

"As certain as I can be, yes." She took another spoonful, watching him carefully,

Overhead, the faerie light orbs continued to sway and move with the gentle waves rocking the *Amshir*. Aran stared at the bowl of stew before him, tilted his head, and then, "Didn't dark fae pour out of the Scathing and attack Kells?"

"Yes, but those dark fae were not the same as the ones in Faeven."

Unbidden memories slammed into her. Monsters of shadow and darkness whose jaws unlocked to devour their victims whole, leaving nothing but bone in their wake. The terrifying creatures who attacked her in her room, with their spindly arms and the spiders that crawled out of their mouths. The ones whose talon-like nails filled her bloodstream with poison. Maeve shuddered against the brutal memory.

Concern glinted in the depths of Aran's emerald gaze, and the flecks of gold there sparked with apprehension. "What do you mean?"

"I mean, I fought the dark fae who attacked the Summer Court, and the ones who ruined Kells...they were not the same."

Aran studied her and when he spoke, his words were clear and precise. "Let me make sure I'm following you." He sat back, adjusting the sleeves of his shirt. It was then Maeve saw he wore the same compass as before, the one wrapped in knots of silk and beads, except this time a piece of rosy pink sea glass was attached to it as well. The sea glass she had given him. "You think the dark fae who attacked Kells are different from those that Parisa controls?"

Maeve nodded. "I do."

"How so?"

"Because the fae I killed in Kells were easy. All it took was one swipe of my Aurastone and they turned to ash." She remembered how easy it had been to kill Madam Dansha, the fortune teller. "But when Niahvess came under attack, I had to aim for their throats. I had to strike true. Any other hit was just a wound. An injury. Killing them took more effort."

Aran shifted in his seat, taking in all she said. "You know what could help you?"

"The will o' wisp?"

"Gods, no." He reared back, affronted by the mere mention of the solitary fae. "Books. You have an affinity for reading, do you not? Surely, answers are kept within the pages of those not yet read."

It was a compliment she would readily accept. There were tons of books inside Tiernan's library she hadn't even touched yet, not to mention the one Rowan had given her about the Aurastone and Astralstone. As soon as the memory of him entered her mind, a horrible twinge wrenched deep inside her. Another fragment of her tortured past meant to wound her. She rubbed her hand along her sternum, shoving the pain away.

She ate a few more bites of her stew and then, once again, curiosity got the better of her. "Are the other Dorai like you?" Maeve snatched one more spiced pumpkin tart. "Do they sail on ships?"

"A good number of them have their own vessels, yes. Some have found homes within other realms and will not live out the rest of their days at sea." His hand absently trailed to the compass around his neck. "As to whether or not they are like me, I suppose that depends on the context of your question."

It wasn't a trap. Not exactly. But she knew what Aran was trying to say, or more so, what he wanted her to say. He wouldn't influence her decision, but how she viewed him was entirely up to her. "Are they good? Loyal? Trustworthy?"

His expression was schooled into one of total neutrality. "And is that what you think? That I'm good, loyal, and trustworthy?"

Maeve reached across the small table and grabbed his free hand. The gesture wasn't lost on Aran and his eyes registered surprise before he could hide it. "Yes. I think all those things. I didn't have a family growing up, I didn't have anyone who loved me. But now I have you, and I think, no matter what, you would lay down your life for me...just as I would for you."

He squeezed her hand and pressed a featherlight kiss across her knuckles. "Then you'd be right." The smile he flashed fell away. "But no, not all Dorai are like me. Some are like me, and others are more forgiving. There are also those who have committed unspeakable crimes and their souls will forever be tainted. They're the thieves among us, the vile ones. They have their own moral code, and I will say they don't set their standards very high."

"What, like pirates?"

"Of a sort."

With her interest piqued, Maeve leaned forward. "Do you speak to them often?"

"Only when I must." Aran watched her, calculating whatever he was about to say next. "We meet fairly regularly on an isle in the Gaelsong Sea, off the coast of Veterra."

She definitely wanted to learn more about that.

He pointed an accusing finger in her direction. "Don't even think about it, Maeve. I know that look in your eye. Save for me, the Dorai are off limits to you." He barged on the second her mouth fell open in protest. "And I know you hate being told what to do, so consider this a plea from your big brother. *Do not* try to seek them out. *Do not* try to learn more about them. Nothing good will come of it, do you understand? If there is anything you want to know, then you come to me first."

Damn it. He was too incredibly smart for his own good.

"Well, then—"

"No." He held up one hand, silencing her. "Promise me right now that you will do as I ask."

Her shoulders dropped but she relented. He was her blood, and she couldn't refuse him.

"Okay. I promise."

He watched her for a few moments longer, waiting, knowing there was more on her mind. She caved beneath his penetrating gaze.

"Do you by chance know where the Furies went? Apparently, they vanished after I...after I was taken."

After she was stolen to Spring by a man she trusted.

After she was tortured in a cell.

"After Casimir brought you to the Spring Court," Aran chose each word with care, "the Furies took to the Moors. With no cause, with no direction or orders to follow, they're just lost souls."

There it was, the confirmation she needed. The Furies would do her bidding if she asked.

Aran lifted one brow. "What are you thinking?"

"I'm thinking I have to go back. To Kells. I have to put an end to the Scathing. I have to find Balor, Tethra, and Dian and return with them to Faeven. Their power is exceptional, and I know the Four Courts will not look kindly upon their return, but they will be under *my* rule." She sat up straighter, ready to defend her response, but Aran didn't argue. "And I have to try and convince Saoirse to come back to the Summer Court."

"Ah." The corners of his mouth lifted into a slow smile. "So, the illustrious warrior lives. Tell me...is she well?"

"As well as possible, given—wait." Maeve studied her brother's face. While he seemed determined to keep his emotions in check, there was no mistaking the glint in his eyes. "Do you have a thing for her?" she teased.

He shrugged and feigned nonchalance. "Call it what you want."

Maeve tucked that little bit of information away to use as ammunition when it came to convincing Saoirse to return to Faeven with her. Perhaps the possibility of a High Prince of Autumn waiting for her would be enough to do the trick.

"If I can bring her back, you'll be the first to know."

He sat back in his chair with his legs propped up on the desk and one ankle crossed over the other. Easing back, he ran his thumb along the cleft in his chin and absently traced the scar there.

"How'd you get that scar?" she asked, knowing he might not tell her but secretly hoping there was a chance.

He grinned. "I fell out of a tree."

Maeve blinked. "You what?"

"I was playing in the forest with Garvan and Shay. We were younger then, reckless and foolish, still in the prime of our youth." He tucked his hands behind his head. "Anyway, Garvan had this great idea that we should go tree jumping."

"Tree jumping," she repeated, and though she wanted to focus on the story, a small part of her was distracted by the mention of their first years. When they were young and Fianna was still a part of their lives. When they were still a family. She had a hard time imagining Garvan and Shay as carefree faerie princes who were simply too caught up enjoying their youth to worry about pressing matters like war.

"It was a sport Shay made up." He sat up straighter, ready to explain. "Basically, we'd just gotten our wings and were learning how to use them, as well as learning how to *fade*." A smile lifted the corner of his mouth, like a memory. "Shay had the brilliant idea that we should jump from the tops of the trees. We were supposed to *fade* first and if we couldn't do it, then we'd resort to our wings."

It absolutely sounded like a game made up by a bunch of immature males, and she couldn't wait to hear more.

"Obviously, because I'm the oldest, I had to go first."

"Obviously," Maeve agreed.

"Well, I jumped, panicked, and couldn't figure out how to *fade*." His rumbling laughter echoed in the small space they shared, and her heart squeezed tight. "My mind blanked and I lost control of my wings. I fell through the tops of the branches and caught myself before I hit the ground. But," he tapped his chin, "the forest made sure I didn't do anything so stupid ever again."

74

"And did you learn your lesson?" she teased.

"I did. The forest disciplined me." He winked. "Garvan and Shay were left to our mother's wrath."

At the mention of their mother, Maeve's soul wept. It was an ache unlike anything she'd ever known. It hurt, not having any of the memories, not being able to share in any of the joy from their childhood. But worse, she supposed, was knowing she was the cause. She was the reason their family was torn apart. Perhaps if Fianna had never fled to the human lands, perhaps if Maeve had never been born, then maybe Dorian would still be around. Maybe Garvan and Shay wouldn't be so cruel.

"I know what you're thinking." Aran's voice was cold and sharp. "Quit it right now."

She sighed, her shoulders rising and falling. "I can't help it."

He stood then and wrapped his arms around her, and she leaned into his embrace. "None of this is your fault, Maeve. Our mother wanted you. She prayed to the goddess for you. So do not ever think her love for you was in vain."

She hugged him back, holding on tight, when her palms lightly grazed the crescent moon scars marring his back, wounds left behind when Carman cut off his wings.

A kindling of hope sparked bright in her mind.

"Come with me." Maeve grabbed Aran's hand and led him out of the map room. "I have an idea."

TIERNAN LOST track of the time since Ceridwen left his room. Seeing her like that, knowing there was nothing she could do to help him...it was more than he could handle. After a few moments of strained silence, she stood and left him to his thoughts.

Which only consisted of Maeve.

If he was smart, he'd put distance between them.

If he was smart, he'd stay far away from her. He wouldn't imagine her in his bed, all flushed and pretty, after he'd pleasured her beyond rational thought. He wouldn't imagine running his tongue between the valley of her breasts, or running his palms up her thighs and over her ass, or burying himself into her so deep she screamed his name.

Fuck.

Raking his hand through his hair, he stalked into the bathroom and turned on the shower. This time, it was ice cold.

Chapter Nine

Maeve led Aran to the back of the *Amshir*, where the wide deck offered glorious views of the Lismore Marin but also space. She didn't know if she was going to be able to help him or not, but if she could bring the Furies back from the dead, then she could certainly regrow Aran's wings.

"Okay." She spread her arms and circled him slowly, fairly sure there would be enough room. Aran was larger than her and his wing-span would likely be far greater, but the stern of the boat looked big enough to accommodate him. Assuming she could do it. "Go ahead and kneel."

Aran's auburn brow quirked. "As much as I love you, darling sister, I kneel before no one."

She rolled her eyes to the crystal blue heavens. "Not like that. Just..." Her gaze darted around, and she dropped onto her knees and sat back on her heels. "Just sit like this."

"Why?" He drew the word out cautiously.

"Because, Aran." She grabbed his hands and squeezed them between hers. "I'm going to try and recreate your wings."

He stared down at her like she'd grown a second head. His

emerald eyes flashed, and some of the color drained from his face. "You're going to what?"

"Well." She stood up and ran her teeth along her bottom lip. "I brought the Furies back. I created a necklace from sunlight." At the mention of that, his brows shot up in surprise. "So, I think I'd like to try and give you back your wings. As much as I love Effie, I know you miss them."

His gaze dipped down to the ground. "I do indeed."

"So, I want to help." Not just help, she thought. But build the bond between them somehow. She was the reason Fianna fled the Autumn Court, the reason she abandoned all she ever knew and loved. Maeve wouldn't let it be in vain. Not when she had an opportunity to rebuild what was lost, to forge a relationship with Aran.

"Do you really think this could work?" Slowly, Aran knelt on the wooden deck. He looked up at her from beneath a swatch of rich auburn hair.

Maeve swallowed down the knot of apprehension building up in the back of her throat. "I think it could, yes."

"Alright, let's give it a try." He bowed his head before her. "Whenever you're ready, High Princess."

"Right." Maeve steadied her nerves and lightly scrubbed her palms against the leather of her leggings. She inhaled and closed her eyes. Magic surrounded her, filled her. She called to the power deep inside her, to the breath of magic swirling and billowing, to the life source coursing through her. Her blood hummed and power rose up, pebbling her flesh with goosebumps. She let her hands splay over his back, where the beautiful wings he'd once possessed had been torn from him.

Ethereal strands of golden light spilled from the tips of her fingers, covering Aran's back like a fine layer of chiffon. It sifted and floated over him, then gathered at the scars beneath his shirt. A powerful force swelled, and Maeve nearly stumbled. It swept over and between them, brilliant and blinding in an explosion of light. Warmth spread over his back, rising to meet her. Beneath her touch,

Aran's body tensed like he was preparing for something. She glanced down to see his eyes were squeezed shut and a tiny bead of sweat had formed along his forehead. Anxiety crawled along her spine, but she ignored it and forced herself to focus on returning the glory of Aran's wings.

Sensations rippled along her fingertips as she imagined the beauty of his wings. They would capture the very essence of him. Strong. Powerful. Magnificent. Intimidating. There was another surge, a rush of magical energy as the air crackled. Aran sucked in a breath as a set of glorious wings burst from his back. They were decadent, deep crimson and gold, draping around him like the mist surrounding a blood moon. He slammed his fist onto the wooden deck, causing the *Amshir* to rock violently. Maeve toppled backward. She tossed both of her arms out to find purchase, but Aran was quicker.

He caught her around the waist with his hands and shot skyward.

A sound of pure elation erupted from him..

Maeve squealed, throwing her arms around his neck.

"You did it!" He coasted through the wispy clouds, spinning her around and around. "Sun and sky, you actually did it."

There was the faintest sheen to his eyes as he held her close, hugging her tightly. "I owe you a debt, dear sister."

"No." Maeve reared back and looked up at his face. "No debt. No vows. No Strands. Just you, Aran. You are enough for me."

His smile was devastating. He kissed her lightly on top of the head. "Ready to fly?"

She ground her teeth and bit out, "Yes." Though to her ears, it sounded like more of a question.

He swung her down swiftly, then hoisted her skyward and let go. She soared above him, shrieking in delight, as warmth tingled along her spine and her wings stretched out behind her. Together they dove through the clouds and then coasted down low toward the sea, skimming their fingers through the cool, cresting waves.

"Soar like this," he directed, and she followed his lead, rising and flying higher. Warm air shifted through her feathers and the breeze carried them over the Lismore Marin. "Now swoop downwind."

He dove and she went after him. Watching. Learning. She matched his energy, tested her own abilities. Aran slowed, flying alongside her, stretching out his arms. "Give me your hands."

Maeve hesitated for only a moment before letting him clasp their hands together.

"We're going to spin."

"Wait, what?" Maeve blinked, suddenly unsure.

"Spread your wings wide," he instructed, demonstrating. "It's a barrel roll, an aerial maneuver used to avoid attack."

Aran was teaching her how to protect herself in the sky. How to defend herself.

"Are you ready?" he asked.

She nodded sharply, and he launched them into a spiral. She yelped, startled as they spun. He held her gaze the entire time.

"I'm going to let go. When I do, I want you to shoot skyward then dive left. Pull your wings in close right before you fly upward. Stretch them wide when you turn, then immediately tuck them on your descent, okay?"

"Okay." She could do this. She could definitely do this.

"On three."

She pressed her lips into a firm line, concentrating.

"One...two..." Aran released her hands, and she was on her own. "Three!"

Maeve bolted toward the clouds, drawing her wings in tight. She funneled up through the sky, far above the sea.

"Left now!" Aran shouted, and she obeyed, unfurling her wings wide as she cut left, gathering them in as she plunged downward.

She pulled up just before she hit the water, sending sea spray shooting out in either direction so the salty mist clung to her cheeks and lashes. She flew back to Aran, where he watched from above, his broad smile beaming with pride.

"Well done." He flew alongside her. "You're a quick study."

She grinned, the sibling bond between them strengthening. "I have a great instructor."

They flew for what seemed like an eternity, an endless flight of exhilaration and freedom. Aran showed her a handful of other moves. He taught her to dodge, to avoid, to keep herself safe in the sky until he was certain she could handle air maneuverability on her own.

Maeve glanced over at Aran. The warm breeze tousled his rich auburn hair. His smile met his eyes in wonder and amazement. Maeve had never seen him so carefree, so untroubled, so full of life.

"How long?" she asked, angling herself sideways beside him. "How long had it been since you had your wings?"

"Too long," he whispered, his voice strangled. "I forgot what it felt like to have the wind sift through my feathers, to feel the rush of exhilaration the second I was bound for the sky. It's been years. There's nothing like it. Nothing."

Minutes bled into hours and eventually they landed back on the deck of the *Amshir*. Maeve's feet barely touched the ground before Aran swept her up into another embrace.

"Whatever would I do without you?" he murmured.

She angled her face up to him. "I imagine you'd be a faerie pirate."

"I still might be," he chuckled. But then his smile faded, and he looked to the sinking sun in the west. The hour was growing late. "You should return to Summer. We wouldn't want to anger the High King."

A fresh heat of annoyance simmered just beneath her skin. "I don't answer to Tiernan."

"Neither do I." Aran stretched his wings, preparing to fly back with her.

"It's okay." Maeve waved him off. "I can go on my own."

He frowned. "Are you certain?"

"Of course. You're not anchored far from shore, and I just spent hours flying with you. Besides, I had a really good instructor." She was grateful for the practice with Aran because she'd have to get used

81

to her wings somehow, and crash landing in water seemed a far safer experiment than on hardened sand, rock, or mountain.

His head tilted to one side. "She'd be so proud of you."

She. Fianna.

"Our mother." Maeve's heart clenched, like it had been pierced with a knife. "Will you tell me about her someday? About both of them?"

The parents she never knew she had.

"The next time we meet," he promised, "I'll tell you everything."

"I'd love that." She stood, reaching for him. "One more thing."

His auburn brow arched in question.

"The compass you wear," she nodded to where it hung from his neck with knotted silk cord, "it doesn't point north."

"It doesn't, no." Sadness crept into his features, and she wished she'd never even mentioned it. He lifted the compass and ran his thumb across the smooth, sparkly glass. "It points to Autumn."

To home.

The unsaid words hung between them.

Aran pulled her into a hug, and as much as she didn't want to let go, she knew she had to return to the Summer Court. He waved goodbye as she took flight from the aft of the *Amshir*, calling upon her wings to carry her back to Summer.

MAEVE GLIDED among the wisps of clouds. She refused to think about how she was basically hanging over the ocean, even if the waves below her were nothing like the terrifying ones that crashed against the Cliffs of Morrigan. She wasn't in a cage, she wasn't trapped. She was free. Her wings were her own and she had to believe in them, to trust in them to return her safely to the Summer Court. She wouldn't tumble to her death and drown out here. There was no wicked sorceress threatening to plunge her to her doom, to hold her underwater until she could no longer breathe. A tremor of unease prickled her skin.

In the darkest corner of her mind, she could still hear the deafening crack of the old oak branch as it groaned beneath the weight of the cage. She could feel the frigid press of metal as it burned into her palms, and she shivered against the bite of the wind as it chilled her skin and bones. But she would not fall victim to the trauma of her past. She shoved it back, locking it away. She didn't want to dwell on memories that continued to haunt her.

The breeze lifted her higher and she shook her head, determined to stay focused. For once, she was in control. She was in command.

She relished in the way the clouds drifted through her fingertips like snowy velvet. Golden sunshine glittered off of the sea. Small waves sparkled like incandescent stretches of gilded turquoise. Her wings flared then soared, letting her rise and fall with the warmth of the breeze, lifting her, carrying her back to Summer's shore. She could just barely make out the towering warrior fae who guarded the coast when a flicker of something in the water caught her eye.

She glanced down and saw nothing, but knowing her eyes did not deceive her, Maeve circled back. This time she let the currents of the sky bring her lower, and that was when she spied it. Clinging to a rock in the middle of the sea was a...child?

The poor girl looked no older than ten years of age, and as far as Maeve could tell, she was definitely human. Threadbare clothes soaked from the sea clung to her bony body. A piece of seaweed was tied into her stringy hair and as Maeve flew closer, she realized the child was crying. Her eyes were rimmed with red, tears slid down her ruddy cheeks, and her whimpers nearly broke Maeve's heart.

She had to save her. But what was a child doing all the way out here? This was the Lismore Marin, and the waters here were magical. Something or someone must have brought her into the realm.

Dorai.

Not Aran, she reminded herself. He wasn't like them. Her

brother was *not* a pirate faerie. She swooped down lower toward the stranded child.

"I'm coming!" Maeve called out, and the little girl's tear-stained face met hers. Her mouth opened and a wail escaped. It was so full of distress and relief, it sent tremors along Maeve's skin. "Just hold on."

The girl waved frantically with one hand, but as another small wave crested around the rock, she clutched the slippery surface and didn't let go again.

Maeve swept down, wings outstretched, and carefully landed upon the rock. The second she touched the rough, gray surface of the stone, the scent of magic mixed with salty sea spray consumed her. Everything around her shimmered. It was exactly like when she stepped through the magical ward surrounding Tiernan's cove.

"What the..."

Wrong. This was all wrong.

It was a glamour.

She hadn't seen it. No, she *had*, but she'd mistaken the shift for the reflection of the sunlight off the sea. Confused, Maeve stumbled forward and reached for the child.

Except it wasn't a mortal girl at all.

Before Maeve's eyes the child morphed into a creature of the sea. Her hair was slick, the color of ink, with skin like a sunken pearl. Onyx eyes were framed by spidery lashes, and bits of crushed coral and shell covered most of her upper body. Her mouth was almost too wide for her face. She gazed back at Maeve, wrinkling her angular nose in distaste.

A merrow, Maeve realized.

She'd seen hand-drawn images of them in her books. They were similar to sirens, but far less pretty and far more terrifying. She couldn't look away, she couldn't stop staring. She'd never seen a merrow before. It was then Maeve saw another flicker as the splash of the merrow's tail cut through the sea. Iridescent scales of black glimmered between the foamy waves, strong and powerful.

Fly.

Every instinct inside of her screamed to flee, to get away as fast as possible, but before she could escape, the merrow whipped her tail into Maeve's side. She staggered toward the edge of the rock, the force of the blow causing her to throw her arms out to recover her balance. But she wasn't fast enough. The merrow snatched her by the arm. Maeve yelped as the creature's nails sank into her flesh like blades.

She didn't even have a chance to catch her breath. They plunged beneath the surface of the Lismore Marin, and the sea was everywhere at once. It was cold and blinding, darker than she ever imagined. Here, the water wasn't comforting and lovely like it was along the shore of Niahvess. It wasn't the glittering turquoise it reflected to the world above. It was a monster. A creature of eternal darkness waiting to swallow her whole.

Panic surged through her, and she thrashed, desperate to get away, to free herself from the merrow's hold. Terror gripped her in its icy hold, sinking into her mind, dredging up the misery of all she'd endured. She kicked and swung at the merrow, but the creature wasn't fazed. The sea swallowed her, and she struggled to grasp her Aurastone, yet every time the tips of her fingers brushed against its hilt, the merrow jerked her deeper into the abyss. She needed to swim back to the rock, she needed to break through the surface, back to where she could breathe. All the fear, all the trauma she'd tried to shove back into the recesses of her memory rushed to the forefront of her mind.

It was her worst nightmare come to life. Everything she'd tried to overcome. Everything she'd tried to defeat was suddenly overwhelming her, drowning her, bringing her down. Her heartbeat pounded, echoing in her skull. Her body twisted and revolted as a bubble of hysteria rose in the back of her throat. But if she opened her mouth to cry out, she'd drown.

Maeve flailed, fought, yet the merrow was too strong. She was simply too fast. Her tail propelled them further into the watery depths where the light of the sun could not reach. Where the sea was dark and fearsome, where there was no way to tell which direction you were going. Maeve clawed at the merrow, but it was useless. Her lungs ached, they screamed for oxygen. Her mind slowly went fuzzy as the darkness pressed in on her. Wave after wave of dizziness swept through her as the crushing weight from the water promised to crush her bones to dust.

She was going to die beneath the sea. A soul lost to the waves. She wasn't brave. She wasn't stronger than her fears. She was nothing. She would die after all, at the hands of her own worst nightmare. Her chest clenched, tightening around her heart. Her body ached and spasmed. Deeper down into the sea they went until the sun was nothing more than a murky memory.

Chapter Ten

Tiernan let the warmth of the sun heal his heart. After confessing to Ceridwen that Maeve was his *sirra*, his room no longer felt like a sanctuary. No matter how many times he picked up his guitar, or how often he steered his thoughts from imagining Maeve's perfect little mouth covering every inch of him, his mind always drifted back to her. It was then he realized he needed someone else to do the talking. Maybe if all he had to do was listen, he could focus on something other than her.

So he'd found Merrick, who not only enjoyed talking, but who also never ran out of things to say.

He'd known Merrick all his life. Merrick's father had been Tiernan's father's most loyal confidant and friend. The two of them, plus Ceridwen were nearly inseparable as children. He'd long since lost track of the number of times they played together in the Summer forest, swam in the cool waters of the faerie pool, and ran along the beaches of Niahvess. As they got older, they would sneak out well past curfew and head into the city, where they would venture into any number of lounges to listen to music, drink until they were stupid, and dance like they weren't Archfae with a swarm of responsibilities. Ceridwen was the only one who ever managed to stay sober enough to get them safely back inside the palace gates without getting caught. Tiernan and Merrick, however, either fell over laughing or found themselves vomiting into a bush. And while their parents seemingly remained unaware of their extracurricular activities, he secretly thought his mother knew. The fact that she'd force them to go train with bloodshot eyes, reeking of alcohol, and suffering through the aftermath of a vicious hangover was reason enough to believe she knew exactly where they'd been all night.

But those were the days of before...

"So," Merrick drawled, pulling Tiernan's attention back to their current conversation. "Are you planning on letting Maeve return to Kells?"

"Maeve does what she wants," Tiernan grunted. Good thing she wasn't here to hear him say *that*.

His friend's bright eyes darkened. "That's not what I meant, and you know it."

"She won't rest unless she sees Saoirse safely back in Faeven with her." A strange tingle prickled over his skin, but he brushed the sensation off. Maeve was with Aran. She was safe. Aran wouldn't let anything happen to her. "You know as well as I do she wants the Scathing destroyed. For some reason she still has a soft spot for the lives of innocent mortals."

"She thought she was one, once."

"I know." Tiernan leaned back in his chair and propped his hands up behind his head. "But yes, she'll be *allowed* to go. And yes, I'll be going with her."

Merrick watched him for a long time, silent and studious. Over lifetimes, they shared everything with one another. They knew each other's greatest achievements, darkest secrets, and greatest fears. Merrick was his best hunter; he could track down anything in less time than it took most. He was also one of the most observant males Tiernan had ever met. So, it made sense when his voice dropped an octave and he leaned forward to whisper, "It's her, isn't it?"

Tiernan spoke the word into his mind. *"Yes."*

Merrick rocked back in his seat and pinched the bridge of his nose. He squeezed his eyes shut. "Fuck."

"An appropriate term," Tiernan agreed. "Yes."

There was another tug this time, a pull of...concern. Or worry. Maybe even a lick of fear. It rushed over him like a wave. The sun slipped behind the clouds, dousing them in shadows and shade. His blood cooled and the hairs along the back of his neck stood on end. Cold, palpable fear slammed into him, so harsh and so fast, it stole the breath from his lungs. Icy panic licked up and down his spine. Sweat broke out along his brow. Terror. There was so much *terror*. He lurched forward, his fingers curling around the arm of his chair until his knuckles turned white.

Merrick's brow furrowed. "What is it? What's wrong?"

Before he had time to recover, Ceridwen *faded* onto the balcony. Her eyes were wild, her lips pulled tight, and it looked as though all the blood had been siphoned from her veins. Tiernan and Merrick were on their feet in a second.

"Where's Maeve?" His twin's gaze sought the skies, looking everywhere but at him.

"She's with Aran." But even speaking the words out loud did little to ease the dread building in his chest. It lodged there and threatened to suffocate him. She couldn't be with Aran. She would never be this afraid in the presence of her brother. Unless someone else was there with them.

"No." Ceridwen shook her head violently. She wrapped her arms around her stomach like she was trying to keep herself from getting sick. "No, I *saw* something. She's not here. She's not with Aran."

A wall of terror slammed into him, fresh and piercing, and its icy grip wrapped around Tiernan's throat and squeezed. This pain, this fear, was dark. It was violent. Like a memory. A terrified gasp ripped from some awful place inside his sister, and Merrick was there in less time than it took to blink, catching her before she hit the ground.

"Something's wrong!" Ceridwen cried and clutched a hand over her chest because she, too, could feel the sheer fright crashing over him. Over Maeve. "This isn't right." She trembled in Merrick's arms and her wide eyes, reflecting dread, latched onto him. "Tiernan, this isn't right."

His gaze stole to Merrick. "Where is she?"

Merrick ducked his head, carefully lifting Ceridwen from the ground and pulling her to her feet. "She left, *moh Ri.*"

"Left?" Tiernan ground the word out, and his tempered rage bubbled up inside of him. Maeve and Aran were supposed to be within the walls of the Summer Court. She wasn't supposed to leave. It wasn't safe. "What do you mean, she left?"

"Don't come at me," Merrick fired back, leveling him with a glare of his own. "You're the one who pissed her off." He jerked his head toward the railing surrounding the balcony. "She jumped off the ledge."

"*What?*" Tiernan boomed.

"She flew, Tiernan. She flew to Aran. I'm assuming they went to his ship." Merrick's blue eyes were frosty and accusing.

His friend was right. He'd been the one to piss her off. He was the one who insulted her, who humiliated her. So, of course, she would take her rage out on him in the worst way possible. By fleeing the protection of his palace. Sun and sky, she was infuriating.

"*Lir!*" Tiernan called to his commander through his thoughts, something he only ever did in grave situations.

Lir *faded* in and appeared right in front of him. He bowed. "Here, my lord."

"Go to the *Amshir* at once." Tiernan directed, then nodded toward Merrick. "Mer, the shore and anywhere else you detect any trace, any scent of her. Ceridwen, you search the cove." His midnight wings exploded from behind him in a burst of wrath. "I'll take the skies."

Another damning surge of terror slicked him with sweat, and he bolted skyward. Fuck, this was all his fault.

"*FIND HER,*" he bellowed so the walls of the palace shuddered, so his call echoed to Summer's furthest edge, so his entire Court kneeled in response to his command.

MAEVE COULDN'T BREATHE.

Her lungs were on fire. Her head was spinning. Nausea swept through her, bile scalded her throat, and right as she was ready to cave, right as she was willing to give into the sea and let it take her, the merrow kissed her. Or it felt like a kiss. Her lips fused to Maeve's briefly—they were slimy and painfully cold—but the wonderful sensation of oxygen, of air, filled her just enough to keep her from drowning.

The merrow continued swimming, pulling her along listlessly, until Maeve spied what looked like an underwater city. Open archways were built into the sides of rock rising from the bed of the sea floor. Pillars of crushed black pearls framed a number of dismal passageways where faerie light barely illuminated the space in an ethereal blue glow. Coral burst from hundreds of sharp, spiraled shells and there were merrows swimming *everywhere*. It seemed almost mythical, too surreal to believe.

She knew merrows existed, or at least, she'd read stories about them. Everything she read claimed they were made creatures, formed from the essence of magic. Long ago, she'd read one particular story where two fae sisters insulted one of the goddesses of the before. Out of spite, the goddess bound them to wooden beams while the tide was out and as the tide came in, they slowly drowned. It was said the sea took pity on them, turning their screams into the calls of sirens, and shifting them into creatures who could live and breathe in the depths of the ocean.

A group of merrows circled around her and she didn't miss the way their glassy, wide-set eyes latched onto her. Some of them swam too close on purpose, inciting her to flinch and recoil in fear. Some of them were even more daring, reaching out and touching her. Groping her. Their cold, rough palms slid over her legs, waist, and feet. Slightly webbed fingers tangled in her hair, and she winced as they snared in her curls. Some of them whispered. Some of them sneered.

The merrow's grip on her wrist tightened, and she yanked Maeve to her side, right as a male merrow was reaching for her breast.

"She is not yours." The merrow's voice was husky. Deep and sultry. She flipped open her hand and sunk her dagger-like nails into the male's shoulder blade. He hissed and jerked away from them. "Don't. Touch."

They swam through one of the underwater tunnels and without warning, Maeve was catapulted forward. She tumbled through the water on a current so strong it tore at her clothing and squeezed her until she thought she'd be ripped in half. The world spiraled around her in a flash of dizzying color. Her body seized and the water surged, hurtling her into a hole barely big enough for her body. The crevice surrounding her opened wide like a mouth and she was dumped onto a pile of shattered seashells and sand, surrounded by...air.

Maeve sucked in a breath and choked. It was oxygen, and it wasn't. It tasted of brine, salty and dense. Her lungs seized and she collapsed onto the jagged chunks of broken shells at her feet. They cut into her palms and stabbed her knees. It was nothing but a dull ache compared to the throbbing in her mind, the constant pulsing at her temples which left her feeling like her head was going to explode at any moment. Her fingers curled into the rough bits of shells, and she gasped. Her stomach heaved, clenched, and the sting of saltwater scraped her throat as she vomited.

She swiped the back of her hand across her mouth and stood gingerly, grappling with her balance on the mound of uneven, crumbling shells.

Maeve called to her magic to see if she could access it. To see if she could somehow save herself. Her power was scarcely a low, dull hum. A breath of response.

Charmed. Wherever she was, whatever she was in, was warded against her magic. Slowly, she let her hand reach for the necklace

Tiernan had given her. She wrapped her fingers around the amethyst and opal, and holding tight, she prayed to the goddess he would hear her call to him.

She was being held in a sphere of some kind, like a bubble of air. It reminded her of the one she made to protect herself while training against Tiernan, but it was different somehow. It rippled around her, yet she could see everything. The merrows who watched her from the darkened alcoves and shadows. The tiny, insignificant fish that swam by without a care. The massive throne made of decadent, glimmering coral. It was then Maeve saw her. Sitting upon the throne, glaring down at her, was a merrow who was just as terrifying as the one who dragged her down from the surface.

The merrow smiled. It wasn't kind, but it wasn't threatening either. It simply looked like it was...uncomfortable for her. Her hair was the same inky shade and piled on top of her head where it was adorned with dark stones that glimmered in the faint glow of faerie light. Pearls encrusted her entire upper body and the scales on her tail were an iridescent black, each one sharpened to a fine point. The water moved, gliding around her so she seemed to float. The longer she stared at Maeve, the more she realized the merrow never blinked. Ever.

It was unnerving, but Maeve found it impossible to look away.

"Where did you get that?" The merrow inclined her head, her eerie gaze focused on the Aurastone strapped to Maeve's thigh as she ran her tongue along her pointy teeth.

She was half tempted to tell the merrow it was none of her damn business, but not only was she outnumbered by opponents, she was also *underwater*. If she wanted to make sure she got out of—wherever she was—alive, she would have to tread carefully. She needed to keep her answers simple. But more than that, she needed to stay calm.

"Do not make me ask you again." The merrow's glittering tail flicked with annoyance.

Maeve stiffened. "I found it."

"Where?" The word seemed to slither from the queen's mouth.

Simple.

Just keep your answers simple, she reminded herself. "In the Moors."

Her response was met with a rise of murmurs, but the merrow sitting upon the throne did not seem impressed. "The Aurastone belonged to my sister. She hid it away before she was murdered by Garvan."

At this, Maeve clenched her fists until the edge of her nails bit into her palms.

"She told me only the one truly worthy of a throne would ever be able to wield it." The merrow's strange smile disappeared. "Yet here it is, claiming a faerie as its truth."

Maeve steeled her spine. She would die before she ever gave up her Aurastone. Some bitchy fae-fish would never convince her that she didn't deserve her dagger.

"It has served me faithfully against those who wish me harm." She let those last few words drop with purpose. "And the dark fae."

The merrow's lips thinned until they looked nonexistent. "The Aurastone has a twin."

"Yes." Maeve nodded. At least of this much, she was aware. "The Astralstone."

Tiernan's dagger.

"The Astralstone belonged to me."

Maeve crossed her arms. She had no idea where this conversation was going, and she was becoming agitated with the passive-aggressive bullshit. It was all too...*fae.* Perhaps she was still more mortal than she realized. They might enjoy speaking in riddles, but she hated it.

"And who are you?" Maeve snapped.

The merrow offered another one of her creepy, unnatural smiles. Her spiked nails tapped against the hardened coral of her throne. "I'm Marella. Queen of Ispomora."

Ispomora. The name vaguely rang a bell. Maeve was sure she'd heard of it in her studies before, but she didn't know much about the place. Except for the fact that it was obviously an undersea realm.

She would have to add it to her growing list of things to research once she returned to the Summer Court.

Assuming she made it that far.

"But you," Queen Marella continued, "are quite the curiosity. You'll have to forgive us for wanting to learn more about the new Archfae who started living under the High King of Summer's watchful eye, whose magic was fresh and ripe, and who suddenly gained wings. All interesting things to those of us who do not venture upon the land. And it would seem you're a novelty to land dwellers as well."

And there it was. Rumors about her were spreading. Aran had been right. The Dorai heard things and word apparently traveled just as fast on the sea as it did below it. But unfortunately, there was nothing to be done. Right now, all she could do was try to survive this interrogation.

"Tell me your name and do not lie," the merrow queen hissed, "or I will gladly have you drowned."

Another spike of panic hit Maeve in the heart. She knew Tiernan and Ceridwen wanted to keep her identity safeguarded for as long as possible. But if speculations were already being made, it wouldn't be easy to deny the truth of her birthright. Not when Queen Marella already knew she was an Archfae with new power and possessed wings. She could tell the truth and risk all of Faeven finding out. Or she could lie and risk dying.

The choice was obvious. "I am Maeve Ruhdneah, High Princess of the Autumn Court."

Murmurs and gasps echoed in her ears, and water currents rippled around her, causing the sphere encircling her to shudder.

"No." Queen Marella shook her head and her tail swished in agitation. "That's impossible. The Autumn Queen vanished years ago. She abandoned her throne."

Maeve lifted her chin. "For me."

There was a roar this time, a collective discussion in harsh whispers and slithering voices. It rose into the cavernous space as each of the merrows fought to be heard.

"She bears a resemblance."

"The eyes, look at the eyes."

"She's the blood of Fianna."

"Enough!" The queen swam forward, and her blackened gaze sharpened. She glided through the water, and it seemed to move for her. "Maeve Ruhdneah. An Autumn Princess come to life...I think you're lying."

Water poured in from the top of the sphere, soaking her. Drowning her. Maeve loosed a garbled scream and shielded her arms over her mouth in a desperate attempt to keep from swallowing more seawater.

"Garvan intends to destroy us." Queen Marella waved one hand and the sphere repaired itself, but the air was thinner now, and Maeve took slow, breathy gasps. "How do we know you aren't in collusion with him?"

"What?" Pressure pounded against Maeve's temples, and she rubbed her fingers there to ease the throbbing pain. "Why does he want to destroy you?"

"He destroys all which he hates or does not understand."

Maeve winced, the headache only increasing with every minute she was trapped inside the bubble. "Fucking prick."

The queen moved around the sphere, forcing Maeve to follow her, to track her. The loose shells slid beneath her boots, and she lost her footing more than once. Queen Marella paused in front of her, coming dangerously close to piercing the shield with her pointy fingernail. "You would speak so ill of your own family?"

Maeve glowered, while the resentment for the brother she barely knew continued to build. "Garvan is *not* my family. I will never swear allegiance to him."

"Good. You shouldn't." The queen's dark gaze roved over her. "He is not king."

To that, Maeve said nothing.

"Do you not find it strange that Garvan is only a High Prince? That even Aran, the Dorai, only holds the title of High Prince?" She inspected her dagger-like nails, then her glossy black eyes shot back to Maeve. "How odd the magic and power of their father, of *your* father, has not yet passed to either one of them."

Maeve stilled. Was it possible? If there was any truth at all to what this merrow queen was saying, then there was a chance. There had to be a chance. "Are you...that is, are you implying that—"

"Dorian, the true High King of the Autumn Court, lives."

"How do you know?"

The merrow's fierce gaze flashed. "You doubt me?"

"Of course not," Maeve answered readily, not wanting to give Queen Marella any more of a reason to drown her. "I'm just...curious."

As always. Another facet of her life that almost always got her into trouble.

Queen Marella swam back to her throne and seated herself, her long black tail sparking and capturing all the light in the small space. "He resides deep within the Autumn forest. It's rumored he is unwell. The loss of your mother did...unspeakable things to him. Drove him mad, some might say."

The merrow queen believed her father was still alive. If Dorian lived, he would be the key to overthrowing Garvan, to uniting the Four Courts, to allying them all against Parisa.

Strange, unsettled silence descended upon the great cove.

"Is there more?" Maeve asked, prodding the merrow queen even further. "Surely you didn't trick me and nearly drown me beneath the sea just to talk to me about Dorian."

Queen Marella coiled the jet-black strands of her hair around one slightly webbed finger. "What do you know of the Aurastone and Astralstone, High Princess?"

"Not as much as I should," Maeve admitted. She'd yet to read the book Rowan had given her, the one full of information regarding the twin daggers.

"Mm." It was a non-committal noise. Or maybe one of disappointment? Maeve couldn't be sure. Queen Marella's face was unreadable, a mask of odd indifference. "I gave the Astralstone to the High King of Summer many years ago in exchange for protection. The Astralstone, though powerful, must be wielded with a certain type of...care."

"Has the High King of Summer not held up his end of the bargain?" Maeve asked.

"He has, and I believe he always shall. However," the merrow's eyes darkened to round orbs of obsidian, "the High King of Summer has no control over the High Prince of Autumn, or his doings, or how he treats his citizens."

Understanding hit Maeve with such force, she stumbled forward a step. Broken shells slid beneath her boots. "You swore allegiance to Autumn."

Queen Marella nodded once.

"And now Garvan has turned on you?"

"Yes." She drew out the word, so once it again it seemed to slide from between her lips. "Garvan has taken to hunting the merrows. While some will argue it's for sport, there are those of us who know better. Once captured, he skins them alive, using their scales for trade to increase Autumn's ever-dwindling coffers."

Scorn boiled through Maeve's blood. Her fury raged. He was a bastard. A vile creature who didn't deserve to breathe within the realms.

"Never again," Maeve swore her own vow, "never again will he harm you in such a way."

The queen's head tilted, and she eyed Maeve coolly, unblinking. "You would stand for us, against your own kin?"

"The High Prince of Autumn may share my blood, but I will never pledge an oath to him." She bristled and crossed her arms, indignation only growing hotter inside her. "I would swear my loyalty to Aran before I knelt before Garvan."

The merrow queen nodded. "You have much to prove, Maeve Ruhdneah, if you are to take your throne."

"Indeed I do."

She snapped her fingers, and two male merrows appeared on either side of the sphere.

"Remember, High Princess, your Aurastone will always prevail."

Maeve opened her mouth to ask what the queen meant, but before she could speak, the male merrows darted into the sphere. Water poured in on either side, freezing cold, nearly sweeping her feet out from under her. Each male snared her by the arm and Maeve sucked in a final breath as they propelled her through the sea.

She broke through the surface of the water, sputtering. On a gasp, she heaved herself onto the stone steps of the verandah leading to Niahvess. Her chest ached as though a boulder had been set atop her. Her throat burned like it had been set on fire. Every breath was painful.

She crawled up the stone stairway, choking, swallowing down gulps of warm summer air. Using the steps for leverage, she staggered to her feet, swaying slightly. Her head throbbed, pulsed at her temples. Even her skin was terribly dry, cracked as though it had been leached of all moisture despite the fact that she was soaking wet. Drenched, with bits of shell and seaweed clinging to her clothing, she wrapped her arms around the nearest pillar, bracing herself for support.

She inhaled. Exhaled. Enjoyed the sweet rush of warm air as it filled her, cleansed her.

And then Lir appeared.

Chapter Eleven

"Hey." Maeve's chest heaved again, and when she spoke, it was like sandpaper had been forced down her mouth. She cleared her throat and tried again, offering a weary smile. "Did you miss me?"

But Lir said nothing.

His silver eyes cut through her, a scowl marred his brow, and she was immediately reminded of the first time they met. He clamped one hand down upon her shoulder, and with no warning, they *faded* into her bedroom.

Deirdre was already there, waiting, spreading a bundle of clean clothing on the bed.

"Cleanse her at once." Lir's voice was low and menacing. He wouldn't even look at her. "She reeks of the sea."

Deirdre bustled past her with competent efficiency, a robe and towel thrown over one shoulder, and displeasure etched into the age lines of her usually warm and welcoming face.

Maeve whirled around to face Lir. "Talk to me."

Nothing.

Just like before...before she thought they were friends.

"No. Don't you dare. Don't you dare give me the silent treatment again." She marched right up to him and stabbed her finger into his chest. He didn't budge. He didn't blink. He didn't even acknowledge her. "You're better than that. I know it."

Deirdre exited the bathroom in a swirl of fragrant steam with her arms crossed. She glanced at Lir, who nodded once and left, shutting the door soundly behind him.

Maeve's chest hurt. There was an ache there, an unfamiliar sensation she didn't recognize. A heavy weight settled around her and nothing she did—no matter how many times she rubbed the sore spot, or how many times she tried to take a breath—eased the increasing pain. Her nose tingled with that burning sensation she hated so much, the one that came with the promise of tears. Unbidden, they slid down her cheeks in silent ribbons. She'd never seen Lir so angry, so mad...at her.

"What did I do wrong?" She swiped at her face, scrubbing away the fallen tears with the back of her hand.

"You had the entire city in an uproar looking for you, dear heart." Deirdre neatly smoothed away the imaginary wrinkles on Maeve's bed. "You jumped off a ledge, spread your wings, and just flew out to sea."

"I was with Aran," Maeve countered, then spread her arms wide, exasperated. "*Everyone* knew that."

"You were with Aran, yes," Deirdre agreed. "Until you weren't. There was no trace of you anywhere, love. I've never seen the High King or High Princess so fearful in all my years." She sighed, pressing one hand to her heart. "The High King sent Lir to the *Amshir* in search of you, only to find out you weren't there. Merrick lost your scent and had no way to track you."

She bustled around the bed, helping Maeve peel her soaked clothing from her skin.

"Lir didn't have to be such a jerk about it," she muttered.

"He was worried, more so than I think he'd care to admit." Deirdre hefted the jeweled top over Maeve's head in one swift tug.

"If there's one thing the commander hates more than anything, it's a mistake. And I believe he's more upset with himself than he is with you."

Maeve snorted in disbelief. "It's not like I did it on purpose."

"Of course not, dear heart." Deirdre's voice was soothing.

"He didn't even ask what happened," Maeve murmured. "Or where I'd been. Or anything."

"Try not to take it to heart. He hasn't always been the best with words." She patted her on the cheek. "Go on and clean up." Deirdre nodded to the shower, laid a turquoise robe upon the bed, and left Maeve alone without another word.

Maeve discarded what was left of her clothing, stepped into the shower, and tried not to think about the way Lir had looked at her with such utter disappointment. Sure, she probably shouldn't have asked Aran to take her to the *Amshir*. But she'd been so desperate to get away. She'd been so angry at Tiernan, so hurt by his words...that she hadn't cared about anyone else in that moment. She'd just wanted to get as far away from him as possible.

In retrospect, she probably should have allowed Aran to escort her home. At least then she wouldn't have been alone when the merrows deceived her. Though if Aran had been with her, they may not have bothered her at all.

If she hadn't been taken to Ispomora, she never would've learned of Garvan's wrongdoings against the merrows. Nor would she have learned some of the truth behind her Aurastone. She'd made progress. She'd learned new information relevant to her cause, and she would hold Garvan responsible for his crimes against the merrows, and anyone else he wronged within the Autumn Court.

Maeve scrubbed her hair and body, rinsing away the salt of the sea. She lathered up the soap and let the lightly sweetened scent of vanilla coat her skin. With her head tilted back beneath the hot spray, scalding water poured over her and enveloped her in a blanket of steam. She stood there, cleansed, and refused to feel guilty for what she'd done. It may not have been the best course of action, but so far, for as long as she'd been in Faeven, all her more reckless decisions had gleaned new information of some kind. And for that, she wouldn't be ashamed.

She dawdled a moment or two longer, until the water cooled, then turned off the overhead faucet. She toweled off, squeezed the excess water from her curls, then glamoured them dry and held up the robe Deirdre had left for her.

It was sheer turquoise chiffon, with matching silk bands at the hems. And while it was exceptionally lovely, she doubted it would be nearly as comfortable as her cotton nightshirt. Wrapping herself into the decadently soft fabric, she pulled open the bathroom door and shrieked.

Tiernan stood before her, his face a barely contained mask of fury, and she was directly in his path.

TIERNAN KNEW HE SCARED HER. But he didn't care. Her pathetic little scream had been a balm to his soul. She'd been the one to scare him. The surge of magic, of all her emotions, had barreled into him. Overwhelmed him. For the first time in a long time, he'd felt true fear. He'd been seconds away from tearing through the realms, from destroying the life and soul of anyone who stood in his way, when Lir had appeared before him and reported that she was safely back in her room.

Now she stood before him, in the flesh and blood, wearing a pretty robe that left absolutely *nothing* to the imagination. He could see each curve, each dip, every inch of skin.

And fuck if he didn't want to take her right then.

Instead, she crossed her arms and cocked one hip to the side. Like she was the one who had the right to be angry. Already his presence enraged her, and he hadn't uttered a word.

She lifted her chin, defiant as always. "Can I help you, my lord?"

"You can start by telling me where the fuck you've been," he growled, enjoying the way her lashes fluttered back in surprise before she quickly schooled her expression into one of disinterest.

She bristled against his harsh tone. "What I do and where I go is none of your concern."

Maeve attempted to shove past him, but he threw his arm out and blocked her escape, barricading her inside the bathroom. "Everything about you is my concern."

She glared up at him. All fire and fury. Smoke and seduction. "Why?"

"Because."

Gods, it was the most pathetic answer, but everything about her made him want to slam his fist into a wall.

"Oh, real smooth, my lord." She rolled her eyes and barreled into him. He didn't give her an inch. *"Move."*

"No." He braced himself for impact in case she threw a punch. "Not until you tell me why you felt the need to vanish for hours without telling anyone where you were going."

"I didn't vanish." She threw her hands up in the air. "All of you knew I was with Aran."

He reached out and curled his hand around the pendant dangling between her breasts, smirking with satisfaction at her sharp inhale. "Then why, High Princess, were you so terrified? Why was your fear so palpable, so consuming, that Ceridwen nearly broke down and I sent every soul in my Court in search of you?"

He would not tell her about the power she held over him.

She ducked her head, and a curtain of curls blocked her face from his view. When she spoke, her voice was soft, laden with something like guilt. "Because I wasn't in your Court."

"Where were you?" He ground the words out and tried to force himself to remain calm, but every muscle, every nerve was wired and strained. All of it for her.

"I was on the *Amshir* with Aran." She flipped her mass of hair from one side to the other. "For a bit."

"And then?"

"And then..."

Tiernan's hand shot out and he captured her chin, so she had no other choice but to look directly at him. "Tell me what happened."

Her lips pressed into a thin line, and she shook her head. "No."

"Why not?"

"You'll hurt them."

Tiernan released her. "It's possible."

"I can't let you do that."

Let. He couldn't remember the last time anyone *let* him do anything. He moved closer, slowly closing the distance between them. He breathed in, inhaled the scent of her, and *let* it consume him completely. "Do not make me delve into your mind for the answers, Maeve."

There was that stubborn lift of her chin again. "It's never stopped you before."

"Damn it, I am trying to be *kind*! I'm doing everything in my power not to rip through the realms and destroy whoever caused you such fear!" Tiernan towered over her, but she didn't flinch beneath his wrath. "But you are so damned stubborn, and you fight me every step of the way!"

She rose up on her toes and jabbed him squarely in the chest. "You call this being kind? You're yelling at me! You're furious. And it doesn't matter what I say. If I tell you I accidentally thought a glamoured merrow was a stranded child, you'd ridicule me for it. If I tell you they dragged me to an underwater city and told me I was worthy of a throne, you'd mock me." She backed away from him then and her shoulders fell, like the battle had already been lost. "And if I dare mention anything about the fact that my Aurastone chose me, you'd humiliate me for all eternity. So forgive me, my lord, if the last person I ever want to talk to about anything is you."

Maeve stormed past him again, and this time he let her go.

Her words were a dagger to his heart. She wounded him. Deeply.

She dropped onto the edge of her bed, crossed one leg over the other, and wrapped her arms around herself. He shook himself out of his stupor from her outburst and approached her again. Slowly, this time. "You were taken to Ispomora?"

Her eyes flashed. "Really? That's all you got from that conversation?"

He matched her energy. "Answer the question."

"Yes," she snapped.

"And they didn't harm you?"

"No." She grabbed a book off her nightstand and flipped it open in a clear dismissal. His blood burned. "Not like you care."

The barb struck true. "I do."

She made a noise of disbelief and continued to turn the pages of her book, not really reading at all. She licked her thumb, swiping at another page, and he tracked the movement. "Sure."

Tiernan couldn't handle it anymore. He couldn't take the way she so easily disregarded him like he was nothing. Like he wasn't a fucking High King of Faeven. She was stubborn and reckless, with just enough audacity that sometimes even looking at her nearly sent him over the edge. He snatched her by the waist and lifted her off the bed in one swift movement.

The book in her hands tumbled to the ground and her bare feet dangled in the air, but her gaze was hyper-focused on him. Relief sank deep into his bones. She was alive. Furious with him, but alive. He'd almost lost her, he'd been panicked, worried she wouldn't come back. That she'd be gone forever. Suddenly, that voice inside his head telling him to put space between them wasn't there anymore.

He glared down at her. "I said I care."

Sparks flickered at her fingertips and cinnamon smoke surrounded them. She demanded an answer of him. "Why?"

"Because you are *mine*." Without thinking, Tiernan drew her in close and fused his mouth to hers. But this kiss was not gentle. It wasn't kind. It was devastating. Torturous. And everything he ever wanted. He tore his mouth away and was met with her damning, lust-filled gaze. "I made you mine when you danced for me in the

Autumn Court. No other will ever touch you. No other will ever mark you. Because you are mine."

TIERNAN LOST track of everything around him when they crashed into each other's arms.

They tumbled onto the bed, and her hands were everywhere at once. Tangled in his hair. Coursing down his shoulders, squeezing the muscle of his arms, exploring his abdomen. Her touch was like fire, hot and dangerous. It set his skin aflame. He climbed on top of her, admired the beauty displayed before him. The only thing keeping him from kissing and tasting every inch of her was the ridiculously sheer robe she wore, and he grinned as she squirmed beneath him, drawing him closer.

He palmed her breasts, using the friction of the fabric to harden her nipples into tiny pink buds. She arched into his grip, a silent demand for more.

Capturing her mouth again, his tongue sought entry, and when she opened for him, the taste of her left him strangled. He bit, and licked, and sucked, all while she writhed underneath him, grinding herself against the hardened length of his cock. Lust filled him, rocked him to his core. He broke the kiss, knowing he wanted more of her, all of her. Her heady desire clung to the air, and it was ambrosia. It melded with his own, and he knew she could sense it as well. This mixture, this mingling of their scents, would be his undoing.

His mind blanked and he forgot everything. He forgot he was supposed to be angry with her. He forgot he was supposed to be punishing her with a kiss. The last thing he'd expected was for her to unravel in his arms. He didn't want to remember anything ever again except for this moment. For how she felt beneath him—like silk. For how she looked up at him—like he was all she ever wanted.

"You should wear this more often." He pulled on the ribbon tied in a bow at her waist, and the robe spilled around her like a faerie pool, exposing her to him completely. He drank his fill of her. Full and lush breasts glimmering in rose gold swirls. The dip of her waist, the curve of her hips. She was glorious. Her skin was velvet beneath his touch and all he wanted to do was glide his tongue over every perfectly smooth inch of her.

She reached up, fumbling, desperately trying to unbutton his shirt. "It's not practical for training."

"Depends on the training," he murmured and sucked her breast into his mouth.

She gasped and bucked beneath him, whimpering when she couldn't free him of his shirt. A simple call to his magic and it was gone. Her robe was gone. Every article of clothing keeping them from each other was gone. His hands stroked her thighs, and he lifted her leg and stretched her wide, planting a kiss just behind her knee. When she hooked her other leg around his waist, he ground himself against her.

The moan that slipped between her lips was all it took. He ravished her. His mouth met the underside of her breast, her neck, her shoulder. Anywhere and everywhere. He gripped her hips. Her ass. And then finally, he let his hand slip between her thighs, cupping her there. It was fascinating, really. How she wiggled and shifted against the palm of his hand, begging for more with a mere thrust of her hips.

"Are you wet for me yet?" The tips of his fingers played along the outer folds of her core, and she jerked her hips, urging him closer.

"I asked you a question, Your Highness."

She looked up at him, all flushed and lovely. Her fingers curled into the bedsheets, and she moved again, grinding against his hand. "Yes."

He bent over her and pressed a kiss just below her ear. "I want to hear you say it."

Her hips lifted, begging for his touch. Her teeth sank into her bottom lip and then, "I'm wet for you, my lord. Only you."

The noise that exploded from somewhere deep inside him was

low and guttural. Primal. He delved two fingers in between the folds of her slick cunt. She was so damn wet. His thumb grazed her clit, pressed down, and she cried out for him.

"Tiernan." His name fell from her lips on a broken sob, and he pressed another kiss to her mouth.

"Not yet, *astora*."

She whimpered and clawed at him, and he relished in the sensation of her nails raking down his back as he curved his fingers just slightly, beckoning her screams. He sucked her other breast into his mouth while he worked her with his hand, twirling his tongue around the sweet little peak of her nipple. She moaned in pleasure, wrapping her arms around his neck and dragging him to her.

"I'm going to fill you full and deep first. And you will only be allowed to come once I'm inside you."

He carefully withdrew his fingers and rose above her. Those sea-swept eyes drank him in, lingering on every inch of him, until they drifted below his waist. Then her lashes fluttered back and her mouth fell open in shock. He glanced at where she stared and grinned.

"Oh, right." He kissed the top of her head. Her cheek. "I may have forgotten to mention that."

"You're...you're pierced." Her cheeks colored to a pretty shade of pink. "There."

"I am."

She reached for him, and the sight of her slender hands barely able to wrap around the full length of him was enough to bring him to his knees. The tips of her fingers trailed along the ladder of piercings adorning his shaft. She touched. Squeezed. Gripped. Pumped. Her curiosity was driving him mad. He expanded in her grip, his cock bulging with need. All he wanted was to slide between her slick folds and lose himself completely. He needed her. All of her. And he needed her now.

"No more." He took her wrist, slowly forcing her to release him. "My turn."

She eased onto her back, spreading her legs readily. She was so wet she damn near glistened for him. He stole one more kiss, branding her with his lips, not caring if the scruff of his facial hair was too rough for her skin. She rubbed her cheek against it, welcoming him. Tiernan nestled the head of his cock at her entrance, held his breath, then plunged himself deep inside of her. She tensed only slightly as he pushed himself further, feeling her stretch to accommodate his size. But shit, she was like nothing he'd ever felt before. She clenched around him, squeezing so tightly he thought he'd spill right then and there.

"Fuck, Maeve." Already beads of sweat broke out along the back of his neck. "You're so fucking tight, it's like you're—"

Tiernan froze above her. All it took was one look at her face, at the way her brow pinched in pain, and he knew. He *knew.*

"Shit." He instantly cupped her cheek, rubbing his thumb back and forth, just beneath her eye. "Maeve. *Maeve.*"

He'd hurt her. Fucking gods, he'd hurt her.

Terrified to move, or even breathe, he searched her face. "Why didn't you tell me?"

Her lashes lowered and she didn't meet his gaze. "You already made your assumptions about me."

"Astora."

Tiernan whispered the affectionate name over and over, like a prayer to the goddess. Each time he spoke it, he carved out a sliver of pain in her heart, carefully replacing it with tenderness. With affection. It was something she never knew she needed, something she never knew she craved. And it was coming from *him.* She thought he hated her. Every callous word, every crude remark, was suddenly wiped away by the press of his lips to her temple, her cheek, her mouth. He loathed her. She was certain of it.

Yet here he was, showing her exactly what it felt like to be adored. To be treasured. To be seen as more than a weapon or a title bestowed upon her. Gods, she'd never known such gentleness; the way he touched her, *looked* at her, it was enough to shatter her soul. Her blood hummed, calling to him, whispering to him. The brush of his lips left her undone. She wanted whatever he was willing to give her. No matter how brief or how fleeting. So long as it came from him, she would want it. She would want *him*.

Tiernan shifted, like he was going to pull out from inside her, and Maeve thought she would die if he stopped now. She hadn't been prepared for him to enter her so fully, she hadn't been prepared for his size, for his length, for any of it. The books had lied. Oh, how they had lied. Or maybe mortal men were simply subpar. Either way, he was halfway inside of her now and even if there had been a pinch of pain, and even if the golden studs lining his cock were slightly intimidating, she didn't want him to stop. She never wanted him to stop.

"No." She gripped his arms, pleading with him not to leave. "No, please."

Worry clouded his eyes, and she'd never seen them such a deep shade of twilight. Like dusk.

Then he was kissing her again. These weren't the hungry, desperate kisses of before. These were different. They were intimate and soft, like gentle explorations. His mouth trailed down her neck, a path of heat, and when he lightly blew on her skin, goosebumps coated her flesh. He sucked her nipple into his mouth again, swirling and nibbling until she was once more squirming beneath him and desperate for more. Warmth pooled low in her belly, but he held firm, not entering her any more than he already had. It didn't matter if her hips rose on their own, angling to urge him deeper inside—he remained completely still and under control. His thumb gently circled the bud of her nipple, and he planted kisses in between the valley of her breasts. For what felt like hours, but was only mere seconds, he continued to worship her with his mouth until she was soaked, and aching, and longing for him.

Only then did he gradually nudge himself deeper inside of her. Inch by excruciatingly slow inch. He stretched her wide and she loved it. Relished in it. She anchored her legs around his back to encourage him until he was fully seated inside of her.

Her name escaped him on a groan, and she tried not to sigh.

He shifted. "Are you okay?"

"Yes." She tried to be firm but was breathless.

"I'll start slow but I cannot..." Tiernan's eyes squeezed shut and when they flew open again, they found hers. "I cannot guarantee it will end that way."

She nodded, ready. "Okay."

True to his word, he pulled out with painstakingly languid movements, then entered her again. He repeated the process, over and over, until gradually he was pumping in and out of her with ease. Their bodies, both slick with sweat, slid against one another, rubbing and causing Maeve to quake with desire. The sensation of the gold studs piercing the length of his cock both teased and tormented her, so each breath became a gasp. And each whimper became a moan. All the while as he moved inside her, as he continued to push her to the brink, he whispered to her in Old Laic.

"I'll worship you till the stars fall from the sky,
Your soul, it answers my call.
The moon, may it shatter
The sun, never rise
Because for you, I will destroy it all."

Not just words, she realized. But a song. A melody. For her.

"Say it again," she whispered as he sank into her once more.

Tiernan hesitated for only a moment before pulling out and gliding into her again. "You understood me?"

"Yes," she gasped. "Say it again, Tiernan. Please."

"Since you asked so nicely," he crooned.

Then he repeated those words in a rich and decadent brogue that wrapped around her skin like layers of silk. He was moving faster now, pumping into her with more force, each time hitting the sweetest of spots that left her teetering on the edge of oblivion. She threw her arms around his neck, let her hands lazily glide over his shoulders and broad chest. Gods, he was beautiful. A sculpted work of art. Chiseled by the hands of a god. He was solid, and gorgeous, and wondrous and—

"You should stop doing that," he muttered above her.

She tightened around him on the next thrust and he groaned. A smile slipped over her lips. "Doing what?"

"Flattering me." His jaw clenched like he was about to break. "Your thoughts are enough to make me erupt inside you right now."

She dug her nails into his shoulder blades. "Then do so, my lord. And take me with you."

"*Fuck,*" he growled.

Tiernan sucked her mouth. Bit her lips. Her body spasmed, his muscles tensed. Again and again, he drove himself deeper inside her. Stars and shadows surrounded them. Fire and violet streaks of lights shattered above them. A shuddering burst of stardust and magic rained down upon them as the orgasm tore through her and he emptied himself inside her.

Chapter Twelve

T iernan couldn't breathe.

He didn't want to move, he didn't want to disturb whatever happened between Maeve and him. As soon as he climaxed, he saw the Strand form above them. He watched as the colors blended together, as the shape of an Autumn leaf emblazoned by the Summer sun branded her skin. It appeared right above her heart, covering the tattoo he'd painted there, searing their bond. Marking her as his *sirra*.

He knew, because a matching one imprinted upon him as well.

Just as he knew that when she asked about it, because at some point she would, he'd have to think of some excuse. Some reason to keep her safe from the truth. It would break him to have to lie to her.

He bent over her and pressed soft kisses to her eyes. Her cheeks. Her temples. Gods, he'd been a dick for not realizing she'd been untouched. However, it filled him with tremendous satisfaction knowing he was her first, and that he would be her only, for all eternity.

Carefully, so not to hurt her again, he slid out from between her legs. She whimpered softly, and he rolled onto the bed next to her, curling her into him as he settled down beside her. Again, his cock was already hardening, wanting her a second time. The sweet and delicious curve of her ass was far too tempting. But he couldn't. He wouldn't. She would need to heal and adjust, so he distracted himself by tracing the curves of her tattoos along her shoulder with the tip of his finger.

Delight slammed into him when she nestled her backside closer against him, and he sucked in a breath, struggling to keep his arousal under control. He started humming instead.

"It was you," she whispered softly.

He detected the faintest hint of an ache in her voice and ceased his tracing. "What was me?"

"When I was poisoned by the dark fae that night they attacked, and I was so sick and delirious," she spoke, her words filling the room. "I heard music and singing...it was you. You sang to me, and I heard it. You brought me back."

"I sang, yes."

He'd been frightened then. The poison from the dark fae had ravaged her body, leaving her weak. Defenseless. Not to mention those damned cuffs Carman had shackled onto her diminished the healing magic of her blood. He'd been terrified of losing her, and he'd only just met her.

He recalled the first time he saw her, when she stood on the verandah overlooking the Lismore Marin. She'd been accompanied by Rowan, Saoirse, and Casimir, and the moment he laid eyes on her, his heart nearly stopped in his chest. His soul sang for her then, called to her, and the sight of her had nearly left him breathless. She'd been all spitfire and fury, demanding he grant her refuge within his Court. She wore her fearlessness like a cloak, and when he'd threatened her, she hadn't even hesitated to stab him with one of those pathetic throwing stars. It had been a pitiful attempt at self-defense, slightly adorable in retrospect, but pitiful nonetheless. It was then, when she'd glared up at him with eyes that reminded him of early morning sea mist, he knew she was destined for him.

Maeve rolled over to face him, and his hand went to her hips, hauling her closer.

"So." She looked up at him from beneath her lashes. "Does this mean you don't hate me?"

He gripped her ass with one hand, let his palm drag and skim along her thigh. Then he hooked her leg over his hip. "I never hated you."

She arched one brow, clearly not amused.

Tiernan grazed his bottom lip with his teeth. "I just enjoy tormenting you."

Her lips twitched slightly and then, "The feeling is mutual."

Seconds stretched into minutes and eventually her lashes fluttered closed. When next she spoke, it was deep and sultry and on the edge of sleep.

"Are you going to leave?"

He ran his fingers through her hair, liking the way the curls wrapped around them. "Do you want me to leave?"

"No."

Another wrench in his heart. "Then I'll stay."

"Do you promise?"

"Yes."

Time slipped by as he lay there with her in his arms. Overhead, stars winked through the glass dome and a river of silver moonlight washed over them. Her eyes remained closed and though her breathing was deep and sound, he knew she wasn't sleeping. She was waiting...to see if he would break his promise.

"*Astora*," he murmured across her cheek, and she pretended to stir. Sun and sky, she was so fucking cute. "May I ask you something?"

With that, her eyes flew open, focused and alert. "If I can ask you something in return."

"You learn so quickly," he mused, then leaned closer, until the tips of their noses touched.

She gazed up at him, the depths of her eyes like pools of the

Lismore Marin. Beautifully green. Mystically gray. Flecked with golden shards of sunlight. He stared, mesmerized, as she said, "I learn from the best."

Tiernan swallowed. He hoped she meant it as a compliment.

Maeve lifted her head and pressed a kiss to the corner of his mouth. "What's your question, my lord?"

He searched her face, unable to find the words. Then he settled for, "May I kiss you?"

She cupped his cheek with one hand, her skin featherlight and soft against the rough scruff of his jaw. Though it was the barest of touches, his blood pumped and he hardened with desire once more.

"You know you don't have to ask. You never ask for anything." She offered him a slow, lazy smile in jest. "What's your real question?"

He shifted, adjusting the length of him, so he settled between her thighs once more. They were still slick and he lightly dug his fingers into her hips so she would know the true effect she had on him. She arched toward him, and he stifled a groan.

"No distractions, my lord."

"Right." Jaw clenched, he settled his raging hormones. Instead of acting like a High King who could control himself in a bedchamber, he was acting like a lust-filled fae boy who'd only just discovered the wonders of sex.

"There's a celebration coming up." A huge party, actually. The last day of summer—the birthday he shared with Ceridwen. "Every year we host a week-long party. The only time we didn't was after the death of my parents, and during Carman's reign."

"And?" Maeve prompted.

"And I want you by my side."

Maeve's nose wrinkled, and then she laughed. She *laughed*. For him. It stole his breath, ripped through his heart, and owned his soul. It was the most rapturous sound he'd ever heard.

"That's not a question," she teased. "That's a command."

Damn her. His mouth was on hers a second later, devouring her.

He sucked on her lips and swept his tongue over hers, determined to lure her into a state of mind-numbing longing. Her nails scoured his shoulder and back. He deepened the kiss and her hips glided back and forth over his cock, soaking him with the proof of her arousal. When he finally broke away, she was breathless, her cheeks were flushed, and those pretty eyes were glazed.

All of it for him.

He pressed another kiss to her temple. "Your Highness, will you please attend Sunatalis with me? As my..."

His mind blanked. He didn't know what to call her, what title to give.

Her glistening lips curved into a seductive smile. "Are you asking me to be your girlfriend?"

"It's more than that." He couldn't say the word *sirra*. It was far too soon. She would panic, possibly try to flee, and then all would be lost.

"I wouldn't expect anything less."

He drank her in, silently dared her to deny him. "Is that a yes?"

She nodded. "Yes."

Content, he pulled her into him.

"My turn," she purred, and his groin pulsed and throbbed.

He blew out a shaky breath. "I was hoping to kiss you until you forgot."

"Another time." She rubbed herself along the length of him.

Wicked little creature.

"Ask away, High Princess."

Her simpering smile fell away and a coil of dread sank low in his gut. "I need to protect the merrows from Garvan. Will you help me?"

That was not at all what he'd been expecting of her. "What's he done?"

"He's hunting them. Enslaving them." Her throat worked, and he bore witness to the distress lining the beautiful features of her face. She was upset. Angry. "He's skinning them alive and selling their scales for money to make up for Autumn's nearly depleted resources."

"That fucking prick." Tiernan's own rage mirrored hers.

"My thoughts exactly."

His fury was enough to smother the desire pumping through his veins. Queen Marella gave him the Astralstone in exchange for protection. Though her alliance was with the Autumn Court, she and the merrows would remain safe so long as they moved between Summer waters. But there was only so much he could do. His power only extended so far until it would be considered an act of war. And maybe that was exactly what Garvan wanted. But why?

"Tiernan?" Maeve's soft voice drew him back from the recesses of his thoughts. She was looking up at him. Expectant. "Will you help me?"

"Yes." Anything. He would do anything for her. "Yes, Maeve. I'll help you."

"What do we do?"

His gaze drifted to the glass dome above them, where the stillness of night coated Niahvess, where the stars kept watch. "First, we sleep. In the morning, we plan."

"Okay." Her body relaxed into him.

Tiernan lay there, watching her until her eyes finally closed, tempted by the pull of sleep. Her chest rose and fell in long, even breaths, a lullaby to his ears. As she slumbered soundly, the tension from all the years of before slid away, and his magic unfurled around them. The cool kiss of a summer breeze. The soft rumble of thunder.

For the first time in a long time, Tiernan slept.

MAEVE WOKE, deliciously sore and comfortably warm. A strong arm was slung possessively across her waist, and she looked over to see the High King of Summer sleeping soundly beside her.

Her heart stuttered.

She'd not expected such tenderness from him last night. He'd been demanding. Punishing. And then...everything had changed. His kisses went from rough and desperate to soft and lingering, like he worshiped every inch of her body. She'd never felt so cherished. So treasured. She wasn't foolish enough to think it was for any reason other than he'd belatedly realized he was taking her virginity.

Even still, she appreciated his concern for her.

Morning sunshine spilled in through her windows from the east and above them the sky was tinged in hues of blush from the glow of dawn.

She studied him while he slept.

Sun and sky, he was gorgeous. She memorized the angle of his jaw, rugged and scruffy, yet classically handsome. She liked the way his dark lashes swept down, was maybe even a little jealous of their beauty. His dark hair fell across his face in long, sweeping pieces. Then there was his full mouth, those delicious lips...

"If you don't stop thinking so loudly, I'll be forced to have you beneath me again this morning." The rich timbre of his voice skated through her mind and chills riddled her flesh.

She inched closer. *"Is that a threat, my lord?"*

"No. It's a promise." Just then, his eyes slowly opened, the mesmerizing twilight of them still full of sleep. His palm coasted over her hip and bottom, squeezing gently. "But last night was your first time, and I don't want to hurt you again."

A frustrated sigh escaped her. "How long will you make me wait, my lord?"

He smiled, but it was sinful. "So eager."

She stretched out, reaching her arms overhead, arching her back, and pointing her toes. Then she pulled back the covers and crawled out of bed.

Tiernan was faster. He snatched her waist, his grip unbreakable. "Where are you going?"

She nodded to the bathroom. "Just to shower."

He made a noise, like a disappointed grunt, but released her.

She slid from the bed and padded softly to the bathroom, knowing he watched her every movement. She turned on the faucet and let ribbons of steam fill the bathroom before piling her mass of curls on top of her head and stepping into the shower. All she wanted was to soak and soothe. The hot water gently poured over the sensitive area between her thighs while she played back every image from the previous night in her mind. Already she wanted him again.

But when she exited the bathroom, fully expecting him to be awaiting her return, he was gone.

Clothes were laid out on her bed. Leather leggings, a cropped corset-style top armored with midnight blue sapphires, and her favorite boots. Her Aurastone was there as well. Apparently, training was in order for the day. Maeve quickly changed, ran her fingers through her hair, and when she opened her bedroom door, Lir was standing there.

Back on guard duty, she presumed. His curved swords were at his waist. He wore black pants, his silver-studded boots, and a deep blue shirt with the cuffs rolled to his elbows. He shifted his weight when he saw her.

"Lir." Maeve closed the door behind her and stared up at the stony-faced warrior.

He inclined his head. "Your Highness."

There was a rub of tension between them, and she didn't like it. It wasn't supposed to be like that, not for them. He was her friend. At least, she'd thought as much.

She twisted her fingers together in front of her, willing her spine to lock into place. "I'm not used to having anyone care about me."

Lir offered her his arm. "I never should have let you out of my sight. I apologize for my foul demeanor yesterday. I was furious with myself for letting you go meet Aran alone."

Maeve leaned into him. "If it makes you feel any better, I don't think I'll be jumping off another balcony any time soon."

"I prefer you let me know ahead of time if you do."

She glanced up to see a ghost of a smile play along his lips before it vanished.

They walked out onto the balcony for breakfast and Maeve realized that was definitely a mistake.

Everyone was there. Tiernan and Ceridwen. Merrick and Brynn. All of them were watching her. *All* of them *knew*. Of course they did; they could probably sense Tiernan's scent on her. She knew for a fact they'd be able to smell her on him. All over him. Her knees softened. Her heart skittered. Heat bled into Maeve's cheeks as she stood awkwardly, her grip latched onto Lir's forearm. She worried if she let go, she'd fall. But then Tiernan was standing, reaching out his hand to her. Lir led her over and she accepted Tiernan's hand, sitting down by his side.

He didn't release her, instead he grazed her knuckles with his thumb in a slow, intentional sweeping motion. His gaze met hers. Held. "My lady."

She couldn't find her voice but lifted her chin anyway. "My lord."

Across from her, Merrick grinned, his dimples on full display. He rapped his knuckles on the table. "Thank the fucking gods, it's about damn time."

Brynn strode forward and her burgundy corkscrew curls glinted like rubies in the sunlight. "Alright, pay up."

She held out her hand to Merrick and Lir. They groaned but reached into their pockets and shoved gold coins into her waiting hand.

Ceridwen smiled, shaking her head lightly. "Always something with you three."

Maeve's mouth fell open. "You placed bets?"

Merrick flashed her a quick wink. "All in good fun, Your Highness."

She kept her expression neutral as she watched him. "You should've told me. I would've helped you win."

There was a shock of heavy silence, and then a roar of laughter. Merrick tossed his head back, wiping fake tears from his eyes.

"Well done, Your Highness," Lir chuckled and rocked his seat backward. "Well done."

Beside her, Tiernan released her hand and slid his own under the table. He found her thigh and squeezed. She tried to ignore the way her nipples hardened in response to his touch.

Again, all eyes were on her. Expectant. A small cascade of serenity drifted over her. Comfortable and caring.

Ceridwen.

She stole a glance at the High Princess seated next to her, resplendent in a gown of liquid gold and turquoise. She nodded in encouragement and the dangling earrings shaped like gilded suns swung freely from her ears.

Maeve blew out a shaky breath. "I wanted to apologize to all of you for—"

"No." Brynn shook her head and grabbed a muffin from the crystal bowl in front of her. "No apologies, Your Highness. You're one of us now." She gestured around the table to all of them. "A part of our family."

"And now you know we care," Lir added gently. Quietly.

A lump formed in the back of Maeve's throat, and she tried to swallow the unexpected rise of emotion. But the prick of tears threatened to fall. From her other side, Ceridwen rubbed her back in slow, compassionate circles.

"Yesterday," Maeve continued, forcing her voice not to shake, "I was on the *Amshir* with Aran. I told him I could fly back on my own, so my disappearance is not his fault. But while I was flying, I thought I saw a mortal child stranded on a rock in the middle of the sea. It was foolish of me—"

"It was compassionate of you," Ceridwen interjected with a kind smile.

Maeve pressed her lips together, then nodded once before continuing, "But when I stopped to help her, I realized it wasn't a child at all. It was a merrow and she...she took me to Ispomora."

Merrick's dark brows shot up, and he tugged on the collar of his shirt. "Holy shit."

Tiernan took her hand again and threaded his fingers through her own. "Garvan is hunting the merrows."

His tone was menacing. He radiated wrath.

"He's skinning them alive," Maeve added with an undertone of a tremor. "And selling their scales for gold."

The glass Brynn was holding shattered, and she didn't at all seem fazed by the way it sliced her skin open. "Fucking bastard."

Maeve sat up and locked her spine into place. "Queen Marella swore allegiance to Autumn. But Garvan's crimes against his citizens are treasonous, and I will not allow his treatment of the merrows to go without punishment."

"Spoken like a true queen." Merrick's bright blue gaze locked onto his High King, but Tiernan said nothing. A look passed between them, one Maeve couldn't decipher.

"Right, kill Garvan." Brynn swiveled her finger in the air like an imaginary check mark. "I'll add that to our list of things to do."

"I haven't yet vowed an oath to any Court." Her throat tightened around the words. "But Autumn's blood runs through my veins. Its essence is in my soul."

Lir leaned forward and adjusted the sleeves of his indigo shirt. "So, what do you wish to do, my lady?"

She would fight for the Autumn Court, she would fight for those who couldn't defend themselves. "I'm going to save the merrows."

"I like it. It's an excellent campaign slogan." Merrick ran a hand through his hot pink hair, shoving it back from his face. "Save the merrows."

"Save the merrows," Ceridwen repeated, and Merrick flashed her a devastating grin.

Maeve could've been mistaken, but she swore the High Princess blushed.

Brynn grabbed another muffin. "Anything else?"

"Yes. The merrows know about me. At least, they know I'm

Archfae and that I'm the daughter of Dorian and Fianna. They don't, however, know about the *anam ó Danua.*" Maeve looked around the table at all of them while Tiernan slowly traced circles over the back of her hand with this thumb. "They had their suspicions already. When they saw me flying, those suspicions were confirmed."

"Which means..." Lir trailed off.

"If they know about me, it's only a matter of time before others do as well." Others, like Garvan and Shay.

Murmurs of agreement sounded from each of them. All save for Tiernan, who'd been almost painfully silent.

"Alright then." Brynn stood and adjusted the straps of her corset, tucking a slim blade into one of the gold leather straps. Then she grabbed a toothpick from the small glass jar on the table and rolled it between her lips. "What do we do first?"

"I want to go to the library, there's a book on—" All thought drained away from her mind when Tiernan grazed a kiss across her knuckles.

In front of them.

"Training first." Another kiss. This time he lingered. "Then reading."

"But..." She sent Lir a pleading look. If anyone would come to her rescue, it'd be him.

"Sorry, little bird." He pressed his lips together to keep from smiling. "The High King has spoken."

Maeve huffed out a breath.

One day, she told herself. One day they'll say, "The High Queen has spoken."

Shivers raced down her spine as Tiernan slowly slid into her mind and whispered, *"Indeed they shall."*

Chapter Thirteen

The waves of the Lismore Marin were calm when Maeve found herself barefoot on the pink sand beach again, facing off with Tiernan. Except this time, Lir, Merrick, and Brynn had joined them.

Just in case, Tiernan had told her.

Right. Just in case she lost control again. Just in case she couldn't let go on her own and they needed to bring her back.

Serenity swept across her cheek. It was a soft caress, like the gentle touch of a palm, and Maeve recognized Ceridwen's magic as she boosted her confidence with affection and support. The sensation swelled around her. Lifted her. Grounded her.

Tiernan tucked a loose strand of hair behind her ear, then lifted her chin with one finger. "I will not go easy on you."

Maeve nodded. "I know."

Her heart raced, so loud that she swore he could hear the thudding of it against her chest. Another swell of tranquility stole away her anxiety and evened her breathing. She appreciated Ceridwen's subtle touches.

"Remember what you are." Then he leaned in closer, so his words were for her alone. "Remember *who* you are—Archfae, the High Princess of Autumn, the soul of the goddess Danua."

All these titles. All these expectations. It was as though everyone knew more about her than she did about herself. She'd gone from a blood-cursed human princess to an Archfae overnight, and though Tiernan had swiftly stepped up to help guide her, she'd never felt more lost. How could she wield such magic, such greatness, when the demons of her past continued to torment her?

She shook her head, crushing the thought. Now was not the time to wallow in self-pity. Maeve braced herself in the soft sand and watched Tiernan walk away. After a few yards, he turned around to face her. The sleeves of his shirt were rolled to reveal his tanned fore-arms and his swirling gold tattoos. Storm clouds gathered in his eyes. The wind swept his midnight hair away from his face as he rolled his shoulders back and cracked his neck. She stole a glance at Lir, Merrick, and Brynn, who had already taken up stances against one another, pretending to fight. They were barely trying. They were waiting for her. For her magic.

Her knee bounced with a restless energy. She stretched her fingers out, let the slow Summer breeze slip through them.

Tiernan dipped his chin, and she fired first.

Bolts of fire clashed against the violet lighting he sent her way. The power inside her surged, an explosion of flame and crackling energy. Smoke swirled around her like the spindly fingers of a skeleton. The long, gray tendrils reached for Tiernan. Thunder exploded around them, so earth-shattering, the ground beneath her feet trembled in fear. Maeve wasted no time. She called to the magic of her soul.

She wouldn't do this alone. She would never be alone again. With one hand, she roped the glittering rays of the sun, dragging them through Tiernan's storm, so they formed a sword of sunlight in her hand. It was brilliant and blinding. The hilt glowed in glorious golden ribbons. The blade was crafted of fire, bronze and crimson, the heat emanating from it strong enough to melt metal and pierce the night. She cut through the bolts of lightning he aimed at her like she was slicing through silk.

"More," he called through her mind.

More? She would give him more.

Her power soared, delighted in the freedom she offered. It was a never-ending well and each time she drew from it, it continued to give without fail. Her tattoos glowed, shimmering and vibrant. The air encircling her hummed with exhilaration, snapping and sparking with each flick of her wrist. The sand shifted beneath her feet. It swirled up around her in a vortex, then compacted into towering, dense mounds. At once, the sand molded to her design, and a dozen fae warriors took shape before her. They lined up, six on each side, crafted from the shores of Summer's coast. She armed all of them with bows of scorching fire and arrows of piercing glass.

Tiernan was relentless, sending violet bolts her direction, and her entire body trembled and shook. Without warning Lir, Merrick, and Brynn were on her, attacking from all angles. But Maeve didn't even have to move, she didn't have to fight back or counterattack. With a flick of her wrist, she merely stood by and watched as her three friends took on her army of sand warriors. They defended her without question. They protected her at all costs. She cast her glimmering bubble of protection and her hair lifted from her shoulders, blown back by the fierce gust of wind Tiernan threw her way.

It was nothing more than a faint breeze to her.

She was the very breath of life.

It was then Maeve decided to call upon the guardian, upon the fae warrior who protected the coast of Niahvess. She beckoned to him, asked him if he thought her worthy enough to serve. She closed her eyes while her magic sought him out, while it entreated him to stand with her. For a second, there was nothing.

The deafening sound of granite and marble grinding against solid earth echoed in her ears. The ground quaked and even Maeve stumbled a step. She spun around and watched, fascinated, as the fae guardian rose from his place atop the hill by the verandah. The helmet upon his head, originally carved from shimmering sandstone, was now the shade of fire rubies. He stood, massive, able to crush palm trees the way one might accidentally step upon a small twig. Sword raised, he bowed to her, ready to destroy all on her command.

"Maeve!"

She whipped back around and saw Tiernan running toward her at a full sprint, his shadows of destruction following in his wake.

She took them.

Called them to her side. The shadows swarmed her, ensconced her in a swath of protection.

He stumbled to a stop before her, eyes wide. He held out his hand. "Let go."

The magic flowing inside her reached a crescendo. Her blood sang, reaching for something she didn't understand. Maeve looked to Lir, Merrick, and Brynn—to her friends, to her family—as they fought the warriors she'd created from nothing more than grains of sand.

"*Let go, astora,*" Tiernan's deep, silky voice whispered into her mind. "*Let go.*"

A breath shuddered out of her, and Maeve released her magic. She tempered it, soothed it, calmed it with nothing more than a change of heart. The guardian stood beyond her, battle ready but unmoving. The shadows returned to Tiernan, back to where they belonged. Her bubble shield evaporated, leaving the heady scent of magic, of orange blossom and cedarwood, floating on the breeze. It mingled with the salty breeze of the sea. Her fae warriors froze right as Merrick cut one down with his blade. It disintegrated, dissolving back into the shore from which it came.

All was still.

Brynn's sword fell from her grasp. "Goddess above."

"Holy fucking shit." Merrick wiped the sweat from his forehead with the hem of his shirt. "She's amazing."

Lir watched her, his eyes glinting with pride, and when she turned to face Tiernan, her soul sang. She felt a pull, as though her very aura was reaching for him. The vibration of it left her breathless.

He was smiling. *Really* smiling. He was the dusk before the fall of night. The essence of a Summer storm. And all Maeve wanted to do was kiss him.

The sand warriors receded, becoming once more nothing but a stretch of beautiful beach. The guardian returned to his kneeling position, where he protected the shoreline of Niahvess. But Maeve would not so quickly relinquish her sword of sunlight. She lifted it up, examined it. It was like holding the beauty of the sun and the force of its flame in her hands. No, this one she was definitely keeping.

Tiernan closed the distance between them in two steps. His hand cupped the back of her neck, and he hauled her against him.

"You," he said, his voice rough and edgy, "are absolute perfection."

Then his mouth was on hers and she was opening for him, needing him, wanting all of him. His tongue glided over hers, hot and velvety. He tasted of summer and violence. Maeve curled one fist into his shirt, wanting him as close to her as possible.

Merrick coughed loudly. "Get a room."

Tiernan broke their kiss but kept his mouth barely a breath away from hers. "If you don't shut up, I'll use yours."

From somewhere beside them, Brynn cackled.

But then Tiernan did pull away. The muscles of his arms stiffened beneath her touch. His jaw locked into place. Tension seeped from him, fierce and dangerous, and the claws of trepidation sank into Maeve's shoulders.

"What's wrong?" she asked. The others had sensed his shift as well. But Tiernan's gaze was focused north, to the Summer forest. "Tiernan, what is it?"

"I don't know." He faced the three fae who would give their lives for him if he only asked. "Lir, ready your forces. Merrick, get your scouts to the forest at once. Brynn, the city."

No one questioned. No one hesitated. One by one they *faded* from sight until it was just the two of them, alone on the beach. He didn't even look at her when he said, "Maeve, return to the palace."

Oh, hell no.

She drew back, ready to stand her ground. "Absolutely not."

Swirling eyes locked onto her. His face was a storm, a violent clash of concern and duty. "I beg your pardon?"

"Whatever it is, I'm going with you." He looked ready to implode, but Maeve refused to let him win. "Don't lock me away. My place has never been inside pretty rooms with pretty beds. I grew up on the training fields, remember? I didn't play with dolls, I played with swords." She pointed to the glittering palace of Niahvess. "*That* is not my place. I belong on a battlefield, the same as you."

He captured her chin, his touch gentle but firm. "I can't let anything happen to you."

"Then don't." She smiled sweetly, and he rolled his eyes to the growing turmoil in the skies. "But you know damn well if you send me back inside the palace walls, back to where it's *safe*, I'll just bribe some poor Summer warrior to bring me along and then you'll be forced to kill him."

He groaned and scrubbed a hand over his face. "Fine. But you do not leave my side, do you understand?" He stole a glance at the sword of sunlight flaring in her grasp. "And bring that with you."

She rose up on her toes and kissed the corner of his mouth, then whispered, "Yes, my lord."

His response was a low and menacing growl. She couldn't be sure, but she could've sworn the corner of his mouth lifted in the faintest of smiles. Then he hauled her against him and they *faded* away to the Summer forest.

MAEVE HAD no idea what to expect when they arrived at the Summer forest, but it hadn't been the sight before her.

Everywhere she looked, there were dozens of fae and all of them were running south, toward Niahvess. They spilled from the forest in droves and while some carried packs filled with their belongings and blankets, others carried small children. There were groups of families and friends, neighbors, and even those who looked to be completely alone. But they all bore the same expression. Fear was etched into the lines of their lovely faces. Tears and wails mingled with shouts as they emerged from the flowering trees and rushed past them without a glance back. In the distance, she heard the familiar rush of a water-fall, and a sharp twinge pierced her heart.

Merrick appeared before them, decked in his armor of cobalt leather and sunshine gold.

"My lord." His cerulean gaze landed on Maeve. "My lady."

Tiernan ignored the fact that his Court was being overrun. "Report."

"Spring fae, *moh Rí.*" He gestured to the fleeing fae, who looked defeated and battered. "They came through the Pass of Veils."

Maeve knew the Pass of Veils was the only way to get from the Summer Court to the Spring Court, but she'd never seen it for herself. It was a treacherous pass that wound its way through the northern mountains, the same ones dividing the border of Spring and Summer. When they considered infiltrating Spring to attack Parisa, that was the path they were going to take. The only other option was to venture all the way around.

"That's incredibly dangerous." Tiernan watched as a female fae struggled past them with one child in her arms and another in tow behind her. Their feet were bare and blistered. The youngest had cuts up and down her little legs. "What are they doing here?"

"Fleeing. Requesting amnesty." Merrick stepped closer and his voice dropped. "They're refugees, Your Grace."

Maeve's stomach clenched. Refugees. If they were running from Spring, then Parisa and her dark fae must be in complete control.

"Shit." Tiernan shoved his midnight hair back from his face as the winds from the storm he called rolled in. "Suvarese must be worse off than we thought."

A scream ripped through the air, and Maeve's blood ran cold. It was the sound of imminent death. There was a crunching sound, like the snapping of a hundred trees all groaning in agony at once. Maeve's knees softened, her grip around her flaming sword tightened, as a flood of terror-filled cries reverberated through the forest.

"Oh yeah. And there's also that." Merrick pointed to where a tree bowed over, its massive trunk wrenched and mangled. Pushing through the forest, shoving the trees out of its way like they were nothing more than a few pesky branches, emerged a monster of impossible size.

Maeve stumbled back a step, and Tiernan's hand instantly went to the small of her back to steady her.

"Giant," she breathed, remembering how Brynn once said they were merely the stuff of legend. How they weren't supposed to exist. Yet there one was, lurching before her. Living. Breathing. Destroying.

Black fur was draped around its boulder-sized shoulders, and its torso was bare and gnarled, marred by scars from years of battle. They wound up his body, wrapping over him like angry red vines. Bands of leather and steel were forged around his upper arms. A leather pouch was slung around his waist, and it hung over layers of mangy gray wool that fell to his knees. His nose was long and bumpy, his eyes were menacing and set back, so his brow jutted out over his face like a ledge. His lips curled beneath a scraggly red beard. Links of rusted chains fell from his neck, and those same chains matched the cuffs on his wrists and ankles, like he'd been a prisoner.

Maeve quickly recounted in her mind anything she'd ever read about giants. They preferred to dwell near mountains, where the air was cool and the thick swirl of mist kept them out of sight. As far as she could recall, they were solitary beings, those who preferred the company of the silence and stillness of their surroundings to living among others of their own kind. They were thought to be created from the earth, from the deepest stone within the tallest mountains, but there was no real record of how or why they came into existence.

They simply *were*. But there was one clear, definite fact she remembered from her studies.

Giants were neither friendly nor unfriendly. They were not friend or foe. For the most part, they were harmless. Unless they were provoked.

And given this giant was hell bent on destroying the fae running at his feet, she bet it was the latter.

"Merrick, go to Ceridwen. Tell her to gather a group and set up camps. We'll deal with the refugees when the time comes." Tiernan kept his gaze focused on the giant slowly ambling toward them. "Right now, we have to make sure they stay alive."

Merrick *faded*, and four of his scouts approached their High King.

"We have to fight him off until Lir arrives with the rest of our forces. More than anything, we can't let him leave the forest. If he makes it to the city, he will destroy Niahvess." He looked down at Maeve. "Protect the innocent, *astora*. The rest of you, come with me."

He didn't even give her a chance to protest. Not that she would have, but still. So much for not leaving his side. Maeve watched as Tiernan and the scouts sprinted toward the lumbering giant, and then she ran in the opposite direction. Toward the terrified fae.

"South!" she shouted over their cries. They rushed past her, clutching their belongings and holding tight to their families. "Run south! You'll be safe in the city!"

She kept her sword of sunlight at the ready and continued to direct the Spring fae toward the safety of Niahvess when a child-like cry raised the hairs on the back of her neck. She whipped in the direction of the sound and realized it was coming from the banks of the faerie pool. Stumbling through the slick grass was a group of fae. Possibly a family. There were three adults. Seven children. One of them was on the ground, his face stained with filth and tears, his small hand wrapped around his ankle. He could scarcely be older than his sixth year of life. But the injury he sustained was not the cause of his cries.

She followed their panicked gazes to the edge of the forest, right before the waterfall, where the mist unfurled.

Then she saw it.

The mass of shadows and night that moved like death. The creature of blood-chilling fear who fed off happiness, a reaper of nightmares. A wall of darkness threatened to descend upon the frightened fae, promising them an eternity of torment and agony.

Maeve would remember that dark fae anywhere. The Hagla. She remembered the bitter cold that seeped into her bones as it swarmed her, as it stole into her mind, warping her senses when she'd been in the Fieann Forest with Rowan, Casimir, and Saoirse. She remembered cowering on the forest floor, lost to the mercy of her memories of the cage and the Cliffs of Morrigan. Of the angry sea and the jaw-like rocks that waited to devour her.

The Hagla would attack them. It would feed off their fear.

Damn if she would let it even get within striking distance of the petrified Spring fae.

Sword raised, she ran toward the shadows with a battle cry on her lips.

Chapter Fourteen

Tiernan knew it was a long shot taking on a giant. It had been close to a hundred years since he last fought one, and for good reason. He'd almost gotten his arms ripped off.

It wasn't that giants were more powerful. In fact, they were far from it. They simply took longer to kill. And once they were raging, they were nearly impossible to stop. This beast was no exception. The ground shuddered as he trudged toward them, knocking fully grown trees out of his way like they were a simple nuisance. Forest animals scattered, darting out of harm's way. The giant smashed a sapling into the ground with his foot; the weight of which would be enough to shatter a fae's bones to dust.

"Watch his arms when he swings!" Tiernan called to his scouts. The giant's movements might be sluggish, but they were lethal. All they had to do was keep him distracted and away from the Spring fae until Lir arrived.

The giant bellowed, baring his yellowed teeth. He stretched his arm back and took aim. His meaty fist, the size of at least two boulders, was lobbed straight at Tiernan. He ducked down and hit the forest floor, rolling out of the way. The gust of air that swept over him reeked of rotten garbage and his gut clenched.

He jumped up from the ground and called upon his magic. Summer churned overhead, clouds of the darkest night roiled, and Tiernan struck out. Slashes of violet exploded from the tips of his fingers, cutting across the space between himself and the giant in jagged bolts of lightning. They scorched and singed his body, charred his skin, melted his face. The giant howled. Destruction rose inside Tiernan, turbulent and demanding, begging for release. But he would not give into the temptation of such power. Not yet. He stole inside the giant's mind, sifted through his garbled thoughts until he found what he was looking for...

Spring fae trying to escape from Suvarese through the Pass of Veils. Dark fae following in their wake, chasing them down and slaughtering them. The giant being whipped and beaten until he was no longer submissive, but instead a rage-filled beast. Fearghal taunting him, torturing him, then releasing him upon the fae attempting to flee the Spring Court. Parisa was bringing ruination upon them all.

There would be no way around it. The only way to stop the giant would be to slay him. If he had more time, he could attempt to subdue the creature, but his mind was too far gone for saving. Except Ceridwen—damn it. If he had her on the battlefield with him, her magic could easily suppress him. But she was back in Niahvess and there was no more time to waste.

Already glamoured in his armor, Tiernan withdrew both of his swords and charged straight ahead. Two of his scouts darted around to the back, maneuvering the barbarian into a position of weakness. If they could flank him, he'd be easier to bring down. The giant roared, raised his fist, and slammed it into the ground, unleashing a wave of tremors that sent all of them sprawling. Tiernan's back collided with the solid earth, and his head smacked hard. Pain coursed down his spine and a glare of stars darted across his vision, temporarily blinding him.

"Move, Your Grace!" a voice shouted from somewhere off to his right. *"Move!"*

Tiernan rolled, his body absorbing the impact of rocks and debris as he looked up just in time to see the giant's fist pounding into the ground where his body had been only a moment before.

That was far too close for comfort.

Jarred from his stupor, Tiernan fought to stand and gain his bearings. Splintering pain tore across the back of his head and temples as he staggered to his feet.

The giant grabbed a broken tree trunk, hoisted it over his head, and snapped it in half. The crack was deafening. He wielded the trunks like weapons, one for each hand.

Shit.

Now they were in trouble.

Tiernan felt him before he saw him. Lir appeared a second later in full armor, with at least fifty of their best warriors, all armed with blades of nightshade. It was ruthless. And lethal. But necessary. There was no other way to bring the giant down, and Tiernan refused to let his Court fall prey to its chaotic destruction.

"What the hell is going on?" Lir called over the clamoring of warriors poised for attack. They surrounded the heaving giant, the tips of their blades ready to strike. Energy filled with an eagerness for bloodshed rippled through their ranks.

"That's a great question." Tiernan blasted his magic again and watched as violet streaks assaulted the giant once more. It exploded from him, crashing, lashing out, casting everything and everyone in a rich purple hue of power. "And one I'll have Merrick explain to you in detail once we return home."

Lir grunted and raised his arm, signaling the warriors to prepare for attack. "Can't wait for that story."

His hand cut through the air like a blade through silk, and the Summer fae warriors began their assault. They hurtled through the forest in a wave of cobalt blue and gold, ready to destroy. To pummel. To kill.

"Not you." Tiernan grabbed Lir's arm before he could storm into the fray. "I need you to protect Maeve."

Lir's silver eyes widened. "You brought her?"

He bit down on the urge to snarl. "Like she gave me a choice."

At that, his commander smiled, the faintest uptick in the corner of his mouth. "Very true." The humor vanished. "Where is she?"

Tiernan jerked his head. "Over by the tree line, she..."

But when he looked to where he'd last left her, she was gone.

STINGING wind whipped past Maeve as she rushed to protect the fae. Her cheeks burned and her face prickled as her hair sliced across her skin. Her heart raced, anticipation and magic pumping through her veins. But she didn't stop. It didn't matter if she was running into danger, she was doing as she'd been ordered.

Protect the innocent.

Tiernan's words reverberated through her mind as she sprinted toward the faerie pool. She leapt over stones and fallen logs, letting the storm of Summer carry her.

The Hagla was moving so fast, much quicker than she remembered that day in the Fieann Forest. Its impenetrable shadows curled around the trees, swallowing them whole. They slithered along the forest floor, devouring the flowers and logs, coating the world around her in the raw grip of empty night.

But Maeve would not let it defeat her. Not this time.

"Finley!" a male fae cried, reaching for the small child who was crawling along the damp grass on his hands and knees, trying to escape. The Hagla was upon him, upon all of them. A wall of nightmares.

Maeve raised her golden sword and screamed. The sound that erupted from her was not of this world. Her wings burst from her back, fueled by magic and fury. Vengeance steeled her heart as she flew toward them. Fingers outstretched, she snatched the boy by his shirt and hauled him into her chest. He threw his small arms around her neck and the scent of his fear set her on fire. Using her wings as a barricade, she shielded the family from the Hagla's onslaught.

Shadows were everywhere at once. Cold seared her skin, stole all the way into her bones. Fear licked around her like white-hot flames. In her arms, the boy whimpered and cried, but she didn't let go. She held him to her fiercely, the way a mother would protect her babe, and she summoned her magic.

Her shimmering bubble appeared, surrounding them. Saving them. Its strength alone far greater than anything the Hagla could throw her way. Its shadowy fingers tried to claw their way in, swarming and snaring, but the bubble didn't yield. It didn't break.

Maeve smoothed the boy's hair back from his face, gently pressing her palm to his cheek to calm him. Then she handed him off into his father's waiting arms.

"Thank you." The fae male cradled his son against him, his eyes filling with unshed tears. "I owe you a life debt."

But Maeve ignored him.

Gaze narrowed, focused solely on the dark fae whose death would belong to her, she lifted her glaring sword of sunlight, stepping out of the shield and into the shadows.

"I fear nothing."

Its cold breath sank into her, trailing along her neck and down her hair. But Maeve didn't waver. Thousands of voices scraped past her ears, whispering promises of nightmares, terrors, and when she didn't tremble, the darkness smiled.

Maeve lifted her chin out of spite. "I fear *nothing*."

Her soul answered in response. She shoved one hand through the seething shadows, through Tiernan's violent storm, and brought down the sun. Brilliant and blinding, she harnessed her magic, empowered her sword, and slashed her way through the Hagla. She ripped and tore, penetrating, ruining the desolate darkness.

The Hagla recoiled against her sword. It hissed and shivered, snaking its way around her ankles, trying to consume her with grief and despair. It wanted to drown her in torment. Images of Rowan dying flashed into her mind. All the swords slashing through the sky like lightning, then puncturing his body while he protected her. All the blood staining his shirt, pants, and feathers. The way he flashed her a broken, bloodied smile. The Hagla wanted to use her memories against her, wanted to watch her waste away until she was nothing more than a shell of a soul.

"You will not take them." Maeve spat the words out and struck true. She aimed the tip of her sword into the heart of the darkness. Through the soul of eternal night.

There was a wail, a blood-curdling shriek so painful it caused the trees to shudder. The rise of power consumed her, lifting her hair from her shoulders. A sudden gust slammed into her, a painful sensation of having all the air pulled from her lungs until she could no longer catch her breath, until her throat tightened and squeezed, and then...the Hagla was gone.

There was no darkness.

No shadows.

No cold.

Maeve gasped, and her chest rose and fell rapidly, heaving from exertion. She wiped a few errant curls away from her sweaty, sticky face and rolled her shoulders back. Cautiously, she kicked the only thing closest to her—a plain gray rock. It bounced twice and then rolled across the flattened grass before coming to a stop. Nothing happened. Nothing responded. There was no rise of dark magic. No crushing of shadows.

The Hagla was dead.

"Fucking fae," Maeve muttered and decided to check on the family. She turned on one heel and froze.

Everyone, *everyone*, was staring at her.

Unease filtered through her, but she quickly waved away the shimmering bubble of protection surrounding the family, freeing them from its ward. They stood there, gaping at her, and without warning, every single one of them fell upon their knees before her. Even the young, injured boy.

Maeve stumbled back a step.

It started like a slow wave. A movement. The swell of acknowledgment spread, the shocking revelation of what she'd done was reflected at her in every pair of eyes she met. Beyond the family, the Spring fae stared at her in awe, disbelieving. But the only one she looked for, the only one she longed to find, was Tiernan.

He stood toward the back of the forest, surrounded by deformed trees and the dead body of a fallen giant. His face was a mask, calm and cool, like always. But there was an emotion swirling in his eyes, one she couldn't read or understand. To his left stood Lir, with the High Army of Niahvess at his back. To Tiernan's right was Merrick, with his band of scouts. They all watched her, observing her like she was a fictional character from one of her stories. Like she wasn't even real.

Maeve carefully trudged over to them, offering a small smile to any fae who met her gaze, but her focus was solely on Tiernan. He was bruised and bleeding a little, but he was alive. And it was all that mattered. She stepped over a bundle of broken branches and kept her eyes focused on the High King of Summer. He kept her steady. Kept her breathing.

Some of the fae murmured as she passed by. Others whispered, their voices soft and reverent. But she heard what they said—what they called her.

Dawnbringer.

Chapter Fifteen

Tiernan stood motionless. Dumbfounded. Awestruck.

There had been one fleeting moment when panic had slicked over him in a cold sweat. But that feeling, that gut-clenching, harrowing sensation, had belonged solely to him. Not Maeve. Not once had the necklace she wore alerted him to any flash of fear or apprehension. Instead, when he sensed her, it had been a different emotion entirely.

Determination.

While his Summer fae warriors struck down the giant with their blades of nightshade, Tiernan witnessed Maeve take on the Hagla.

By herself.

Her wings had burst open and spread wide, like a rose-dusted barrier, protecting the Spring fae who took shelter behind her. With incredible speed, she'd vaulted over to them and snatched a child from death's grasp. When the dense wall of shadows loomed over her, threatening to overtake her, and she held the babe in one arm with her sword of sunlight hoisted high and blazing bright, she'd looked like a fucking goddess.

She'd shielded those Spring fae, who weren't of Summer or

Autumn. She'd faced down death for them without a second thought. Without question or hesitation. She glowed with power then, magnified by the sheer force of her will and courage. Her magic shimmered like an aura around her, a wave of stunning power bright enough to shut out even the darkest of nights. He only felt relief when her bubble of protection appeared, encasing her and the Spring fae family, and shutting out the Hagla's seething shadows. But then his heart had stopped the moment she'd walked right through it and straight into the mouth of danger.

Tiernan had almost gone to her then. He called her name, screamed for her, and would have destroyed all in his path to reach her. To save her. Because the Hagla was one of the most devastating dark fae to ever roam the realm.

But Lir had snared him by the shoulder and held him back. Told him to watch. To wait.

It killed him.

But damn if his commander hadn't been right.

Golden light slashed through the Hagla, brought down from the sun itself. The creature ripped and roared as she gutted it from the inside out. The strength of her power, of her magic, of *her*, devastated the writhing shadows and purged the darkness from the Summer forest.

He'd held his breath and watched as Maeve, as his *sirra*, emerged victorious. When she kicked that rock, he almost laughed out loud. She had no idea the strength of her power or the magnitude of her worth. He realized it the second she spun around to face them, looking like what she'd just done was all in a day's work.

His heart soared, but pride kept him anchored in place on the battlefield, waiting. His soul called to hers...and he could've sworn hers answered.

The whispers floating among the Spring fae reached his ears before she returned to his side.

Dawnbringer.

Maeve walked up to him, alluring and radiant. Her post-battle windswept hair curled down around her shoulders and back. Her cheeks were flushed pink, her breath slowly regulated with each rise and fall of her chest. Unmarred by any new injuries, her skin was flawless, and her shoulders glistened with the faintest sheen of sweat. She was pure radiance, glowing from the rush of fighting and the thrill of power.

If she'd reached inside his chest and clenched his heart to cease its beating, he would've been no less surprised. Now, more than ever, he found it difficult to even breathe around her.

She tucked a lock of hair behind her ear and peered up at him. "They're all staring at me."

Her voice was a throaty whisper that had him wanting to tangle his fingers in her hair and devour that pouty little mouth. But he abstained, and simply said, "So am I."

She rubbed her lips together. "But why?"

He lifted her chin with the hilt of his sword and kissed her lightly, the barest meeting of lips. "Because you are power and magic unlike anything they have ever beheld. A true faerie queen."

Rosy heat spread across her breasts, all the way up her neck, to the tips of her pointed ears. Then she snorted, and it was ridiculously unladylike yet downright endearing. "I don't even have a Court."

"Tell that to them." He placed both of his hands on her shoulders and slowly turned her around to face the fae she'd gone to battle for, the ones she'd been ready to die for if it meant keeping them alive.

Her body jerked with a sharp inhale as every fae, every Summer warrior, even Merrick and Lir, lowered themselves onto one knee before her.

"Sun and sky," she breathed.

"Indeed." He slid his arm around her waist and pulled her close to him. "Come on, let's get them safely to Niahvess...Dawnbringer."

MAEVE ROLLED her shoulders and neck till the ache from exertion passed. She was drained, exhausted from battle and a bit sore, but energy pumped through her and kept her from collapsing.

Lir installed a rack for weapons in her bedroom, since she seemed to accumulate them. Her Aurastone remained in its revered position under her pillow, but she'd hung her sword of sunlight on the new wall unit, and it emitted a soft, pulsing glow as the rise of late afternoon washed in through the doors leading to her balcony.

Tomorrow they would go into the city to check on the Spring fae refugees. It would be Maeve's first time venturing into Niahvess and though she wasn't nervous, she was worried there would be tension between the Summer fae who lived there and the Spring fae who abandoned their own Court. But Ceridwen had assured her all was well. With help from Brynn and a few others, they'd been able to set up shelters and provide the Spring fae with food, clothing, and a safe place to sleep.

Maeve wasn't fully aware of all the details, but it was apparent that Suvarese was falling beneath Parisa's rule. The fae who'd fled on foot through the treacherous Pass of Veils had left everything behind save for a few possessions. Many of them only wore the clothes on their backs. They'd abandoned their homes. Their livelihoods. All of it to escape her and the dark fae.

Tiernan had sent Merrick and his scouts to see what other information they could uncover about the situation in Suvarese, and while it left her feeling uneasy—Maeve knew he and the other scouts were highly skilled at what they did—it helped to have Ceridwen remind her that Merrick knew exactly what he was doing. It was just like Brynn said...they were family now. And she'd come to care for all of them.

Maeve was just sliding her Aurastone under her pillow when a knock sounded outside her door. "Come in."

Deirdre bustled into the room, balancing a tray on one hand. "Hello, dear heart."

It wasn't exactly time for dinner and usually Maeve wouldn't have minded when Deirdre brought her a snack. But wariness crept through her, distinct and chilling, when she saw the plate full of chocolate chip cookies and the steaming cup of tea.

Maeve didn't drink tea.

Ever.

"You're the talk of the town tonight, Maeve dear." She set the tray down on the bedside table. "Taking on the Hagla by yourself? The mother in me wants to reprimand you, while the other part is simply bursting with pride. I wish I'd been there to witness it."

"It wasn't anything special." Maeve eyed the tea and shrugged out of her jeweled bodice, opting for a loose-fitting maroon cotton blouse instead. "Just a dark fae."

"*Just* a dark fae?" Deirdre fisted her hands on her wide hips. "My sweet, darling child, do you have any idea about the nature of the Hagla?"

"I know some, only what Rowan told me." It still hurt to speak his name out loud, and a sliver of guilt carved its way into her heart. Maeve swallowed, but it was like stuffing parchment down her throat.

"Then you better read that book your brother gave you," Deirdre continued, oblivious to Maeve's discomfort. "And after you learn the history of the Hagla, then you can come back and tell me if it's still *just* a dark fae."

Maeve offered her a small smile. She knew an order when she heard one. "Yes, Deirdre."

A wrinkle of concern formed across the older woman's brows. "Is something wrong, Maeve?"

"It's the tea." Maeve removed her boots and Deirdre took them from her, placing them at the foot of the bed. "I can't drink it."

Deirdre shuffled over to the bedside table and sniffed the tea. "You don't like it?"

"No, it's not that. It's just my moth—I mean, Carman—used to put darmodh root in my tea when I was younger. To encourage memory loss."

Deirdre shape-shifted into a round ball of fury. "Of all the wretched, awful, terrible things to do to a child!" She wrung her hands in front of her and sucked in a stifled breath. Her shoulders relaxed and she nodded toward the tray. "But I'm afraid this tea is necessary."

"What for?"

"It's to help with..." She stole a glance at the door leading to Tiernan's room and lowered her voice to a whisper. "...your moon cycles, dear heart."

Maeve blinked. "What?"

Deirdre leaned in closer. "To prevent you from being with child."

"Oh!" Maeve reared back, mortified, and her cheeks turned scarlet. So hot, she felt like she was on fire. "I didn't...that is, I didn't realize—"

"Think nothing of it." She waved away Maeve's embarrassment. "But female fae have a tendency to be exceptionally fertile, and you'll only have to drink this tea once a month, unless of course you plan on trying to—"

"No!" Maeve grabbed the cup of tea and blew on it, then took a hasty sip. It wasn't good, but it wasn't awful. It tasted earthy, with a hint of ginger. "At least, not for a long time."

Not for a very, *very* long time. Like maybe one hundred years.

"Well, I'll leave you to freshen up before dinner. I imagine it'll be quite the feast, given the events of the day." Deirdre gave her a gentle pat on the cheek and left without another word.

Maeve finished the rest of her tea and peeled off her leggings, which were still covered in mud and grime from the forest. She debated on showering before dinner, but then she caught sight of her reflection in the ornate mirror on her vanity. The blouse she wore dipped low in the front and that was when she saw it. There was a tattoo over her heart. A new one. At least, she thought it was new. She had so many marking her body now, she supposed she could've easily overlooked it. But this one was different. It resembled an intricate leaf set inside a spiraling sun.

She tugged her blouse off one shoulder and examined the mark more closely. It was definitely not like the rest of her tattoos. Where those were all rose gold, this one was deep red and outlined in gold. Her brow furrowed.

When did she get that one?

Instead of heading into the bathroom, she found herself staring at the door separating her room from Tiernan's.

Her teeth skated along her bottom lip. They never discussed the particulars. Like if she could go to him if she wanted, or if he would be the one to choose when and where. She didn't know if they were exclusive, if he would sleep with other females whenever he felt the urge, or if they were even a thing at all.

She padded softly across the wooden floor and braced both hands as quietly as possible upon the door. Then she leaned in, pressed her ear to its carved surface, and listened.

From the other side came the low, gentle rumbling of a baritone paired with the soft strumming of a guitar. He was singing again, a more haunting melody this time. It was enough to cause her knees to soften and her blood to thrum. There was just something about listening to him play, listening to him sing, that carried her to another time. Another world. What she wouldn't give to have him touch her while he sang.

Maeve melted into the alluring tune, and her forehead came to rest on the door between them, content to let his music take her away.

A moment later, the door swung open, and she tumbled directly into his arms.

Chapter Sixteen

Tiernan caught Maeve in his arms, and she stared up at him with beautiful, glassy eyes. He supposed he could've ignored her, but he'd heard her thoughts through the wall, and as soon as he'd sensed her silent call to him, he'd gone to her. How lucky for him she was wearing only an ill-fitting blouse that fell dangerously low off one of her shoulders, revealing inch after glorious inch of creamy flesh.

His arms easily slid around her waist, drawing her flush against him. "What were you saying?"

Maeve shook her head, and he saw the moment her eyes cleared. "I wasn't saying anything."

He inclined his head and let his gaze dip down to her mouth. "Weren't you though?"

"No." Concern lined her brow as he waited for her to understand. "I was just thinking that—"

Her gaze shot to him, all fiery and hot. "I thought you were going to stop doing that?"

He bent down to her, smiled to himself when she melted against him, then casually nuzzled her neck, letting his next words skate across her skin. "Apparently I can't help myself when it comes to you."

Her resolve weakened then, and her arms slowly wrapped around his neck.

"Now, tell me again, Your Highness." He pressed his mouth to her throat, where her pulse jumped for him. Then he kissed her just below her ear, before moving his lips to her jaw. "What was it you wanted me to do?"

She let loose one of those breathy little sighs that drove him absolutely mad. He let his hand trail from her waist to her rib cage, then he cupped her left breast and squeezed. She was like the sand from his beach in his arms. Soft. Pliant. Warm. Already his blood rushed to his cock, already their mingling scents of heady arousal filled the air around them. His other hand palmed her ass, clutching her, rubbing her against him so she would know, beyond a shadow of a doubt, that he wanted her. That he desired her.

"To sing." She pressed her lips together like she couldn't remember what she was going to say. Her eyes fluttered closed when she spoke again. "I wanted you to sing for me."

"Mm," he growled, rubbing his thumb back and forth across her little bud of a nipple. "I could've sworn it was more than that."

He slid one hand beneath the hem of her blouse. His fingers floated along her warm thigh, then closer still to where he knew she was already wet for him. Gods, she wasn't even wearing any intimates. There was nothing keeping him from the slick folds of her cunt.

"Do you *always* go bare?"

"Yes." Her hips angled toward him in a silent plea for more. "I hate lace."

"As do I." He scraped his teeth along her bottom lip, and her fingers coiled into his hair, urging him closer. He chuckled softly. "Not until you tell me what it is you really want, *astora*."

"I want you to sing and..." A strangled gasp escaped her when he shoved one finger inside of her and her head lolled back. "Sing while you touch me."

Tiernan stilled and waited for her lustful eyes to open. "Is that a command, my lady?"

He delved another finger deep inside her, moved them both in and out with agonizing patience.

"Yes," she panted. She anchored herself to him, lifted her leg, and effortlessly guided his fingers further inside her. "Yes, it's a command. Sing for me until I cry for you. Touch me until I beg for you."

His cock surged to life. Ached for her. Throbbed for her. "You are the bane of my existence."

"I'll take that as a compliment."

"As you should."

He pulled his fingers out and she whimpered. He smothered it with a kiss. Her mouth opened readily for him, and she tasted of forbidden fruit, hidden secrets—all things dark and delicious. Her tongue was velvet against his own. His hands coasted up her body. Her abdomen, her breasts, to the necklace dangling between the valley of them, until his palms settled gently, firmly, around her neck. Her teeth sank into his bottom lip, not hard enough to draw blood, but strong enough to make him want to fall to his knees before her.

She tugged on the buttons of his shirt and broke apart their kiss, only to say, "Why are you always fully clothed?"

Laughter rumbled from inside his chest. "An excellent question."

Before he could think, all his clothes were gone, and his cock sprang free. He blinked. Her blouse vanished as well. Maeve had glamoured them off. His boots, pants, shirt, even the silk black shorts he wore as undergarments. They stood naked, wrapped in each other's arms, consumed with one another, and everywhere her hands touched left him burning for her.

"Nicely done, Your Highness."

Her misty, green-gray eyes sought his own. "Again, I learn from the best."

Then her mouth was on him, *everywhere*. Her lips scorched his neck and shoulders. She planted a trail of hot kisses on every ridge of muscle across his stomach and all the way to the sensitive dip of flesh just beneath his waist. Her tongue licked and flicked, and his body coiled with tension. His blood pounded, echoing in his ears. His soul begged for her. But she took her time. Curious and cautious, she kept every touch featherlight, and it nearly shattered him. Her fingers explored his back, hips, and thighs. And when she got down onto her knees before him, he swore to the skies, to the heavens, to anyone who would listen, that he would die for her.

Maeve's hand moved over the hardened length of his shaft and this time it was his head that rolled back, desperate for her to touch. To taste.

She trailed the tip of her finger along the five golden studs piercing him and when her pretty lips opened, and her tongue glided over the tip of his cock, it took every ounce of Tiernan's self-control not to thrust himself down her throat.

"Is it okay if I kiss you here?" Her voice was hushed, like a whisper.

"Yes," he ground the word out through clenched teeth. "Kiss. Lick. Suck. Just no biting."

He glanced down and she smiled, the curve of it so feline and so perfectly female. "Yes, my lord."

Fucking gods, he was going to die. And if this was the way he went, so be it.

She did exactly as he instructed. She kissed. Licked. Sucked. And she sucked *hard*. If he wasn't careful, he'd come before her, and that was something he refused to do. He'd had every intention of moving slowly with her this time. Of worshiping her. Now all he wanted to do was bend her over a table and drive himself into her until she was screaming his name.

That smart little mouth was taking him deeper and faster, and as much as he hated to do it, he pulled himself out. She glanced up at him with glossy, wet lips and he scooped her up into his arms before she could protest. He would not take her hard and fast again; he'd made that mistake the first time. No. She wanted him to sing to her and touch her, and that's exactly what he was going to do.

Tiernan laid her down upon his bed and covered her body with his own. Her golden pink hair sprawled over his midnight pillow like the dying rays of the sun. Her breasts rose to greet him and she shifted her hips, spreading her legs so he could settle himself between them. While his fingers traced every swirling tattoo covering her body, he started to sing.

A song meant only for her.

"Eyes like the Lismore Marin,
    She stole hearts, and it was more than
    Any had seen in o'er a hundred of years.
    She's both moon and she's sunlight,
    And the stars, they will burn bright,
    For her alone they will catch all of her tears."

Tiernan kissed her lips, her legs, her stomach and shoulders. It was excruciating to watch her wiggle and writhe beneath him, but he was determined to take his time and savor every inch of her satin skin. He needed her to know, to *understand*, this was more than a casual bedding. He wanted to burn himself into her memory, so every time she closed her eyes, she would know she belonged to him. He nudged her thighs wider to make room for his broad shoulders, and this time when he sank two fingers deep inside her, he suckled at her clit. Her hips bucked, but he held her down and a broken sob escaped her.

Tiernan shifted, brought himself directly over top of her, and whispered along her cheek, "Cry for me." Maeve shuddered and it was then he saw the misty sheen in her eyes. "Beg for me."

"Please, Tiernan." Her fingers dug into his shoulders, held onto him like she was about to fall apart. "Please."

"As you wish."

The head of his cock pried her open for him and she tensed, so he continued to sing softly and move slowly, to ensure she could take all of him without pain. Each tender thrust took him further inside her as she stretched to accommodate him, molded to fit him like she was made for him. Her hands roved over his shoulders and arms and gradually, her body relaxed, and he filled her fully. But she was still so tight that it set his teeth on edge.

In one swift movement, he flipped them over so she straddled him. Her eyes widened in shock, and she reached for his chest. "What do I do?"

"Like this." Tiernan gripped her hips and drove himself upward, plunging himself inside her.

The sound she made was nothing short of satisfying. Pleasure overtook her, so much so she practically glowed with it. Then she was riding him with ease, and watching her full, round breasts bounce was positively delightful. His name spilled from her lips, over and over like a prayer. Eyes closed in ecstasy, she lifted her hair from her shoulders and let him take her, let him guide her. She was incandescent. The familiar scent of magic overwhelmed him, smothered him, and if he'd ever been one to believe in fairytales, he would've sworn sparks were flying.

Fuck.

Sparks *were* flying. Sweetened cinnamon smoke swirled around them. Flickers of fire scattered from the tips of her fingers, and as he brought her closer to climax, the flames burned brighter.

"Shit." He tightened his grip on her hips; she was so fucking reckless.

Calling upon his own magic to counter hers, he brought the storm, the wind, and the rain. He watched through the glass dome ceiling above them as lightning splintered across the sky and the clouds rolled in. His cock thickened even more, relishing the rush of power and the hunger for release. The doors to his balcony swung open, carrying a gust of cool Summer wind and rain. He let it pour over them, soak them, as he drove her higher.

"Tiernan!" she screamed his name, grinding herself against him, and in a crack of thunder loud enough to terrify the heavens, he filled her with his seed.

Maeve collapsed on top of him, slick and smoking. Her fire had faded to embers. He held her to his chest and let the rain cool their heated skin.

"I...I'm sorry." Her words were a breathless pant and her heart thudded wildly against him.

He refused to release her and instead kissed the top of her head, all while trying to steady himself. To keep himself calm and collected. "There's nothing to apologize for, *astora*."

She turned her head to face him. "But the fire, and the smoke—"

"Was the sexiest thing I've ever seen."

He silenced her turbulent thoughts with a kiss. He hadn't lied...it was sexy. And utterly terrifying. Never in his life had he borne witness to such a thing.

Maeve had been so consumed by desire, by lust, that she'd lost all control.

For him.

And damn if he didn't want to see her do that for him every day for the rest of his life.

Maeve didn't want to move. She wasn't sure she could, even if she tried. She simply lay there, sprawled on top of Tiernan, while he held her in his arms. The mattress and linens were soaked with water. The wooden floor looked flooded. She and Tiernan were drenched from the rain he'd called to them after she'd nearly set fire to his bedroom.

She couldn't understand what had happened. The feel of him had been too much; everything about him was too much. The song he sang for her had fractured her heart and brought tears to her eyes. He'd done exactly as she'd asked of him. And when he'd placed her on top—the way he watched her, like she was his only reason for living—she'd never felt such an emotion.

So, she stayed where she was, lounging upon his chest, and eventually the rain ebbed away, and the cool breeze of Summer drifted through the open doors.

She shivered and goosebumps pebbled all over her flesh.

Instantly she was dry, the bed was dry, and a fire roared to life in the hearth of Tiernan's room.

He rolled her over with him and pulled a soft velvet blanket over top of them. She curled into the warmth of his body, and he reached down, carefully brushing back a lock of hair from her face. But her nerves were frayed, and her body was still spiraling, and she didn't have the courage to look him in the eyes after...

After *that*.

Tiernan said nothing. He just continued to wind each curl around his finger, one by one, then let them bounce free. She was tempted to trace the golden tattoos covering his bronze skin when she caught sight of the one over his heart.

It was an exact match to the one on hers. An Autumn leaf. A Summer sun. The realization slammed into her, and her throat tightened. They weren't tattoos at all. She looked up into his eyes, whirling with a storm of intensity she couldn't understand.

"We have matching Strands."

He gazed down at her, his face impassive. "We do."

Maeve arched one brow. "Did I make a bargain with you I'm not aware of?"

"Not a bargain, no." He paused, then twirled another curl around his finger. "A bond."

"A bond," she repeated, rolling the words around in her head.

"Yes."

He really wasn't going to give her anything unless she asked. "What kind of bond?"

"A mating bond." When he spoke, his words were precise. Careful. Cautious. "The one I told you about. The dance in Autumn."

Right. The one he'd forced upon her.

His brows drew together, and she knew he'd heard her thoughts. Guilt shamed her. She hadn't meant for it to sound so cruel. Though at the time, it had been nothing short of it.

She placed her hand on her heart, over the Strand that must've formed from the magic that happened between them the first time they had sex. "This is from when I agreed to be yours."

It wasn't a question.

"Yes." Again, Tiernan showed no emotion.

"Then that means," her gaze dropped to the Strand covering his heart, "you're mine."

"Yes." His voice was softer this time. Strained.

He was hers. Tiernan, High King of the Summer Court, was hers. He'd bonded himself to her as well. So, this was more than just casual sex. This was permanent. Lasting.

He ran his finger over the necklace she wore. "You're conflicted."

"No. I mean, yes, but no." She winced at how foolish she sounded. "I suppose I'm just confused."

"Why?"

It killed her to say it, but there was no other way around it. She had to know, and he was the only one who had the answer. "I don't know why you'd choose me."

He pressed his mouth to hers, lightly. Affectionately. Like that of a lover.

"That is not always up for us to decide." His thumb followed the line of her lips. "Just because something is written in the stars, doesn't mean it is sealed by fate."

Maeve wasn't sure she'd ever heard anything so terribly romantic in her life. If she was still a mortal, she might've swooned for him right then and there. "You think we're fated?"

"I think—"

He moved so quickly, Maeve didn't have time to react. He wrapped her in the blanket, shoved her behind him on the bed, and was dressed in full armor before she could form a coherent thought.

Just then, the door to his bedroom burst open and Maeve clutched the velvet blanket to her chest. She peeked around Tiernan's broad shoulders and spied Merrick and Brynn standing in the doorway.

"What the fuck happened in—" Merrick's question evaporated when Brynn swiftly jabbed him in his rib cage with her elbow.

His bright blue gaze shot to the bed. They both bowed quickly, but Tiernan didn't move. He was quiet. Deadly quiet.

"Apologies, my lord." Merrick glanced over at Maeve, then softer, "my lady." He straightened. "Ceridwen had a vision, but it's too late."

Tiernan shifted, blocking Maeve completely from view, and all she heard was Merrick say, "We've got company."

Chapter Seventeen

Tiernan lifted Maeve off the bed, blanket and all, and carried her into her room.

Anger radiated from him. His muscles were taut against her body, stiff with suppressed rage. But there was something else as well. Worry?

"Who is it?" Maeve asked when he carefully lowered her to the ground.

His eyes darkened to a midnight Summer sky. "Shay is paying us a visit."

"What?" Maeve croaked, and the spindly fingers of panic trekked down her spine. She knew it was only a matter of time until he and Garvan learned about her, but she hadn't expected it to be so soon. Now Shay was here, obviously to see her, but she had no idea what he could possibly want. And she wasn't entirely sure she wanted to know, either. Anxiety crawled over her skin. What if he tried to take her away? What if he tried to bargain with Tiernan for her? Would he give her up if it meant he received something in return? What if Shay threatened the Summer Court?

She unraveled herself out of the velvet blanket and handed it to

Tiernan, who tossed it over the edge of the bed. He gripped her by the shoulders and his gaze dipped down to her breasts. No, not her breasts. The necklace.

"Breathe, *astora*." He swiped his thumb gently along her chin. "Breathe."

She stood there, still naked, and inhaled slowly. She exhaled the paranoia. The concern. The overwhelming number of possibilities.

"You fear nothing, remember?" He kissed the top of her head. "Less than three hours ago, you took out the fucking Hagla. All by yourself." Another kiss, this one on the corner of her mouth. "You fear *nothing*."

Maeve nodded. Right. She'd done that. She could handle facing one of her brothers. But then another disturbance slinked into the far recesses of her mind. "Is Garvan with him?"

Tiernan was quiet for a moment. "No. Just Shay." His gaze swept over her, up and down, lingering on the area below her navel until her skin heated once more. "You'll need to dress."

Clothing. Of course. "Should I shower?"

"No," Tiernan bit the word out. "Let him smell my scent on you." When he smiled, it was purely wicked.

Thousands of butterflies swirled in her stomach, a sensation she hadn't felt in far too long. Ducking her head to hide her blush, Maeve turned away from him and walked over to the wardrobe. She grabbed a pair of leggings, but Tiernan's hand came down upon her shoulder.

"No leggings, Maeve. Tonight, you're Archfae."

"But you—" She spun back to face him, ready to argue the fact that he was in full armor...except he wasn't anymore. Words escaped her. There was absolutely no way to describe the male who stood before her. His dark hair fell over one side of his face like a midnight wave. The collar of his cobalt shirt stuck up with the top two buttons undone. A trim, stormy gray coat fell to his knees and stitches of swirling gold ran down the length of the sleeves. His sleek black pants were tucked into his boots and a belt slung low across his waist, prominently displaying both his swords. His leather vest was embroidered with Summer's crest, the sun rising between twin mountain peaks. On his pinky finger was the same ring he always wore, the one that reminded her of his eyes, set in a gilded sun. He looked exceptionally royal, and the sight of him left her throat dry.

He was stunning.

Her soul fractured. Shattered.

The corner of his mouth lifted into a slow half-smile. "If you keep staring at me like that, I'll be forced to bed you again."

Heat pooled between her thighs at the mere thought of it.

"But there will be plenty of time for that later." He winked. "Tonight, you're Autumn High Fae. Pick something worthy of your birthright, something that will leave no question, no doubt in their minds, that you're a High Princess."

When she nodded, he gestured to the door and added, "Lir will escort you."

Without another word, Tiernan *faded* out of her room.

Maeve steadied herself. She could do this. She flung open the doors to the wardrobe, sifted through the bounty of gowns Deirdre had made for her and chose a gown the color of Autumn's leaves. It was strapless, with heavy gold beading that formed crescent moons all over the bodice. Silk dripped from her waist down in shades of shimmery gold, burnt orange, and rich crimson. One slit on the side came all the way to her hip. She twirled once in front of the mirror, grabbed a pair of annoyingly high heels and then glanced at her vanity.

High Fae, she reminded herself.

She painted her lips blood red and left her curls wild, but wove tiny, golden leaf charms into a few of them. She chose scarlet rubies for her ears and a few thin bangles that had been a gift from Ceridwen. As a final touch, she strapped her Aurastone to her right thigh, ensuring it was visible for all to see.

I fear nothing.

Rolling her shoulders back, she raised her chin to a level of utter defiance and opened the door to her bedroom.

Lir stood before her, decked in armor of Summer's colors. But this time, bands of gold hung from his shoulder and were pinned into place by matching suns, displaying his rank within the Summer Court. Commander of the Summer Legion, General of the High Army of Niahvess. His curved swords glinted like starlight, almost as silver as his eyes. He bowed.

"Your Highness."

Maeve inclined her head. "Commander."

His dark brows rose in acknowledgment, and he offered her his arm. When her fingers curled into the crook of his elbow, he lowered his head and whispered, "We won't let anything happen to you."

Maeve didn't look at him, but whispered back, "I know."

He led her to a part of the palace she'd never seen before. It was a decadent ballroom, exposed to the elements. Stars twinkled overhead and wispy clouds floated by in the inky sky. The flooring was iridescent marble and glittered like cresting waves out at sea. All around her were pillars of soft ivory wrapped in bright florals. Faerie lights draped from the tops of them, casting the space in an ethereal, moonlit glow.

There were fae everywhere, far more than she thought would be present. Summer fae warriors lined the outer edges of the space and in the center stood the arriving Autumn fae in a clash of vibrantly jeweled reds and golds against the cool tones of Summer. At the far side of the outdoor ballroom was a dais with a singular throne. Beams of gold exploded from it, mimicking the sun's dazzling rays, and each of them was encrusted with diamonds and sapphires. Upon it, sat the High King of Summer.

Ceridwen stood to his right, with Merrick and Brynn on his left.

Tiernan rose when she entered, and every set of eyes in the room landed on her.

Tremors skittered down her spine, and she clutched Lir's arm. A delicate touch of serenity soothed her like a caress, and she'd never been more grateful for Ceridwen.

Lir escorted her across the ballroom floor, and the crowd of fae

163

parted for her. Shay stood out among them, with his crown of golden hair falling to just below his jaw and his greenish gray eyes, similar to hers in color. She couldn't bring herself to look at him again. One fae, however, caught her eye.

Her fiery hair was pulled back into a long braid, and her gown of smoky quartz fell around her in ripples of satin. Honey-colored eyes, so much like a fox's, locked onto Maeve.

She was the Autumn fae from the Ceilie. The one she'd danced with around the bonfire. The one who'd been warm and welcoming and had expected nothing of her in return. She smiled broadly and her pert nose crinkled.

Maeve lifted her hand, giving the smallest of waves in return.

Tiernan's brow arched in question at the exchange, but he said nothing, continuing to watch her every move. At least until Lir helped her up the dais, then released her to Tiernan.

He bowed and she lowered herself into a curtsy. When he held out his arm, she lightly placed her hand on top of his forearm, silently grateful to have him by her side. His muscles bunched beneath her touch and though he looked unbothered, tension lined his hardened jaw. Beneath his cool façade, he fumed. Together, they faced the crowd of onlooking fae. They shuffled closer, each wanting a closer look at the supposed High Princess of Autumn. Shay moved to the forefront of the group and stood only a few feet away from the edge of the dais. Maeve held her breath.

From her other side, Merrick straightened. "The High King of Summer, Tiernan Velless. And the High Princess of Summer, Ceridwen Velless."

Maeve watched in silence as all the fae bowed or curtsied in a show of respect. Then Tiernan stepped forward, and she went with him.

When he spoke, his voice was low and menacing, a thunderstorm in the making. "Shay Ruhdneah, High Prince of the Autumn Court, may I present to you, Maeve Ruhdneah, High Princess of the Autumn Court...your sister."

164

SHAY BOWED before her and Maeve curtsied in return, but she didn't take her eyes off him.

He straightened and faced her, and there was no denying the similarities between them. They possessed the same eyes, the same mouth, and jawline. There was the faintest tug in her chest, the same one she felt whenever she was with Aran.

Like calls to like.

Maeve steeled her heart against the resemblances. She was nothing like him.

"Sister, you're looking rather well since the last time I saw you." His smile was wide and beautiful.

"Since the *only* time you saw me," she corrected coolly.

She could play this part. At that, Tiernan released her arm, and she appreciated that at least one of them had confidence in her.

"Yes, I suppose you're right." He stepped forward, toward her, and both Lir and Merrick matched him, closing in on either side of her. "I want to offer you my sincerest apologies for our...previous introduction."

To that, Maeve said nothing. She simply met his gaze and held it. Unwavering. Unflinching.

She clasped her hands together in front of her, keeping her chin held high. "Why are you here?"

An emotion shadowed his face, but when she blinked, it was gone. "I wanted to see you for myself."

"Well." She spread her arms wide, graceful and elegant, befitting a princess. "Now you've seen me."

"That's not what I meant," Shay countered, a line forming across his brow.

"Then perhaps you should be more precise in your words, my lord."

A deep, rumbling chuckle echoed in her mind, and Tiernan's voice slipped into her thoughts. *"Good girl."*

165

Maeve didn't falter.

Shay adjusted the lapel of his garnet coat and the obsidian stones lining the border reminded her of the Black Lake. "I've come to warn you that Garvan is aware of your existence."

"How thoughtful of you."

Tension simmered between them, stifling and dense. He straightened and when he spoke again, his voice was strained. "Would you prefer I let him attempt to kill you?"

Thunder rumbled, the threat of Tiernan's might, but Maeve didn't need him to come to her rescue. Not this time. She met Shay's icy glare with one of her own. "You didn't seem too interested in stopping him the first time he tried."

Much to her surprise, the ballroom erupted in a swell of strangled gasps and hushed whispers.

"I caught you before you fell," he ground out, his hands coiling into fists at his sides.

"Then consider me grateful," she countered smoothly.

Shay opened his mouth, likely to offend her with a caustic retort, when she noticed a shimmer in the back of the ballroom near the ivory palace walls. She stormed forward. "What's that?" she demanded.

He balked. "What?"

She pointed to the glamour, to where the world seemed too bright, too purposeful. "What *is that*? What have you glamoured?"

Tiernan was on his feet a moment later, and Shay's mouth fell open. He stared at her, eyes wide.

"You see through glamour," he breathed.

From somewhere behind her, she heard Brynn mutter the words, "Oh, shit."

Shay swiveled to face Tiernan, his eyes accusing. "Are you honestly going to tell me you didn't know she possessed such an ability?"

Tiernan shoved his hands into his pockets and rocked back onto his heels. "I wasn't aware."

She took a step forward, ready to defend herself, but Merrick snared her by the arm and held her back.

"Easy tiger," he mumbled.

"I can't see *through* glamour." Maeve faced them, nodded once to Merrick, in a silent promise to be on her best behavior. He flashed his dimples in a wide smile and let her go. "But I can sense it. I can see it. I know when it's being used to deceive. Reveal it at once."

Shay's back snapped straight like she'd slapped him. Tendrils of smoke curled around him, and his eyes burned with irritation.

Tiernan idly fiddled with the ring on his pinky. "Be very careful in your next choice of words, High Prince."

The warning was clear. He would tolerate no disrespect.

"It was meant to be a gift," Shay muttered.

Maeve showed him no sympathy. "Reveal it."

Shay waved a hand, and the shimmering object was brought forward. Whatever it was, it was massive, and the other fae moved out of the way, stepping aside to make room for it. In an instant, the glamour fell away to reveal a stunning wardrobe. The dark oak door was carved with a crescent moon and beneath it, a tree with spiraling roots and branches that extended past its hinges. Inlaid rubies and yellow diamonds outlined the intricate leaves, and when Shay pulled the door open, a rack hanging with at least a dozen ball gowns sparkled in the faerie light. Satin and velvet. Silk and chiffon. There were shelves with glittering crowns and tiaras, and drawers filled with jewels in rich Autumn colors.

"What..." Maeve's voice cracked. "What is this?"

Shay didn't look at her, instead running his fingers along one of the purple velvet cushions holding at least half a dozen rings. His voice was low and tinged with remorse when he said, "It belonged to our mother, the High Queen Fianna. Garvan wanted it destroyed but I...I refused. So, I kept it out of sight." He faced her then, his expression solemn and unreadable. "She would have wanted you to have it."

Silence fell around them. A surge of pain struck her chest, and she absently rubbed the area with her palm. She'd been expecting a number of things—blackmail to get her back to Autumn, promises of vengeance and war, maybe even hurtling insults. But she hadn't been prepared at all to have Shay stand before her and give her something that belonged to their mother.

She could almost see her, could almost envision their mother. Distorted images pieced together in her mind, though whether they were from her memories or her imagination, she couldn't be sure. But Maeve could see her. She could see Fianna dancing across a gilded ballroom, twirling beneath a harvest moon, and hosting lavish parties throughout the year. Her face wasn't clear; it was like looking at a moment captured in time. Whenever Maeve tried to focus, her mother looked away, becoming a blur of the past.

A strong hand gently cupped her elbow and steered her from her dismal thoughts. She glanced over to see Lir gazing down at her.

"My lady?" He nodded toward the wardrobe. "Do you wish to accept?"

"I..."

The one time she actually wanted Tiernan to slip into her mind and offer her guidance, he was exceptionally quiet.

She faced her brother, the one who'd been willing to save her when the other was content to let her fall to her death. "I would like very much to accept your gift, Shay."

Emotion clouded his eyes when she used his first name. There was hope in the faint smile he offered her.

"But first, I'd like to know what you want in return."

He nodded in understanding. "In exchange for the wardrobe, I want only a few minutes of the High King's time."

Tiernan stepped toward the edge of the dais. "Agreed."

Relief settled into Maeve's bones, but she held herself upright. She couldn't afford to be swayed by his kindness and generosity, by his attempt to forge an alliance or build a relationship with her. She would be polite and respectful, but she would not trust him. Not until she had reason to do so.

"Perhaps we all might be more comfortable with some food and beverages," Tiernan mused.

He gestured between them, and long tables draped with sheer turquoise fabric appeared. There were large platters of meats and roasted vegetables, baskets of breads and rolls, bowls of sugared fruit and lemon tarts. Music started to play, jovial and spirited, and after a moment, the awkward tension melted away. Summer and Autumn fae began to talk, to laugh, and to dance, their voices carrying upward to the moon and filling the starlit sky.

Lir offered her a glass of sparkling wine with fizzing berries, and she took a hasty gulp. The golden liquid tasted lightly of pear, strawberry, and vanilla. It was absolutely delicious, and it went down entirely too quickly.

She could sense Shay watching her, and she had a feeling he probably wanted to speak to her, but for whatever reason, he stayed away. It was the other Autumn fae, the one from the Ceilie, who approached her.

"Lady Maeve." She curtsied and her fox-like eyes glinted. "It's a pleasure to see you again."

"It's you." Maeve smiled, pleased to have been remembered. "I didn't catch your name the last time we met."

"I'm Aeralie Kindling." Her gaze swept over Maeve. "That dress suits you well, my lady. But then again, you looked ravishing caked in mud and filth as well."

She winked and Maeve's cheeks heated. She tossed a casual glance over one shoulder and spied Tiernan watching her, amusement flickering in his stormy gaze. Then Shay approached him, and the two males left the outdoor ballroom.

The music transformed from a low melody to a livelier rhythm that had Maeve tapping her toe along with its beat.

"Want to go dance?" Aeralie asked and waved a thin stick in front of her, one that Maeve knew would emit a puff of pink smoke.

"Yes." Maeve lifted her glass and Lir filled it again. "But I'll stick to the sparkling wine this time."

Aeralie grinned when Lir silently offered her one as well. "Your pick, High Princess."

Together, they clinked glasses. When Aeralie whirled her away, Maeve noticed Lir watching her, a bemused expression on his usually impassive face. He smiled, barely, and shook his head, encouraging her to go and enjoy herself. But his silver eyes were sharp, a steadfast reminder that she was safe within Summer's walls.

With bubbles from the sparkling wine still dancing on her tongue and its unwinding effects loosening her limbs, Maeve stole away with Aeralie and went to go dance.

Chapter Eighteen

Tiernan was exceptionally wary of the Autumn High Prince. It was unlike any Autumn fae to arrive unannounced, and not only had he shown up without notice, but he'd brought along a small entourage as well.

Tiernan led Shay to his study and walked over to the gold cart positioned in the corner, stacked with crystal glasses and various liquors. He poured them each a shot of whiskey.

"Let's get this over with, shall we?" Handing one shot glass to Shay, he nodded, and they downed the liquor in unison. It burned down the back of his throat and he leveled him with a hard stare. "What do you want, Shay?"

"It's just as I said before, I—"

"Cut the bullshit." Tiernan poured them each another shot.

"Alright." Shay finished it without question, then dropped onto one of the chairs across from Tiernan's desk. He propped his ankle up on his knee and his grip on the leather arms of the chair was so strong, his knuckles whitened. "Garvan wants her."

Tiernan's blood turned to ice in his veins. The darkness inside him stirred to life, growling, ready to seek and destroy. Like hell he'd let that prick of a prince have her. He grabbed the decanter and poured Shay another shot.

"Have you come to negotiate, then?"

"As if I'd waste my time," Shay scoffed. He inspected his nails and ran his tongue along his teeth. Then he swirled his whiskey once before taking another slow sip. "He's planning something. I know he's been working with Parisa, and they've been speaking to one another regularly, but he's shut me out of those conversations. I hate to say it's due to lack of trust because I sincerely doubt it, but I imagine it has more to do with the fact that Garvan thinks me incompetent."

In the distance, thunder rumbled, but Tiernan kept it at bay. He inclined his head, calculating the fae male across from him. "Are you expecting me to believe you're no longer in your brother's confidence?"

"I am..." Shay began, like he was tossing the idea around, "and I'm not."

"What the fuck does that mean?"

At Tiernan's fierce tone, Shay stood, matching him. "It means Garvan is a bastard and I want no part in what he's doing."

"But you don't want him to cut you off," Tiernan finished for him, eyeing his empty shot glass.

Shay's arms spread wide, palms up. "Can you blame me?"

He couldn't, but he didn't say as much. If Shay spoke out against Garvan, he'd have a target on his back and a bounty on his head.

A dull ache formed at Tiernan's temples. "Why are you really here, Shay?"

"I don't want anything to happen to her."

"Bullshit."

"*No.*" When Shay spoke, it was in earnest and laced with vehemence. His hands coiled into fists as his side and his magic—death magic—swirled around him, permeating the air with the earthy scent of damp leaves and decay. "Something happened during the Autumn Ceilie. Yes, Garvan dropped her from the fucking sky because he's an asshole, but I *caught* her. I wasn't going to hurt her. I couldn't. You think us similar, but I am not my brother. When she asked me to put her down, I heard a voice in my mind."

Shay's gaze sought the floor and when he looked up again, his eyes were bright with the blaze of loyalty. "My mother's voice."

Tiernan didn't want to believe him, but he recognized that loss and related to it all too well. There were times he heard his own mother as well. She whispered to him, called to him, and guided him. But whereas Tiernan's mother had been taken from him, Shay's mother had abandoned him. She'd left him and all she loved behind... to save Maeve's life.

"What did she say," Tiernan asked quietly, "your mother?"

Shay's angular features were tight. His brow drawn. But he held Tiernan's gaze when he said, "Protect her."

Interesting. "And that's why you're here?"

"Yes." The High Prince's shoulders dropped, and it was then Tiernan saw the lines of fatigue pulling at him, the way the weight of exhaustion fell across him like a burden. "I know he's up to something, but there's only so much I can ask without appearing overly interested in politics." Shay flicked the cuffs of his coat and straightened to his full height. "Which, as I'm sure you're aware, is not really my thing."

Tiernan dipped his head in acknowledgement. "I would agree, yes."

"Garvan hasn't always been a dickhead, but it's worse now. He's turning on our own people. I mean, he's taken to hunting merrows, skinning them, and selling their scales. They're citizens of our own Court and he's stalking them." He pointed to Tiernan, not accusingly, but more in a general vagueness. "You saw how out of control the Autumn Ceilie was...it never used to be like that. Not when my parents ruled."

Indeed. Tiernan remembered it well, though not for the reasons Shay thought.

He remembered watching Rowan sneak Maeve behind a stone wall covered in overgrowth and moss. He remembered them reemerging with her coated in the scent of Rowan's lust, her eyes glazed, her cheeks flushed, and there hadn't been a damn thing he could do about it. He remembered watching her cry when he used his power to take control of her body and then forced her to perform a mating dance in a last-ditch effort to keep Fearghal away from her.

But it hadn't been enough.

The butcher fae had gotten his hands on her anyway.

Tiernan's jaw ticked, and he kept a stranglehold on his emotions. "And you don't agree with Garvan's ways?"

"No. Never." Shay scowled and his mouth turned down in disgust. "My parents would disown him."

"And what would you have me do?"

Shay glared up at him and his eyes shifted to something wild. Feral. His magic illuminated him, glowing with a haze of power, the epitome of Autumn.

"Protect her," he growled.

Tiernan nodded. The bond he shared with Maeve was unmistakable then, even if she wasn't ready to accept it. But that fierce protectiveness, that determination, it was the exact same feeling he shared for Ceridwen.

"I will continue to protect Maeve and I will offer you protection as well. In exchange," Tiernan gestured between them, "you will give me information."

"On?" Shay prompted.

"Garvan's movements. His dealings." Tiernan offered his hand. "Anything you think may help us prepare against Parisa and remove both of them from power."

Shay gripped his hand. "Agreed."

A Strand formed between them, a crashing wave upon a harvest moon. He felt the sensation of it take form around his bicep, hidden from view. It floated over his skin, then branded him.

Shay examined his own arm, the same Strand having taken form on him as well. "I'm assuming the invitation to Sunatalis still stands?"

"As it has for years." The Autumn Court rarely appeared at the celebration of his and Ceridwen's birth, but with Maeve in the picture, Garvan and Shay's attendance was almost guaranteed.

Tiernan headed toward the door of the study and paused with his hand on the handle. "One more thing."

Shay waited, expectant.

"Why the wardrobe? Was it all for show?"

"No." Shay swallowed but kept his chin high. How interesting it was that Maeve often did the same thing. "No. I believe with every fiber of my being that my mother would've wanted her most prized possessions to go to her only daughter."

Without another word between them, Tiernan and Shay returned to the outdoor ballroom. It appeared the Summer and Autumn fae had settled tensions just fine on their own as music exploded around them, accompanied by boisterous laughter and excitement. The very last thing he expected to see, however, was Maeve right in the midst of it all, dancing as though she didn't have a single worry in the world.

MAEVE WAS ALIVE.

The ballroom had become a swirl of bodies and movement, of incoherent giggles and too many glasses of bubbly wine. She'd lost count of the number of drinks she'd consumed and found she no longer cared. The music flowed through her, lifting her. She soared to its spirited beat and danced with abandon, and all around her, Autumn and Summer fae twirled, spun, and swayed to the wild rhythm. Beside her, Aeralie whirled with her head tilted up to the starlit sky, and every now and then she'd glance over at Maeve and grin.

It had taken a lot of pleading and she may have entered into a teensy contract or two, but she'd finally convinced Merrick and Brynn to join her on the dance floor. Lir had outright refused, but she'd caught him smirking as she carted Merrick and Brynn away by the hand. Though she wasn't entirely sure that dragging Brynn from the dais was such a good idea. She moved and twisted her body like she was trying to avoid stepping in a pile of mud.

Maeve snorted.

"Don't mock me, Your Highness," Brynn called over to her, struggling to shake her hips. "I haven't had nearly enough alcohol for this sort of thing."

Merrick laughed. "I don't think the alcohol is going to help."

Brynn gave him the finger and turned away from them to join Aeralie instead.

Maeve stilled and watched Brynn take Aeralie's hands while trying her best to figure out how to dance without looking like she had no idea what she was doing.

"Do you think she's mad at us?"

"Eh, she'll get over it." Merrick reached out and grabbed her hand. "Come on, Your Highness. Let's show them what you've got."

Merrick, on the other hand, was an exceptional dancer. He looked like he walked on air. Every motion was so easy and fluid, like second nature. He guided her along, leading her through a sequence of intricate steps. The music seemed to flow into him, through him, and on more than one occasion, Maeve caught herself staring.

He whirled her around in a sweeping circle of spins, keeping her hand clasped above her head the entire time. Her cheeks ached from smiling so much and her heart was so full, so happy, it almost burst. But then the tempo slowed into a gentle cadence of highs and lows, like that of a ballad or love song, and fae couples started drifting off into pairs. Just as easily as he'd spun her around, Merrick pulled her in for a slow dance. He kept his distance, holding her hand to guide her while his other hand barely grazed the small of her back.

The easy melody gave Maeve enough time to catch her breath, the bubbles from the sparkling wine having finally caught up with her. "You're an incredible dancer, Merrick."

"Thank you." He anchored his leg and dipped her slowly until she arched all the way back, then gradually pulled her upright. "I've got two older sisters, so it was forced upon me. When Tiernan and I were younger, my sisters dressed us up as princes and made us attend imaginary balls."

Maeve leaned back and gazed into his cerulean eyes. "You've known each other that long?"

He grinned down at her, and his dimples illuminated his face. "We grew up together." Merrick spun her out, twirled her once, then dragged her back to him. "I've known Tiernan my whole life."

"I've bet you've got some stories."

She tried to imagine Tiernan and Merrick as children; as young males who were reckless and impulsive, who probably had no idea the world was at their fingertips. Her imagination dreamed up the adventures they went on and the trouble they likely caused in their youth.

The calming beat of the music floated over her, reminding her of an intricate waltz. She stifled a yawn. But her body was warm and fuzzy, and though she knew she was slightly intoxicated, she wanted to learn more about baby Tiernan.

"Did you two spend all of your time together?"

"There were actually four of us for a while. Myself, my oldest sister Ciara, Tiernan, and Ceridwen. For the longest time, we did everything together." Merrick dipped her low this time, and the world spun in a blur of colors. "But things got weird after Tiernan and Ciara slept together, so then it was just Ceridwen, Tiernan, and me."

Maeve tried to ignore that annoying bit of information. Obviously, he'd had multiple partners over the course of his lifetime. He was fae. She couldn't blame him. But it didn't make her any less jealous. She opted to take the high road and not the one paved in envy.

"Tell me stories about what it was like when you were younger."

Merrick laughed, pulling her in. She let her head come to rest upon his shoulder while he swayed them back and forth. Her eyes were heavy with sleep, and his voice was like a lullaby.

"Which ones? Our adorable youth?" He chuckled softly. "Or when we were careless rebels?"

"Any of them. All of them."

The music pitched and Merrick spun her out once more. Maeve twirled away from him, but her hand slipped from his grip. She reached out blindly, and he caught her wrist, gently bringing her back into the dance.

Maeve let a small sigh escape her. "I would've liked to have had a childhood like yours."

"It would've been even better if you'd been there with us." A deep, velvety baritone coasted past her cheek and her head snapped up.

She wasn't dancing with Merrick.

It was Tiernan.

Maeve glanced over Tiernan's broad shoulders and spied Merrick standing back, watching. He flashed his dimples in a wide smile, then disappeared into the crowd of bodies.

"Are you tired?" Tiernan's whisper skated across her cheek.

"Mm." It was a noncommittal agreement.

"Then let's get you to bed."

Maeve held onto his arm and pressed the back of her hand to her mouth to disguise another yawn. "Don't I have to say good night?"

"Just wave." Tiernan guided her toward the exit. "I'm sure they'll understand."

Maeve waved to no one in particular, but she caught Shay's eye. He watched her from across the room, not daring to step her way, not risking speaking to her again. Maeve gave him a little smile in what she hoped he would perceive as a truce, and the one he flashed back her way was shining.

Once they were out of the ballroom and in the halls leading back to their rooms, Tiernan scooped her up off her feet and into his arms. She instantly relaxed, melting into the strength of him. She listened to the sound of his heart beating against her ear, and she enjoyed the way his chest rose and fell. Steadfast. Confident. Sure. She remained silent when he carried her into his room and not her own.

She said nothing as he slowly undressed her, carefully unraveling every article of clothing like she was a present on Yuletide morning. She removed her Aurastone and handed it to him, and Tiernan placed it beneath the pillow where she would lay her head down to sleep. A shiver danced across her skin and the fire in the hearth that was once nothing more than a few dying embers flickered to life at his command. With her mind fuzzy from too much drink and the promise of sleep tugging on her eyelids, Maeve crawled into Tiernan's bed.

He took off his clothing and climbed in next to her, drawing her up close to him so her back fit against his chest and her bottom nestled against his hips. He stroked her hair, twirling each curl around one of his fingers. The last thing she remembered before succumbing to sleep was Tiernan serenading her with a song about magic, dreams, and faerie queens.

Chapter Nineteen

Maeve had never been to Niahvess before.

She'd roamed the palace and the stretch of pale pink sand, but she'd never been down into the city that seemed to float upon the many canals running through it. It was situated in the valley with the mountains in the distance, and turquoise river ways separated the pretty shops and homes rather than roads. There were cobblestone walking paths and ornate foot bridges, colorful buildings with bright awnings stretching over outdoor cafes. Flowers bloomed on every corner, the air was warm and sweetened by the scent of the sea and fresh florals, and Maeve had never seen anything quite so lovely.

She ventured down into the city with Tiernan and Ceridwen. Though she would've preferred the comfort of leggings and a bodice, she understood she was Archfae. When she participated in any sort of public appearance, gowns were required. She opted for a chiffon dress that fell off her shoulders and flowed around her legs. It was the color of an Autumn sunrise, a striking contrast to Tiernan's midnight blue clothing and the soft gold of Ceridwen's dress.

Tiernan paused before one of the paths that split into three separate bridges dividing the city. "Ceridwen has a few places to stop in the Market District, and if you want to visit the Spring fae, she can take you to them."

Maeve looked up at him and shielded her eyes from the sunlight. "You're not coming with us?"

He nodded toward the bridge leading to the right. "I'm needed at an appointment in the Shadow District this morning, but I'll meet up with both of you afterward."

"Shadow District?" Maeve's brow arched and he gestured vaguely to the path leading toward an area of Niahvess that did in fact look cloaked in shadows. "How many districts are there?"

"Three." He pointed them out to her. "The Market District, the Pleasure District, and the Shadow District."

Her mouth fell open. "You have a Pleasure District?"

Ceridwen laughed and Maeve could've sworn Tiernan blushed.

"Not *that* kind of pleasure, Maeve." Ceridwen swatted at her playfully. "Pleasure as in food and drinks, different kinds of entertainment, and self-care."

"Oh." Now it was her turn to have her cheeks heat with embarrassment.

"Come on." Ceridwen looped their arms together, still giggling. "There's a shop here in town I've been dying to show you."

"I'll see you soon." Tiernan bowed his head, just slightly, and pressed a featherlight kiss to her forehead. Then he strode off to the right without looking back.

"Must be some pretty important business," Maeve murmured.

"Everything with Tiernan is important." Ceridwen laughed, a soft, tinkling sound. "Let's go through the city first and then I'll take you to check in on the Spring fae."

Together they strolled over a few bridges and wound their way into the heart of Niahvess. Magic seemed to vibrate and thrive within its beautiful shops and quaint little homes. It floated over her skin, carried by the breeze. There were restaurants and taverns, shops bursting with the wares of crafters whose magic allowed them to create any number of useful items. Art, glassware, trinkets, tapestries, lighting fixtures...all of it made with faerie magic.

Ceridwen stopped in front of a pretty shop with a pastel pink awning adorned with summer roses. "This is the one."

When they stepped inside, a bell announced their arrival, and Maeve knew exactly why Ceridwen wanted to take her there.

It was a dress shop. A gorgeous establishment filled with an array of gowns, jewels, shoes, and crowns. Tiaras glittered behind glass cases, jewelry spilled from velvet boxes, and there was a gown for every color of the rainbow and then some.

A cute fae with a perky nose and kind eyes popped from behind a dress form. A tape measure tied to a navy sash hung from her waist, two pencils were stuck in the bun on top of her head, and she dusted her hands off on her cream-colored skirt before coming to greet them.

"Your Highness." She curtsied before Ceridwen and then her eyes found Maeve. They widened, and when she smiled, it was bright and welcoming.

"Imogen." Ceridwen reached out and clasped the shopkeeper's hands. "Such a pleasure to see you again."

"And you as well, my lady." Her pale brown eyes slid to Maeve. "I see you brought a friend this time."

"I did." She gestured between them, her movements effortlessly graceful. "Imogen, I'd like you to meet Maeve Ruhdneah, High Princess of the Autumn Court."

Imogen's smile brightened even further, if such a thing was possible. "It's an honor to meet you, Your Highness. Your reputation precedes you."

Maeve blinked, hoping she meant her words as a compliment.

As though sensing where her mind had wandered, Imogen continued, "What you did for the Spring fae in the Summer forest... we're all in awe of your valor."

Maeve blushed. She'd hardly call what she'd done to protect them an act of valor, but she appreciated the acknowledgment nonetheless. "I only did what anyone else in my position would've done."

Imogen's features softened. "That's what all the great ones say."

Ceridwen draped her arm around Maeve's shoulders. "I've come to pick up my dress for the Sunatalis celebration and to convince Maeve that she needs one as well."

"Oh, Cer, no. I don't need another gown." Maeve waved the notion away. She had plenty, not including the ones she'd just received as a gift from Shay—the ones belonging to her mother. "Besides, you know I prefer leggings."

"But Maeve," Ceridwen crooned. "If any occasion calls for a new dress, it's Sunatalis. Not only do we celebrate the end of summer for the calendar year, but it's also my birthday. And Tiernan's." She clutched Maeve's hand and leaned in conspiratorially. "Surely you'd want something new for such...festivities."

Imogen's eyebrows lifted in surprise at the painfully obvious implication.

Heat spread across Maeve's chest, all the way up her neck, to the tips of her pointy ears. "I really don't think a dress is necessary." She sought something, anything to change the subject. A jewelry display on one of the counters caught her eye. "Maybe a bracelet. Something to match the necklace you made me."

Ceridwen clapped once. "An excellent idea."

Grateful for the distraction and pleased she'd satisfied Ceridwen to some extent, Maeve wandered over to the array of jewels spread out on tiers of black velvet while Imogen's tape measure whirled around Ceridwen. There were a few bracelets made with amethyst, but most of them were aquamarine, sapphire, and other gemstones. Then, tucked behind a stack of bangles, she discovered a bracelet of fiery opals wrapped in gold. It wasn't a perfect match to her necklace, but it was certainly close enough.

She picked it up just as Ceridwen called out to her. "Maeve?"

"Hm?" She glanced over her shoulder.

"When is your birthday?"

The simple question was a punch to her gut. She tried her best to smile, but the truth was, she didn't know the exact date. "I don't know. To Carman, it was never anything worthy of discussion. But Casimir told me he found me when the season of autumn took its final breath."

"Then you must've been born during Samhwyn, the end of autumn right before winter." Surprise lit the High Princess's delicate features. "That's only a few weeks away. We should have another celebration!"

"It's fine, really." Maeve shook her head and waved the notion away. It was a kind thought, but the only soul who likely knew the true date of her birth was her mother. And she was dead.

Ceridwen paid for her dress, insisted upon buying the bracelet for Maeve, and then they bid farewell to Imogen. On their way to the outskirts of the city, they picked up a few paper bags loaded with pastries and other baked goods to bring to the Spring fae.

The camp was easy to spot. Large white tents were set up as temporary shelter. There were a handful of small fire pits, plenty of chairs and tables, and even some overhead shower stalls had been installed for their use. A few fae were sorting through bags of donated clothing and goods and handing them out to those in need.

Maeve ducked into the largest tent with Ceridwen behind her. As soon as she entered the space, every fae inside dropped onto one knee before her, from the oldest to the youngest. Unease caused her palms to slick with sweat, but the second discomfort overwhelmed her, a lulling swell of soothing calmness and composure swept over her. Beside her, Ceridwen winked.

"You're her." A child fae with springy blonde curls approached Maeve, her crystalline blue eyes wide with wonder. "You're the Dawnbringer."

"I..." Maeve stole a glance at Ceridwen, desperate for assistance.

Ceridwen set down her bag of treats and started passing them out. "The Dawnbringer was a demi-goddess who lived in the before, hundreds of years before any being, mortal or immortal, ruled the realms. Legend has it she was the creator of the most ancient fae race."

"Yes!" The fae girl squealed then carefully accepted the coconut tart like it was a piece of treasure. "The Dawnbringer and the Night-weaver worked together to forge the fae realms, with the help of Danua and Aed. In my studies...well, when I was allowed to study before the Dark Queen banned it, I learned—"

"I'm sorry to interrupt." Maeve knelt down in front of the girl so they were eye to eye. "The Dark Queen?"

The girl looked over her shoulder at an adult, presumably her mother. The female nodded once and the small girl leaned in close, then whispered, "Parisa."

Ceridwen and Maeve shared a look. For the first time, Maeve wished Ceridwen shared the same powers as her twin. In a moment like this, speaking thoughts within the minds of one another would've been exceptionally useful.

"She banned your studies?" Maeve prompted, and the child's head bobbed in agreement.

"She did. She outlawed magic and banned education of any kind." This from the female Maeve assumed was the child's mother. "She burned all the books."

Maeve's heart nearly gave out and her balance faltered. If not for Ceridwen's arm on her back, she would've fallen on her ass.

"She...*burned* the books?" Maeve's chest ached and her soul cried. So many beautiful words, so many tomes of knowledge, so many stories, lost to the grip of power. "I...I don't know what to say."

"Say you'll destroy her," a male fae piped up from somewhere in the back.

"You're the Dawnbringer," echoed a female. "If anyone can rid the Four Courts of the Dark Queen, it's you."

Hesitation clawed down her spine. "I don't know about that."

"No." When the girl with the bouncy blonde curls spoke, her

185

voice was reverent. She took Maeve's hand; it was so small compared to hers. "It's you. I know it."

"We all know it," answered another amidst murmurs of agreement.

"I had a vineyard, Your Highness." A male fae stepped forward and weary lines of exhaustion haunted his handsome face. "I watched it burn to the ground. The Dark Queen is destroying all that Spring ever was. She's ruining it, spreading her darkness and letting it fester. She sends the dark fae out to wreak havoc upon us. There's nothing for us there anymore. We left everything behind. Our homes. Our trades and professions. Parts of our soul. We abandoned it all and in doing so, we revoked our vows to the Spring Court."

Ceridwen gasped.

Maeve wasn't entirely sure, but she imagined rescinding a vow to one's Court was kind of a big deal. She turned to Ceridwen and lowered her voice, so only they heard the words she spoke. "I didn't realize it was so bad."

"Neither did I." Ceridwen shook her head, her waves of golden hair spilling around her like a sunlit waterfall.

"Will Tiernan accept them?"

"If they swear allegiance to him and Summer," she paused and pressed her lips together, "then yes."

Maeve faced the Spring fae. She rolled her shoulders back, shifting easily into the role of an Archfae before addressing them. "The High King will protect all those who seek amnesty and vow their fidelity to the Summer Court."

The fae who'd lost his vineyard straightened. He shared looks with those around him and when he spoke, his voice was low and firm. "With all due respect, Your Highnesses, we don't want to pledge allegiance to the Summer Court." He bowed. "We wish to swear our devotion to *you*."

Maeve balked. "Me? But I...I don't even have a Court."

"It makes no difference to us." He spread his arms wide, encompassing the Spring fae as a whole. "We've all agreed. We want no other as our queen. Only you."

"I..." Maeve stammered, lost to the rise of emotion clogging her throat. Queen. These fae wanted her as their *queen.*

The mother of the curly-haired fae moved to the front of the crowd. "You saved us."

Their praise was too much for her to bear. "It was nothing."

A male stepped up and placed his fist upon his heart. "You destroyed the Hagla for us."

"The High King took down the giant," Maeve countered while struggling to control the rapid rise and fall of her chest. Her heart hammered, and her breath barely escaped under the crushing weight of expectation pressing down on her lungs.

"He did so to protect the Summer Court." The male fae bowed to her. "You went after the Hagla to protect us. You stormed into the shadows for *us.*"

"You saved my son's life!" shouted a male from the back and she looked up, recognizing his face. He was the father of the small fae child she'd held when the Hagla attacked.

Dazed, Maeve stepped back, and Ceridwen stepped right up to save her. "Let us speak with the High King and see what we can do. I'm certain he'll be sympathetic and understanding to your cause."

The Spring fae agreed and nodded. They would wait for the High King's word. They would ask him to hear their plight. Maeve offered to find them employment and homes, to create whatever they needed. Whatever their heart's desire, she would find a way to bring it to fruition.

"You are a gift from the goddess, Lady Maeve."

"A true Dawnbringer."

By the time they left the Spring fae shelter, Maeve was spell-bound. She wasn't accustomed to being the recipient of so much love and respect. Those fae wanted her, they chose her, and their simple kindness and gratitude left her head spinning. Their utter devotion to her was beyond anything she ever dreamed of for herself. She'd always wanted to be a queen, she'd been determined to take the crown she was owed, but she'd thought such aspirations vanished when the truth of her blood came out. Yet now...now it was suddenly within her grasp, and the thought of it was petrifying.

Maeve drifted to Ceridwen's side and the High Princess draped her in a cloak of tranquility. Easy, gentle waves of composure coasted over her to help calm her mind.

When Maeve finally caught her breath, she took Ceridwen's hand. "What just happened?"

Ceridwen laughed, airy and musical. "I think it's safe to say you've been anointed High Queen."

"But how? That's impossible." Maeve couldn't even think clearly anymore.

"Nothing's impossible."

"What do you think Tiernan will say?" Maeve wasn't even sure she wanted to know. She'd only just received the title of High Princess; she knew absolutely nothing about becoming a High Queen.

Ceridwen gave her shoulders a comforting squeeze as they walked back toward the palace, and she laughed again. "I think there's only one way to find out."

TIERNAN LISTENED while Ceridwen gushed about her gown for Sunatalis as her overall general excitement had spiked once she realized guests would be arriving for the celebration in the next two days.

Maeve, on the other hand, was strangely quiet on the way back to the palace.

He watched her walk beside him silently, chewing on her bottom lip. Even though he didn't dare slide into her thoughts, they were loud enough that he had to intentionally block them out. She fiddled with her loose curls, squinted up at the sky every now and then, and adjusted the sleeves of her gown. All tells of someone who was troubled by something.

They entered the arching gateway of ivory stone, and the main courtyard welcomed them with swaying palm trees and the rippling sound of pools winding their way through the palace grounds. Maeve's gaze was focused on one of the palms, but she was distant, lost somewhere he couldn't quite reach.

He bent toward her. "And what did you think of the Summer Court's Crown City, my lady?"

Her eyes flicked up to his. "It was lovely."

"But?" He knew she was holding back.

Maeve glanced over at Ceridwen. His twin inclined her head, then turned away, leaving them alone. Maeve searched his face, and he would've done anything to erase the worry harboring along her brow.

"Will you walk with me for a minute?"

"Gladly." He captured her hand and entwined their fingers. An intimate gesture. Something he rarely did for anyone.

They moved to the inner courtyard where Maeve destroyed a palm tree in a fit of rage a few weeks prior. It was slowly coming back to life, but it served as a constant reminder to never piss her off. She continued to let him hold her hand, but she bounced in her high heels with a restless, fitful sort of energy. "Talk to me, *astora*."

"Something happened when I was checking on the Spring fae." The words tumbled from her mouth, and Tiernan instantly went on alert. His body stilled, and his muscles bunched.

"What happened?"

"Nothing bad," she amended quickly and clamped her hand over his forearm. "But they said something to me and I'm not sure what to make of it." She rubbed her lips together again and crackles of nervous energy sparked around her. "I don't want to upset you."

"You won't." The words were out of his mouth before he could take them back. It wasn't like him to make foolish promises. He couldn't guarantee he wouldn't get upset. What if they'd done something absurd, like insult her or humiliate her? He certainly wouldn't have been able to remain calm and collected then.

"The Spring fae...they've revoked their vow to Parisa. She calls herself the Dark Queen now and they want nothing to do with her. She's destroying all that is good, banning magic, and outlawing education. Tiernan, she *burned books*." Her throat worked, and it was then he saw her struggle. The pain haunting her eyes. The way her chest rose and fell in small gasps. It was as though speaking the words ripped her heart out. "But they...they don't want to swear allegiance to you, to Summer."

He thought as much. Spring aligned more with Autumn when it came to values, traditions, and beliefs.

"They wish to swear allegiance to me."

Tiernan froze. Maeve was staring at the ground and playing with the chiffon sleeves draping off her shoulders. She wouldn't look at him, but instead of delving into her mind, he focused on her necklace. On her emotions.

"This bothers you?" he asked, unsure why she would feel so insecure at the mention of such an honor.

Her sea-swept eyes, clouded by concern, landed on him. "Doesn't it bother you?"

"No. Why would it?"

"Because I'm fourth in line for the Autumn throne. I have no Court, no Crown City." She gestured to the south, to where Niahvess was prepping for evening activities. "Yet these Spring fae want me as their queen, and it's terrifying."

He brushed a fallen curl back behind her ear. "You were born to rule."

She sighed then and her shoulders dropped underneath what he could only assume was defeat.

"You fear nothing, Maeve." He let his arm snake around her waist and pulled her so she was flush against him. "If it is a Court you need, then I'll find you one."

"What? No, I—" She stopped herself. "You can't just create a Court."

"I said I'll handle it."

He silenced her nonsense with a kiss. Her lips were soft and smooth, and she opened her mouth readily for him, letting his tongue sweep across hers. Letting him taste her. When he pulled away, her eyes had fluttered closed. He took her hand once more and this time he escorted her back to her room.

She wrapped her arms around his neck, and he pressed her back against the door.

"Don't forget," he whispered across her neck, then let his tongue slide where his words lingered. "We have training today."

Her brows arched in interest, and she ground her hips against him. "Which kind?"

He caressed her breast and palmed her ass, wanting every inch of her lush body in his hands.

"Wicked creature," he growled.

She arched into him, and he damned the fact that unless he wanted to hoist her entire dress up to her hips, there was no easy, inconspicuous way to touch her. He planted a rough kiss on her mouth, then dragged himself away from her. He had to stay focused. There were certain things he had to take care of before he could take care of her. Yet already his cock was straining against the fabric of his pants.

"Don't forget." He raked a hand through his hair, hating the fact he was leaving her there, all soft and pliable and fully aroused for him. "Training. I'll see you on the beach in thirty minutes."

"You're leaving?"

"I have some other..." he drank in every sensual inch of her, "far less tempting matters to attend to."

She stuck out her bottom lip in a pout and it took every ounce of his self-control not to drag up that godsforsaken dress, pin her to the wall, and bury himself inside of her. As if sensing the direction of his thoughts, she smirked.

"Training," he ground out. "Thirty minutes."

She rolled her eyes. "Fine."

Tiernan was far more impressed with his willpower to walk away from Maeve than he was with his ability to stay focused on the matters at hand. He mused over the idea of Maeve becoming a High Queen in his mind. It was doable, especially if the Spring fae demanded it. There was also no doubt in his mind about her being the Dawnbringer. He'd never witnessed anyone take on a Hagla and survive to talk about it.

The walk across the palace eased the intensity of his lust, and when Tiernan opened the door of his study, he found Lir, Merrick, and Brynn waiting for him.

The three of them stood at once, each one bowing.

"Moh Rí," they said in unison.

"Sit." He gestured to the chairs and sofa and sat behind his desk. He focused on his hunter first. "What were you able to uncover, Mer?"

"She's ruining it all, my lord. Parisa calls herself the Dark Queen and spreads destruction like a plague. She's banned magic completely, devastated livelihoods, and prohibited learning of any sort." Merrick leaned back in his seat and shoved his hands through his hot pink hair. "It's far worse than we expected."

Tiernan nodded, keeping his expression schooled into one of calm composure. Parisa was wrecking the Spring Court from the inside out.

"Son of a bitch," he muttered, squeezing his eyes shut.

"I heard from Aran this morning," Brynn piped up, and Tiernan let his gaze drift to her.

"Good news, I hope?"

She shrugged. "I suppose you could call it that. But he confirmed that the Furies are indeed inhabiting the Moors."

"So, they never left Kells?" Lir asked.

"They did not." Brynn's eye color shifted from a pleasant gold to a deep magenta. "I imagine they're waiting on orders from Maeve."

"And what of the merrows?" Tiernan asked.

"Shay already sent word that Garvan is intent on hunting down more of them." Lir ran his thumb along his chin, back and forth. "It seems to be Parisa's doing."

Tiernan scrubbed his hands over his face. This was not what they wanted. This was not what they bargained for. They wanted peace. They wanted an alliance between the Four Courts, but Parisa had wanted more. She always wanted more. It had been so long since they'd been without war. So very long.

He leaned back in his chair, and the leather groaned beneath his weight. Blowing out a breath, he faced his three closest friends. The commander. The hunter. The healer. He told himself he would be honest with them. Always.

"I went into Niahvess today." His hands coiled into fists and he forced himself to relax. "I tried to find an oath breaker."

Silence descended upon them.

Lir leaned forward first and steepled his hands together. "Maeve. She bears your mark now."

"Yes." Tiernan confirmed his suspicions.

"Shit." Brynn's eyes darted around them, and her nails dug into the fabric of the sofa. A line of apprehension formed across her brow. "It wasn't supposed to happen."

"No," Tiernan agreed. "It wasn't."

He wasn't worthy of the one fated to him. He never intended to bind himself to another, and certainly not through a mating bond, because he knew his time was finite. His days had been numbered since he made that deal with the god of death. Eventually, Aed would return, and when he did, he would take *everything* from Tiernan. His magic. His power. His life.

"Were you able to find one?" Merrick stretched his legs out, crossing one ankle over the other. "An oath breaker?"

"Not exactly." Tiernan recalled venturing into the part of Niahvess that wasn't quite as pretty as the rest of the city. The area shrouded in shadows, where magic of a darker nature was discussed in whispers, where those who dared to show their faces went only out of desperation. "It was a fae who specializes in verbatim."

Meaning, he could help Tiernan work around his deal with the god of death, but for now, there was no way to break their bargain.

"Have you told Maeve?" Merrick asked.

"Have I told her what?"

"Any of it?" He gestured vaguely around the room. "All of it?"

"No."

Brynn jolted upright. "Why the hell not?"

"And what, exactly, do you suggest I tell her?" Tiernan cut through the tension simmering between them.

"The truth, *moh Rí.*" Brynn crossed her arms and agitation rolled off her in thick waves. "She deserves to know. It could make things...easier."

A ridiculous notion. "I don't see how."

"If she doesn't yet know the magnitude of the situation," Lir began, choosing his words carefully, "it will be all the more devastating for her."

"That's a good point. You've already told her about the mating bond between the two of you." Merrick tucked his hands behind his head. "Just expand on everything that implies."

"No." Tiernan stood then, firm in his convictions. "I won't have her living in fear for my life."

Brynn fumed and scowled at him. "You can't keep her in the dark."

Anger bubbled beneath the surface of Tiernan's skin. She had no idea the depths he would venture to protect Maeve from harm. But telling her the truth, telling her about his vow with the god of death, could end everything he'd worked so hard to preserve.

"I'm not keeping her in the dark. I'm protecting her."

"You're deceiving her." She shot to her feet, face flushed with frustration, and her eyes sparked to a deep shade of crimson. "How do you think Maeve will feel when she uncovers the truth? When she learns you've been lying to her and keeping secrets from her, just as Casimir and Rowan did?"

Thunder erupted around them. It cracked so loudly, the glass doors leading to the balcony rattled in their frames. "You *dare* compare me to them?"

She fisted her hands on her hips. "Explain to me how what you're doing is any different!"

"Hey now, easy does it." Merrick jumped to his feet, separating the two of them. The air roiled with the threat of violence as their tempers flared. "Let's take a step back." He shot Brynn a hasty look. "Breathe."

Brynn glared at Tiernan. Fury radiated from her. His strongest healer and third-in-command held his stare for minute after agonizing minute, until finally conceding. "She deserves to know."

"I promise to tell her." Tiernan softened his tone. "Eventually."

Brynn dropped back down onto the sofa, defeated.

"So," Merrick drawled. "Sunatalis?"

Tiernan ignored the ache taking form at his temples. "Still happening. As far as I know, everyone on the invitation list plans to attend. I imagine this year will be the one when Garvan and Shay decide to grace us with their presence."

Merrick tugged on the collar of his shirt. "And the Winter Court?"

Tiernan met his gaze. "Confirmed."

Lir, who'd been decidedly quiet during the previous outburst, straightened in his seat. "That will be another problem."

"I'll handle it." Tiernan waved off his concern. "Anything else?"

When his commander, hunter, and healer didn't respond, he nodded sharply. "Good. We'll tackle everything else as it comes to us. Right now, I have to go meet Maeve for training."

He was already twenty minutes late and would likely have to endure a verbal lashing from her as well.

Tiernan *faded* from his study to the strand of shoreline where they usually met to practice, but when he arrived, he found the beach empty. Except for a note scrawled into the pale pink sand. By the looks of it, she'd either used her finger or her toe.

I WAITED. You're late. If you need me, you know where to find me.

TIERNAN CHUCKLED, rolled his eyes to the sunny sky, then *faded* to the library.

Chapter Twenty

Maeve waited for ten minutes for Tiernan to show up to their scheduled training. The one he demanded of her. Then another five before she finally gave up and flew back to the palace. She passed a few Summer warriors, some servants, and she said hello to Deirdre as she was strolling by with a bundle full of glittering decorations in her arms.

She stopped by her room and grabbed Aran's book of fairytales and the book Rowan had given her on the Aurastone and Astralstone, then made her way to the library. If Tiernan really wanted to train, he would have to come to her.

Maeve nudged the door open and stepped inside.

Its resplendence set her heart racing. Shelves upon shelves were brimming with books. Above her head, the mural shifted from an image of the Summer Court with its floating Crown City to that of mountains, forests, and mist. The way it moved and changed of its own accord was nothing short of disconcerting. She'd never asked if the ceiling of the library was sentient; she'd always assumed it was magic of some kind. But now, she wasn't so sure.

Her footfalls were soft against the hardwood floor, and the toes of her boots followed the inlaid spirals of the sun. She scanned texts at random, with no direction or sense of purpose. There were worn bindings and spines with titles in a language she couldn't understand. Her fingers grazed the edges of the tomes, lightly brushing over both linen and leather. She didn't really know what it was she was looking for...dark magic, maybe. Or something.

She ventured further into the library's vast collection, through a maze of books, when she discovered an alcove barely illuminated by faerie light. Goosebumps prickled along her flesh and a certain chill clung to the air. A row of books was positioned upon a black shelf, their spines bare, their pages untouched. A thin layer of dust coated each of them. There were no markings and no emblems, but the closer Maeve got, the more they seemed to pulse with magic. Deep and dark, like a never-ending well. A tempting lure to all that was outside the realms of the living.

It was as though death itself ran its bony fingers across the back of her neck, and Maeve shuddered.

She stepped away from the alcove. Those books were not for her. Not yet anyway.

Maeve returned to where the light from the windows flooded the room and dropped into a chair at one of the tables. She flipped open Aran's book first, determined to distract herself. She turned the pages, bypassing all manner of creatures, both lovely and frightening, until she found the one she sought.

The Hagla.

It was created from the shadows, from the absence of light. In the before, when magic itself was reactive and capable of response, the Hagla was born from darkness. It craved the weak and destructible and fed off emotion and happiness. It thrived on nightmares and relished the suffering from the inconsolable terrors of its victims' minds. So many had attempted to destroy it, to vanquish it from the realm of the living. But none had succeeded.

Maeve startled as words appeared before her on the page in an inky, flowing script.

. . .

ONLY ONE HAS EVER TRIUMPHED *over the Hagla. Only one has ever been able to send the shadows back into the deep depths of the earth from which they were born. Maeve Ruhdneah, High Princess of the Autumn Court, the Dawnbringer, and her sword of sunlight.*

SHE SHOVED the book away from her.

How in the seven hells was such a thing possible?

"Magic," a rich voice sounded from behind her.

Maeve jumped out of her seat and whipped around to see Tiernan standing there. His hands were shoved into the pockets of his slate gray pants and the sleeves of his shirt were rolled to his elbows, revealing inches of marvelously tanned skin and golden tattoos.

"Some books have certain magical properties that allow them to record history as it happens," he continued, as though he hadn't scared the shit out of her. "I have no doubt that your brother's book is one of such quality."

"Aran is quite talented," she agreed, keeping her eyes on him.

Tiernan remained quiet, and Maeve couldn't read him. His mannerisms were cool and icy, but his eyes were a swirling storm of... chaos? Anger? She flipped through a few pages of her book and examined the notes she took while reading, then repeated the process when he continued to stare at her and not speak.

"Why are you looking at me like that?"

"You were not at training." His voice was low and menacing.

Affronted, Maeve reared back.

"And you were not on time," she countered. She shrugged then, flippant. "I got tired of waiting."

His gaze flicked to the open books spread before her on the table. "What have you learned so far about the Aurastone and Astralstone?"

"Admittedly, not much." She hadn't even opened Rowan's book yet. "I was getting ready to read about them and then you barged in looking all..." She waved her hand up and down at him.

"All what?" He sidled up to the side of the desk and casually leaned his hip against the hard oak. He towered above her and the flecks of gold in his eyes sparked like the banked embers of a flame.

"Aggravated. Annoyed." Maeve looked up at him. If he was intentionally trying to fluster her, she refused to let him win. "Angry."

"I'm not any of those things." Tiernan folded his arms and scraped his teeth along his bottom lip.

Her gaze betrayed her and dipped down to his mouth. To his perfect lips. "Then what are you?"

"Aroused." He hauled her out of the chair, pulling her against him. His hands gripped her hips, and he jerked her forward, grinding her against the obvious bulge straining against his pants. She braced her hands against the solid frame of his chest. Her knees quivered and a distinctive heat pooled between her thighs. He inhaled deeply, then lowered his head so his lips barely brushed against the sensitive skin between her neck and ear.

When he spoke, his deep voice skated across her cheek and prickling tingles of awareness caused her to shudder in his hold. "Since you felt the need to skip training today, then I think we should work on other things."

Maeve's fingers trailed up his arms and around his neck. "Such as?"

"Your ability to thwart unwanted advances."

She bristled in his arms. "Excuse me?"

"Fae, especially male fae, can be very convincing." He grabbed her wrist and planted a kiss just below her palm. Then he trailed those scorching kisses all the way up her arm to her shoulder. Maeve's thighs clenched together. "At Court, when the world is their stage, they're usually on their best behavior. At parties, however, when distractions are at their finest, they are often at their worst."

Maeve's head fell back as his hot tongue swirled up the column of her neck. "You mean like the Autumn Ceilie?"

"That's an extreme example," he paused, "but yes."

"Will your party be similar in style?"

"Not exactly." He edged her backward until her heels bumped into the wall behind her and she was pinned between his body and smooth, cool stone. Above them, the mural began to ripple and change its form again. "It's a masquerade party as well, but it will be less—"

"Crude?" she suggested. "Primal? Sexual?"

"Yes."

She arched a brow. "Then what's the problem?"

His hand slid from her hip to her ass, then squeezed. "I want to make sure you're aware of your surroundings at all times."

An odd request. "And what will you be doing, my lord?"

"I'll have other matters to attend."

If he hadn't been pressed up against her, she might not have noticed the way his muscles tensed. If he hadn't been so close, she might not have seen the clench of his jaw, or the way his eyes narrowed ever so slightly. But he was barely a breath away, and she saw all of it.

She studied the handsome planes of his face. The way his brow was drawn, the way he carefully crafted every emotion and kept them in check behind a cool façade of indifference.

"I see." Above them, the mural mimicked that of a summer storm. Dark, broody clouds. Slashes of bold lightning. The hiss of cold rain against overheated rooftops. "I thought you said no other male will touch me since I bear your mark?"

"That won't stop them from flirting," he countered.

"And what of you?" Her head tilted in question, daring him to contradict her. "Am I to assume my mark upon you will deter other females? Or will they still attempt to bed you?"

He grazed his knuckles across the swell of her breasts and played with her necklace dangling there. "Are you feeling envious, High

Princess?"

It didn't slip her attention that he avoided the question, and she locked her spine into place, angling her chin. "No."

She wasn't jealous. Not really. But if he was hers, if they were fated to one another, then she'd be damned if she'd let another female touch him. The guests for Sunatalis would arrive soon. A day or two at most. And if their current conversation was any inclination, she would be prepared to stand her ground.

"So tell me, High Princess," Tiernan barricaded her against the wall, giving her no space to escape or even breathe. He planted both of his hands on either side of her head, trapping her. "What will you do if a male corners you when you're alone?"

"What makes you think I'll be alone?"

"Answer the question."

She lifted one shoulder and let it fall. "I'll call to you."

There was a flash of emotion in his eyes, but he blinked, and it was gone. "What if I'm unable to answer your call?"

She did *not* care for this discussion at all.

Maeve was already well aware of how completely out of control fae celebrations could get, especially if what she'd witnessed in the Autumn Court was any indication. But what she didn't like was the way Tiernan implied that she would somehow fall victim to a male's sexual desire.

She was no damsel in distress. She wasn't a princess in need of rescuing from an ivory tower. She'd proven time and again she could handle herself. Maeve Ruhdneah feared nothing. Yet the fact he broached this topic made her gut seize.

She glared up at him. "What are you implying, Tiernan?"

"I'm High King of the Summer Court, Maeve. This is *my* party. I have to play the part of a proper host." He tucked a curl of her hair back into place. "I simply want to make sure no harm comes to you just because someone thinks I'm not looking."

Her hands clenched into fists at her sides, ready to strike. "You know damn well there will be blood on my hands before anyone, male or female, dares to touch me."

The lines of his face hardened. "Humor me."

"Fine." She huffed out a breath of frustration. "I'll ask him what game he thinks he's playing, because I will never be someone's pawn ever again."

"And if he persists?"

"He won't."

"What if he does this?" Tiernan grabbed her wrists and yanked them over her head, holding her in place with one hand while the other stole down the front of her leggings, groping her.

"Then I'll tell him to fuck off." Maeve's jaw clenched until her teeth ached. She refused to be deterred. If he wanted to know the true strength of her ability to defend herself, then she would show him exactly what to expect. "Or face my wrath."

She slammed her head into the bridge of his nose, grinning when he muttered a vile swear under his breath. His grip loosened for barely a second and it was the only opportunity she needed. She twisted out of his grasp and ducked low, swinging her elbow so it collided with his stomach and even though he grunted, it felt as though she'd hit a brick wall. Pain rippled up her arm, but she ignored it. Dropping onto the ground, she snatched her Aurastone from its sheath, popped up behind him, and leapt onto his back. Tiernan stumbled forward, and she twisted her hand into his hair, jerking his head backward. Without hesitation, she pressed the blade of her dagger to his throat.

Chest heaving, she spoke softly into his ear. "Do not trifle with me, my lord."

"You're entirely too tempting when you're pissed off." Tiernan laughed but recovered faster than she expected. He reached overhead, snared her by the shoulders, and threw her over top of him.

She landed on the desk, wincing as the impact stole her breath. Before she could retaliate, he spun around and covered her body with his own. With both hands, he clutched the fabric of her bodice and tore it in half. Beads and gemstones skittered around her and onto the floor like a shattered rainbow. Roughened palms grabbed her breasts, and she locked her legs around his hips. He flicked his thumbs back and forth over her nipples until they turned into perky pink buds. Maeve arched into his touch, desperate for the feel of him. He sucked her nipple into the hot confines of his mouth. His tongue swirled and when his teeth lightly scraped and bit the sensitive flesh there, Maeve ignited.

"You won't let anyone touch you like this," he growled.

Not a question. A command.

"No." Her fingers tangled in the strands of his midnight hair, urging him back to her breast. "Only you."

"Only me."

She inhaled the scent of magic, of cedarwood and orange blossom, and he glamoured her leggings away, leaving her in nothing but her necklace and knee-high boots.

"You...are exquisite," Tiernan rasped and eased back, drinking in every inch of her.

Her blood hummed and heated beneath the intensity of his gaze. He spread her thighs wider, splaying her open like one of her books, and rubbed his thumb over her swollen clit. Maeve whimpered, but once again, she was naked and completely at his mercy, while he was fully clothed.

This time, she would take control. She would be the one to make him ache for her, to make him beg.

Maeve shoved up from the table and hooked her fingers into the belt loops of his pants, drawing him closer. The corner of his mouth lifted in a smirk, and she couldn't wait to watch it fade away, until his breathing grew ragged, until he suffered insatiable desire at her hand. With precise movements, she unbuckled his belt and unbuttoned his pants until his cock sprang free from its confines. It was larger than she remembered, but maybe that was because it was right in front of her face. The ladder of gold studs that pierced the length of him glinted in the wash of late afternoon sunlight, and she longed to lick it, to suck all of him into her mouth.

But she would make him wait for that. Instead, she cupped her own breast.

Tiernan's smile fell away, and he went still, like he'd been carved from stone. He didn't move. He didn't breathe. He simply watched. *Good.*

She rolled her nipple between her fingers, then slowly let her hand glide down her sternum, over her belly, then lower still. Tiernan inhaled sharply, and storm clouds shadowed his eyes. She didn't take her eyes off him as she stroked herself, as she soaked her fingers with her own wetness. She let her eyes close and tipped her head back, relishing in the pleasure she gave herself.

Tiernan's rumbling voice infiltrated her haze of lust. *"Mine."*

She blinked up at him and smiled, purely feline. *"Wait your turn."*

His chest rumbled like thunder rolling in from the coast. Magic swelled in the air around them, vibrating with an intensity that left her shaken and breathless. Worried she'd lose him if she took too much longer, Maeve reached out, gripped him firmly in her fist, and started to pump.

The fucking fae *roared.* Books toppled from the shelves, falling like rocks off the Cliffs of Morrigan. The walls shuddered and thunder cracked, and the table she sat upon splintered and snapped. Maeve jolted and Tiernan deftly plucked her off the table.

"Bend over," he growled and snatched her by the hips, whipping her around so her back was flush against his chest. His throbbing cock nestled itself directly between her legs and then his hands were on her thighs, stretching her wider for him. Maeve reached over, shoving aside the books, pressing her breasts into what was left of the solid wood. His hoarse whisper echoed above her. "Grab the edge of the table and do not let go."

Her fingers curved over the ledge and her nails bit into the grain. The head of his cock slid against her slick core and the cool metal of his piercings sent a rush of anticipation shivering down her spine. He grabbed her hips and squeezed. His hot breath left a trail along her lower spine, then she felt the sharp bite of his teeth as they scraped her left ass cheek. Maeve gasped, the shock of his bite reverberated through her, and her knees turned to liquid. Then he was molding his hands to her hips, opening her for him. Maeve sucked in a quick breath and Tiernan slammed into her, filling her fully as she stretched to accommodate his size.

She cried out as her cheek pressed onto the table. There was no time to recover, he simply drove himself into her over and over. With every push, the head of his cock and the studs along his shaft reached the deepest part of her. Desire exploded inside her, rippled around her in a flurry of need. The wooden table dug into her skin, but Tiernan didn't seem to care if her breasts were smashed, if she couldn't catch her breath. He simply carried her, taking her higher and higher, driving her closer and closer to the brink of collapse. He hoisted her up so that she no longer touched the floor, deepening the angle. Her body convulsed against him, and she squeezed, using her inner muscles to torment him. The full length of him stroked her every nerve, tantalized her, tormented her, until the building bubble of tension quivering with the need to release exploded like an array of shooting stars.

She shook violently as the orgasm overtook her until she was gasping and crying his name like he was the only one who could save her. From behind her, Tiernan groaned—a feral, guttural sound— then he sank into her one final time, emptying himself inside her. He peppered featherlight kisses along her spine while his hands coasted up and down her waist, and when he finally pulled out, the heated mixture of his seed and her own juices slid down her thighs. She heaved herself up from the table, ignoring the slight ache in her breasts, and turned to face him.

He brushed her hair back from her damp forehead, kissed her lightly on the temple. "I didn't hurt you, did I?"

Maeve shook her head. "No. I'm fine. More than fine." Her gaze slid to the mess of beads and gems on the floor by their feet. "That's more than I can say for my bodice, however."

He smiled, a real one, and it was so devastatingly beautiful her heart nearly fractured. "I'll get you a new one."

He glamoured her some fresh clothing and a towel so she could clean herself. As she adjusted the new cropped bodice of rubies and gold beads, she looked up at him and asked, "Am I done with training today, my lord?"

Tiernan laughed. And it was so rich, and loud, and unexpected, that Maeve could do nothing but stare. She'd never heard him laugh before. Not like that. Not like he was actually...happy.

Her gaze flicked to the mural on the ceiling. It displayed a clear night with a starry sky. Endless.

Tiernan took her hand and pressed a light kiss upon her knuckles. "Can I escort you to dinner?"

"I think I'll take my dinner in the library tonight." At his look, she continued quickly, "There's more I need to understand."

He nodded once. "I'll see that it's done."

The scent of orange blossom and cedarwood surrounded them at once as the library righted itself. The books returned to their proper place; the ones she'd been reading reopened to the pages she'd left them on, and the table replaced by a new one.

He turned to go, to leave her to her books, and Maeve gathered up the last of her nerves to call out to him. "Tiernan?"

He paused and faced her. "My lady?"

Maeve couldn't find the words. Everything between them recently had been so fluid, so easy, and she didn't want to ruin it. But she didn't know how to ask the one question that constantly seemed to haunt her. She just wanted to know where they stood with one another. What, if anything, their relationship meant. But words failed her, and she found it far more difficult to ask if she was allowed to sleep in his bed each night, or if she should go to her own room instead. She didn't want to assume, but at the same time, she didn't want to offend him either.

His voice echoed in her mind, a soft, subtle caress. *"You are always welcome in my bed, astora."*

Her mouth curved into a smile.

Tiernan bowed, and when Maeve sat down to read, all she could hear in the back of her mind was the delightful sound of Tiernan's laughter.

MAEVE SPENT the next two days in the library, leaving only to check on the Spring fae and to share Tiernan's bed.

Her mind was frazzled, but she knew she was on the cusp of discovery. Tiernan must've sensed it as well, because not once did he request her presence for training, though he often sent plates of food to where she sat, surrounded by a tower of tomes.

She'd devoured the book on the Aurastone and Astralstone; she learned they did indeed belong to the merrow queen, Marella, and her sister, Delphina. They'd been forged in the depths of the Lismore Marin, made of stardust and sunlight taken from above the sea, and imbued with ancient celestial magic belonging to heavens. The Aurastone and Astralstone were gifted to Marella and Delphina from the gods as a symbol of their alliance with the skies, with the condition that when the time came, the daggers would be relinquished to those who were worthy of defending the realm from the rising darkness. At least, that much had been prophesied by Delphina.

But Tiernan had been gifted the Astralstone from Queen Marella in exchange for protection. The Aurastone, once belonging to Delphina, had presented itself to Maeve.

She wasn't entirely sure why she'd been deemed deserving of the Aurastone, but she'd already promised to defend the merrows against Garvan's tyranny, so surely that had to count for something. So, she researched as much as possible, taking notes and delving deeper into the lore surrounding Faeven, while the rest of the world seemed to carry on without her.

Every now and then, Ceridwen, Merrick, Lir, or Brynn would pop in to check on her and keep her company. They would make general small talk or scribble little notes for her to find later among the pages of some of the books she scoured. In the back of her mind, Tiernan's earlier suggestion prodded at her, nudged her, whispered to her.

She would write her own book as well. A book on the magic of creation and the *anam ó Danua.*

But not yet. Right now, there was another book that required her attention, and it sat within the dim alcove of the library. She returned and stood before the shelf that housed the books. The air was cooler somehow, and she could almost see her breath on each exhale. Dark magic lived here, alluring and ancient. There was a reason those books were cloaked in shadows. There was a reason layers of dust a hundred years old coated their bindings. An icy breeze kissed her cheek, like the hand of death.

Those books were glamoured.

The mural was moody now, foreboding, depicting nothing more than a swirl of shadows and mist. It was a sign. A warning, quietly reminding her to proceed with caution. Carefully, she closed her eyes and reached out. Whichever book called to her, whichever one begged her to listen to its stories of old, was the one she would choose to read.

Trusting only her intuition, Maeve selected a book from where the temperature seemed coldest. Her fingers closed around the cracked, aged leather, and she gradually removed it from the alcove. Opening her eyes, she looked down, and silvery shapes on the cover took the form of words. Her heart stuttered as she read the title and the tiny hairs along the back of her neck stood on end.

Legends of the Puca.

The Puca.

The same fae who had attacked Tiernan and his parents. The fae who murdered the former High King and High Queen of Summer. The fae who left Tiernan for dead.

Maeve opened the book and read.

The Puca were shifters, neutral in temperament but also frenzied. They could be persuaded to do good and wondrous deeds or coerced to commit the most atrocious of crimes. Their loyalty was to whoever could pay them the most, to whoever had the highest offer. Their magic was neither dark nor light, good nor evil. It was only a matter of how they chose to wield it. They were master metalsmiths and often used their power to turn their weapons into portals. Notorious for falling to corruption, they would easily devote themselves to a life of servitude if it meant they would be rewarded.

Bastards, Maeve thought. No wonder they'd been so quick to murder Archfae. They must've been paid handsomely for it. To them, it was a means to an end. A promise of fortune.

Puca were tall fae creatures with two curved horns protruding from the top of their head. Their hair was long and unkempt, and they could shift into various animal forms. Which animal they chose, however, varied greatly depending upon their mood and surroundings.

She flipped the almost translucent page, and her breath caught in the back of her throat.

Someone had drawn a pencil sketch of a Puca. The lines were haphazard and rough with no clear definition, but the face...the face was the same one that she saw every time she closed her eyes.

Fearghal.

She would recognize his sadistic smirk anywhere. Black corded veins bulged from his neck, and his curving horns looked like they were splattered in blood. He was drawn with a swath of fur draped around his waist and in his hands he held his blade, the same one he'd used when he carved her up deep within the dungeons of the Spring Court.

Maeve slammed the book shut. Like interlocking pieces of a puzzle, everything she knew, everything she'd read, snapped into place. Fearghal was a Puca, a wielder of a more sinister form of magic. He was also Parisa's henchman, which meant he'd obviously been lured to her side with the guarantee of a worthy bounty. And if he was a Puca, he was a metalsmith. Weapons could be portals. The Scathing was a portal.

Her mind whirred, and the book tumbled from her grasp, slamming against the wooden floor of the library. She jumped, jarring herself out of her stupor, and when she glanced down, the book displayed Fearghal's image once more. His mocking eyes looked up at her, laughed at her from the papery thin pages.

The words of the will o' wisp echoed in her mind.

The only way to save your kingdom...is by destroying the magic source of the Scathing.

The magic source. The one who *made* the Scathing. Not Parisa.

Fearghal.

"Shit."

Maeve had to find Tiernan. She abandoned her books and notes and rushed from the library in search of the High King. Decorations for the Sunatalis celebration caused her steps to falter. She'd almost forgotten about it. Gilded suns crafted from gold and sapphires floated in every corridor. Fully bloomed plumeria in shades of magenta, violet, soft yellow, and white floated in the fountains and streams running through the courtyards. Tiny orbs illuminated with faerie lights hung from the palm trees and flickered, dancing and playing, illuminating every surface in a soft glow. As much as she wanted to idle and take in all the lovely decor, finding Tiernan was more important.

He wasn't in his study or out on the patio where they usually dined. She went to the opposite side of the palace to check the outdoor ballroom, but he was nowhere to be found. Running out of options, she headed toward the far wing, to their bedrooms. If he wasn't there, then she'd go to the beach next.

She rounded the corner and found Merrick lounging in the hall, propped up against the wall with one ankle kicked over the other. At the sight of her, he jolted upright.

She waved. "Hi, Merrick."

"My lady." He maneuvered himself so he was between her and Tiernan's door.

Her brow arched in question. "What are you doing?"

"Oh, nothing." His shoulder fell against the frame, casually blocking her path.

"Right." She tried to sidestep him, but he moved with her. "I need to speak with Tiernan. It's important."

Merrick's face blanched but he recovered quickly. "He's ah...busy."

"Busy," Maeve repeated dully. She could sense the lie fizzling between them. He was hiding something.

"Yeah. High King stuff." He blew a strand of hot pink hair out of his face. "Really boring."

Maeve stepped up, closing the distance between them. To his credit, he didn't back down. "I'm sure he can spare a few moments for me."

He laughed but it was off. Forced. "Why don't we go grab some of those pumpkin tarts you love so much?" He reached out to take her hand, but she jerked away from him.

"No." Her gaze slid to the door he barricaded. "What are you hiding?"

His cerulean gaze pleaded with her, begging her not to ask. "Maeve."

She bristled. Whatever he was keeping from her, it involved Tiernan. Knots of trepidation twisted inside her stomach as an empty, hollowed-out sensation gripped her. Her pulse kicked up, thundering in her ears, and she crossed her arms to disguise her apprehension.

"Step aside, Merrick."

He hesitated, torn between whatever duty he'd been assigned and giving in to her request.

Her magic thrummed in warning. "If you don't let me pass, I'll blast a fucking hole through this wall."

"My lady, please. It's not—"

Bolts of fire shot out from the tips of her fingers and scorched the wall behind Merrick, narrowly missing his legs.

"Shit. Fine." He stepped out of her way.

Maeve grabbed the handle and wrenched the door open. Her chest heaved and her heart tumbled into the acidic pit of her stomach. Her mind screamed and her blood roared. Tiernan was there, but he wasn't alone. A half-naked female fae was wrapped around him like a vine. Her hair was the color of freshly fallen snow and stopped just above her bare shoulders. She wore a gown of satin with slits up to her wide hips. Liquid silver fabric pooled around her waist, and her perky breasts were crushed against the solid frame of Tiernan's chest. Her arms were coiled around his neck, drawing his mouth close to her own, and on her head was a crown of snowflakes.

"Maeve." Tiernan's voice was strangled and raw as he tried to pry the female off of him to no avail.

White-hot fury scalded her from the inside out. Cinnamon smoke clouded the air around them and she swore if she took one more breath, she'd suffocate.

"So," the female fae purred. "This is the pretty little Autumn princess?"

Maeve said nothing. She couldn't move, couldn't speak. She could only stare, unable to look away. Something dark and vile contorted inside her. Trembles wrecked her body, but she kept herself locked into place. She would not show her pain to him. She wouldn't show anger. She wouldn't show weakness. She would give him nothing.

The female ran her finger down Tiernan's neck, and he visibly stiffened. She tossed a careless glance over to Maeve. "Did you need something?"

Maeve cut her down with one hard glare. "Not from you."

The fae startled and her blue eyes widened in disbelief.

"Maeve," Tiernan tried again, his voice firm. But the female was latched onto him, and he couldn't disentangle himself from her lithe body. "This is Ciara, the High Queen of Winter."

Ciara.

Merrick's sister. The one Tiernan had fucked.

She whipped around to face Merrick, and the cruelty of his deception cut through her like the sting of a frostbitten blade. He ducked his head, a flush scalding his cheeks. He at least had the decency to look ashamed.

"Well." Maeve crossed her arms to protect her heart. "At least now I know where we stand."

Tiernan's voice filled her head. *"Maeve, listen to me."*

"Get the fuck out of my head." Her voice was breathy and low as her power surged, radiating around her. Fury boiled her blood. "Whatever bullshit excuse you're about to give me can be said out loud."

"It is not what it looks like," he ground the words out.

"It sure as hell doesn't look like anything else." Humiliation burned her, branded her. She'd given herself to him. Fully. And this was the treatment she'd received in return? "Is this what you meant by having to play host? Is this how you plan to show all the females your appreciation for coming to your bullshit birthday party?"

She shook her head. Her nose tingled, and the burning threat of tears pricked the corners of her eyes. But she wouldn't blink. She wouldn't let them fall. Not for him. Another horrible thought slithered its way into her mind. No wonder he came into the library, demanding she defend herself against him, asking her how she would handle sexual advances.

"It makes sense now, you know. Why you wanted to ensure I wouldn't let another touch me, but why you carefully avoided promising the same thing to me."

She stormed toward the open door of his bedroom, determined to put as much distance between them as possible. If she never saw his face again, it would still be too soon. Perhaps she should blast a hole through his wall anyway; he'd be lucky if she didn't incinerate him right then and there.

"Where are you going?" Tiernan demanded.

"None of your fucking business." She didn't look back.

Merrick's arm shot up to stop her, and she raised both of her hands in response, ready to fight. "Don't you dare, *High Prince*. You knew. You knew and you said *nothing*. You're no better than him."

Maeve shoved past him and barreled down the hall toward the main courtyard, half-tempted to set fire to everything in her path. Her magic raged, her power ignited. She stalked across the stone path, heading for the palace gates, as flames spat from the tips of her fingers. Out of nowhere, Lir appeared and fell into step beside her. She could sense his silver eyes upon her, reading her, gauging her.

She held up one hand. "Not a fucking word."

He nodded, following her in silent consent.

Anger.

Goddess above, the anger consuming her was enough to summon the wrath of the realms. She hated Tiernan for what he'd done to her. He made her think there was something between them, a mark worthy of the fates. She thought he *cared*. It was a foolish mistake, one that would haunt her. She might be fae now, but maybe she was still in possession of a mortal heart. Or at least, what was left of it. Being heartbroken shouldn't hurt this much, it shouldn't ache to the point of despair. Sun and sky, the bastard had crushed her, then did nothing but watch her inner turmoil.

A single tear burned down her cheek and she hastily swiped it away. No, she would not cry for him. He would never be worthy of her tears. She hated their stupid bond, hated the fact that he'd forced it upon her with that godsforsaken mating dance. She wanted to burn it from her skin, to watch the pretty Autumn leaf and the gold sun of Summer catch fire until there was nothing left but charred flesh. She wanted to scour it from her, carve it out of her, just like Fearghal had done.

Shards of lightning ripped across the sky as Tiernan's voice grated through her mind. *"Stop those vile thoughts at once."*

Maeve fired back. *"If you slip into my mind one more time, I'm*

215

going to cut off your dick and force Merrick to wear it as a fucking necklace."

Silence answered her.

Good.

She hoped he never spoke to her again.

Chapter Twenty-One

"**D**amn it, Ciara." Tiernan grabbed the Winter High Queen's wrists and yanked her off him. It took all his self-control not to toss her across the room. She dragged up her dress that had "mistakenly" fallen right as Maeve walked in the door. "I told you to stay away."

"As if I could." She slid the straps of her gown up over her shoulders, all demure and feigned innocence. "You know how much I adore you."

Her slender fingers skated around his throat, her touch like ice. He reared back, away from her. "No."

"You're serious." She blinked, then looked over to Merrick and her deep berry lips started to pout. Years ago, he might've fallen for such a trick. Years ago, he'd been a fool. "Mer, why doesn't Tiernan want to play anymore?"

Merrick stiffened. His spine locked into place and his eyes darkened to the color of the Lismore Marin's deepest trench. "Because he has a mating bond, Ciara. Because that High Princess who just walked out of here is the best thing to ever happen to him, and you tried to ruin it. On purpose."

"I'd say I was fairly successful." Ciara rolled her eyes to the ceiling and continued to sulk. "I was only trying to have some fun."

Tiernan glowered down at her. "You lost that privilege long ago."

She huffed, clearly annoyed, but he didn't care. After she accepted the invitation to Sunatalis, she'd reached out to him, claiming she needed to speak with him regarding an urgent matter. He'd agreed, but he assumed she meant to hold an audience with him. He hadn't expected her to show up in his damn bedroom.

He'd told Ciara about his mating bond with Maeve and still she thought they could carry on as they left off. It didn't matter if he'd fucked her multiple times; back then, he thought they meant something to one another. The pull to Ciara had never been as strong as it was with Maeve. There was no bond between them, no connection. But he'd remained faithful to her, only to find out she was far more interested in testing the waters and wasn't nearly as devoted to him. He'd caught her one day with her back against a tree and her legs wrapped around the waist of a Winter warrior while he pumped himself inside her.

Ciara fiddled with the silver hoops swinging from her pointed ears. "When did you become so boring?"

Tiernan tempered his rage. "When I realized my entire Court was worth more than anything I could ever get from you."

Her harsh laughter rang out, and Tiernan ground his teeth together.

"What can she possibly offer you?"

"Her heart. Her soul. She's given herself to me completely. No bargains. No questions. No ultimatums." Tiernan quieted his mind and reached out to Lir.

"How is she?"

No response.

"Lir." He would be kind before attempting to command. *"Please."*

Strained seconds ticked by and then finally, *"She's safe."*

His commander was pissed at him and for good reason. He never should've agreed to see Ciara. He never should've asked Merrick to deter Maeve when the High Queen showed up in his room unannounced.

Ciara folded her arms, and a thin scowl etched its way across her brow. "She obviously needs training of some kind."

Tiernan considered explaining they were working on that until she continued with, "You should whip her for the way she spoke to me. Insolent little brat. Add in the fact that she's no better than a mortal whore—"

Tiernan had never seen Merrick move faster in his life.

He slammed his sister against the wall and the glass doors leading to the balcony shuddered in their panes. One hand gripped Ciara's neck and her toes barely touched the floor. His magic swarmed, thick and menacing. The only time Tiernan ever saw such a flash of brute strength and power from Merrick was on the battlefield.

When Merrick spoke, the flowers wilted. "Do not *ever* speak ill of the Dawnbringer."

Ciara gasped and tried to swallow a breath. "What?"

"You heard me." His threat was clearly implied.

Tiernan stepped forward. "Mer."

It was just his name, but it was laced with enough authority that Merrick released her. He glared at his sister and if his eyes were blades, they would've sliced her to pieces. "The High Princess of Autumn has done more for Faeven in her brief life than you have in your entire existence."

Ciara's skin turned scarlet at the insult, and faint bruises marred her neck. She rubbed at them absently, and though her frown deepened, she relented.

"Fine." She drew the word out so it dripped with sarcasm. "Apologies for insulting your High Princess."

Merrick said nothing, but the room quaked with power and violence.

She whirled away, mumbling something about finding some Summer soldier to fuck instead.

"Take your pick," Tiernan called after her.

She gave him the finger and stalked out of his room. As soon as they were alone, Tiernan turned to look at his best friend.

"I shouldn't have asked you to distract Maeve. I apologize."

Merrick's shoulders rose and fell. He pinched the bridge of his nose with his thumb and forefinger. "You're not the only one to blame. We both thought it was the right decision."

He looked to his hunter, hoping to ease some of the worry from his mind. "Where is she?"

"Niahvess." Merrick paused, inhaling deeply, tracking the scent of her. "Some kind of shop."

Tiernan nodded; at least she was with Lir.

His hunter took another breath, then added, "She's pissed."

"I'm aware." He pressed his lips together in a firm line.

Merrick shoved his hands into the pockets of his pants, looking like a schoolboy who'd been caught thieving lollipops from a candy store. "I think we should apologize."

"Separately," Tiernan amended.

"Agreed." Merrick headed for the door. "I'll try and make sure she's back in time for the party."

"I wouldn't." He shook his head, knowing Maeve would refuse him. She was stubborn, if anything, and with how furious she was at the both of them, sending Merrick off on an errand like that would likely end with him being injured. Or maimed. Or burned. Possibly all three. He gradually paced the wooden floor of his bedroom, his boots clicked noisily against the hard surface. "Ask Ceridwen instead. Maeve is liable to set you on fire."

Merrick blanched. "Noted."

Tiernan ran a hand through his hair. His frustration was mounting. Guests were already arriving for Sunatalis and he'd have to welcome them and show face. But he needed more time. He needed to make amends with Maeve, and soon. He had to prove the depth of the bond they shared. But tonight, time simply wouldn't allow for it.

Righting all the wrongs with Maeve would have to wait.

He could only hope he wouldn't regret it.

Chapter Twenty-Two

Maeve stalked through the floating city with Lir following closely behind. She tried to stay mad, to hold tight to her anger, but the beauty of Niahvess melted it away. She couldn't frown at the darling fae children who smiled up at her with shining eyes. The array of blossoms bursting over the bridges softened her glare. Even the air seemed to sense her frustration and sent a warm breeze to tickle her cheek.

She opened the door to the dress shop she'd visited earlier with Ceridwen and the bell jingled, announcing her arrival.

Imogen came out from around a counter showcasing an array of jewels and tiaras, with a bright smile on her face.

"My lady." She bobbed a curtsy. "It's a pleasure to see you again."

Her gaze shifted to Lir, and she lowered her eyes. "Commander."

Maeve's brow quirked. "You two know each other?"

Imogen offered a small, shy smile and answered, "Everyone knows the commander, my lady."

Of course, everyone would know Lir. He was unmistakable. He was patient. Compliant. Quiet and calm. He never wavered. Never panicked. He fought with a kind of ruthlessness that was only accomplished by those in possession of a stone-cold heart.

Imogen fiddled with the measuring tape dangling from her hip. "Have you changed your mind about a gown for the party tomorrow night?"

"As a matter of fact, I have." Maeve slowly took in the shop and her gaze trailed over the racks of colorful gowns in varying fabrics. Delicate silks and shimmering satins hung from glittering hangers. Rows of eye-catching lace and flowing chiffon billowed from different displays.

"Did you have anything in mind?" Imogen asked, inclining her head toward the multitude of dresses.

"Yes." Maeve turned and focused on the spritely fae. She lifted her chin and the corner of her mouth curved upward. "I need a gown that will bring the High King to his knees."

Imogen's smile widened and a wicked gleam sparked in her eyes. Her nose crinkled. "I thought you'd never ask."

AFTER IMOGEN TOOK Maeve's measurements and came up with a rough design that was nothing short of devastating, Maeve and Lir left the shop and returned to the city's cobblestone paths. Niahvess was vibrant, alive with laughter and a fizzing energy, as it seemed everyone was readying for Tiernan and Ceridwen's birthday.

Maeve was considering going to the beach to train and avoiding the palace at all costs when a distinctive tug pulled on her magic. She looked around but saw nothing out of the ordinary. She scanned her surroundings, checking behind them. No one was following them. There were no signs of a threat, and except for an occasional smile and wave, no one seemed to pay them any attention. She shrugged off the strange sensation and continued walking, but as they neared the final bridge leading to the pathway back to the palace, the draw calling to her was stronger. More insistent.

She stumbled to a stop, and Lir almost collided with her.

"Sorry," she mumbled and stole another glance over her shoulder. "Something is just..."

"Something is what, my lady?" he prompted, his silver eyes instantly scanning the skies and canals.

"Just off," she finished weakly. She didn't know how to describe it, this puzzling awareness wanting to lure her to something or someone.

They crossed the footbridge to where the cobblestone paths from the three different parts of the city met. The other day, when she'd come to Niahvess with Tiernan and Ceridwen, Tiernan had gone down the one on the far right, while she and Ceridwen had taken the one to the left.

It was the path on the right that caused her magic to hum.

"I think I want to go this way." She pointed to the part of the city where the sunlight didn't quite hit, where shadows darkened the streets, despite there being no clouds in the sky.

"I'm afraid I have to advise against that, my lady." Lir's brow was drawn as he looked in the same direction. "You have no need to associate with those types of dealings. The Shadow District is no place for a High Princess."

Her curiosity was instantly piqued. Lir was warding her away from that section of the city, but Tiernan had gone there for an appointment. "Is it unsafe?"

"Not unsafe, no." A breeze swept over them, almost through them. It was cooler now and his dark twists of hair fell in his face. He shoved them back. "Fae only go to the Shadow District when...when they need particular types of magic. Charms and bindings. Lifting curses, breaking vows, things of that nature."

The sort of magic no one liked to talk about, but that everyone knew existed.

Maeve's gaze slid to the area of Niahvess that didn't shine as brightly as the rest, the area where the wind carried the hushed whispers of dark secrets, where the buildings stood witness to any number of clandestine deals. Where she hoped to find the one thing she sought more than anything else.

She leaned in close to Lir. "What about a memory keeper?"

He bristled. "No."

"No, I can't find one there? Or no, you don't want me looking for one?"

"Both."

"That's not fair."

"I don't know what business you seek with a memory keeper, High Princess. And it's not my place to ask. But if you go in search of one, I will report it to the High King." His voice was firm and final. She had no doubt he'd hold true to his word. But then he added, softer, "Memory keepers are dangerous, my lady. No one associates with them, and for good reason."

She appreciated his concern for her well-being, but she wouldn't let a few words of foreboding discourage her. "The High King already knows. We've talked about it."

He crossed his arms over his broad chest, ever the fierce protector. "I still won't let you go."

Indignation tingled through her. "And why not?"

"Because if you enter into any sort of unsavory accord, Tiernan will take my head." His scowl deepened, daring her to contradict him.

"What if I promise not to strike a bargain with a memory keeper?" The tug on her magic yanked again, stronger this time. "I only want to see if one exists and maybe talk to them. I have my reasons, same as anyone else. We all have things we long to forget."

Lir squeezed his eyes shut, like he was dealing with a petulant child. When he opened them, the silver pools of his irises had darkened. "It's not a good idea."

"Nothing I do is ever a good idea." But her attempt at humor failed miserably. Instead of cracking a smile, he simply glowered down at her. "That being said, you can either come with me right now and keep me safe, or I'll just sneak out and go without you. Because either way, I'm going."

Lir offered his arm and she accepted. "Has anyone ever told you how incredibly stubborn you are?"

She looped her hand into the crook of his elbow. "It's an excellent trait to possess."

"More like a flaw," he muttered and shook his head, his face grim. "If the High King finds out about this—"

"Then I'll handle it," Maeve cut in, trying to put his mind at ease. Caring about what Tiernan thought of her escapades was the furthest thing from her mind.

Lir glamoured them in hooded cloaks of softly spun cotton, and they treaded quietly into the Shadow District. She wasn't sure which direction to go or what exactly she was looking for, but the tug on her magic was more prominent now, so she was certain they were going in the right direction. At least, she hoped as much.

The air was cooler in the Shadow District. It sifted in through the thin fibers of her cloak, chilling her skin. Lir must have sensed it as well, because he moved closer to her side. They wandered through the streets, carefully avoiding the uneven bumps, the rising swells of the cobblestones. The scent of magic was strong, pungent and tinged with crushed herbs. There were interesting shops with oddities and curiosities. Potions and runes. Charms and baubles. There was even a bookstore, but the windows were all dingy, so Maeve forced herself to keep going. They passed only a handful of other fae. All of them wore cloaks or coats to keep their faces discreetly hidden from view. They walked with hasty steps, never once looking up.

The grip calling to her magic ceased and Maeve paused in front of a nondescript building.

"Here." She looked at the shop that resembled an old, abandoned home instead of a storefront. It was plain with a crumbling brick exterior, and its pale gray shutters were peeling from the salty ocean breeze. "This is the place."

Lir's hand instantly went to the hilt of one of his swords. "You're certain?"

"Yes." She glanced up. Creaking in the faint breeze was a wooden sign with faded lettering that read *Recollections*. She nodded sharply. "Yes. I'm sure this is it."

Lir stepped in front of her and walked inside. The door groaned open, announcing their arrival, and Maeve followed behind him.

The inside of the store was just as unadorned as the outside. It was a small room with a shabby, cushioned bench placed in front of the bay window. There were two chairs sitting across from it, their leather cracked and splitting. A round table was set in between the seating arrangement. On its wooden surface was a half-melted candle. Actual fire, Maeve noted. Not faerie light.

An elderly fae male appeared from a back room, ambling toward them with a lopsided gait. His knobby knuckles curled over a cane that looked to be made from an ash tree. His clothing was ragged and fraying, his skin tanned like aged leather. He had a tuft of white hair on his head with a snowy beard to match. Wrinkles lined his face, but his eyes were clear and bright.

"Can I help you?" he asked, and those eyes of his seemed to stare right through her, like she was a mirage.

She snagged Lir's hand in her own as an unexpected jolt of nervousness shot through her. "I'm looking for a memory keeper."

The older fae nudged his wire-framed glasses further up his nose. "Is that so?"

She nodded stiffly.

"Then you've come to the right place. The name's Cormac." He hobbled over to the table and a thick tome materialized before him. Its bindings were falling apart, and the pages of parchment looked nearly translucent. The book flipped open, and he pulled a pen from his front pocket. "What sort of memory work are you needing?"

"I want to know how the process works first." Maeve hedged away from the book, whose pages had begun to flip on their own. "Before I enter into any sort of arrangement."

"Of course." Cormac set the pen down and the book closed.

"Happy to help."

For a fae whose magic was spoken of in hushed murmurs, he really didn't seem too bad. He was more unsettling than anything.

"Memories are tricky business, so the cost is usually rather high." He settled himself into one of the old leather chairs and something cracked; she hoped it wasn't his bones. "Some only want to erase a moment in time, others want more. As fae, our memories can span hundreds of years, so it makes sense we'd want to ease the worries of our minds. We all have something we'd like to forget."

An eerie sense of trepidation settled around her, heavy and dense like fog rolling in from off the coast. How odd it was he'd nearly repeated her exact words back to her. But he was right. In her mere twenty-four years, she already had dozens of memories she wouldn't mind doing away with for good. It was bad enough she was reliving Rowan's death, the dungeon of Spring, and the haunting cage from her childhood every time she closed her eyes at night.

"And then there are some fae who wish for new memories alto-gether," Cormac continued. His breath wheezed in and out, like he hadn't spoken to anyone in years. "That's a rather extensive process, but worth it all the same, so long as you're on the receiving end."

She adjusted her cloak, pulling it tighter around her shoulders. "And do I get to choose the exact memory you take?"

Cormac smiled, displaying a set of slightly yellowed teeth. "Usually."

That didn't sound very promising.

"So..." He glanced over at the book, and it opened once more, an eerie blue glow highlighting what could've been a ledger. "Would you like to get started? I know he troubles you."

He...Rowan? Fearghal?

How in the hell did Cormac know that?

Beside her, Lir's entire body went tense. His hand squeezed hers.

"Um, not today." Maeve was relieved when the book closed once more and Lir visibly relaxed. Barely. "But if I were to return, what's the cost for a moment in time?"

Cormac chuckled, but it was a craggy, rough noise. "Well now, that depends."

"On?" she prompted.

"On the pain associated with the memory." He leaned forward and rested his hands upon his knees. "Foolish mistakes and embarrassments are easy to dispose of, but memories of heartache, terror, and sorrow...those things take time."

"Of course." Maeve nodded slowly. He made it sound like it was the easiest thing in the world to understand. "Well, I might return."

"You might indeed, Dawnbringer."

Maeve stumbled backward. Lir drew his weapon, ready to slay the old fae with a single blow.

"No need for that, commander." Cormac's keen eyes focused on Maeve. "I'd recognize you anywhere. You're pure radiance. There's no mistaking your identity."

She supposed Cormac's words could've been a compliment. But she wasn't so sure, and she didn't want to ask. Nor did she want to spend any more time in his presence.

As if sensing her discomfort, the fae nodded to the door. "Fair winds."

Lir didn't waste a second. He grabbed her upper arm and hauled her out of the store. She didn't know what to make of the exchange with Cormac. He certainly didn't seem as horrible as everyone made him out to be, but the way he spoke to her set her nerves on edge. He acted like he knew her, like he knew the memories that haunted her very soul. She tried to shrug off the peculiar weight of foreboding that settled around her shoulders, yet it lingered as they walked down the uneven cobblestone street. She had every intention of researching as much as she could on memory keepers before she made any sort of deal with him.

Lir was painfully silent the entire trek back to the three bridges, and when Maeve couldn't take the strained tension between them, she finally spoke. "I didn't know fae could age like mortals."

The look he gave her turned her blood cold. "They don't."

Chapter Twenty-Three

After her trip into Niahvess, Maeve returned to the glamoured lagoon, except this time she brought Lir with her. She refused to go back to the palace. Even though Niahvess helped to dull the ache in her chest, the closer she got to the palace gates, the more anxiety clawed its way through her. The more pain harbored in her heart. So, she opted to take a slight detour and train instead.

Lir, at least, was a willing participant.

"No magic," Maeve reiterated. She worried if they fought with magic, she'd do something drastic. Like burn the entire place down. Or create a new realm, thousands of miles away, and catapult Tiernan into it. "I don't want to hurt you."

His dispassionate expression never changed. "Whatever you throw at me, I can take it."

She nodded.

Swords were better. Safer. For the most part.

Lir stood across from her in the crescent-shaped cove with his curved swords at the ready. Maeve called to her sword of sunlight, and it appeared in her hands. She wielded it, raising it in front of her, and it burned like the dawn in her hands. Rolling her wrist, the fiery blade arced and wove before her. It cut through the air like the trailing blaze of a falling star. She calmed her breath, slowed her heartbeat. Lir had never been her opponent before, but she'd seen him battle against the dark fae. His speed was no match for lightning. His footwork was featherlight, like he walked on water. Every time his strike was true. He never wasted a breath, a moment, or opportunity. He never looked back.

She would have to remain on guard.

"Attack," Lir commanded, and she launched herself at him.

Their swords met in a deafening crack of magic and metal, the force of it enough to reverberate through her whole body. She twirled away from him and struck again, but he blocked her blow in one swift movement. She parried, jumping to the side to avoid the curve of his blade as it swung above her head. Hitting the ground and rolling, Maeve maneuvered to pop up behind him. He whirled, dodging her strike.

Already, sweat slid down her temples and stung her eyes, but she didn't quit. Together, they assailed one another like two partners trapped in a death dance. He evaded the heat of her blade. She avoided the slice of his swords. Her muscles screamed, ached, begged for reprieve, but she ignored them. She disregarded the pain, the way her arms spasmed as their weapons collided time and time again.

Beads of sweat dripped down his neck and chest, glistening like pearls against the jewel-toned umber of his skin. But whereas Maeve thought her legs would give out at any moment, that her knees would soften like the damp sand beneath her feet and send her careening to the ground, Lir moved like a ribbon of satin on the wind. Graceful, flowing. Not once did he falter.

Until he stopped moving completely and jerked his head toward the entrance of the lagoon. "My lady."

Maeve sucked in a few gulps of the sea-tainted breeze and looked to where he nodded. On the outskirts of the cove stood Ceridwen.

She wore a gown of ruby to match her lips and golden suns were pinned to the silk pooling around her shoulders. She stepped forward and though her smile was bright, her eyes darted between Maeve and Lir and nervous energy crackled between them.

She clasped her hands in front of her. "I thought you might be here."

Maeve wiped her brow with the back of her hand. "I took a break from the library."

"I can tell." Ceridwen's smile softened, and this time it reached her eyes. "Watching you train is rather inspiring."

"Care to pick up a sword and join us, my lady?" Lir asked, the faintest tease in his voice.

"Oh, I could never." A wicked gleam flickered in Ceridwen's eyes, and she gestured to the belt of jeweled daggers wrapped around her waist. "You know I prefer to be more...up close and personal."

Lir barked out a laugh. It was rough, but genuine.

Maeve's gaze dropped to where the High Princess fidgeted with the beading trimming her gown. "What is it, Ceridwen? It's not like you to be so uncertain."

Her dusky eyes slid to Lir once more, but the fae commander gave nothing away. "Are you coming to the welcome party tonight?"

Ah. So, Tiernan sent his twin to do his dirty work for him. Such a typically male thing to do. Maeve peered up at the hole gaping through the ceiling of the cove, where the sky was already painting itself in shades of magenta, teal, and periwinkle. She sheathed her sword, calming the flames. Then she piled her curls on top of her head, twisting them into a messy, lopsided bun. Tiny hairs clung to her damp skin. It wouldn't take her long to freshen up and show face at the Sunatalis celebration, but she much preferred to make Tiernan squirm.

"No." She inspected her nails, thinking maybe she'd venture into the Pleasure District for a proper manicure. "I don't think so."

Ceridwen waited, but when Maeve offered no further explanation, she asked, "Did something happen?"

"You could say that."

Her gaze narrowed. "Was it Tiernan?"

"Isn't it always?" An uncomfortable twinge of guilt harbored inside the heaving walls of Maeve's chest. It wasn't Ceridwen's fault her brother was a dick.

"He wants you to be there," Ceridwen urged, casting a glance toward where the palace waited just beyond the glamoured cove. "They'll be asking about you."

"Let them ask." Maeve would not be swayed to act like nothing happened, to carry on like she hadn't walked in on him with another female wrapped around him. "Perhaps the High King should've thought about that before he invited Ciara into his bedroom."

Color flared up Ceridwen's neck and bled into her cheeks. "He didn't..."

"He did." Maeve called on her magic, summoned the gentle lapping waves of the lagoon, and created a new sword, one that mimicked the sleek, curved blades of Lir's scimitar. Hers, however, had a hilt of gold and a blade the color of the Lismore Marin. "You can tell the High King I'll make an appearance at the ball tomorrow night. But I will not be by his side, and I won't partake in any other...festivities."

The explicit meaning was implied, and Ceridwen ducked her head at the same time Lir blew out a low, calculating whistle.

Ceridwen nodded, resigned. "I understand." Without another word, she *faded* out of the glamoured cove.

Maeve eyed the sword she'd created. The one made from sea foam, crystalline waters, and magic. The one she would gift to Queen Marella of Ispomora as a means of protection against Garvan. She held it, turned it over in her hands, ran two fingers along the smooth, flat edge of the blade. Perhaps she would create more weapons. Enough to outfit all of Summer's warriors. Enough to destroy Fearghal.

Lir returned his swords to their sheaths and strode over to her. "What's on your mind, my lady?"

"I figured out how to defeat the Scathing," the words tumbled out of her mouth before she could stop them.

He stumbled. The poised, steel-faced Commander of the Summer Legion actually tripped over his own two feet. "Have you told the High King?"

She cut him down with a look. "I tried."

She knew the second he pieced it all together. A scowl formed across his brow and the corners of his mouth pinched in displeasure. "You were going to tell him when you caught the High Queen of Winter in his room."

Not exactly a question but Maeve appreciated his bluntness. "Yeah."

He studied her and if Maeve didn't know any better, she would've sworn he could hear her thoughts the same way Tiernan could. The fae commander tilted his head and his silver eyes turned molten, like liquid stars. "You already have a plan."

She looked away from him then. She wasn't ready to see the disappointment in his face when she confirmed what he already knew. "I do."

"And you weren't going to tell me?" Accusation lit his tone, and his words stabbed her like scorching daggers.

"No." Maeve forced herself to meet the intensity of his stare. "Not because I don't trust you, because I do. With my life. But I know if Tiernan asks, you'll feel torn between your loyalty to him and your promise to me." She shook her head and tucked an errant curl back behind her ear. "I can't ask you to do that."

"Ask him to do what?" A low baritone rumbled from the shadows of the cove, and she was suddenly overwhelmed with the scent of *him*. Warm sandalwood. Palm leaves. Plumeria.

She spun around to see Tiernan lounging against one of the cavernous walls. He looked so carefree, so godsdamned gorgeous, and she hated him for it. "Leave."

He reared back at the demand but recovered quickly. A scowl marred his handsome face. "No."

Lir took a cautious step toward her in the sand, and she remembered his vow, his oath to protect her from everyone, no matter the cost.

"Get away from me, Tiernan," Maeve warned, and the magic in her blood thrummed to life. "Get away right now, or else."

He had the balls to smirk. That callous, cruel, manipulative smirk. The same one she faced down daily before...before the mating bond made its mark.

"Or else what?" he taunted.

She didn't even warn him. She blasted him. With all her strength. All her energy. All her magic. It rose in her like a tidal wave and came crashing down with brute force. Her power slammed into him, this intense eruption of fire and smoke, of absolute creation. Tiernan was thrown backward, and his body slammed into the cavern wall. Bits of rock and stone crumbled around him. He bit out a swear and the look he sent her, that vengeful, furious glare, told her all she needed to know.

He was pissed.

And she couldn't be happier.

Maeve didn't wait for him to fire back. She summoned her sphere of protection, but it was more than that this time. Not only did it keep her safe, but it kept him out. It shimmered over Lir and herself, enveloping them, blocking out all sound so the world within was still. There was no birdsong echoing outside the alcove. No gentle lapping of the waves along the sandy shore of the lagoon. Even the whisper of the wind had vanished.

But Tiernan...he *raged*. Over and over, he tried to walk through her bubble, to force entry, but her magic held firm against his onslaught. He was yelling, she was sure of it, demanding she let him in. She watched in silence as he paced the outer edge, gesturing wildly, likely pleading with her to stop her foolishness. But she didn't care. Not really.

Maeve looked over to where Lir stood, his mouth slightly agape, like he couldn't quite believe she'd just thrown his High King into a damn wall. Her shoulders fell.

"I understand if you need to go with him."

Lir snapped his mouth shut. He shook his head once. "I'm sworn to protect you."

"Very well, then."

Maeve stood, hands fisted on her hips, until Tiernan slowed his pacing. Until his withering looks of disdain morphed into something that could be mistaken for sorrow, or regret. He stretched his arm out and placed one hand on the shield. It shimmered but it didn't give way, and his chest rose, then fell in defeat. He ducked his head, pressing his lips into a firm line. The shadow in his eyes resembled shame, but she held her ground. She wouldn't be swayed by him or his sad eyes. She wouldn't be guilted into feeling remorse for blocking him out, for protecting herself and her heart from him.

Seconds dragged by into minutes and eventually, the High King *faded* out of the cove.

Exhausted, Maeve collapsed onto the sand. She pulled her knees into her chest, wrapped her arms around her legs, and looked out to sea.

Lir lowered himself to the ground beside her. He leaned back on his hands and stretched out his legs, kicking one ankle over the other. "Do you want to return to the palace?"

"No." Her voice cracked.

"Do you want some company?"

Maeve rested her chin on top of her knees. "Yes."

The sphere remained in place around them, drowning out all sound, all remnants of the outside world. Together they sat on the shore, watching the sun as it sank deep into the western sky, its vibrant colors bleeding across the horizon and painting the Lismore Marin in shades of gold, deep violet, and crimson. Slowly, stars dotted the heavens and wisps of inky clouds rolled by like tufts of cushiony velvet. But Maeve wouldn't go back to the palace. Not until the promise of sleep could drag her under, leaving the day as nothing more than a distant memory.

TIERNAN ASSUMED the role of dutiful host; and hated every minute of it. Every forced smile caused his jaw to clench and his temples to pound like they were being crushed between two boulders. Every nod and incline of his head made his fingers curl into white-knuckled fists. His magic simmered and clawed beneath the surface of his skin, and he silently dared anyone to look at him the wrong way.

Plus, his back hurt like a motherfucker.

When Maeve threw him into the cove's wall, he'd seen millions of tiny black stars. The air had been siphoned from his lungs. Pain had exploded up and down his body. And then she'd shut him out. Her little bubble of protection had morphed into an indestructible shield, and he hadn't been able to reach her. He hadn't even been able to speak to her.

And he deserved it.

He deserved all of it.

Tiernan sat upon his throne while the welcome party carried on without him. The outdoor ballroom was in full swing with partygoers drinking his sparkling wine, laughing and acting as though they hadn't a care in the world, while he sat brooding over the female he'd wronged. Music played as the sun traveled across the sky, but in the distance, thunder rumbled and the storm inside him continued to brew and stir, ready to lash out at a moment's notice.

He silenced all thoughts around him, tuned them out, and debated on taking control over every soul within his palace walls and sending them all away. But such a feat would expend his magic to no end, render him useless, and he couldn't afford to let down his guard. A small part of him debated on sneaking into Maeve's mind, just to *check* on her, and make sure she was well. But now more than ever, he knew she'd kill him if he tried. Of that, he had no doubt.

To his left and right, standing guard, were Merrick and Brynn. Lir had not yet returned with Maeve. His agitation flared, and he rapped his fingers on the glossy, curved arm of his throne.

He hated that she was not by his side.

A shadow fell over him and he glanced up to see Ceridwen staring at him, her eyes alight with a kind of rage he hadn't seen from her in many years. But she hid it well. She smiled, sparkling in her gown of gold, and waved to anyone who passed by them. She stood next to him, her hands primly clasped in front of her.

"Whatever you did," she spoke from the corner of her mouth and not once did her perfectly placed smile falter, "I suggest you fix it."

"I'm working on it," he ground out. He gestured lazily around the space before them where fae from all the Four Courts mingled, reveling, completely oblivious to his inner turmoil. "I'm a little preoccupied at the moment."

Her piercing gaze cut to his. "Do better."

Tiernan entered his twin's mind. *"I'm doing what I can, Cer. I have to be here. You know as well as I do there will be rumors if I walk out."*

She wasted no time firing back at him. *"Maeve is more important. She is your sirra, Tiernan. Fix it. Tonight."*

"I will."

Without another word, Ceridwen spun away and floated down from the dais, the epitome of elegance and beauty.

His sister melted into the crowd, and from the corner of his eye, Tiernan saw Shay approach the dais. The Autumn Archfae was dressed in his finest attire and armed to the hilt. As was to be expected. Even though it was a celebration, there was no such thing as neutral territory within the Four Courts. At least not anymore. He bowed regally and Tiernan nodded in kind.

"Your Grace." Shay adjusted the lapel of his coat when he spoke, his voice was barely a whisper. "Garvan arrives tomorrow."

Tiernan nodded sharply. "Understood."

They would be prepared for the Autumn High Prince, and he wouldn't be allowed to come within arm's reach of Maeve.

As if sensing the direction of his thoughts, Shay scanned the dais and the ballroom. "Where's Maeve?"

"Training." Tiernan bit the word out with a little too much force, and the High Prince's brows rose in question.

Fuck.

A knowing smirk twisted up the corner of Shay's mouth. "Pissed off my little sister already, have you?"

Tiernan allowed his gaze to drift. It wasn't as though he was the only male to ever have female problems. "It's not the first time."

"It better be the last."

Tiernan's head snapped up, a scowl furrowing across his brow. But the High Prince's smile had vanished and in its place was a look that promised death.

"She's my blood." He pretended to inspect his nails, then brushed them lightly against his coat. "I will defend her at all costs."

On that, at least, they could agree.

"It was a misunderstanding," Tiernan muttered.

Shay watched him without saying a word and waited silently for an explanation.

"Ciara paid me an unexpected visit...in my bedchamber." Remembering the look on Maeve's face, the utter disbelief and devastation, nearly sent him spiraling into the darkness inside him. "Maeve walked in just as her dress decided to fall from her shoulders."

Shay's eyes, so similar to Maeve's, skimmed the crowd and landed upon the High Queen in question. She stood beneath a palm tree, a frosty ice queen covered in pearls and wearing an excessively dark lip color, surrounded by starstruck males.

Shay's lip curled in disgust. "Bitch probably did it on purpose."

"She did," Tiernan confirmed.

The High Prince turned back to face him. "As much as it pains me to say this, I'm trusting you to keep her happy. If you hurt her, I *will* come for you."

Tiernan sat there, dumbfounded, as Shay stalked off. It had been many moons since he'd been insulted, and no one ever had the audacity to threaten him within his own Court, yet...he understood Shay's implications. He accepted the warning without retaliation. He would've defended Ceridwen in a similar manner. And also, because as much as he hated to admit it, Shay was right.

Tiernan had hurt Maeve.

Her pain and anger were all because of him.

He could only pray to the heavens it wasn't irrevocable; he would fall on his knees and beg for forgiveness if he must. And even though she wasn't near, and his mind was silent save for his own thoughts, he could've sworn he heard Maeve laughing at him.

Chapter Twenty-Four

Maeve avoided Tiernan the entire next day. He sought her out multiple times in the morning, but she refused to see him. She spent the afternoon in Niahvess with Lir, visiting the Spring fae who, despite being beaten down and broken during their escape from Suvarese, remained upbeat given their current circumstances.

After ensuring the Spring fae were in good spirits and not in need of anything, Maeve made her way to Imogen's dress shop to pick up her gown.

Imogen ushered her into a dressing room and when Maeve slipped into the gown, her heart almost stopped. It was remarkable.

Maeve stepped out of the dressing room, ready to show Lir and ask his opinion.

She had her answer when his silver gaze locked onto her and his jaw fell open. He stared at her, blinked as though remembering who stood before him, then snapped his mouth shut. Even Imogen gasped.

She clutched one hand over her heart. "You look..."

"Captivating," Lir finished for her. "Absolutely captivating."

Maeve's cheeks heated. "Thank you, commander."

He nodded.

Imogen clapped her hands together. "I cannot wait to see the High King's face once he gets his fill of you."

"Him and everyone else in attendance." Approval illuminated Lir's face. "They won't be able to take their eyes off you."

Maeve thanked Imogen, and the darling fae refused any kind of payment. "Just knowing you'll be wearing my creation is all the payment I need, my lady."

"Are you sure? I don't want you to—"

"High Princess, it was my highest honor to make this gown for you." Imogen curtsied. "But if anyone asks—"

"I'll send them to you." Maeve took the faerie's hand and squeezed gently. "You deserve all the praise, Imogen."

The fae blushed furiously, and with her new gown for Sunatalis in tow, Maeve and Lir took their leave and headed back to the palace.

Maeve took her time preparing for the celebration. She soaked in her bathtub filled with silky bubbles and fragrant water. She applied a lightly scented oil all over her skin, so it glowed and smelled faintly of sweetened spice and earthy woods. After she styled every individual curl on her head, Deirdre arrived to help her dress.

"Good heavens, child." The older woman sighed and placed Maeve's new crown on top of her head. "You look stunning. Positively breathtaking."

"Thank you, Deirdre." A slight flush spread across Maeve's chest and Deirdre handed her the intricate mask.

Deirdre flicked her gaze to the glass doors, where night had already fallen upon Niahvess and the stars danced in the sky. She made a clucking type of noise. "You're going to be late, dear heart."

Maeve smiled while applying a light gloss to her lips. "That's the plan."

Deirdre snickered. "There is nothing I wouldn't do for my High

King. But I must admit, every now and then it is rather fun to watch him be bested. Especially by you."

She opened the bedroom door, allowing Maeve to pass through first, and there was Lir, waiting for her. He was painfully handsome in his uniform of cobalt and gold, with rows of medals glinting upon his chest, proudly displaying all his achievements. Even though it was a masquerade, he wore no mask, and it was then she noticed the way his armor had been fashioned to resemble more formal attire. He was prepared for an attack, for battle, as always.

"Your Highness."

"Commander." She took his arm and even though she'd planned for this, even though she knew her intent was to hurt Tiernan as much as he hurt her, a stab of nervous energy pierced her.

"I should warn you." Lir leaned down conspiratorially as he escorted her through the courtyard. "Garvan is here."

Her steps stuttered.

"I will not leave your side."

"I appreciate that." Maeve looked up at him. "I should warn you I have every intention of making the High King realize he made a grave mistake by insulting me."

"I wouldn't expect anything less." Lir shared one of his rare smiles with her.

The doors to the open-air ballroom stood before them. Maeve's heart raced with the speed of a thousand wild horses. Her blood rushed, her magic sang, and anticipation wound its way through her. She released a ragged breath, then held her chin high.

She was Archfae. A High Princess born to the Autumn Court. She submitted to no one.

Beneath her hand, Lir's forearm tensed. He peered down at her. "Are you ready?"

Maeve nodded. She would always be ready.

"Very well."

Lir shoved the doors open with enough force to rattle them on their hinges. The resounding boom silenced every voice, the music halted, and all eyes in the ballroom latched onto her. Gasps and murmurs echoed in her ears and filled the night sky. Everyone stared at her. Some with admiration. Some with desire. And even some with envy. She was the epitome of Autumn, a queen in her own right, though she ruled over no Court.

And they all knew it.

Off to her right, Merrick loosed a low, approving whistle.

Her lip curved into a seductive smile, and she scanned the room, intentionally avoiding the dais where she knew Tiernan stood, watching her. She could feel his eyes upon her, the way his cool, stormy gaze lingered on the exposed flesh of her tattoos and then some.

Good, let him watch.

Mingling with the crowd, she spied Shay, his grin an exact match to her own. He dripped with excess but wore it well. His burnished gold hair was smoothed back and swept over the left side of his chiseled face. He lifted his hand in a small wave and Maeve smiled in return. But it fell the moment she saw who was standing next to him.

Garvan.

He was only a few inches taller than Shay. His auburn hair tumbled to his shoulders and his eyes—a deeper, emerald green—were cold and empty. His face remained impassive, and he ran a hand over his smooth jaw, as though he still couldn't quite believe she existed. As much as she despised it, the same familiar bond she experienced with Aran and Shay pulled on her heartstrings. She wanted to refuse it. To deny any kind of relation to him. The corners of his mouth turned up, cruel and intentional, and she knew he experienced the same awareness binding them as family.

She dipped her chin, glowering at him, challenging him.

With an air of flippant indifference, Maeve rolled her eyes to the open sky as she looked away from him and sought the perfect victim.

She found him standing by one of the gurgling fountains. From the looks of it, he was a Winter fae. Decked in silver and white, his uniform shimmered like freshly fallen snow. The mask he wore was made of gray fur and followed the shape of his pointed ears, so he resembled a snow wolf. He was decidedly handsome, with winning dimples and eyes that reminded her of barren, misty mountains. A few other Winter fae soldiers stood nearby, but this particular male... he held a glass of sparkling wine in his hand, swirling it absently, and was damn near drooling at the sight of her.

Yes. He would do perfectly.

Maeve sauntered over to him, and the throng of bodies parted for her, giving her a clear and direct path. As she approached, the Winter male's brows lifted in surprise and he pressed his lips together, drinking her in. His lascivious gaze dipped to her breasts, then further still, before slowly returning to her face. She stopped right next to him and stood closer than necessary, ensuring her shoulder grazed his uniform. He smelled of frosted pine and juniper berries and for a moment her heart ached for the harsh winters of Kells, when snowflakes fell from the sky like lace and the wind howled through the frozen trees.

She shut the memory away and focused on the task at hand. Her gaze flitted to the glass of sparkling wine in his hand. "I don't suppose you have another one, do you?"

He bowed deeply and handed his glass to her, his movements as smooth as ice. "Anything for you, my lady."

She took a sip and fizzy bubbles flavored with sun-ripened berries danced across her tongue. She winked. "It's a pity there's no more music."

As if on cue, the string quartet started back up and lively notes echoed in the outdoor space. Gradually, conversation picked up, laughter rang out, and the merriment from before continued. Except this time there was a distinctive undertone of inquisitive whispers and stolen glances.

"I'm Maeve Ruhdneah." She held out her hand and he accepted, brushing the lightest of kisses across her knuckles. From somewhere in the distance, thunder cracked.

"Oh, I know exactly who you are, High Princess. Your name has been spoken like a prayer among the Spring fae and whispered as lore throughout the Autumn forest. So much so, the testament of your beauty and prominence has reached even the furthest corners of the Winter Court." The Winter soldier's eyes glinted with mischief. "My name is Malachy Brannon, Commander of the Winter Legion, General of the High Army of Ashdara."

"My, how fancy." Maeve allowed him to hold her hand for longer than was appropriate. "And should I address you as Commander or Malachy?"

He inclined his head and locks of jet-black hair tumbled forward. "For you, my lady, my name is Malachy."

"Then it's a pleasure to meet you, Malachy."

His wide smile oozed charm. "The pleasure's all mine."

Another rumble of thunder sounded overhead, louder this time, so the palm trees trembled and the lights hanging from them swung on the breeze. But Maeve didn't bother sparing Tiernan a glance. She knew he watched her; she knew if she turned around, his gaze would be shooting violet-flamed daggers her way.

Around them, the string quartet's upbeat melody gave way to a haunting ballad. Maeve's gaze cut through the fae all dressed in masks and costumes of grandeur, and from the corner of her eye, she caught Garvan prowling toward her.

"You know, Malachy," she drew his name out with layers of sultry innuendo. "This song is perfect for dancing, don't you think?"

Amusement flickered in his slate eyes. "Is that a hint, my lady?"

She closed the distance between them, then whispered, "Only if it's one you're willing to accept."

He laughed, deep and rumbling, and the sound was so seductive that more than one female looked their way. "Would you care to dance, High Princess?"

"I thought you'd never ask."

Malachy took their finished glasses of sparkling wine, set them down on the fountain's ledge, and led her out onto the center of the dance floor, just as Garvan came into view.

Other fae couples moved around them, unintentionally barricading her from his reach.

Malachy captured her hand while the other slid around her waist possessively, drawing her so close her breasts brushed against the fabric of his coat. She followed along effortlessly as he guided her around the ballroom in complex spins and turns, each one more intimate than the last. Whenever she twirled, he drew her in closer, so their bodies moved as one. Seamless and elegant. Whenever he spun her outward and pulled her back in, his hand slid lower. From the small of her back, to that sensitive area of flesh where her backside dipped then curved.

"Everyone is talking about you," he murmured into her ear, his lips so close, they grazed her skin. "About the High Princess of Autumn who was hidden away in the human lands, only to return more powerful than any before her. They say you're the Dawnbringer, for the likes of your magic is unrivaled."

Maeve looked up at him from beneath her lashes and fluttered them shamelessly. "I'm sure not all have such nice things to say about me."

"Perhaps, but I am not one of them. I can understand their obsession." His lips moved near her cheek and the warmth of his breath skated across her skin. "You are exquisite."

She leaned back in his arms, cleverly arching herself in his hold. "And you are incredibly charming."

He spun her away, then drew her back in as the music pitched through the air around them. "I can be other things as well."

Maeve played along with his game. "Such as?"

"Tempting. Wicked. Seductive."

"All admirable qualities." Her gaze drifted past him, to where Lir stood on the outskirts of the dance floor. He wasn't scowling, but his silver eyes flashed once, warning her to be careful.

She glanced back up at Malachy and found him staring at her breasts. Or rather, her heart.

"You bear his mark." An undercurrent of tension weighted his words.

Maeve jerked her chin upward, defiant. "And yet he still let your queen tempt him."

Malachy's eyes darkened to resemble Winter's longest night. "A mistake on his part. One he's sure to regret."

"I couldn't agree more."

The finale sounded, and Malachy lowered her into a sensuous dip, letting his palm glide from her hip to her thigh. When at last he righted her, she curled her fingers around his arm, and she enjoyed the way he flexed beneath her touch. Tiernan was bound to be trembling with rage, but not once did she seek him out to ensure her scheme was working. He'd made himself perfectly clear in the library that she was not to allow another soul to touch her, and after Lir's look of caution, she debated abandoning her purposeful dalliance altogether. Until she saw Ciara glowering at her from across the room. The sump-tuous Winter Queen sneered in her direction and looked posi-tively murderous.

Maeve watched her with matched loathing. "Is your queen always so angry?"

"No. Not always." Malachy guided her through the other dancers, back toward the fountain. "Right now, I believe it's jealousy that vexes her. She's taken me to her bed many times and afterward she throws me out, barely even giving me enough time to grab my boots and pants before she slams the door in my face."

Maeve's lashes fluttered back, then he chuckled, patting her hand. "Have no fear, High Princess. Her enjoyment of my services is nothing more than that of a child playing with her favorite toy, then tossing it aside when she is bored of it. For Queen Ciara, it is shame that forces her to shun me. She's Archfae...and I am not."

"How callous." Irritation flared hot and Maeve's temper spiked. She wound her arms around his neck and rose up on her toes, pressing her full breasts into his chest. "Perhaps we should make both the High King of Summer and the High Queen of Winter regret their treatment of us?"

Malachy smiled, and he gripped her hips, grinding her into him. The bulge in his pants nudged against her. "Your determination is admirable, but I don't wish to die."

Thunder erupted around them, a deafening crack that left her ears ringing and almost sent her careening into the fountain. She jerked back and whipped around to find Tiernan towering above her, his eyes a violent storm of clouds and chaos. Fury radiated from him, and a thin sliver of panic shivered down her spine. There was a small, insignificant chance that she *may* have pushed him a little too far.

The entire ballroom had once again fallen silent. All of them watched with bated breath to see if the High King of Summer would unleash his wrath upon her.

Even though he looked like he was ready to destroy the entire fucking realm, Maeve flashed him her best smile and held her ground. She looked up at him, expectant.

"Might I have a word, my lady?" Malice laced his voice.

Oh yes, she had definitely pissed him off. But she didn't move an inch.

"Of course," she said coolly.

When she failed to step forward, he leaned down, so the tips of their noses almost touched.

"*Alone.*"

Maeve looked over at Malachy and deliberately held out her hand. He accepted without hesitation.

"It was wonderful to meet you, Malachy Brannon, Commander of the Winter Legion, General of the Army of Ashdara."

"I hope to see you again in the future, my lady." He pressed a firm kiss directly onto her knuckles.

The temperature around them dropped, and Tiernan was so tightly wound, violet sparks shot out from his fingers and scorched the earth at their feet. He looked ready to combust. Tiernan's arm shot out, a demand for her to accept her place by his side. She stared, counted to ten in her mind, then placed her hand so it just hovered above his forearm.

Tiernan escorted Maeve from the open-air ballroom, and at their exit, rumors rose like the swelling tide behind them. He led her through the courtyard without speaking and when they made the turn down the corridor that would lead to their bedrooms, the wrath of Summer was unleashed upon her.

TIERNAN GRIPPED Maeve's arms and hauled her up against the nearest wall. Her frightened gasp sent a surge of need straight to his cock, but he was so fucking pissed, he could barely focus. It was bad enough she'd refused to see him all day, and he had tried to be patient. He was ready to admit his mistake and apologize. He'd been willing to give her the space she demanded. Then she'd shown up wearing *that* dress.

She was flawless. It was entirely nude, displaying the tattoos *he* gave her for all to see. Gold beads that shifted to crimson when she moved in the light. The beadwork swirled over her breasts and other intimate areas, forming the shape of sun, crescent moons, and stars. Strands of rubies draped from her shoulders, tinkling like soft music whenever she twirled. Her mask for the masquerade was beaded just like the gown, shifting from soft gold to deep red. She even wore a new crown of rubies and black diamonds, as though it had been made from the very breath of Autumn.

He'd been tempted to go to her, to drop upon his knees in front of everyone, and beg her forgiveness. She walked with the grace of a queen, and all he wanted to do was throw her over his shoulder, toss her onto his bed, and bury himself inside her until she saw stars. But then she pulled that stunt with Malachy, knowing damn well every soul in attendance tonight would be watching her; it had been enough to summon the destruction inside him. Each of his muscles was so tightly wound with tension, he wanted to snap. Her brutal act of indifference toward him and her flirtations with Malachy called upon the darkness welling within him and that ravaging beast he kept locked away stirred to life.

Maeve's initial shock faded to anger, and she lashed out. "Put me down, you bastard."

Tiernan released her, but he didn't let her go. Instead, he used his magic to pin her into place. To still her movements. To keep her up against the wall because his magic would not harm her, but his fingers could indeed leave bruises.

Alarm fired through him, hot and swift. But it belonged to Maeve, not to him. Her emotions drowned him in a wave of anguish, heartbreak, and panic. Her eyes were wide with betrayal. She struggled against his magic, fought it valiantly, but she couldn't break the charm. So, she remained splayed against the ivory stone, completely at his mercy.

"Tiernan!" Her voice pitched in fear, but he lifted one finger to silence her.

"A moment, please." He turned away, closing his eyes, calming the chaos inside him.

The magic of destruction could overwhelm him if he wasn't in complete control of his thoughts. He shoved it back down into the darkest part of his soul. With a shaking, shallow breath, he centered himself. Then he waved a hand, releasing his hold on Maeve, and she sagged against the wall. He slowly turned to her.

"Do you take pleasure in mocking me?"

"I could ask the same of you," she spat. Her chest heaved and the harsh accusation in her glare sliced through him like a thousand blades dipped in nightshade.

He'd hurt her far worse than he'd realized.

But he'd kept Ciara at arm's length. He hadn't allowed her to touch and fondle him like she would've liked, instead he'd pushed her away. It wasn't until the moment before Maeve burst into his bedroom that Ciara had wrapped her arms around him like some gnarled vine and let her breasts spill from the confines of her ill-fitting gown. Maeve, on the other hand, had blatantly aroused Malachy. She'd allowed his hands to rove over her body for everyone to witness.

"You bear my mark and yet—"

"And you bear mine!" she fired back. "Yet you had no problem letting Ciara hang all over you."

"You are gravely mistaken." Tiernan's blood turned to ice. "I kicked her out."

"You never should've invited her in," Maeve snapped and spun on one heel.

Tiernan snatched her arm and dragged her against him. "Do not walk away from me, High Princess."

She wrenched herself free from his hold and her eyes frosted over. "Don't tell me what to do." She jabbed him in the chest with one finger. "You don't get to choose when you want me or when I'm enough for you. I lost everyone, Tiernan. *Everyone*. Every soul I cared about was taken from me. My entire life was stolen from me! Then there was you and you offered me whatever this," she gestured between them, "thing is between us. And I wanted it because I wanted you."

Smoke furled around her like ribbons of gray velvet, and Tiernan brought the rain, a light sprinkle, to soothe the fire raging inside her.

It wasn't enough.

"But you," she accused, "you didn't even think well enough of me to tell me your ex-girlfriend was coming to town. And to make it worse, you had Merrick cover for you."

A terrible mistake.

"I only did what I thought was right, Maeve. I knew Ciara would purposefully try to hurt and insult you." He spread his arms wide. "I was trying to protect you from her."

"I am perfectly capable of protecting myself!" She fisted her hands on her hips, glowering at him. "You of all people should know that."

Tiernan raked a hand through his hair. She was maddening.

Absolutely infuriating. Fiercely independent and stubbornly foolish. Of course she could handle herself, he was fully aware of the fact, but no matter how many souls she slayed, no matter how many times she ran into a battle alongside him, none of it would ever be enough to keep him from protecting her. He would rather die, multiple times over, if it meant she was safe.

"All I know is that Garvan is here. And I've seen the way he watches you. He's waiting for us to make a mistake, for us to falter. Just one time is all it will take." Tiernan nodded vaguely in the direction of the ballroom. "He's looking for an opportunity. I'm sure he wants nothing more than to drive a wedge between us."

"It looks like he didn't have to." She cocked one hip to the side. "You did that yourself."

"Gods damn it, Maeve!" Tiernan slammed his fist into the wall beside her head, and she jumped. Pieces of stone and rock tore into his flesh, staining his hand red with his own blood. "I told Ciara to leave me. I told her there was nothing left of what we used to have, and even *that* was dozens of years ago. I only care for two things in this life." He gripped her chin and angled her face to his. "You and my Court. Nothing else."

His hand fell away from her. "Yet tonight you mocked my fidelity to you by showing up in a dress that would make every male within a five-foot radius want to fuck you."

She didn't flinch. She didn't waver. "As was my intent."

Wind howled through the corridor, and vicious bolts of lightning ripped across the sky. "We are going back into that ballroom, and you are going to stay by my side for the remainder of the night."

"No." Her dismissal was clear.

"You. Are. Mine," he growled. "I won't have you acting like a shameless flirt and throwing yourself at the feet of unworthy males just because you think it's my jealousy you crave. Those are not the actions of an Archfae. It's the behavior of a common whore."

"Fuck you."

Her hand collided with his face, and the stinging pain from her palm burned his cheek. He stumbled back as fire erupted from her, blasting toward him. His magic surged and the rain poured down, dousing her flames. Her eyes flashed, wild with fury. Cloying smoke clouded his senses. Overhead his storm raged against the wall of power building between them. Her skin glowed and she opened her hand, calling her sword of sunlight to her. It burned bright, its flames licking the space between them. Her gaze narrowed and she took aim.

He drew his own sword, wary. "You really want to do this right now?"

"Do not ever call me that again." It was the only warning he had before she attacked.

Their swords crashed into each other in a deafening crack. He blocked her every strike, dodged her every assault. All of her rage came down upon him and he matched it, absorbing all of her anger, giving her the fight she craved. They maneuvered as one, swords arcing and clashing, but not once did he challenge her in return. He simply took it.

Energy spiked between them, crackling like the roar of a bonfire. She struck again and he parried, avoiding the cut of her blade. Her face twisted in anguish and her aggression faded as her movements grew careless. Her thoughts were a violent storm, a mental siege upon his mind. When she raised her sword high, he rushed her and sent her careening backward in those damned heels.

She stumbled into the stone corridor, chest heaving. Her crown sat lopsided upon her head and hair fell around her in a mess of tangles and curls.

Gods save him, all he wanted to do was kiss her.

But the look of raw anguish on her face...it was enough to rip his heart from his chest.

She lowered her weapon and the sword vanished. He took a hesitant step toward her, but she threw up one hand, halting him.

"Let's make one thing perfectly clear, Tiernan Velless." Her eyes were too bright, glossy with what he knew to be tears. "I might be yours, but you are *not* my king. I don't answer to you." She sucked in a ragged breath. "I don't answer to anyone."

The heady scent of orange blossom and cedarwood permeated the air around them. Magic amplified the space between them. But there was no smoke or fire. It was something else.

She was *fading*.

"Maeve." Her name fell from his lips, but the sound was all wrong.

It was fear.

His fear.

There was one fleeting look of terror upon her face, and the tears she kept at bay slid down her cheeks. He lunged for her, but then she was gone. There was nothing but the scent of cinnamon woods, Autumn bonfires, and toasted vanilla left in her wake.

Chapter Twenty-Five

The air pulled from Maeve's lungs and silenced her screams on a gasp. Her magic swirled and compressed, squeezing around her tightly before finally letting go.

She'd *faded*. Literally faded. And she'd gone to the first place that appeared within her mind's eye.

The Black Lake.

Maeve had returned to the Autumn Court. It was just as breathtaking as she remembered. The surface of the lake was smooth, untouched by even a ripple, and it glimmered like obsidian in the silver wash of the moon. The forest surrounding her was silent and still, a beating heart, a living creature, as here the magic seemed to breathe and thrive on its own. Jewel-toned leaves decorated the long, ancient branches of the trees, creating a canopy of ruby, gold, and amethyst. A crisp breeze wrapped itself around her, carrying with it the scent of damp earth, sweetened spice, and woodsy smoke. Leaves rustled. Branches swayed. And it was as though the entire forest released a collective sigh, welcoming her home.

Here, Maeve felt no fear.

Garvan was back in the Summer Court, and no one had any idea she was gone. Except for Tiernan, who would probably be furious.

Yes, she may have gone to the extreme in her quest to make him suffer, but damn it...she'd been pissed. And hurt. She placed her hand over her heart and the Strand marking her warmed beneath her touch. It wasn't the worst thing, being bound to him. The first pang of remorse left her heart aching. She clutched the necklace he'd given to her and hoped he could sense that she was safe. That returning to Autumn, to the quiet edge of the Black Lake was giving her the serenity her soul craved.

Hopefully, he wouldn't worry *too* much.

She dropped onto the soft, cushioned shore and pulled her knees to her chest. Her gown did very little to keep the chill from her bones, but she didn't mind. Autumn was her home. It recognized her as its own. It remembered her.

From somewhere off to her left, a twig snapped. Maeve's hand instantly went to the Aurastone strapped to her thigh. She waited. One breath. Then two. Her gaze scanned the tree line, searching for a threat. A possible attack. Her blood hummed, but not in warning. This was different. For a moment, there was nothing. Then she spied it. Slinking toward her from beneath a bush bursting with berries was a beautiful red fox with eyes that shone like the darkest emeralds.

It approached her slowly. Maeve held out her upturned hand, allowing the woodland creature to sniff her.

"Hello, there."

The fox's ears perked up and its clever gaze locked onto her.

Her heart surged. Images bombarded her; scenes of a magical ball on an Autumn night, a fae couple dancing, gazing up at each other in love, the scattering of leaves and a burst of color.

Unable to move, Maeve stared at the fox.

"Dorian?" she whispered into the cool night.

Its ears flattened, its sharp gaze narrowed, and the fur along the back of his neck stood on end. The fox backed up, lowered its head like it was ready to attack.

"It's okay if you are him," Maeve spoke in hushed tones, refusing to show fear. "You're safe with me."

Its whiskers twitched and it took one step closer. Then another, before finally curling up onto the ground beside her.

"Do you know who I am?" Maeve asked, and those emerald eyes focused on her. "My name is Maeve. I'm your daughter."

The fox blinked.

Alright. So maybe it wasn't Dorian after all. She felt stupid sitting on the shoreline talking with a fox, but right now, she appreciated the company. "She still loved you, you know. Fianna. She left you and your sons to save me. To keep me as far away from Carman as possible."

Unfortunately, it hadn't been enough.

At the mention of the dead sorceress's name, the fox growled, and a shiver pricked its way down Maeve's spine. He'd recognized it. She reached out and gently patted the top of his head to settle him down.

"Don't worry. She's not a threat anymore. But there's another who's just as bad as her, if not worse." Maeve wondered if he knew about Parisa too, if he knew about her exploits. She wanted to be the one to end Parisa. She wanted to watch the life fade from her eyes, wanted her death to be slow and painful. "But if you are Dorian, we could use your help. Autumn needs you. Your Court needs you."

The fox nudged her hand with his little black nose. Definitely just a forest animal and not at all a respected High King. Maeve sighed.

But then the fox jumped up on all fours and his green eyes shot to the sky, fully alert.

"What is it?"

He darted toward the forest's edge and whipped back around to face her, jerking his small head to the cover of the trees, urging her to follow.

The abrupt beating of wings echoed overhead, and Maeve scrambled to her feet, her heart plummeting to the pit of her stomach.

Garvan.

She rushed to follow the fox and the tree branches pulled back, revealing a small space to hide among some bushes and hollowed-out logs. As soon as she crossed into the safety of the forest, the branches closed in behind her, the leaves overhead thickened to a layer so dense, they blocked out any shred of moonlight, hiding her away. Protecting her. Guarding her. The fox stood watch at her feet, bunched and ready to launch itself at the intruder.

Dense magic filtered through the air and the trees shuddered, bowed, but they did not break. And they did not reveal her. She crouched down and peered through a sliver of leaves just large enough to peek out into the clearing by the lake. Piercing the night sky, with wings like blades of golden brown, was a dragon. His scales were a charred gray and smoke puffed out of his nose in long, winding tendrils. His eyes were amber, the pupils tiny black slits that reminded Maeve of a cat.

She'd read about dragons in some of her books. They were the fire-breathing beasts that once used to rule the skies and mountains. Not a soul had seen one in the flesh in years.

He soared high above them, those observant eyes searching for something.

Then he swooped down, his wing shredding the air like a blade through satin. He clambered up a stone rock near the lake, kicking up earth and leaves in his wake. Chest swelling, his nostrils flared as he inhaled deeply, and Maeve shrank inside her skin. Smoldering clouds of gray surrounded him, hiding him away from her view, and when the mist cleared away, Maeve clamped one hand over her mouth to quiet her gasp.

Casimir.

He tossed his hood back and stood upon the rock, looking out over the lake. He wasn't facing her and though the distance between the forest's edge and that of the lake was not far, she could see how his clothing was worn. Tattered. Scars littered his back and arms, the work mimicking those of her own. Blackened and bulging, the scars of a blade marred his flesh, as though he'd been cut open, then roughly stitched back together.

He shoved his hand through his dark hair, pulling it back from his face, then turned. "I know you're here."

Maeve's body convulsed at the sound of the voice that was once a balm to her heart. Her throat tightened and she held her breath, unsure why the burn of hot tears suddenly threatened to spill down her cheeks. The last time she'd seen him, he'd broken her out of the dungeon beneath Parisa's palace, even though he'd been the one to sentence her to the torture she'd endured. But he'd come back for her. Despite it all, he'd come back. He'd wrapped her bleeding, battered body in a blanket and ran. Then he'd handed her off to Rowan for safekeeping. Rowan, who'd died trying to save her.

Sweet goddess above. The memory of that night came crashing back in all its horror and anguish. The permeating metallic scent of her blood. Fearghal's hot breath along her neck as he whispered into her ear all the ways he was going to hurt her. Casimir taking her away, rescuing her, and Rowan...gods, *Rowan.*

There'd been so many swords and so much blood. His wings had been mutilated, his body punctured over and over.

She pressed her lips together and stood, slowly.

The fox, alert to what was happening, nipped the hem of her dress with his teeth and tugged, desperate to keep her within the safety of the forest.

"I can smell you, Maeve." Casimir sounded exhausted. Empty. "Please come out."

"You stay here." She patted the fox on the top of his head and though he watched her with pleading eyes, he released her. "I can handle him."

Maeve straightened, ready to face the one who taught her every-thing she knew...whose ultimate betrayal nearly ruined her.

The branches of the trees lifted and groaned, revealing her to him. He turned at the sound of the noise and faced her. One trem-bling step at a time, she made her way to him.

"Maeve," he croaked.

"Casimir."

"You look..." His gaze swept over her, over the dress. "Really nice."

She swallowed. "I wish I could say the same for you."

He laughed but it was strained and unnatural.

"But the dragon stunt was pretty impressive," she amended quickly. "How did you know I was here?"

"The real question is, *why* are you here?"

Maeve didn't answer. She didn't want to tell him she'd gotten into an argument with Tiernan and had accidentally *faded* herself into the Autumn Court. "It doesn't matter."

The fox circled between her ankles, then planted himself directly in front of her. He loosed a low growl.

Casimir spared him a glance, clearly unimpressed. "Friend of yours?"

The fox glared at Casimir and bared his teeth. "Yes. I'm pretty sure if I gave him the word, he'd tear you limb from limb."

Casimir took a step back. "I got lucky finding you here. I'd come to see Garvan and was informed he'd gone to the Summer Court for a celebration. Imagine my surprise to see you by the Black Lake instead."

Maeve shrugged, dismissing any of his speculations. "I just needed to get away."

"I understand."

She eyed him, studied him. But where once she could so easily read the male standing before her, where once it seemed his movements and thoughts were merely an extension of her own, now stood a stranger. "Why were you going to see Garvan?"

"He's working with the Dark Queen," Casimir answered coolly, without hesitation.

Maeve angled her head and noted the fact that Casimir now addressed Parisa as the Dark Queen. So much for true love. "And does Tiernan know?"

261

Casimir's gaze shifted to his scuffed boots. "I don't know."

"You're lying."

"I would assume he knows. I've caught glimpses of Merrick and his hunters snooping around Spring's borders." When he looked upon her again, the lines of his face were deep, riddled with tension and fatigue. "The High King may only guess that Garvan and the Dark Queen are in close confidence with one another. But it's safe to say he's fully aware."

"I see." It seemed there were a number of things Tiernan was keeping from her. "But why? Why is Garvan working with her?"

Casimir scrubbed a hand over his face, the only part of his body left untouched by a blade. "Because he thinks if he hands you over to her, he'll get the Spring Court in return."

Maeve's brow furrowed. "And what of Autumn?"

"He'd take rule of both. Their plan is to separate Winter from Summer, to divide the Four Courts and force them to kneel." He shook his head and his rich brown hair fell into his face. "The Dark Court is strong, Maeve. Stronger than anyone realizes."

She stepped closer to him, the fox on her heels. "Why are you telling me all this, Cas?"

"Because you were right." His voice cracked, like he'd been broken. And the look on his face—the torment and despair—it caused a devastating ache inside her. Soul deep. "She's too far gone. Not even I can reach her anymore. There's no trace left of the faerie princess I once loved." Then, softer, "She perished long ago."

Maeve wanted to reach out to him, but she held back and kept her arms locked around her waist. "Do you know what she's planning?"

"Not exactly." He blew out a frustrated breath. "I fell out of trust with her after helping you escape. But what I can tell you is this...you are the only one who can stop her."

"Me," Maeve repeated weakly.

He nodded. "You have...certain abilities that others lack."

Abilities. Like giving life and bringing souls back from the dead. Creating magic. "Do you speak of Balor, Tethra, and Dian?"

His shoulders shifted, nonchalant. "Among others."

"But I haven't used that kind of magic on anyone else." Maeve shivered as the cold of Autumn sank into her. "I haven't brought any other beings back to life. Not since the Furies."

"Not yet," Casimir countered.

The fox sniffed at a fallen leaf and bounded off, chasing another one as it fell from a branch. Casimir's brow quirked in question, but he said nothing.

"Will they fight for me, Casimir?" She strode up to him then, as close as she dared. "Balor, Tethra, and Dian?"

"They will."

"And who else?" Because there was no way in hell she would work with Queen Ciara.

"Those who roam the skies among the storms. Those who foretell of battles and strife." He placed one hand on her shoulder. Firm. "The eternal warriors of the night."

Maeve had never heard of them, but as soon as she returned to Summer, if she could figure out how to get back, she would go directly to the library and find out all she could about these supposed eternal warriors.

The temperature was dropping, and she clamped her hands together to keep from shivering.

"And what about you?" Goosebumps riddled her flesh. "When the time comes, whose side will you stand on?"

He looked at her, and those eyes she'd memorized since she was a child still glinted with the strength of a battle-hardened warrior. "I will fight for those who cannot fight for themselves."

She nodded. It was enough for her. It would have to be, for now.

Maeve shuddered and her teeth chattered in the chilling breeze.

Casimir shifted his weight from one foot to the other as his gaze scanned the forest. "You should go."

She gave him a half of a smile. "I don't know how."

"Call upon your magic, Maeve. Picture where you want to be in your mind." He did not share her smile. "See it. Take it. And you'll go."

"Okay." She summoned her magic, imagining the Summer Court. She recalled its warmth, its beauty, its tantalizing scent.

"I'll see you again, Maeve." He stepped away from her. "When the stars align."

"Until then." She lifted her chin as the rise of magic crowded around her, ready to sweep her away.

Tiernan struggled to remain calm. Maeve had *faded* right before his eyes, and he hadn't been able to help her. He'd waited in the corridor, praying to the heavens she'd return, but seconds had ticked by into minutes, and still there'd been no sign of her.

Then he'd felt it.

The pulse she sent him through the necklace she wore. Wherever she was, she was safe...for now. But she could be anywhere. On the *Amshir* with Aran. Or lost in another area of the Four Courts. Or even Kells.

His gut seized. He didn't want to imagine her back there, in that mortal shithole of a realm. Unless she'd gone to Saoirse...

No. He wouldn't think of it. She was alive and unharmed, and those were the only two things that mattered. Her necklace would alert him if something happened, or if she was in danger, so he forced himself to return to the party. To save face. He knew everyone in attendance would be watching and wondering why she hadn't returned with him. There'd been no mistaking the might of his storm. Anyone with half a brain would know they'd argued and that he'd been on the losing end.

He strolled back into the ballroom, completely aware of the way gazes shifted and whispers floated past him. Tucking his hands into the pockets of his pants, he radiated cool composure and unequivocal indifference. He was the fucking High King of Summer. He was never flustered or thrown into a state of frenzy, even if he was, at the moment, mildly panicked. Climbing the steps of the dais, he headed straight for Merrick.

His closest friend read his demeanor, understood the significance of what he was about to say, but maintained a relaxed posture for the sake of anyone watching their exchange.

"*Moh Rí,*" he drawled, inclining his head just slightly.

"Maeve has *faded.*"

"She *faded?*" Merrick sent a casual glance around the ballroom, as though they were having the most mundane of conversations. "I didn't think she knew how to do that yet."

"Apparently neither did she." Tiernan shoved his black hair from his face, remembering the way her eyes widened when she realized what was happening. "It came as a shock to both of us."

"Where is she?" Merrick asked.

The one question he dreaded. "That's the problem. I don't know." He glanced to Lir and Brynn, who were both standing nearby, close enough to hear, and they walked over. "She used her necklace to relay her emotions to me. As of now, she's calm. And she's not afraid."

"Have you tried to reach her through her thoughts?" Brynn's fingers tapped restlessly against the hilt of the sword at her waist.

"You know that magic only works to a certain extent."

His ability to hear the thoughts of those around him did not cross borders or realms. It was only useful to him if he was within a limited distance of the one he wished to hear.

"But she's bonded to you." Lir's gaze skimmed the crowd. "Perhaps you should try. Mating bonds are a more powerful sort of magic."

Tiernan blew out a breath. "She hates it when I do that."

"Maybe this one time would be an exception?" Brynn suggested.

"I don't know." He shook his head. "If you'd seen how angry she was—"

"Oh, trust me." Brynn's eyes changed from her usual brown to sympathetic gold. "Everyone saw."

He would never doubt Maeve's abilities, and he wouldn't put it past her to learn now, but if she ever found it necessary to block him from her mind...the devastation would be immense.

Tiernan looked at Merrick. "We need to find her."

Merrick nodded sharply.

"Find who?" Ceridwen's soft voice floated in from behind him.

Shit.

"Maeve. She *faded* and we don't know where she went," Brynn supplied, sending Tiernan a look that told him there was no way out of this one.

Ceridwen's cheeks flushed pink with frustration. "What did I tell you? Tier, we've gone over this a dozen times. Between her stubborn pride and your ruthless arrogance, your tempers are bound to clash. The both of you are far too powerful for such quarrels. If you're not careful, you'll bring down the entire realm." She fisted her hands on her hips, clearly annoyed. "You have to be *calm.*"

"I *was* calm." He ground the words out. "Up until she told me she wore that dress on purpose."

Ceridwen's eyes rolled to the midnight sky above. "Of course she did. It was her way of getting back at you for the whole Ciara debacle and, quite honestly, you deserved it." His twin's eyes burned bright. "Did you even apologize?"

"I—"

Fuck. He hadn't apologized to her. Not once.

"Tiernan," Brynn groaned, smothering her face with her hand. "Will males ever learn?"

"Hey, now." Merrick raised both hands in innocence. "Some of us know when to admit we're wrong."

The bastard cut him a cunning grin.

"I will make this right. But first, we have to get her back." His gut seized at the thought of her being anywhere alone, where he couldn't reach her. "If anyone asks, she claimed a headache and returned to her room. No one needs to know anything is amiss, no one needs to suspect any sort of weakness from our Court."

"My lord?" Brynn's voice was quieter than usual, and a grating sense of unease carved its way down his spine.

Tiernan focused on her. "What is it?"

She shifted her weight, unable to look him in the eye. "What if she can't figure out how to get back?"

"We'll get her back. I swear it." He looked to Lir. "Keep a steady eye on the grounds in case rumors circulate and Garvan thinks he can sneak his way out of here to find her." He searched the throng of people dancing and drinking, oblivious to anything else but their own personal happiness. "Where is the bastard anyway?"

"The last time I saw him," Ceridwen sneered, disgusted, "he had his hand up the skirt of an Autumn faerie."

A stream of unsavory curses spewed from Lir and then he walked away, following his orders.

Tiernan faced his hunter. "Merrick, gather your scouts. If that fails, I'll try and reach for her through the bond instead."

He nodded once, then *faded.*

"Brynn, secure the palace. No one is to go beyond the outlying courtyard," Tiernan ordered, and she bowed before heading off to secure the doors. "Ceridwen, do what you do best."

"Of course." She pretended to inspect her manicure and then there was a shimmer of magic and a rise of gaiety among his guests. The music pulsed through the air. Laughter rang out and drinks flowed more freely as her power sifted its way through the crowd. She eased their minds, evaporated their worries, and gradually sedated them with the need to do nothing but dance the entire night away.

Tiernan dropped onto his throne. He rubbed his temples, trying to force away the dull ache that had been inconveniencing him all night.

Yet again, Shay approached the dais, and Tiernan stifled a groan. He did not want to deal with the princeling right now.

Shay swirled his glass of sparkling wine. "Pissed her off again, have you?"

"It was an accident."

"Where is she?"

"Her room." The lie tasted sour and Tiernan grimaced. "She asked me to tell everyone she had a headache."

Shay's lips drew into a thin line. He didn't believe a word of it. "I see." Then he sat on the edge of the dais and downed the rest of his drink.

Tiernan's gaze cut to him. "What are you doing?"

But Shay didn't respond. Instead, he stared out over the sea of bodies, and swiveled his empty glass between his fingers.

Tiernan slid into his thoughts. *"What is it?"*

To this, Shay answered. *"I overheard Garvan speaking with Parisa."*

"I see." Tiernan crossed one leg over his knee and surveyed the ballroom. Garvan was nowhere in sight. *"Continue."*

"They're planning an attack on the Winter Court in two weeks' time."

"Shit." It would seem as though Parisa was growing more confident, and her lack of patience was getting the best of her if she was already planning an attack. *"Do you have any details?"*

"She intends to invade from the southern border with her Dark Army." Shay plucked another glass of sparkling wine off the tray of a passing attendant.

"Does Queen Ciara know?"

Shay lifted his glass to the light so the bubbly liquid turned gold. *"Not yet."*

"I'll ensure she's prepared." Tiernan motioned for his own glass, preferring whiskey as his poison. He knocked it back in one gulp. *"I appreciate your information."*

Understanding their silent discussion had ended, Shay stood from the dais, stretched, then stumbled forward, feigning intoxication for anyone who may have been observing.

Brynn appeared to his left, one hand positioned on the hilt of her sword. "Secure, my lord."

He spared her a glance. "Send word. We call a meeting in the morning. Away from prying eyes and listening ears."

"Yes, *moh Rí*." She dipped her head.

Tiernan rapped his knuckles against the hardwood of his throne. He longed to reach out to her, but he knew that doing so would only drive her further away from him. Instead, he let his head fall back against his throne. All he could do was wait.

Where was she?

Chapter Twenty-Six

M aeve didn't *fade* into her bedroom as expected. But she
did make it back to the Summer Court. The balmy air
warmed her chilled flesh, and she rubbed her hands up
and down her arms to rid herself of goosebumps. She took in her
surroundings and realized she was standing in the eastern courtyard
where she used to train with Casimir and Saoirse. Off to her left was
the battered palm tree she'd shredded after getting into an argument
with Tiernan.

She supposed she should go to him, to let him know she'd
returned and that she was safe. But she wasn't entirely sure she was
ready for the confrontation that would ensue when he discovered
she'd gone to the Autumn Court and Casimir had found her.

Maeve plucked a leaf from her hair. She was debating on
whether she should return to the Sunatalis celebration or just go back
to her room and wait for Tiernan to come to her when she heard
someone crying.

Choking, broken sobs fill her ears, the sounds of *pain*.

"Shut the fuck up, you filthy whore." A rough and slurred masculine voice came from the furthest corner of the courtyard, near one of the gurgling fountains. "Or I'll slit your pretty little throat."

Oh, hell no.

No one was going to threaten another, not while she was around.

Maeve pulled her Aurastone from its sheath and listened, following the crying. She crept across the courtyard, clinging to the shadows of the towering palms overhead. She spied the vulgar male crouched behind one of the flowering plumeria trees, its branches and blooms so thick they could hide anyone from view.

Except it wasn't some random, drunken dickhead.

It was Garvan.

He had pinned a female beneath him, her skirts hiked up around her waist. Tears and dirt stained her cheeks, and there were healing scratch marks along the side of his face, like she'd tried to fight him off. He held her down, one large hand clamped around her throat, while the other fumbled with the button on his pants.

Maeve raised her dagger. "Get the fuck away from her."

Garvan's head snapped up, and he whipped around to face her, eyes glazed with the sheen of too much alcohol. He smirked and sat back on his heels, swaying.

"Well, well. If it isn't our little wild one."

"Get away from her." Maeve twirled her dagger, flipping the blade and hilt between the tips of her fingers. "Now."

He snarled and looked down where the female fae continued to whimper, trying in vain to pull down the layers of her skirts. Without warning, he heaved his elbow back and slammed his fist into her face. Her head lolled back, the blow knocking her unconscious. Blood sputtered from her nose and lip and the crunch of his knuckles against her skin set fire to Maeve's magic.

"You fucking prick!"

He grinned, flecks of the female's blood scattered across his cheek. "Can't have any witnesses for when I snatch my little sister and hand her over to the Dark Queen."

Maeve laughed, but it was harsh against her own ears. Grating. "You'll never get your hands on me."

"Is that so?" He stood abruptly and his wings burst from his back as he took a menacing step toward her. "Shall we play another game, sister?"

This time, Maeve spread her own wings, letting them unfurl and beat, ready to match him. She kept her Aurastone aimed for his heart. "What kind of game did you have in mind?"

He was impressed. There was no mistaking the gleam of astonishment in his eyes, but he hid it well.

The female groaned in pain, rolling over onto her side, and his gaze slid to her again. "I've got the perfect idea."

Garvan grabbed her wrist, wrenching her arm behind her so she yelped, and shot into the night sky.

Damn it. Maeve was left with no choice but to follow. She darted into the air behind him as he soared with the female dangling in his grip. He dove and spun, tossing her around like a child's doll. Her cries carried on the wind, but Garvan didn't care. To him, she was nothing but a toy. A means to an end. He flew carelessly, dragging her through the air, flying higher and flinging her about so her body jerked back and forth like it was caught in the tangled strings of a marionette.

Maeve hovered near him, her Aurastone in her hand. "Give her to me, Garvan." They were above the terracotta rooftops of the palace now, with the courtyard far below. "She's not a part of this and you know it."

"But you are, dear sister." He swung the fae back and forth as she struggled in his hold. She would rather fall to her death than be used by him. "And for some reason, you care about everyone."

"You're wrong," she hissed the words, and he blinked at her venomous denial. "I don't care about you at all."

"Your insults are pathetic." His laugh was bitter and laced with malice. "Ready for our game, little wild one?"

Her jaw clenched and her grip around the hilt of her Aurastone tightened, poised to strike.

Garvan hoisted the girl up, hanging her between them in the air like a lure. "Answer me in truth, and this wretched little creature's life will be spared."

"And if I refuse?"

"Then decay will spread throughout her deplorable body. I'll kill her from the inside out. Her veins will turn black, worms will carve their way through her organs, festering and feeding until there's nothing left. The agony of it will be insufferable. Her screams will echo to the furthest corners of the Four Courts." Clouds crawled across the light of the moon, dousing him in vicious shadows. "And by the end the rot of her own blood will suffocate her to death."

Maeve fought down the urge to retch.

He was vile. Grotesque. And deserved all the pain he would endure beneath the tip of her blade. "You're heinous. A disgrace to the faerie race. And I will make you pay for your crimes against the innocent."

His mirthless smile peeled back over his teeth. "So, you agree?"

He jerked the female mercilessly and a loud popping sound reverberated in Maeve's ears. The fae screeched in anguish as she hung from an awkward angle, her shoulder dislocated by his blatant cruelty.

"Fine!" Maeve shouted and flew closer. "I'll play your stupid little game. But do not harm her again."

"Good." Garvan regarded her, angling his head. "Now tell me, do you indeed possess the *anam ó Danua* like Parisa thinks you do?"

Goddess above, of course that would be his first question. Maeve's teeth ground together. "Yes."

His wings beat and he shifted, taken aback. "Interesting...and what of the Hagla? There are rumors you were the one to destroy it."

She lifted her chin in defiance. "I did."

The fae female began sobbing.

"You're hurting her!" Maeve's accusation didn't faze him.

He shrugged, uncaring. "So what? I never said I wouldn't hurt her, just that her life would be spared."

Flames exploded from the tips of her fingers and smoke curled around her like venomous snakes.

Garvan chuckled. "Temper, temper. Last question..."

Maeve held her breath, her gaze darting down to the female whose face was pinched in despair. "What is it?"

"Are you in love with the High King of Summer?"

Maeve blanched.

That wasn't at all what she was expecting him to ask. "What?" Her voice sounded hoarse, like she'd suffered too long in the cold.

Garvan's face remained impassive. Unreadable. "You heard me."

Love. Was she in love with Tiernan? She didn't even know what true love felt like, not really. She knew she held love in her heart for Saoirse. And not so long ago, for Casimir. But that was more of a deep affection, a sworn loyalty. Nothing of the romantic kind. Then Rowan had come along. Rowan...she'd loved him, hadn't she? She'd warned herself not to fall for him, told herself over and over not to trust him, but in the end, hadn't it been the breaking of her heart that destroyed her when he died?

Did she feel the same for Tiernan now?

Garvan swung the fae back and forth like a pendulum. "Time is ticking, sister."

"No!" Maeve cried out. "No, I don't love him."

The words tumbled from her mouth before she could stop them, and her voice cracked. She didn't know, she didn't know how she truly felt about Tiernan. But she'd be damned if she admitted her love for him to Garvan first.

Her brother paused his torture, eyeing her suspiciously. "I think you're lying."

Rivers of black oozed their way from his hand into the female's veins and her scream was so harrowing, Maeve's blood turned to ice.

"Stop, stop it! I'm not lying!" Maeve's voice pitched with frantic urgency. "I don't love him!"

"Hm." His gaze dipped to the ground that was so, so far below them. "Very well."

Then he dropped the female.

"No!" Maeve made to dive after the falling fae, but Garvan slammed into her in a blow of brute force and wings. The air pulled from her lungs as he collided into her midair, sending her tumbling. Her wings sought purchase on the wind but suddenly he was behind her, his rough hands clamping down upon her arms, forcing them to her sides and binding her wings behind her. She cried out in pain, struggling and straining against him. Power rose inside of her, the lifeblood of magic. There would be time to fight him, but she could not let the female die. She reached, desperate to save the falling faerie.

As the fae's body plummeted from the sky, leaves of burgundy and citron circled around her in a whirlwind. They layered and multiplied, stretching out above the courtyard like a canopy, and Maeve's breath hitched as she watched the girl topple into the pile of leaves.

Garvan's hold on her arms loosened, stunned by what she'd done. It was the only opening Maeve needed, and she never wasted an opportunity. Rearing back, she jabbed her elbow into his face.

"You bitch," he hissed and yanked her around to face him.

Wings thrashing, Maeve glared up at her brother. "Fuck you, Garvan."

Blood poured from his nose and stained his teeth red. She raised her Aurastone, prepared to plunge it into his blackened heart, but he was faster. He pulled something from his pocket, a small blade, and stabbed it into her shoulder.

Maeve screamed.

Searing hot pain scorched her skin, branding her like a sword whose blade was still glowing with the heat from a forge.

She was losing feeling in her body. Numbness spread from her fingers, across her chest, and down her legs to her toes. Her wings drooped; they were failing her. The Aurastone slipped from her grip, and she yelped, helpless to stop it from falling to the ground. Her wings vanished, the warmth along her spine dissipating. She grasped at her magic, her only means of defense. And though her heart continued to beat and her blood thrummed with the pulse of power, it did not answer her call. With every breath, she became more limp. More lifeless. For one terrifying second, she thought he'd poisoned her just as the dark fae had done the night they attacked the Summer Court. But this wasn't poison. It was something else entirely. She was aware, alert, but her body was unresponsive.

"Dark magic is a powerful thing," Garvan murmured as his grip on her tightened, bruising her flesh. He clutched her to him. "You should learn to accept it."

"Never," Maeve spat.

The dense scent of orange blossom and cedarwood overwhelmed her, and a jolt of hysteria bubbled up in the back of her throat. He was going to steal her away. He was going to *fade* and if he handed her over to Parisa, she wouldn't be able to escape. At least not alive. Even the fates weren't so kind when it came to granting second chances.

"Let me go!" she shouted.

His laughter was mocking. "Not a chance."

A streak of violet, cobalt, and gold careened into them. The last thing Maeve heard was an eruption of thunder so tumultuous, the mountains trembled, the sea floor shuddered, and skies split open as the tempest of Summer, the essence of destruction, rained down upon them.

Then Maeve was falling, just like before, except this time there was no one to catch her.

Chapter Twenty-Seven

Tiernan barreled into Garvan with all of his strength. The brunt force of his shoulder slammed the Autumn High Prince in his torso, hurtling them through the air. He hauled himself backward, wings beating, pummeling the prick with every shred of power inside him. The sky roiled, pitched black with the storm he had unleashed. Violet bolts of lightning tore from him and struck their mark, slashing across the Archfae's body in vicious streaks.

Garvan snarled, red hair whipping in front of his face, and shot toward him. He swung violently, knuckles just grazing Tiernan's jaw. The metallic taste of blood filled his mouth and slid down his chin. Tiernan slammed his fist into Garvan's face, and the ring he wore cut across his skin, ripping the flesh. Blood dripped from his nose. Fists collided with faces and the heavens roiled, pitched with the storm he unleashed upon them. Rain slashed into them. Darkened clouds billowed around them, magnifying the sound of chaos as they brawled against the night sky in a clash of wings and power.

When the stirring of destruction took a breath inside him, when the absolute ruination he could inflict upon Garvan began to rise,

Tiernan locked it away. He shoved it back down into the recesses of his soul and seized the High Prince's body with his venomous coils of magic.

Garvan jerked and his muscles spasmed in a poor attempt to fight off the intrusion, but Tiernan held firm, immobilizing the bastard until Garvan bared his teeth and sneered, "You'll pay for this."

"Maybe." Tiernan glided toward him and plucked the small dagger—the one he's used to prick Maeve's skin—from the breast pocket of his coat. "But not today."

He could kill him right now. It would be so easy to watch the life fade from his eyes, to watch him gasp and beg as he took his final breath. But if he did, Parisa would come for them, and they needed more time to prepare. He still needed to warn Queen Ciara about the impending attack on Winter. He needed to find a way for Maeve to ask the Wild Hunt for assistance before the upcoming war. Right now, he needed Garvan alive and would have to glean as much information as possible from him because there were too many unknowns.

Like the numbers of Parisa's Dark Army.

He raised his sword to Garvan's throat, to where his veins throbbed, to where the killing blow would take very little effort at all. "Count your blessings that I don't destroy you right now. That I don't rip your limbs from your body and feed your intestines to the creatures of the sea, and then skin you alive...just as you've done to the merrows."

Garvan's face leached of color, but hardened determination lined the sharp angles of his face. "I don't know why you care so much," he spat. "She doesn't love you."

Tiernan faltered. It was brief, hardly noticeable, but Garvan pounced.

"She told me so, right before you came flying in to rescue her." He grinned, bloody and bruised. "You will never earn her love. You tricked her into a mating dance, marked her against her will. She

278

deserves better. She deserves someone worthy of her. Someone willing to *die* for her...someone like Rowan."

All he saw was red. An unruly swath of rage and wrath. He was on the High Prince so fast he couldn't stop himself even if he tried. His hand wrapped around Garvan's throat and squeezed until his eyes bulged and his face turned as purple as his vest. Unable to defend himself against Tiernan's magic, he laughed, but it was garbled and choking.

"Go ahead and kill me, High King," he sputtered. "Put me out of my lifetime of misery."

Tiernan's wings beat against the storm, and the wind howled around them. Garvan's words raked under his skin, chilled him to the bone, and he swallowed hard.

"Stay the fuck away from her."

Garvan's hoarse whisper scraped from his throat. "She'll never stop. She'll never quit until she has Maeve in her clutches."

Tiernan released his hold on Garvan's body, tossing him down, and he stuttered in the sky, falling. His wings twitched and thrashed as he clawed his way back up into the air.

"Leave. Now." Tiernan aimed his blade at the High Prince's heart. "Before I carve you from the tip of your dick to your tongue."

Garvan's lip curled in disgust, but without another word, he *faded* from sight.

The storm ebbed but Tiernan remained sky-bound. Chest heaving, he hovered in the cover of his clouds, aching for something he couldn't name. It was as though his heart had been ripped out by the claws of death, and there was nothing but a gaping hole, a sucking chest wound. He stole a glance down at the ground, to the courtyard. The remnants of the storm shielded him from view as he sought out a fae with hot pink hair.

There.

There was Merrick, striding down a corridor with Maeve in his arms. Brynn was tending to the female fae Garvan had attacked. Ceridwen and Lir were busy intercepting the guests who'd thought it smart to leave the ballroom. As if they heard him speak their names, they both looked up at once.

"Party's over."

Lir nodded sharply and took charge, ushering guests out of the courtyard while Ceridwen politely smiled and bade everyone a good night.

Tiernan could've returned to help assist, but instead he soared to the rooftops. There was a harrowing pain splitting through him and it had nothing to do with the gash along his cheek, or his split lip that was still bleeding, or the cut searing across his forehead. No. This was not that kind of pain.

It was agony.

Pure, raw agony.

Because Garvan was right.

Maeve did not love him.

He'd heard her scream the words, and the second before he plowed into Garvan, his heart—the one he thought he'd carved out long ago—had broken.

"ARE YOU ALRIGHT, HIGH PRINCESS?"

Maeve glanced to her right and saw Lir; he stood in the doorway of the balcony where they usually dined, his silver eyes as sharp as ever, roving over her and looking for any other physical wounds or injuries. She sat in a chair, still wearing her painfully revealing gown, with a blanket draped around her. Brynn had healed her with some sort of crystal device after she finished treating the female fae Garvan had used as a plaything. She used a tool Maeve had never seen before to draw out the "dark magic venom," as Brynn had so thoughtfully dubbed it. Though it had taken some time and was more than a little uncomfortable, feeling was finally returning to her fingers and toes. In the meantime, Brynn studied the magic used on the seemingly harmless blade to figure out how it had rendered her motionless.

"I'll be okay, Lir." She sent him a confident smile, something that was easier to do since Merrick returned her Aurastone to her. "I appreciate you asking."

Ceridwen stepped out from around behind him with a mug in her hands. "I brought you some coffee. With two lumps of sugar."

"You're a goddess." Maeve gratefully accepted the steaming cup of dark deliciousness. "How's the female?"

"Physically, Brynn says she'll be fine. Her shoulder is already on the mend." Ceridwen's twilight eyes darkened to midnight and her curtain of blonde waves fell in her face. "Emotionally, I cannot say."

Merrick sat in the chair opposite of her, his chiseled face clenched in anguish. He cracked his knuckles and surged forward. "I swear to the gods, if I see Garvan again—"

"He'll regret his first breath," Lir finished for him.

Brynn strode out onto the balcony, and faint smudges of exhaustion marred the delicate skin beneath her eyes. Healing had taken its toll on her.

Ceridwen turned toward her. "Has everyone left?"

"Yes, my lady." Brynn's gaze landed on Maeve. "Shay sends his regrets that he wasn't able to say goodbye to you in person."

Maeve nodded. She would've liked to have spoken with him more. Maybe even have gotten to know him better. Perhaps Tiernan could arrange a meeting and...

The moment she thought of him, he swooped down and landed on the stone floor of the balcony. There were cuts and bruises all over his face, and blood slid down from the corner of his mouth. His hair was wild and unkempt, sticking up in all directions. Scruff lined his battered jaw and lines of stress tugged at his handsome features. He'd fought for her. Saved her. And now...he wouldn't even look at her.

He scrubbed a hand over his face, smearing some of the blood there, and his gaze slid to Lir. "I'm calling a meeting now since we're all in attendance."

His beautiful wings vanished, and he dropped into a chair as though the weight of all the realms was upon his broad shoulders.

Still, he did not look her way. "Shay informed me tonight that Garvan and Parisa are planning to attack the Winter Court in two weeks' time."

Lir crossed his arms. "Can we really trust him, my lord?"

"What choice do we have?" Tiernan gestured vaguely to the north. "If we ignore his warning, we risk seeing Winter overrun by dark fae. But if we show up in force, then we at least stand a chance of keeping another Court out of Parisa's clutches."

"What if it's a trap?" Brynn countered.

Tiernan squeezed his eyes shut, and when he opened them again, they were focused and clear. "Let's hope it's not."

"This supposed attack," Lir spoke the words carefully, "this is not the war."

"No." Tiernan let his head fall back against the chair. "It's not."

"Shit," Merrick muttered and strummed his fingers along the edge of the table. "I'll return with my scouts to Spring. To Suvarese. We need to know what she's planning, what kinds of weapons she's utilizing." He nodded in Maeve's direction. "Especially since he stabbed Maeve with a rather insignificantly sized blade and almost incapacitated her completely."

Maeve glanced at the wound from the blade. It was still pink and raw, but healing.

"Should I call upon the Furies for assistance?" She directed her question at Tiernan, but he didn't spare her a glance.

Instead, he stared blankly at the railing and the calming call of the sea beyond. No one else spoke. They all waited for him to acknowledge her, but uncomfortable tension swelled in the space. Stifling and suffocating. He looked so...defeated. Maeve shifted in her seat, uneasy.

She tried again. "My lord?"

Finally, he dragged his gaze to her, and she may as well have been looking at a stranger. His eyes were empty when they landed on her. There was no emotion. No anger or lust. Just a void. He looked at her like he didn't recognize her, like she was nothing. Like anything that had happened between them over the past few days was nothing but a myth, a story from another time, in another world.

It stole the air from her lungs.

He sighed, dismissive. "Whatever you wish."

Merrick's gaze darted between them. "I understand there's some underlying friction with the two of you, but these are the Furies we're talking about, my lord. Balor. Tethra. Dian. Destruction, darkness, and death. The last time they set foot in Faeven, we were left in ruination."

Maeve looked down into her mug of coffee, then drained the entire thing, scalding the back of her throat so it burned and ached.

"You're right," Tiernan agreed, angling his body toward Merrick and away from Maeve. "I do think the Furies will be useful against Parisa. But right now, we must focus on the upcoming battle in Winter. For all we know, we may not find the Furies in time. Mer, I want your scouts ready to head out in two days. Take your best and find out any information you can." Tiernan stood and Merrick followed suit, bowing swiftly before walking away. "Lir, I want every soldier armed with blades of nightshade. Brynn, ready as many healers as you can, then report to your post."

In a matter of seconds, everyone was standing and moving, knowing exactly what they were supposed to do. Everyone except her.

"Cer, send word to Queen Ciara about the impending attack. She'll need to ready her army."

Maeve flinched at the Winter queen's name, but no one paid her any attention.

"Of course." Ceridwen dipped her head and her gaze slid to Maeve.

Tiernan headed for the door and Maeve stood, clutching the blanket around herself and lifting her chin out of spite. "And what of me, my lord?"

He stilled, one hand on the door. Then, "You do not answer to me, High Princess. So, you may do as you wish."

His words were a slap across her face. "Tiernan, please..."

But he was already gone, and he didn't bother looking back.

Maeve's mouth fell open, and she caught Ceridwen's lingering gaze. "Cer, I—"

Ceridwen lifted one slender hand, quieting her. "I love my brother. Very much. And I agree he made a terrible mistake when he allowed Ciara into his quarters. And you had every right to be furious with him. Honestly, I would've extracted petty revenge myself if I'd been in your place." She smoothed her hands down the front of her gown, then clasped them together, and when she faced Maeve, she was Archfae. Resilient. Elegant. Final. "But tonight...you showed him the truth of your heart, and that is not something even I can repair."

She dipped her head, a look of pained remorse flitting across her face, then slowly turned to walk away.

Maeve had never felt more alone.

Chapter Twenty-Eight

Maeve returned to her room.

Alone.

Gone was the rich laughter and sounds of celebration that once filled the air. Everyone had been sent home, Sunatalis was over, and a distinctive stillness had settled throughout the Summer Court.

She kicked off her heels and padded across her bedroom to where the double doors of her balcony were wide open in welcome. The warm summer breeze kissed her skin, enveloping her in a comforting embrace.

She'd broken Tiernan's heart.

But she hadn't done so on purpose. She'd only wanted him to wallow in a murky pool of guilt for a while. She'd wanted him ripe with envy. Her plan failed miserably. From the clash of tempers between them, to her accidentally *fading* to the Autumn Court, to the fight with Garvan, everything unraveled so quickly, and she hadn't been able to stop it. She hadn't been able to stop herself. She'd been so consumed by saving the life of an innocent that she tossed aside her own feelings for the one male she...enjoyed? Adored? Admired?

Cared for? Did she love Tiernan? Was that why her heart was suddenly splintering like shards of broken glass? Was that the reason the Strand between them burned so badly that her chest literally *ached* for him?

He was good and kind. All the things she never thought she'd find in a mate. He protected those he loved, and the depth of his loyalty was unlike anything she'd ever seen or experienced, save for Saoirse. She'd almost lost count of the number of times he'd saved her life. When she'd been on the brink of death from poisoning, he'd stayed by her side. When the Spring fae wanted her as their High Queen, he hadn't balked at the idea. Instead, he'd offered to help build her a Court.

It was Tiernan who was constantly forcing her to face her fear, encouraging her, reminding her of who she was and what she'd become. She was Archfae. The High Princess of Autumn. The *anam ó Danua*. The Dawnbringer. All these things defined her by her magic and that alone should've been enough to save her from the trials and trauma of her past, from her suffering.

An uncomfortable sensation squeezed inside of her heart, her foolish mortal heart. Her singular weakness. Even Rowan had known it. When they'd stood on the edge of the Shores all those months ago, he'd told her it didn't matter how well she fought or the depth of her bravery. She would always be weak...because of her heart. Perhaps he was right. She had all this magic, all this power, yet it never seemed to be enough.

Her footsteps carried her out onto the balcony, and she leaned over the railing to gaze up at the stars. They twinkled and sparkled like diamonds against the velvet of the night. The fates were cruel, she decided. It seemed unfair that she would be forced to choose between loving the one taken from her and loving the one destined for her. Whatever the gods and goddesses had planned, whatever was written in the stars, was more of a punishment than anything else.

Fearghal had nearly broken her once, and she'd vowed to never yield to another. Yet this feeling, this sense of being torn, of relentless remorse, was fracturing her soul.

Her nose tingled. Burned. The tears slid down her cheeks before she could stop them.

Maeve let them fall.

She'd hurt Tiernan, far worse than he'd hurt her. She'd acted out of rage and bitterness, she'd wanted him to know the pain he'd caused her. Foolishly, she thought she'd feel better for it. She'd been so terribly wrong. This was not better. This was worse. A thousand times worse.

She gasped as a strangled sob escaped from the back of her throat. Tremors wrecked her as she sniffed and her shoulders shook, the tears falling more freely now. With one hand pressed to the Strand, the bond marking her heart, Maeve cried.

"*Astora.*"

Maeve whipped around to see Tiernan standing just outside the doors of the balcony they shared. He was so devastatingly beautiful. The wounds he'd received during his fight with Garvan were already beginning to heal. He'd removed most of his royal garb and was back to wearing his usual simple attire. A crisp button-down shirt cuffed to the elbows with the top two buttons undone, exposing his glorious chest and the golden tattoo crawling up his neck. His hands were shoved into the pockets of his pants and when he stepped toward her, his boots clicked softly against the stone floor.

Her chest rose and fell in short, ragged breaths.

He moved closer until mere inches separated them, and he simply stood there, watching her. Not touching. Just looking. So close yet so very far away. His distance nearly severed the bond between them, and she gave a startled cry.

She didn't want this. She didn't want to spend an eternity away from his side. She never wanted to feel such heartache, such tremendous loss, ever again. Without him, her heart was empty. Cavernous and sweeping, cold and desolate.

The Strand binding them together warmed. It was a promise. A vow. And it was in that moment she knew, with every fiber of her being, she loved him. Fiercely. She loved this male who offered her his soul, who would do anything for her. Through it all, she would do the same for him. She would burn the heavens and scorch all the seven circles of hell for him. She would rather die than live in a world without him.

"Tiernan." His name fell from her lips on a sob, and she threw her arms around his waist, burying her face in his chest.

For a second, he was motionless, and she feared she'd lost him forever.

But then he drew her close and one hand slowly stroked her hair. She looked up and blinked, his face still blurry from the outpouring of tears.

He started to pull away and panic coursed through her, hot and fast. "Tiernan, wait," she begged. "I'm so sorry, I—"

"No, *astora*. I'm the one who must apologize to you." The High King of Summer dropped onto his knees before her. He captured both of her hands in the security of his own. "I hurt you. I allowed you to think you meant nothing to me, gave you cause to doubt the Strand between us. It is something I will always regret, and I will *never* let it happen again. You..." He paused, drawing in a breath, gazing up at her in agony. "You are my everything." He kissed each one of her fingers. "You are the sun within my storm. The star in my eternal night and the glowing ember of my soul. And I will cherish you until the fates decide I am no longer worthy of the dawn."

Chapter Twenty-Nine

Maeve slid down into his lap and cupped his cheeks in both of her palms. Her thumbs lightly glided across the faint scruff lining his jaw. She whispered across his lips, "You are mine."

Fire lit within the depths of his eyes and passion sparked to life in flecks of gold. His warm lips found hers, and he wrapped his arms around her, tugging her closer to him. His kiss was soft at first. Sweet. Romantic, even. But his hands...his hands were everywhere.

Her hips and thighs. Her waist and breasts. Groping. Squeezing. Heat flared at her core, and she clenched her legs together, wishing he'd slide his hand beneath the slit of her gown and touch her where she wanted him most.

"Gods, this dress of yours," he mumbled as one hand encircled her neck, tipping her head back so he could graze his teeth along the column of her throat. "All I've wanted to do, all night, is take it off."

He was already hard. The press of him nudged against her and she nestled herself against him further, relishing the way chest rumbled in response.

"I had it ordered especially for you." Maeve tangled her fingers into his dark strands of hair. "I wanted to bring you to your knees."

His laughter caused her heart to soar. "It worked."

Suddenly she was in his arms, and he was standing on the balcony. His wings, twilight and midnight, unfurled, and he spread them wide. On instinct, she wrapped her arms around his neck.

"What are you doing?"

"Taking you somewhere special." Tiernan darted into the night sky, soaring above the floating city of Niahvess, toward the twin mountains.

Wisps of clouds drifted past them like ribbons of silver satin, and the breeze lifted them higher as he flew closer to the mountains bordering Summer and Autumn. The sharp slate peaks jutted upward across the horizon.

Maeve memorized his outline. Chiseled jaw. High, prominent cheekbones. Pointed ears. Full lips that curved into a smirk. "I can fly too, you know."

"Yes." He grinned and his fingers pressed into her thighs and waist. "But carrying you gives me an excuse to touch you."

"Fair enough."

He touched down on a balcony in a small, inviting house near the top of one of the twin mountain peaks. Looking around, Maeve wasn't even sure she would classify it as a house. It was mostly just a room with floor-to-ceiling glass windows on either side that faced the east and the west. There was a fireplace in one corner and across from it was a sofa piled with pillows. A plush indigo rug was spread out across the hardwood floors, and tiny faerie lights danced across the ceiling encased in glass orbs of violet. There were a few shelves filled with books and a leather chair with an ivory throw tossed over it. In the far corner was a plush bed piled with blankets and satin pillows. The space was cozy. Comfortable. The kind of place where she could sit and read from sunrise until sunset.

Carefully, Tiernan set her down, and her gaze trailed out the eastern windows in wonder. From their vantage point, she could just see the snow-kissed peaks of the mountains in the Winter Court. And below her, bordering the other side of the mountains, was the Autumn forest.

It was breathtaking.

She turned to face him, outlined in silver pools of moonlight. "What is this place?"

"This is The Vista." He shoved his hands into his pockets, gently rocking back onto his heels. "I come here sometimes."

"Just sometimes?"

Tiernan shrugged. "When I need to gather my thoughts."

"I can see why." Maeve folded her arms over her chest, sensing he was showing her something special to him. Something secret. Like his own slice of heaven. "It's lovely."

Easy silence filled the space between them, and Maeve glanced out the window to the west once more before facing him.

"I need to tell you something."

He stilled and a line creased his brow. "What is it?"

"It's Fearghal."

The air whispering in through the room cooled and she shivered. Thunder rumbled and Tiernan's gaze darkened, clouded by the storm rising inside him.

"What of him?"

Maeve told him everything she'd learned in the library. She told him about Fearghal and how he was a Puca, a shifter, a creator of portals. How she'd misinterpreted the will o' wisp's words; the source of the Scathing wasn't Parisa. She had no magic. It was Fearghal. She told him about *The Legend of the Puca* and how she'd found the drawing of Fearghal sketched onto one of the pages, how he seemed to mock her.

Tiernan's shoulders were rigid, strained with tension. "Then we must plan to go to Kells at once. The sooner we get rid of the Scathing and find the Furies—"

"And bring back Saoirse," Maeve added.

"And bring back Saoirse," he smiled, but it didn't reach his eyes, "the sooner we can focus on defeating Parisa."

"I agree." Maeve pressed her lips together. "And having the Furies on our side will be helpful against her."

"Yes." Tiernan studied her and reached out, rubbing his hands up and down her arm. "How long have you known about Fearghal?"

"Since..." Maeve's voice trailed off, not wanting to remember how badly she'd wanted to speak with him and share the news of her discovery, only to be thwarted by Merrick. Only to discover Ciara in his bedroom.

He read her face and he *knew*.

"I'm sorry." He tilted her chin up to him and kissed both of her cheeks. "I'm sorry." His lips brushed along her forehead. "I will never hurt you like that again."

Outside, the stars were slowly winking out and the faint glow of dawn lingered on the horizon in tempered shades of pink and bronze.

She entwined her arms around Tiernan's neck and drew him down to her. He peppered kisses along her jaw and neck all while his fingers skimmed down the length of her. His mouth slanted across hers, his tongue gliding over the seam of her lips, seeking entry. She opened for him readily, sinking her teeth into his bottom lip. He growled and cupped her ass with both hands, jerking her hips forward and pressing her into the stiff proof of his arousal.

Beneath the delicate fabric of her gown, her nipples hardened, and she rubbed them against his chest. The friction of lace and flesh spread a rush of heat through her. Everywhere he touched set her skin on fire, and the sensitive area between her thighs throbbed with desire. She was hot. Wet. Dripping with need.

The rubies dangling from her shoulders tinkled softly as she latched onto his shoulders and he gripped the heavy beading of her gown, gathering it in fistfuls and hiking it up to her waist. "This fucking dress."

"It's my new favorite." She licked the tattoo spiraling up his neck. "Don't ruin it."

"Of course, my lady."

One hand moved between her legs, and he dragged his calloused palm up to her inner thigh. His fingers thrummed against her heated flesh, playing against her skin the same way she watched him strum his guitar. She squirmed beneath his velvety touch.

"Any other requests?" he murmured, gliding his thumb back and forth along her slick folds.

"Yes," she gasped and looked into his eyes. Desire rippled through the pools of violet and sapphire, the gold flecks glinted with heat. He ran his teeth along his bottom lip and his gaze darted down to her mouth. "I want you. All of you. From now until dusk gives way to the dawn. Until stars dance between us."

"As you wish."

Tiernan removed his hand and grabbed her legs, lifting her. He pinned her backside to the window, bracing her, anchoring her. He glamoured away all his clothing, and for once, he was the one who was deliciously naked while she was fully clothed. A second later, the pads of his fingers bit into the flesh of her thighs as he spread her legs wider, making room for him. The metal studs climbing along his shaft were a cool shock against the burning heat of her core. Shivers of anticipation raced down her spine and she wriggled in his hold, urging him closer, desperate for him to fill her.

"Are you ready?" Lust thickened his words.

"Yes." Her tongue darted out, swiping along his neck. "Yes."

He kissed her soundly and slammed into her, swallowing her gasping cry. Again, he stretched her, and she took the full length of him. Her head fell back against the glass door. Every thrust took her higher and higher. She locked her ankles around his back, beckoning him to drive deeper inside her. Her chest rose and fell in ragged, heavy breaths, but it wasn't enough. She needed more. Wanted more.

"Do you trust me?" His whisper caressed her skin.

Her muscles clenched, tightening around him, gripping his cock while he pumped inside her. "I trust you."

She felt it then, the stirring of his magic as it reached for her. Silky tendrils of power slipped through her, taking control of her body, leaving her mind untouched. He wrapped her in the velvet of the night as his magic stroked her, fondled her from the inside out. Maeve cried out, the pleasure unlike anything she'd ever experienced. His hips jutted forward, filling her completely, and the windows of the room opened, chilling them with a cool Autumn breeze. Beautiful wings unfurled behind him, and he lifted off the small balcony, taking to the skies.

His wings continued to beat soundlessly as he suspended them between the twin mountain peaks with the glow of the morning sun on the rise behind them. He placed a kiss on her lips, and then her body was arching backward, obeying his every command. Her arms fell away from him as he dipped her further still, intensifying the angle, and clouds of silver sifted through her fingertips. Grasping her hips, he began pumping inside her once more. With each thrust, his magic intensified, teasing her. Taunting her. She could feel the power of him in her breasts and nipples. His magic coursed down her spine and up her thighs, until the force of it centered upon her clit, sliding and stroking so she gasped and screamed his name.

"Fuck," he ground the word out between clenched teeth, driving himself into her so hard and fast that the burning orgasm ripped through them both.

She cried.

He roared.

And the last remaining stars in the sky shattered, falling down around them like crushed diamonds.

Chapter Thirty

Tiernan carried a sleeping Maeve back to the palace, and while he was able to catch a few hours of sleep, his mind refused to let him fully rest.

Tomorrow, they would venture to Kells to defeat the Scathing. But he was no fool. He knew whatever lay in wait for them there would not be easy to overcome. They would have to go to the Moors and enlist the help of the Furies, the wrathful beings who he hoped did indeed answer to Maeve. Then, as promised, they would find Saoirse. There was no doubt in his mind the silver-haired warrior would want to fight alongside them in the Scathing, so putting off trying to find her was out of the question. If she remained in the castle like Merrick said, then bringing Saoirse with them would be the easiest part of their journey.

Once they returned to Faeven, their focus would shift on Parisa's impending attack against the Winter Court.

Unable to lie in bed any longer, Tiernan dressed and slipped out the door of his room, quietly closing it behind him so as not to disturb Maeve.

It was still early, and he expected half of the palace to be asleep given the previous night's events, but when he strode out onto the balcony where they usually dined, Lir, Merrick, and Brynn were already there. A basket of rolls with an assortment of jam and a bowl of ripe berries and cream were spread before them.

"Morning, sunshine." Brynn poured a steaming cup of coffee, then set it down on the table in front of him. "Sleep well?"

Tiernan's brow quirked.

"Hell of a thunderstorm we had last night." Merrick stretched his legs out before him and kicked one ankle over the other. He took an obnoxiously large handful of grapes and popped one into his mouth, smirking. "Anybody else hear it?"

"Oh yeah," Brynn drawled, and her eyes changed colors from their usual golden brown to a shade of mocking blue. "Absolutely raging."

Lir ducked his head, but there was no mistaking the way his shoulders shook in silent laughter.

Merrick smiled, flashing his dimples. "Sounded like a *fucking* good time."

Brynn snorted and swiftly jabbed her elbow into his side. Merrick cracked up and Lir just shook his head.

Tiernan lowered himself into his chair and met Merrick's laughing gaze from over the rim of his coffee cup. "Jealous much, Mer?" He took an intentionally slow drink of the scalding liquid.

"You're fucking right, I'm jealous." His grin only widened. "Not all of us are lucky enough to find our *sirra*."

Brynn tossed an arm around his shoulders. "Don't worry, I'm sure you'll find someone who will put up with your bullshit."

Merrick snorted.

"Moving on from the fact that our king's sex life is none of our concern," Lir said, all humor vanishing from his face, "when do we leave?"

"Tomorrow at first light." Tiernan quickly relayed everything Maeve told him about Fearghal and the Scathing, and was only slightly disheartened to learn Lir had already known all of it. But the consequence of not being the first informed was his own doing, so he let it drop without another thought. "Lir, Maeve, and I will fade to the Moors first in search of the Furies. Then we'll go to Kells for Saoirse. After that, we'll move on to face the Scathing and rid it from the continent of Veterra once and for all."

He twisted the ring he wore on his pinky—the one that belonged to his mother—back and forth. He'd been born to fight. To lead. To win wars and maintain peace. And now, in part due to her death, he'd been gifted the ability to destroy. And so he would. He would destroy Parisa. He'd destroy the army she created and the Court she'd built. He'd destroy it all.

"Ceridwen will be in charge during my absence. Merrick, I want you and your best scouts to unearth any information you can about this new Dark Court and Parisa's plans." Tiernan downed the rest of his coffee. "Brynn, I want you to secure the Court and ready our forces. There will be no time to waste once we return from Kells."

Merrick snatched another roll. "If I leave after breakfast, we should return before dawn."

Tiernan nodded sharply, then focused his attention on Lir and Brynn. "We need to find a way to protect Niahvess while we're gone. Our borders are strong and secure, but they are not impenetrable. And until we learn the depth of Parisa's forces, no risk is too great."

"I can do it."

He sensed Maeve lingering just outside the doors to the balcony before she spoke. His gaze snapped up and there she was, as lovely as ever.

Her hair was piled on top of her head; he thought it might've been the first time he'd ever seen her with it up. With a hesitant smile, she tucked one loose tendril of hair behind her ear. Tight black leggings clung to the curve of her hips and legs, and she wore a cropped top that was so heavily beaded, it could've been mistaken for armor. Her eyes were still slumbrous and hazy with a sheen of lust, and he was taken back to that moment last night, when he'd fallen on his knees before her and bared his soul.

"My lady." Brynn nodded in acknowledgment.

Lir and Merrick all stood as she entered the balcony, and Tiernan's chest tightened when she surprised him by sitting upon his lap instead of the empty seat beside him. His arm instinctively curled around her waist.

Maeve propped her forearm up on his shoulder and looked up to the sky. "I can create a sphere of protection to encase the entire city while we're away."

"We can't ask you to do that." Tiernan shook his head, but she caught his jaw in her palm.

Her eyes, so much like a misty morning on the Lismore Marin, were soft when she said, "You don't have to."

The corner of his mouth curled into a smirk. "You do love your little bubbles."

"Mind your tone, my lord." She swatted at him playfully and nestled her tight ass against his thighs. His cock hardened instantly, wanting to partake in its own kind of banter.

Maeve's thoughts were loud enough for him to hear. *"Be nice, or I'll make you pay for it later."*

His teeth scraped along his bottom lip, and her gaze instantly dropped to his mouth. *"Is that a threat, High Princess?"*

"No, my lord." Her hand moved to his thigh. Squeezed. *"It's a promise."*

Merrick coughed. Loudly. "You two want to go mind fuck elsewhere? Some of us are trying to eat." He held up his half-finished roll as proof.

Maeve flushed to a beautiful shade of pink, and Tiernan seized the opportunity to glide his hand from her waist, right in between her thighs. He cupped her, his thumb coming to rest on her clit, and she became very, *very* still. She knew. Oh, she knew. One move, one shift, and he'd have her soaking those shiny leather leggings of hers in a matter of minutes.

Tiernan flashed an unapologetic grin. "Apologies, Mer."

Lir leaned forward across the table and addressed Maeve, deftly deterring the conversation. "Will the sphere hold?"

She tilted her head to the side, a ghost of a smile upon her lips. "Do you doubt my abilities, commander?"

Lir's silver eyes lightened. "Never."

Her smile evaporated and determination hardened her voice. "It will hold."

Ceridwen strolled out onto the balcony, carrying a small dagger in her hand. "I spoke with a healer in the Market District." Her penetrating gaze locked onto Maeve. "He concurs with Brynn's assessment of the blade used to pierce Maeve's skin. It is indeed a form of dark magic."

Brynn straightened in her seat and all traces of her previous humor vanished. "Did he elaborate?"

Ceridwen held out the dagger for everyone to see. "It was a spell of sorts, and it was used to imbue an ordinary object with potions. Similar to how a blade is dipped in nightshade, yet vastly different. This particular dark magic venom, as Brynn calls it, can cause paralysis while leaving the victim fully conscious and aware of their surroundings."

Every muscle inside Tiernan wound tight with tension. He didn't even want to think what could've happened if Garvan had used the dagger on the fae girl. It had been a stroke of fate that Maeve *faded* in at the right time to stop him. Then again, the bastard had stabbed Maeve with it instead. If it wasn't for the bond he shared with Maeve and the necklace she wore overwhelming him with merciless vengeance, he might not have been able to get to her in time.

Merrick's gaze slid to Tiernan. "If she can paralyze her enemies, who knows what else she's capable of doing."

"But the dagger." Brynn crossed her arms, debating. "Garvan had to be up close to use it on Maeve. That won't be so easy to do in a fight."

"Unless that same venom is used on arrows," Maeve muttered.

Fuck.

"Shit," Merrick said, echoing his sentiments.

Lir scrubbed his hands over his face.

Maeve twisted in his lap to face him. "Are you aware there's an area of your library that's glamoured?"

He shared a look with Ceridwen, then patted Maeve's thigh, letting his thumb trace lazy circles. "Yes. It's glamoured for a reason. Dark magic can be tempting to those whose minds are too weak to resist."

She reared back, affronted. "Are you calling me weak?"

"Not at all." The corner of his mouth twisted out of spite. "Reckless, yes. But never weak."

"It's where I learned about Fearghal," Maeve admitted and ducked her head as a wash of pink flooded her neck and crawled up her cheeks. "And the Puca."

"I assumed as much." Tiernan planted a kiss at the base of her neck. "Your curiosity often gets the best of you."

"I can go back to the library and see if I can find more information on dark magic," Maeve continued.

"Once we return from Kells." He slid his hand back between her thighs, maintaining control, relishing the fact that her body froze again. "And only if Merrick's scouts uncover no new information for us."

Tiernan was fully expecting her to fight him on it. To argue that the library was just as necessary as anything else, but shockingly enough, she agreed, and only curled further onto his lap. Arousal pummeled through him. If they were alone, he'd take her right here, on the balcony, in the glorious rays of late morning sunlight. He could imagine how perfect Maeve would look wrapped up in nothing but the silk of the sun.

"So," Merrick drew the word out and pushed up from his seat. "I'm going to go...find something else to do."

Brynn laughed and stood with him. "I believe there's a tavern in the city offering half-priced drinks." She flicked a glance to the timepiece on her wrist. "We'd be four hours early but I'm sure they won't mind."

"Alas, duty calls." Merrick raked a hand through his hot pink hair. "I'll take you up on a drunken stupor after this shit show is over."

"Deal."

Lir stood as well, and Maeve glanced up at him. "You're leaving, too?"

He nodded solemnly. "I have swords that need sharpening for tomorrow's adventure."

"Of course."

Right as Lir walked off, Ceridwen sat down. Tiernan shot his twin a menacing look.

"Yes, Tier, I'm fully aware that you need some alone time with Maeve." Her eyes steeled. "But this can't wait."

Threads of apprehension stitched their way down Tiernan's spine. "What is it?"

Ceridwen fiddled with the ribbons of gold silk at her waist. "I've had another vision."

From under the table, Maeve squeezed his hand, and he looked up sharply at his sister. "What happened?"

"It wasn't clear. At least, not completely. I've never had a vision like this one before, where the images continue to shift. But there was a massive storm. The sound...it was the thundering of a thousand hooves and shadows tore across the sky in an abundance of roiling clouds." Her lips pressed together, but she held his gaze, firm and elegant at once. "It was the eternal warriors."

"The Wild Hunt," Tiernan murmured.

"Yes." Ceridwen's eyes darkened like dusk before the fall of night and her gaze slid to the female seated upon his lap. "Maeve was among them."

"It's a sign then, right?" She angled her head and glanced at him from over her shoulder. "That they will fight alongside us if I ask?"

"Yes." Concern heightened his ever-increasing awareness. "But how did you know about the Wild Hunt?"

"Casimir told me when I—" Maeve clamped her mouth shut and her entire body went rigid in his hold.

Ceridwen's lashes fluttered back, and she looked at Tiernan before stealing a fleeting glance at the stone floor.

Tiernan blew out a low breath, steeling himself. He must remain calm. If Maeve had seen Casimir recently, and hadn't told him, it was likely his own doing. With one finger, he guided her chin up and lifted her face to him.

"Continue, Maeve."

Words poured from her like a violent, rushing river. After their argument during Sunatalis, she'd somehow managed to *fade* to the Autumn Court. That piece of information alone was enough to cause him to lose his grip on control, but then she mentioned a fox and how the Autumn woods seemed to respond to her. To recognize her. She told him how Casimir appeared first in his Drakon form and then shifted, knowing she was hiding in the forest. He processed everything she told him, and though he was furious at the prospect of her being alone within the boundaries of the Court that would see her handed over to Parisa, he was also grateful it'd been Casimir who'd discovered her and not some trooping fae. Yet he couldn't gauge whether speaking with Casimir was such a good thing. It was difficult to discern if the Drakon would tell Maeve the truth or not, but he *had* been the one to rescue her from the Spring dungeon.

He was debating whether to ask Maeve if she trusted Casimir's word when Ceridwen spoke instead, and her train of thought was elsewhere entirely.

His twin's eyes were round with something that could've been awe. "You met a fox?" she asked.

Maeve nodded once. "I did."

Ceridwen's brow furrowed in thought. "And what did he say?"

"Nothing." Maeve shifted and Tiernan wrapped an arm around

her waist, his hand splayed open across her upper thigh. "He was a fox."

"Was he though?" Ceridwen's head tilted in that thoughtful manner of hers when she knew she was right, and everyone else was wrong. "Truly?"

"I..." Maeve opened her mouth, then closed it.

Ceridwen waited, her features soft and calming. "Speak freely, Maeve."

She tucked another loose curl behind her ear. "I thought it could've been Dorian. My father."

"Your father," Tiernan repeated. He had to admit, the odds weren't likely. But at the same time, Garvan was not the High King, and neither was Aran. The shift of power had never occurred, which meant Dorian couldn't be dead. His magic granted him the ability to shape-shift into any number of creatures, most notably a fox. Maeve's theory could be proven, except for the fact that Dorian hadn't been seen in dozens of years. He'd disappeared completely after Fianna vanished from Autumn.

"Fox form *was* his favorite," Tiernan mused, mulling the idea over in his mind. "And Queen Marella mentioned he lived, did she not?"

"She did." Maeve leaned back, rested her body against his chest. "I mean, I thought there was a connection. He recognized Carman's name when I said it. And he attempted to protect me from Casimir when he circled above us in his Drakon form. But then he chased a leaf..."

Ceridwen snorted and Tiernan laughed out loud.

"Perhaps just a fox then?" he teased, tugging playfully on one of Maeve's curls.

"Maybe." Ceridwen's shoulders rose and fell. "Maybe not. Either way, I'll bid the two of you a good afternoon and prepare for tomorrow." With that, she twirled away from them, her footsteps more hushed than a whisper in the wind.

Tiernan wasted no time.

He wrapped his arms around Maeve, crushed her to him, and together they *faded*.

When they arrived at their destination, Maeve gasped and smacked him soundly on the chest. "A little warning next time, Your Grace."

Tiernan didn't miss the way she'd used his more formal title. She'd never done so before. In fact, it was rare for anyone to address him as such. But she did it as a sign of respect. Of loyalty. And it left him brimming with an emotion he couldn't quite name.

She gazed at their surroundings in wonder, one hand pressed firmly to the Strand branding her heart. "Where are we?"

He bowed his head. "The home of your future Court."

MAEVE COULDN'T BREATHE. Wherever Tiernan had taken her, it was beautiful. They were still within the borders of Summer yet one glance upward and there was nothing but devastating mountains. On the other side lay Autumn. The air was brisk here, cool against her heated summer skin. Overhead, the leaves were just beginning to change colors on the trees at the foothills and a river of emerald green cascaded down through the mountains. The same one, she realized, that broke off into dozens of smaller canals once it reached Niahvess, giving the Floating City its namesake. Here, the mountains looked grayish purple, a stunning backdrop to the lush beauty caught between two seasons.

And here, here was where she would build her Court.

She could almost envision it. A pretty little palace and the Spring fae—now her citizens—all living and thriving in a city full of shops and restaurants. They could rebuild their lives here. They could find happiness and purpose here. Perhaps there was even enough room for a vineyard.

"What do you think?" Tiernan's voice hovered above her, and she turned to look up at him.

"It's perfect."

"But?" he prompted.

"You...you would just give me some of your land? You'd build an entire Court here?" She searched his eyes, his soul. "For me?"

He reached down and ran his thumb along the top of her cheekbone. "Why wouldn't I?"

"Because I'm not..." How could she possibly tell him she still didn't feel like she was Archfae? That she barely recognized herself anymore.

"Maeve, listen to me." Tiernan captured her shoulders in his strong hands. She could drown in the deep sapphire and violet of his eyes. "The Spring fae were chased from their homes. They were attacked, assaulted, and oppressed. They renounced their oath to the Spring Court and in doing so, they chose you. They chose *you*, Maeve."

"But I—"

"You will be their queen." He spoke the words with such ease, such conviction. Like it was so easy to accept. "And you will need somewhere to rule."

A Court. She would need a Court.

She pressed her lips together, scraped her teeth along the inside seam. She should be happy. Thrilled, even. Despondency gnawed away at her. It wasn't that she didn't want a Court, because of course she did. She wanted to protect the Spring fae from any who would cause them harm. But she also wanted Tiernan.

A line formed across his brow. "Something is bothering you." His gaze dipped to the necklace he'd given her. "What is it?"

"It's nothing." She shook off the trepidation growing inside her.

"You're lying."

"Yes, but it's not important," she countered.

"Anything you have to say is important."

The air she held pinched inside her lungs left her in a rush. She dropped down onto the grassy bank by the river's edge, beneath the shade of trees just kissed by Autumn. Absently, she plucked a blade of grass and twisted it between her fingers.

"This is what I always wanted. When I was in Kells, I tried so hard to prove myself worthy of a crown. Of ruling. I just never expected..."

Tiernan continued to stand. Watching. Waiting.

"I never expected to do it alone." Her voice sounded hollow.

"You're not alone." He lowered himself down on the soft grass beside her. Stretching out, he crossed one ankle over the other and propped himself up on both hands. "I'm right here with you."

"But you have your own Court."

At that, he remained silent, and she knew he understood what she was so poorly trying to convey. That maybe she didn't want to be just *any* High Queen. "I can't expect you to abandon your own duties and responsibilities to Summer just to help me figure out what the hell I'm doing. I was raised in Veterra, trained and prepared to rule a kingdom of mortals. I'm only twenty-four years old, not..."

She gestured vaguely in his direction, and he chuckled.

"We won't mention my age again."

Maeve lay down, letting her head come to rest in his lap. "I had all these plans for Kells. I was going to form a better alliance with Cantata, maybe even expand the city all the way down to the border of the Cascadian Mountains. Protect the Moors, improve the Gael-song Port, and open trade routes with some of the eastern realms." Her eyes drifted closed. "I would've been tolerant. Merciful. Kind."

The tips of his fingers skated up and down her arm. "You can still do all those things here."

She opened her eyes. "What if I'm not any good at it?"

"You've already proven your worth to so many, Maeve." He took her hand into his own and placed a kiss inside her open palm. "You are a High Princess of Autumn. Are you really going to sit here and tell me the idea of becoming a queen has never crossed your mind?"

"Of course it has," she muttered. "But I have three brothers in line before me."

"Let me ask you this," he looked up to the mountains, to the brilliant blue sky where low-lying mist started to take shape, "if you were queen tomorrow, what would you do?"

Maeve tugged up three more pieces of grass and began to plait them together. "I'd work on building the infrastructure of my Court. There would be a central market square with shops where local artisans could showcase their wares. I'd build homes and I would help the faerie who lost his vineyard open a winery, and there would be a library for everyone to access, not just those who live in a palace." She glanced up at him and smirked.

"Noted, my lady." He snapped a flower off a nearby rose bush; the petals were the deepest shade of red she'd ever seen. After inspecting it for thorns, he fashioned it into her curls. "And what about you?"

Maeve lifted herself into a sitting position so she faced him, breathing in the sweetened fragrance of the rose. "What about me?"

"Would you want a palace?" he asked.

"I suppose it would be necessary." She shifted her shoulders. She honestly had given little thought to where she would live. "But I wouldn't need anything fancy."

"You may not need one, but you deserve one." He moved closer. "What would it look like?"

"I don't really know. I always assumed I would rule Kells." If she ever had her own palace, it would look nothing like Carman's fortress. It would be welcoming and beautiful, not intimidating and macabre. "A throne, however...I think I'd like one that resembles the Aurastone. Something that shimmers and reflects the glow of the dawn. A throne of beauty."

Tiernan was barely a breath from her now. "A throne of dreams," he murmured.

"Yes." She sighed when his lips hovered over hers. "A throne of dreams."

Chapter Thirty-One

Tiernan brushed a kiss along Maeve's jaw while his hand lazily encircled her neck. Her skin was like velvet beneath his touch. Decadent. He stroked his thumb up and down the column of her throat and her head dipped back, allowing his tongue to trail over the tattoo painting her flesh. The breathy little sound she made caused his pulse to hammer and his cock to throb.

"Did you know," he drawled, while he lightly kissed her lips once, then twice, "I knew you were mine the moment I first saw you?"

She drew back. Her sea-swept eyes, almost hazy with lust, suddenly cleared. "But you were so awful to me."

"I was." Guilt toiled through him. It carved him up from the inside out.

She looked up at him from beneath her feathery lashes. "Why?"

This was the moment. He could tell her everything. He could tell her the real reason he pushed her away. He could be honest about his snide remarks and callous insults. But there was no telling how she would react when she discovered she was fated to someone who was destined to die. She'd already lost so much of herself; he didn't want to make it worse.

"I have done many things in my life that I am not proud of, but there are very few things I would ever lament." He pressed his mouth to hers, firm, then broke their kiss apart. "Treating you the way I did is one of them. It's a regret I'll live with for all eternity."

He could see her mind working, almost hear her thinking, but he shut out her thoughts. Now was not the time to intervene, to break into her mind without permission.

She gnawed on her bottom lip and then, "Does this have anything to do with the fact that you'll lose everything if you fall in love?"

Tiernan felt the blood drain from his face. An unsettling kind of dread locked tight inside of him. "Perhaps. But falling in love has nothing to do with it." He studied her. "What do you know of it?"

She played with the pieces of braided grass in her hands. "Deirdre may have mentioned an ancient prophecy..."

Ancient prophecy indeed.

He would have to tread these waters carefully to keep them both from drowning. "I'd say she romanticized things. It's not exactly a deal...it's a vow I made a long time ago."

"How much of it is true?" There was a tremor in her voice.

"I suppose that would depend on how much she told you." The harrowing grip of dread took hold of him and refused to let go. He was torn between wanting to tell her everything and keeping her locked in the dark, if only to keep her heart safe. "When my parents were slain in the Autumn woods, grief tormented me. I called out to the gods, to any who would answer, to let me have my vengeance."

Her breath hitched. "Who answered?"

"The god of death."

Maeve's face fell as she processed what he'd told her. She chewed her bottom lip again, thinking, and he found it painfully difficult to stay out of her head.

"This deal you made," she began, considering each word with care, "what were the exact words?"

Every muscle in his body tensed. It was now. He could tell her now or spare her. "In exchange for the power of absolute destruction, I would lose everything in return."

A ripple of fear washed over her face. It slammed through him like a gust of wind at the onslaught of a storm, strong and powerful.

"Everything?" She paled. "What do you mean, everything?"

"My power. My magic." Tiernan's throat seized. "My life."

He couldn't take his eyes off her, not even when a single tear clung to her lashes before falling down her cheek.

"When?" She whispered the word, like the gods were listening.

"Any time of his choosing."

Maeve clamped one hand over her mouth and shook her head. "Tiernan." Her voice broke and her shoulders trembled. "How could you make such an awful deal?"

"I was desperate, Maeve." She climbed into his lap, straddling him, and threw her arms around his neck, burying her face in his chest. He stroked one hand down her hair. "I wanted nothing more than to kill those who killed my parents. I wanted to see their lives destroyed, and I was willing to pay the price, no matter what."

He cradled her for a moment, enjoying the way her body fit perfectly against his own. She was everything he ever wanted in this life. Powerful. Fearless. A dreamer with tenacity and almost too stubborn at times. His Strand warmed, burned with longing for her, answered only to her. To the other half of his soul. To his *sirra*. He eased her back, gently cupping her face in his hands.

"It's not fair," she protested. "I've only just found you."

"And I will give you all of me for as long as I can." He pressed a kiss to her forehead. "You are perfect, *astora*. So wholly perfect."

"Not always." Her lashes were damp. She was fighting back tears. "I was broken, once."

"I know." This time, her mind was too loud for its own good. He knew where her thoughts wandered, and he understood the depth of her trauma. Her past still haunted her, and he supposed it would for quite some time. So, if he could help ease some of her suffering, at least for a little while, then he would. Tiernan forced himself to speak his next words. "I do believe he loved you."

Maeve froze in his arms and all her breath left her at once. She looked at him, wide-eyed. Nearly hopeless. "What?"

"Rowan loved you, Maeve." It killed him to say it. To admit. "But he also knew that you..."

"That I was fated to you," Maeve finished for him, her eyes clouded with uncertainty. Confusion warred across her lovely face. "But you let him kiss me. You let me think my feelings for him were real."

"Your feelings for him *were* real. Whether it be a matter of fates or stars, I cannot sway your emotions." Tiernan ran his fingers through the silky, pink-gold strands of her hair, then twirled them around one of his fingers. "So yes, I let him kiss you and touch you. I let you tumble headfirst into something I couldn't control because I thought I was sparing us both from something far worse. I didn't realize I would torture myself in the process."

"But what if he hadn't died?" Maeve pressed her hand to the Strand on his chest, the one matching her own. "What if Rowan had lived—"

"I would not have interfered." At least, not too much, he told himself. "I would have suffered in silence."

Doing so would have wrecked him.

She glanced down at her chest. "And the bond?"

"Would only form once you chose me."

Her brow arched in question. "Even with the mating dance?"

"Even with it." He kissed her slowly. Softly. "I would've waited for you until the stars fell from the sky."

"And now?" she asked, her lips moving over his.

"I would shatter the realms to remain by your side."

The corner of her mouth lifted in a wicked smile. "Good."

She unbuttoned his shirt deftly, shoving it away, letting her warm hands rove over his bare chest. Lips pressed together, she grabbed his shoulders, urging him to lie down on the soft blanket of grass. He tucked his hands behind his head and flashed her one of his haughtiest, most arrogant grins. "Taking control already?"

"You know me so well," she purred.

Then she was sliding further down his legs and only when her fingers unbuckled the belt on his pants did he realize her intent. Already, he strained for her, wanting to bury himself deep inside of her. The pure scent of her arousal sent all of his blood rushing to his cock, and he craved her touch. She worked slowly, one button at a time, until the full and hardened length of him sprang free from the confines of his pants.

He watched her every movement, taking notice of the way she looked up at him, both curious yet confident. He enjoyed the way her hair tumbled down around her like a waterfall of satin as her full mouth hovered inches away from the gold studs piercing him. She was gazing down at him, marveling over him, and staring at him in such a way that conceit almost swallowed him whole. He couldn't help himself. He stretched and flexed, causing every muscle to tighten and ripple for show, and he bit the inside of his cheek to keep from smiling when her eyes widened at the sight of him.

But then her little pink tongue flicked out from between her lips and she barely, *barely*, tasted him, and he nearly exploded like a youth just discovering the pleasures of a female for the first time.

"If you continue to tease me, Your Highness," he spoke the words through gritted teeth, "I will be sure to return the favor."

"Oh, forgive me, my lord." Her breath coated his sensitive flesh and he throbbed, damn near burned for her. "I didn't mean to tease. Let me try again."

She took him, all of him, into her mouth, and Tiernan's eyes rolled back in his head.

Fuck.

Her tongue glided and swirled around his cock, sucking, taking him all the way to the hilt. His hips bucked of their own accord, but she didn't falter. She continued to lick and taste, drawing him deep into her throat. He knew her eyes likely burned with the threat of

312

tears; sucking his dick was...intimidating. But she grabbed his waist, digging her fingernails into his skin, and held on. Her beautiful head bobbed up and down, and he coiled one fist into her hair, driving himself deeper with each thrust as he fucked her pretty pink mouth.

Gods, he was going to lose it. He was going to erupt inside her, and he knew she'd take every last drop of him.

But he refused to let it happen.

Under no circumstances would he ever find release before her.

As much as it pained him to do so, he clasped her shoulders and pulled out of her mouth.

Maeve blinked up at him, lashes damp. "Is everything alright?"

"Fucking perfect." He glamoured away their clothing, so they were nothing but flesh upon heated flesh. "So fucking perfect."

In one swift movement, he lifted her off him, so she lay flat on her stomach in the grass beside him. Her back dipped when she attempted to push herself off the ground, displaying the tempting curve of her ass.

"Tiernan, what—"

But he was already moving behind her, bracing himself on his knees. He snared her hips with both hands, jerking them upward to meet him. She gasped, and his palm slid around her, to the smooth planes of her stomach. Gradually, he moved them even lower until he plunged two fingers inside the sweet folds of her center, moving them in and out quickly, driving her closer to the edge.

She tossed her head back and cried out. Then she was panting, and she arched her back, urging him to continue. "Oh, gods."

"No gods would dare answer your plea here, High Princess. Only me." Removing his fingers, he spread her legs wide, and plunged his cock deep into the folds of her slick cunt.

"Yes," she gasped.

Holding onto her hips, he thrust himself into her, over and over. Her fingers threaded through the grass, her nails pulling the blades up from their roots. Her cries for more echoed in his mind; her thoughts were a storm of desperation and pleasure. Goddess above, he wished he had a fucking mirror. What he wouldn't give to watch her pant out his name. To see her eyes glaze with lust. To admire the way her full breasts swung back and forth while her nipples formed into delectable little peaks.

She clenched around him, the sensation maddening, as her wetness soaked every inch of him. His cock bulged, swelled with the need for release. But not yet.

Her first.

She would always come first.

Tiernan reached around her hips and pressed one finger hard against Maeve's swollen clit, and she screamed his name. Her body jerked and tightened, dragging him over the ledge. Fire sparked. Cool rain began to fall. And the deafening crash of thunder sounded above them as the orgasm ripped through him and he finally poured himself into her.

Maeve didn't remember *fading* back to the palace.

But there she was, in Tiernan's bed, sated and overcome with a feeling of everlasting bliss.

She thought he offered her food, some of those pumpkin tarts she loved so much. Maybe even some wine. But the pull of sleep called to her, beckoning her like an old friend.

Without a fight, she caved, and tumbled into a world without dreams or nightmares.

In some hazy corner of her subconscious, she knew she was preparing for what would come next. For what they would face together. The unknown. A sinister kind of evil. A place to which she never thought she would return.

In the morning, they were going to Kells.

Chapter Thirty-Two

S leep was impossible for Tiernan.

Even though Maeve was curled up beside him, sound asleep, he found no peace. His thoughts were at war with one another, each one demanding his undivided attention. There was so much at stake. Their venture to Kells to locate the Furies, ridding the land of the Scathing, and destroying Fearghal were not small tasks. All of it would require time, effort, and energy. If Shay's tip on Garvan and Parisa's doings were any indication, they were on the cusp of a major battle.

As of now, Merrick had still not returned with any details regarding weaponry or numbers. He had no doubt his hunter would come back with all the information they sought, but until then, they were going in blind.

He watched the stars vanish through the glass dome of his ceiling. He watched as the night sky faded away to the glowing watercolors of early dawn, like brushstrokes across a canvas. The sun rose in the east, its brilliant beams striking up from between the twin mountain peaks of the border. By the time Maeve roused from slumber, he was already dressed and waiting for her to awaken.

She stretched her arms up over her head and gave him a sleepy smile. "You're up early."

Tiernan walked over to her and lowered himself onto the edge of the bed. "Yes."

"You didn't sleep, did you?"

"No."

He waved his hand and a pile of neatly folded clothing appeared. A blouse and leggings, her boots, but also...armor. There was a corset and leathers for her arms and legs. He thought the color suited her. Aubergine, Ceridwen had called it. The stitching was a fine rose gold, a perfect match to her tattoos, and it was embellished with tiny rare faerie stones that shifted colors from purple to crimson, depending upon the light.

She sat up at once and blinked down at the stack of armor, her fingers carefully touching the material as though it was a fine silk and not leather made to protect her from a blade.

"Do you like them?" he asked.

"Tiernan, they're beautiful." She lifted the corset and admired it in the early morning light. "But..."

"But what?" Doubt needled its way through him. Perhaps he'd made a mistake in commissioning them for her.

Her brow furrowed. "They're not Summer colors."

"No, but they are colors that suit you."

Her gaze darted to him.

Shit. He'd gone a step too far. He couldn't read her face, he couldn't analyze her expression. For the first time, she was a blank page. Void of any emotion.

"You're right. That was out of line, even for me. I shouldn't have assumed." Tiernan hastily scooped up the leathers. "Let's just toss these out, then you can choose whatever you want and—"

"Tiernan, stop." She snatched them from his hold and pulled, clutching them to her chest. "They're perfect for me and...my Court." She leaned over and pressed a kiss to his cheek. "Thank you."

"Your gratitude," he warned.

"Is never wasted on you," she countered. "But if there's something I can give you in return..."

She shimmied a little, allowing the bed linens to pool around her, showcasing her breasts and abdomen, and lower still. He reached out and gently lifted the opal and amethyst necklace dangling between the valley of her breasts. Her skin was warm against the gentle graze of his knuckles.

"Wicked little queen." He released the necklace and pulled back. "But I'm afraid your offer will have to be postponed until we return from Kells. The others are already waiting for us."

Maeve jolted out of the bed. "What? Why didn't you wake me?"

"As if I would." He smirked. "A female suffering from lack of sleep is damn near a death wish to anyone who approaches her." His gaze slid to the door, and then, "You've seen Ceridwen..."

"Point taken." She pulled on the leggings and blouse, then laced up the heavily beaded corset. Tiernan helped her with the leathers, and by the time he stepped back to admire her, his blood started to hum.

She did a little twirl. "What do you think?"

She was a warrior. A queen. And all he wanted to do was put her right back into his bed where she belonged.

"You know," he drawled and gave her ass a gentle smack, "I think we can make them wait a few minutes more."

He made to grab her, but she twisted out of his reach.

"Not a chance, my lord." She pulled her Aurastone from under the pillow and sheathed it on her thigh. Then she stalked into her adjoining bedroom and reemerged a few moments later with her sword of sunlight at her hip. "Ready?"

"As ever." He offered his hand and she accepted.

Together they strode through the open-air corridors toward the main courtyard of the palace, passing a handful of soldiers and servants, but none dared to look up. They knew what was happening, where they were going. They knew what was coming.

Tiernan and Maeve rounded the corner, and Ceridwen, Lir, and

Brynn were there, standing just inside the palace gates. Merrick had not yet returned from Spring. Lir was decked in full armor, as he was the only one coming with them, but a weight of worry had settled upon Tiernan's shoulders, and it was something he couldn't quite shake.

Ceridwen focused on him immediately. "What's wrong?"

Maeve, Lir, and Brynn all turned to watch the exchange.

He glanced at each of the faces looking at him in expectation. "I'm thinking."

"That you don't want to leave Brynn and me here alone." Ceridwen's guess was accurate.

"Exactly."

Brynn bristled and stepped forward. "*Moh Rí,* with all due respect..."

He held up one hand in quiet command. "I know, Brynn. You're one of my best warriors. There is no doubt in my mind of your ability to lead the High Army of Niahvess in my absence."

Pride left her glowing, and her eyes shifted from golden brown to blue.

"But," Tiernan continued, and her face fell. He grabbed her shoulder and squeezed lightly, then let his hand fall away. "You are also my strongest healer. If anything happens while we're gone, I need you saving lives, not issuing orders."

Brynn opened her mouth to object, but Tiernan overrode her unsaid words. "That being said, when we go to war against Parisa and her supposed Dark Court, you *will* be on the battlefield with us. I will not leave you behind to care for the wounded."

Ceridwen draped an arm around Brynn's sullen shoulders. "It's just his way of saying he doesn't want me left alone in case something happens. It's too much of a risk without having Lir or Merrick here with us."

"Of course, my lord. I understand." Brynn straightened and inclined her head. "I will ensure no threat breaches our Court and I will protect the High Princess at all costs."

Tiernan's gaze slid to Lir, to his Commander of the Summer Legion. He bowed in kind and his silver eyes flashed to Maeve, to the life he'd sworn to protect. "You're certain you wish for me to remain behind?"

"Yes." The weight bearing down upon him slowly lifted. "Ceridwen will see to the Court while you and Brynn ensure the city does not waver while I'm gone."

"Very well, my lord." Lir looked at Maeve and offered her—and only her—a smile. "Promise me you won't leave his side, little bird."

Maeve's face illuminated with undulated joy. "I promise."

Tiernan noted the exchange. He couldn't recall the last time he'd seen his commander genuinely smile and to know Maeve had been the one to do it, to bring such lightness to the shadows that haunted Lir...a sense of pride swelled inside him. She truly was radiant, the Dawnbringer in every sense of the word.

"Debrief Merrick as soon as he returns," Tiernan continued, drawing his attention to the task at hand. It was another slight concern. Merrick should've been back by now. But when Tiernan reached for his hunter, only silence answered, which meant Merrick was still somewhere inside the Spring Court. "Watch the borders. Watch the skies. Trust no one."

Lir and Brynn snapped to attention. Brynn bowed as Lir said, "Consider it done."

After a quick farewell, Brynn and Lir walked away, seeing to their respective duties. Neither would fail him. Neither would falter. They knew what must be done, and the safety of his Court was in the best of hands. They would risk their own lives before they allowed any harm to come to Niahvess and its people.

Ceridwen clasped his hand and then took Maeve's in her other. Her jaw was set, her red lips pressed into a hard line. She fought back the shimmer of tears but failed miserably. "Return to us. Both of you."

Maeve's smile faltered, and Tiernan curled her into his side. He bowed deeply before his twin. "On my honor."

With one hand encircling Maeve's waist, he looked down at her. "Let's go."

Right before they *faded*, Ceridwen's thoughts called out to Tiernan, and he heard her final words as the scent of magic overwhelmed them and the world of Summer blurred to nothing but a memory.

"Come home to us."

WHEN MAEVE OPENED her eyes after *fading*, a gasp fell from her lips, and she stumbled into Tiernan's strong embrace.

They stood just outside the Moors. Or rather, what remained of it.

Everything was swathed in a coat of darkness. Clouds boiled across the sky, blocking out the sun, stealing any shred of warmth. The blustery wind stung her cheeks and burned her nose, and though the bite of autumn was still weeks away, the trees were already dead. Stark and bare, the branches shuddered silently against the stiff breeze. The leaves had fallen and died ages ago. There was no lush greenery, no gorgeous flowers with overly perfumed blooms, no beauty left at all. It looked as though life itself had been sucked from the land until all that remained was a hollow husk.

The Moors were dying.

Decay lingered across what once was a vast forest. Where tall trees once sighed and swayed, offering shade and respite, now there were only deteriorating trunks and scattered leaves. Bushes had shriveled up, marked by the scourge of the Scathing. A permeating stench of rancid earth and rot clung to the air as well. Tainted ground spread as far as the eye could see. Nothing had been untouched. Nothing had been spared. There were no animals. No call of birdsong or even that of an owl. There was just a deafening stillness. So quiet, it seemed to have settled into the bones of Veterra, the silence of it all was almost grating.

Kells, it seemed, had been marked.

By the hand of death.

An emotion bubbled up in the back of Maeve's throat. She tried to swallow it down, to no avail. She gasped, sucking in short breaths of air as she absorbed what remained of the world that was once her home. Her fingers curled into her armor, and she clutched her arms around herself tightly as she struggled to get air. Her chest heaved, and her lungs refused to fill. Whatever this sensation, this grip held over her, it was crippling.

"Tiernan." She gasped his name, and his arms swiftly hauled her against him. Panic. She was having a panic attack. This used to be her home, the remnants of her former life. Her childhood was spent here. The Moors were her refuge. Her haven. And now there was nothing.

"Tier," she cried.

"Breathe, *astora*." He gripped her chin and angled her head up so she faced him. His velvety voice slid into her mind. *"Breathe. Take a breath in with me."*

Her body quaked as she struggled to inhale.

"Now let it out slowly."

Her soul shuddered.

"Again," he commanded softly, and she did what he demanded of her.

Slowly, her heartbeat steadied and instead of short, panicked breaths, she could draw air and fill her lungs completely. The ache in her heart eased. Just slightly.

"We are here to end this, Maeve." Tiernan ran his thumb along her jaw, caressing her skin. "We are here for what remains of Kells. For all of Veterra. For you."

"It's so much worse than I thought." The words tumbled from her mouth, and she wiped away the fallen tears with the back of her hand. "I wasn't expecting—"

"Neither of us were."

Maeve gazed up at him. There was a sharpness to his voice,

though it wasn't directed at her. A severe line marred his brow as he took in their surroundings. Not even he had thought it would be so bad. He slid his hand into hers and together they started walking headfirst into the fray.

The devastation of the Moors was nearly unrecognizable.

"When the Furies invaded Faeven with Carman," Maeve began, but she couldn't keep her voice from trembling, "did it..."

He nodded solemnly. "It looked much like this."

Maeve didn't want to believe it. She didn't want to believe that what happened to the Moors was because of the Furies. This was the fault of the Scathing. It had nothing to do with Balor, Tethra, and Dian. They were simply the byproducts of a spell gone horribly wrong.

As they walked further into the Moors, the sky overhead seemed to darken. The world around them grew quieter, if such a feat was even possible, so the only sound to be heard was that of their own breathing. Tiernan traced small circles onto the back of her hand with his thumb. The movement was hardly noticeable, but it offered her comfort.

She could do this.

She *would* do this.

I am the Dawnbringer. Maeve's free hand lingered over the hilt of her glowing sword. *I fear nothing.*

She froze and beside her, Tiernan's body instantly went on alert. He drew both of his swords at once, the blades blackened with a sheen of glossy violet. Nightshade.

"Well, well." A masculine voice cut through the dead quiet of the Moors. "If it isn't the fae bitch who murdered our queen in cold blood."

Maeve spun to her right and Tiernan whirled to the left.

Twelve guards, outfitted in the black and gold of Kells, rushed to surround them. They were outnumbered in bodies, but not in strength. Maeve knew she and Tiernan alone could take down the lot of them. The trouble was these were not just ordinary soldiers. They were faces she recognized. Names she knew. Men she trained with daily under Casimir's guidance.

She lifted her chin, refusing to cower. "Your queen was a monster."

The same soldier—Berne—called out, "As are you, fae bitch."

Thunder cracked, so loud it sounded like the earth had split open once more. The ground trembled beneath the might of its rumble, the force of it enough to shatter cliffs and crumble boulders. Tiernan glided forward, the tip of his sword aimed at the soldier's throat.

"Mind your tongue. Before I cut it out and feed it to your men."

The soldiers laughed. Either too foolish to believe him, or too broken to care.

Berne turned his attention back to Maeve. He was a rotund man with a red beard and ruddy skin. Lines of weariness haunted his eyes. He sneered at Maeve, daring a step closer, and Tiernan met his stride with one of his own.

"Carman was right when she said you would never learn your place. You weren't worthy of the throne then, and you aren't worthy of it now."

Tension coiled through her, pulling so tight it threatened to snap. "I'm not here to take her throne. I'm here to get rid of the plague on this land."

"A plague you brought upon us!" he fired back, and his soldiers edged closer. "You're nothing but fae filth. Didn't she used to keep you in a cage?"

Maeve's gut clenched at the memory, and the soldier jeered, his men laughing in response. He knew he'd hit his mark.

Lightning splintered across the sky, violet and raging. Thunder exploded in ear-splitting cracks as Tiernan's storm brewed and churned above them.

But the soldiers had a death wish. Berne took another step toward her, his lip curling in disgust. "I've heard stories about you, fae bitch."

Another soldier ambled forward. Coghlan was his name. He was as pale as the moon, with hair the color of night. He smiled, his teeth crooked and yellowed. She'd seen him before on the training grounds, though he looked far worse for wear now. "Word travels through the realms. I heard you were tortured, cut up with a blade so badly that not even your precious magical blood could heal you...tell me, did you scream? Did you beg for mercy?"

"Shut your mouth," she hissed.

"Is that what all those pretty little tattoos are covering?" he asked, smirking. He nodded to Tiernan. "Is he the one who tattooed you?"

Another one laughed. "I bet she spreads her legs for him, too. Filthy little whore."

Maeve didn't hesitate. She didn't think, she didn't prepare. She pulled her sword of sunlight, and as a battle scream ripped from the back of her throat, she launched herself at the offending soldiers. Tiernan was right beside her, his movements nearly a mirror image of her own. Back-to-back, they fended off the attacks of the soldiers. She would fight them and made sure they knew, right before the life left their bodies, that they died at the hand of a warrior.

Sword after sword clanged and rattled, crackling with a fissure of energy as a storm raged overhead, and she hated it. She hated she was killing men she once fought alongside. Each swipe of her sword, each cut of her blade, was like a dagger being thrust into her own chest.

She kicked and spun, eliminating one opponent, ready to strike down another, when a fiery streak of heat caught the back of her thigh. It was a direct hit, and she gasped as the blade ripped into her flesh. She fell hard, hands slamming into the dirt of the barren forest floor. She rolled over and through the haze of battle, she saw Berne looming over her, his sword poised to pierce her heart.

The toe of his boot slammed into the side of her face, shattering her cheek. Blood spurted from her mouth and she screamed. Pain burst from the back of her skull, splintering before her eyes until she saw tiny black stars. From somewhere, she heard Tiernan roar her name. Berne heaved his sword back, ready for the killing blow, but then the ground erupted beneath her. Shadows of darkness engulfed them all. Cold stole into her bones and froze her heart. Through the terror of screams filling the air, she heard three distinct voices laugh with the promise of death.

The Furies had arrived.

Chapter Thirty-Three

Tiernan was blown back by the explosion of magic.

"Maeve!" he shouted her name over the screams. The last thing he saw was her being struck down by that fucking soldier, but then darkness descended upon them, destruction ripped through the chaos of battle, and death lingered in the wake of it all.

Darkness. Balor.

Destruction. Tethra.

Death. Dian.

The intense shroud of night cleaved, and Tiernan witnessed the Furies ravage the soldiers, tearing them limb from limb, unleashing the might of their wrath upon those who dared to harm Maeve. His gaze stole across the ground, finding her, mouth pouring blood, gaping up in terror as Balor ripped the spine from the soldier who kicked her in the face. Horror and dirt were streaked across her features, and he bolted to her side. With one hand, he hauled her to her feet and clutched her to him.

"Don't look," he murmured, holding the back of her head firm and keeping her face buried against his chest.

She may have made a noise in response, but he couldn't be sure, and he didn't care because she was safe in his arms. And by the gods, he would die before he allowed her to see the havoc the Furies wreaked upon the soldiers of Kells.

Balor, the darkest night.

Tethra, the ending ruination.

Dian, the hand of death.

The screams were the worst. It was a sound unlike anything Tiernan had ever heard. He'd seen the Furies at the full extent of their capabilities, but this...the noise these mortals made...it was as though their very souls were being flayed open. It unnerved him down to his core. Then there was silence, worse even than when they first arrived at the Moors. The utter quiet was the sort he'd only ever experienced on the battlefield after tremendous loss, when the vultures circled overhead and the only sound heard was the trudging slop of footfalls from those sent out to collect the dead.

But no one would come for these men.

Hostility sank its claws into Tiernan's back and he stiffened, his arms tightening around Maeve, as he came face to face with the Furies. He stared into the hollow faces of the men who were no longer the same ones who'd destroyed his world. They were how he remembered them, yet different. Their bodies were made of shadows, cloaking them completely. They hovered when they moved, as though their feet never touched the ground. But it was their faces that would etch and burn themselves into his nightmares for many moons to come.

Their faces were sunken, almost skeletal, with eyes that burned like embers of a banked fire. Veins of the same glowing color defined what little remained of their flesh and each of their foreheads bore the mark of a different rune representing their paths. Darkness. Destruction. Death.

Dian drifted forward, his blazing eyes zeroing in on Tiernan. "Unhand her."

Tiernan shoved Maeve behind him. "Never."

"No, don't! He's with me." Maeve's voice cracked and when he caught sight of her face, the fire of vengeance ignited inside him. Though the wound to the back of her thigh was already healing, her face was still brutally bruised and discolored as her cheek bones mended themselves while her bottom lip was crusted with dried blood. Her hand wrapped around his arm, gripping him, holding onto him like he was the only one who wouldn't let her fall.

She trembled when she said, "That is to say, the High King of Summer is mine."

The Furies shared a look and together they knelt before her.

"Maeve Ruhdneah, High Princess of the Autumn Court. Keeper of the *anam ó Danua*. Dawnbringer." This from Balor, whose fiery gaze slid to Tethra.

"As we said once before, we answer only to you." When Tethra spoke, even what remained of the trees trembled in fear. "But we will defend you...and yours."

Silence enveloped them once more, and Tiernan found himself too stunned to speak. Not that he didn't believe Maeve when she said the Furies would answer her call, he'd known even then she spoke true, but he had to admit, he hadn't expected the depth of their vow.

After all, he was the reason they'd been banished from Faeven through death. He was the one who'd ventured to Maghmell, the eternal paradise, and pleaded to the goddess Danua for her assistance in defeating them and Carman. He was the one who was responsible for their ultimate demise.

To hear them agree to protect him as they would Maeve was unsettling.

She took a small step toward them, and it took all of Tiernan's willpower not to haul her back to his side.

She raised her bloodied chin, wincing as she spoke. "I need your assistance."

They rose before her.

"As I'm sure you've heard, Parisa is threatening all of Faeven. Her army of dark fae continues to grow." Her shoulders rolled back, and she was incandescent. "I know while you were under Carman's control, you were commanded to ruin the Four Courts. I would ask you to stand with me and defend the realm you once sought to destroy against a more sinister threat."

Tiernan bit the inside of his cheek to keep from smiling. He was so fucking impressed by her. Maeve was the epitome of a queen.

She was born to rule.

Balor crossed a fisted hand over his chest and his brothers followed suit. "We will fight for you and all that you wish to protect, Your Grace."

Maeve blinked. "I'm not—"

"You are." Tiernan cupped her elbow, offering her his support.

"We've heard the rumors of your greatness." Dian bowed. "Of how you single-handedly destroyed the Hagla. How you fought for those who were not your own."

Balor spread his shadowy arms wide. "Such worthiness could only ever be found in a true faerie queen."

Tethra nodded. "We pledge our lives unto you, *moh Rienna*."

My queen.

If only Tiernan could find the strength to utter such words in her presence.

Maeve looked over at him then, uncertainty warring across her fractured features. He took her hand, encouraging her to accept their oath.

With lips pressed together, she faced the Furies without fear. "I am honored to be your queen. But before we return to Faeven, there is another task at hand."

The Furies watched her. They did not speak. They did not argue. They simply awaited their orders with silent patience.

"First, we must go to Kells." Maeve lifted her eyes, and he knew she sought Kells in the distance or what remained of the forsaken city. "I need to find Saoirse Doran."

Balor pointed in the same direction as her line of sight. "The silver-haired warrior resides within what's left of the castle upon the Cliffs of Morrigan, Your Grace."

329

Maeve nodded once. "And then we must go into the Scathing." Hardened determination gripped her, and any shred of warmth faded away. "And defeat the source of power there."

The source of power.

Fearghal.

The Furies bowed at once. "We are yours to command, Your Grace."

Maeve captured Tiernan's hand with her own and linked their fingers together. "To Kells?"

He pressed a kiss to each of her knuckles. "To Kells."

TIERNAN *FADED* Maeve and himself onto a balustrade that jutted over the Cliffs of Morrigan. Behind them stood the castle that once belonged to Carman. It was quite possibly the only structure still in one piece in the whole of Kells. Its towers remained intact, as did all its windows and stone walls, but as far as he could tell, there were no signs of life.

Wind howled in from off the coast, biting through his layers and carrying with it the scent of the sea. He pulled Maeve closer to warm her. The Furies appeared a moment later, never touching the ground, their shadowy bodies hovering as though they lingered between this world and the next. Tiernan's gaze stole across the city below them. From his vantage point, he saw the port and everything below, everything that had once been thriving and flourishing before the assault of the Scathing.

The absolute destruction of Kells was far greater than Tiernan could have imagined. Devastation was everywhere. What he supposed was once the city's center was now a crumbling pile of ash and ruin. Buildings were burned down to cinders, footpaths were blackened, and a light mist hung from a blanket of low-lying clouds, covering the fallen city in shades of gray.

Maeve's hand, tucked into his own, tightened in his grip. She stared down at the roughened stone flooring of the balustrade, and as he watched her, he knew. Her skin had lost some of its pallor and her bottom lip trembled, but he knew this was the place where she killed Carman. This was where she'd brought the Furies back and where blood had been spilled. This was where Casimir had stolen her away to the Spring Court.

He wanted to offer her encouragement. Strength. Anything he could possibly give her. Yet words failed him. Instead, there was only more of the dreadful, empty silence of a place marked by death. No sound could be heard, save for the rush of wind whistling off the Gaelsong Sea and the thrashing of angry waves against the rugged shoreline.

The hairs along the back of Tiernan's neck prickled.

An otherworldly sensation thickened the air. Beside him, Maeve stiffened.

The Furies sensed it as well. Their fiery gazes prowled the castle and the derelict city below.

"Dark magic," Balor murmured, inhaling deeply.

"Darker than that. Vile." Dian shook his head, his eyes narrowing. "Ruthless and cold."

He was right. The magic brought here by either the Scathing or by Fearghal himself was something straight out of a nightmare, promising nothing but terror.

"Come on." Tiernan nodded toward the massive archway of obsidian stone. "Let's go see if we can find her."

"The throne room." Lines pinched around Maeve's bloodied mouth. "If Saoirse is anywhere, she'll be there."

Tiernan led the way, and the Furies followed them into Carman's former throne room. Surprisingly enough, it looked to be in perfect condition. The floors were gleaming bronze and stole the dwindling light from the few sconces that were lit. A throne with three spears pointing up to the sky stood empty, abandoned, and the number of lifelike statues carved from ivory set his nerves on edge.

Tethra glided forward. He scooped up a rock and tossed it at the throne, not even caring when it shattered into dozens of tiny pieces that skittered in every direction.

In the distance, the slamming of doors crashed through the solitude of the castle.

"On your guard," Tiernan murmured, withdrawing his weapons.

The Furies surrounded Maeve, each of them taking up a position, protecting her from all angles.

Footfalls sounded against the solid flooring, growing louder with each passing second. Murmurs echoed down the hall just beyond the throne room and a rise of voices reverberated off the walls with alarm, the sounds of those readying for battle. A moment later, the carved wooden doors of the throne room burst open, and three soldiers barreled into the space, armed with their swords drawn.

One soldier had hair the color of moonlight.

"Drop your—" The silver-haired warrior faltered, her eyes widening. Her breath expelled from her in a rush. "Maeve."

"Saoirse?" Maeve darted out from between the barricade of Furies and sprinted across the throne room, her boots sounding in time to the rapid pace of Tiernan's heart.

Balor made to chase after her, but Tiernan's arm shot out, holding him back. "Leave her."

"Saoirse!" Her voice broke.

"Maeve!" Saoirse rushed forward, running into Maeve's open arms. The two beauties crashed into one another, falling into an embrace so strong, it brought them both to their knees, each one holding the other as though nothing, not the skies nor the seas, could ever tear them apart again.

MAEVE'S HEART NEARLY BURST.

Saoirse was alive. She was flesh and blood. Still as strong as ever. Tears stung at the corner of her eyes, but she blinked them away, willing herself not to cry.

Saoirse pulled back, grabbing both of Maeve's hands and holding them in her own. A withering pink dahlia was tucked behind her ear. "I told Merrick to keep you far away from here."

"You know how I feel about being told what to do." She bent her head over their joined hands and kissed the top of her friend's hands.

A broken smile fractured Saoirse's laugh. "But, how? And why?" Her sapphire gaze slid to Tiernan and the Furies, her brows raised in question. She held Maeve back at arm's length, taking in the handful of tattoos that were visible beneath her arm. Most notably the one in the shape of a rose on her battered cheek. "What's happened since you've been in Faeven? And why are you bleeding?"

"There will be time to explain all that later." Maeve rose, bringing Saoirse to her feet. "We're here to destroy the Scathing."

"It's too dangerous." She shook her head and wisps fell free from her silver braid, framing her face. "Many have entered and none have returned. I don't know what sort of evil dwells there, but it's a place not even the light of the sun can reach."

Determination fired through Maeve, hot and fast, as she remembered the numbing burn of Fearghal's blade while he carved her up in the dungeon of Suvarese. "I do. I know the evil that lurks beneath its surface."

Saoirse blinked, mouth parting slightly. "And you know how to defeat it?"

"Yes." Maeve tossed a glance over her shoulder at Tiernan. He nodded in support, her eternal champion. "And I'm not leaving here until I do."

"Alright." She looked back at her own soldiers, faces Maeve didn't recognize, and adjusted the strap of daggers hanging from her waist. "When do we leave?"

"Now." Tiernan's low timbre echoed up into the domed ceiling. "The sooner the better."

Saoirse lobbed her sword over one shoulder, ever casual about war. "Very well." She faced her soldiers. "No one leaves the castle until I return. And in case I don't...Finnigan, I leave you in charge."

The soldier righted himself to attention and saluted Saoirse. "Understood, Captain Doran."

Maeve jabbed her friend lightly in the ribs. "Captain now, is it?"

She winked. "Somebody had to take over since Captain Vawda abandoned his post." Her brow furrowed, and Maeve blanched at the mention of Casimir's former title. "Where is he, anyway?"

"You and I have a lot of catching up to do."

There was no way to ignore the wrath emanating from Tiernan, but Maeve would tell Saoirse all that she endured another time. Her past was a burning memory in the back of her mind, one she didn't care to dwell on too often. Especially not right now. So instead, she linked her arm through Saoirse's, and they started down one of the vaulted corridors that would lead them to the Ridge.

Together they headed toward the stone steps with Tiernan and the Furies following closely behind. Where once moss and emerald blades of grass crawled along the roughened stone, there were now only smears of grime and ash. The closer they drew to the Scathing, the more the air seemed to throb, ripe and dense with malicious intent. The quiet that dwelled within the Moors was even worse here, and though Maeve attempted to keep herself composed, her breathing grew shallow. Life had been snatched from the very earth, a demise so great it left Maeve's skin crawling with a sense of impending doom. Of dread.

"What happened...after?" Her whisper sounded harsh against the onslaught of complete nothingness.

Saoirse's eyes darkened to the shade of the deepest part of the sea. "When Carman fell to your blade, your friends back there murdered anyone who dared to speak ill of you or highly of her. Most of the city was evacuated beforehand, to Cantata, and those who stayed behind took up arms against the Scathing."

Maeve wasn't sure she heard correctly. She shook her head and her gaze slid to Saoirse. "Citizens stayed behind to fight?"

"Kells is their home." She looked straight ahead to the ruins, refusing to make eye contact. "Just as much as it is mine."

There was something in her tone, about the way she spoke of Kells, and it gouged out a part of Maeve's heart. It wouldn't be easy to convince Saoirse to return to Faeven with her, to beg her not to stay in this desolate place. She'd assumed Saoirse would want to come with her, that she would have no qualms about abandoning Kells and leaving the fallen city behind. But now, she wasn't so sure. If Saoirse didn't want to leave, she wouldn't, and there would be nothing Maeve could say or do that would be enough to change her mind. As much as it hurt to admit, she would understand her friend's reasoning. Because not so long ago, she felt the same way.

Defeated, her shoulders fell. "I should've done more."

Tiernan was by her side a second later. "You did enough."

"The High King is right, my lady." Saoirse looked up at him, nodding firmly. "You did all you could do. Any of us would've done the same if we'd found ourselves in your situation."

A situation in which an evil sorceress-queen wanted to kill her.

Their reassurances only alleviated a small amount of the remorse she held inside of her. "I feel like I abandoned my home."

"You may not remember, but I do." Saoirse's voice was soft. "I remember vividly how quickly the soldiers of Kells turned their back on you when they learned you were fae. If you had stayed behind, even with your heart of pure gold, they would've killed you. And all of it would've stemmed from the hatred ingrained in them since their birth."

She remembered, too. The way they shoved her down. The looks of disgust that rippled across their stern features. She remembered all of it. She'd seen that same loathing from the soldiers they killed in the Moors.

Fae bitch.

Maeve gritted her teeth together. She wouldn't soon forget that soldier's boot slamming into the side of her still-tender face. "I suppose you're right."

"Of course I'm right." Saoirse gave her a knowing smile, then stumbled to a stop.

Maeve held her breath.

Malevolence slithered through the air. Menacing and chilling all at once.

"My lady." Saoirse nodded then, looking at Tiernan. "Your Grace." She gestured to a gaping hole in the ground, a wide chasm that looked like it had ripped through the earth with a mouthful of blades for teeth. Steps of rot descended into a barren cavern where it was so dark, not even a shred of light could penetrate the blackness of night glaring back at them. "Welcome to the Scathing."

Chapter Thirty-Four

Although Tiernan had been in worse places before, he shuddered when they entered the Scathing.

He could barely see two paces in front of him, so all-encompassing was the darkness. Next to him, Maeve lifted her sword of sunlight, casting a burning glow so they could see where they were walking. Bitter cold clung to his skin like a cloak of ice and his breath swirled up before him in puffs of mist. The air was leached of any warmth, yet it was heavy with the pulse of dark magic. It was dank and unsettling. A foul stench greeted them, reeking of excrement, urine, and sweat.

Evil lived here.

"Stay close," he murmured, drawing up to Maeve's side. Dian took the lead into the portal, with Tethra and Balor bringing up the rear. Saoirse was to his left, her sword drawn and at the ready.

"This place is cursed." Tethra's voice rumbled from behind him.

Saoirse's breath floated in front of her. "There's rumors it thrives on fear."

"Much like the Hagla," Balor said. "Even I can feel its deathlike grip upon my shadows."

"Yes," Tiernan agreed.

This place was all too similar to the dark fae known for preying on terror and nightmares. But he couldn't understand how. He didn't know how Parisa had become so powerful. The god Aed had stripped her magic from her after she murdered her mother, High Queen Brigid, yet whatever she dabbled in now must be dangerously strong.

Maeve paused, raising her sword higher. "It looks like someone... lives here."

Tiernan glanced around their surroundings. She was right. There was a thatch of hay that resembled a bed, along with a pile of books covered in grime and dust. Beyond that were two passageways, each one branching off in a different direction.

Maeve peered down at the books. "What do you think—"

Dian gripped her shoulder, and she spun to face him. He pressed a finger to his mouth, urging her to be quiet, then tapped his ear.

Tiernan strained to listen. At first, there was nothing. Then he caught the faintest sound of whimpering. Without speaking, he motioned all of them forward, to the passage on the left, following the muffled sounds of crying.

The passage opened into a vast room with no light, and the ceiling was composed of dirt and stone. Metal bars protruded from the ground up to the earthen cave above them. Broken sobs and pleas sounded in his ears, echoing all around them.

Saoirse gripped Maeve's hand "Are these—"

"Cages," she finished for her and crept over to the one nearest her.

There were seven cells altogether, each one crammed full of bodies. Faces peered up at her, sunken eyes squinted against the abrupt light source. Filth matted their hair, cuts and bruises marred their ashen skin, and their cries grew frantic as malnourished limbs jutted out from between the bars, desperate for release.

"Help us!"

"Gods save us, please!"

The frenzied voices of the innocent keened and begged for freedom.

Maeve knelt before one of them, whispering promises she couldn't keep. "Tiernan." She glanced over her shoulder back at him, hoisting her sword to spread the light between them. "They're mortal."

"Right you are, High Princess." An ominous voice reverberated through the dungeon and the humans trapped inside the cells wailed.

The color drained from Maeve's face as she shot to her feet.

Tiernan's blood ran cold, then pumped full of fury. The destruction swirling inside him roared to life.

Fearghal.

"On your guard!" he shouted, withdrawing both swords. He snagged Maeve's arm, yanking her to him. Tethra and Balor swarmed around them, and Dian took up Saoirse's opposite side.

Menacing laughter bounced off the walls. Fearghal's voice assaulted them from every direction. Though Maeve's sword shone brighter than the dawn, the darkness lashed against it, attempting to snuff it out completely. She raised her arm in a slashing arc, cutting through the pitch threatening to engulf them. Sparks exploded through the underground room, illuminating it in its entirety. But Fearghal was nowhere to be seen.

"It's interesting, is it not?" His voice slithered through the space and climbed the damp walls. "How a meek and nearly useless creature can become a monster."

Maeve spun, trying to find the source of his voice. "What are you talking about?"

"Don't these *mortals* look familiar?" Fearghal crooned. "They are the same as the dark fae you destroyed the night the Scathing ripped through Kells."

"No." Maeve edged closer to one of the cells, eyeing the humans who clawed over one another in despair and anguish. She shook her head. "No, it can't be true."

Another unpleasant chuckle scraped throughout the chamber like nails being dragged down a stone wall. "Allow me to demonstrate."

The scent of magic permeated the air. The once familiar smell of orange blossom and cedarwood was polluted, rancid, suffocating them with the stench of wilted flowers and rotten wood.

Tiernan lurched forward and grabbed Maeve, hauling her away from the cages as the mortals were glamoured and transformed into beings of the night. They howled, their panicked cries shifting into angered shrieks. Their bones cracked, their jaws dislocated, their limbs elongated. Before his eyes, the humans morphed into dark fae. Dozens of them bore sharpened teeth like daggers and hollowed, glowing pits for eyes. They became vicious. Rabid. Hungry for blood. Some of them grew nails the length of a sword, others climbed up the walls and sank their pointed teeth into the metal bars, gnawing at their enclosure the way a pack animal might devour its prey.

"Impossible," Maeve breathed, her eyes widening in horror.

"Nothing is impossible," Fearghal scoffed, "with the right kind of magic."

Saoirse spat, disgusted. "You sick fuck."

Another smug laugh sounded, this one closer than the last. "I like your mouth, pretty warrior. Perhaps when all this is over, I'll claim it with my own."

Maeve swung violently, and her sword slashed through nothing but air.

"Come now, Maeve." Anticipation dripped from Fearghal's words. "I believe you owe me a dance."

At once, the bars barricading the cell doors vanished, and the dark fae descended upon them.

340

"THEY'RE ONLY MORTALS!" Maeve screamed even as three attacked her head on. She blocked two and kicked the other, refusing to strike them down. "Don't hurt them!"

A flash of silver darted before her eyes and Saoirse rolled to the ground before jumping back to her feet.

"If we don't kill them," she shouted in return, using her sword to fend two of them off, "they'll kill us."

Agony ripped her heart in half. They were innocents. Captives stolen against their will only to be used as weapons in a war that was not their own.

"Orders, *moh Rienna!*" Tethra bellowed from somewhere off to her right.

Maeve reared back, slamming her elbow into one of the creatures, then shoving another to the ground. She stole a fleeting glance at Tiernan.

The look in his eyes told her there was no other way.

"Make it swift!" she cried out. "Do not make them suffer but kill them. Kill them all!"

Darkness swarmed them, attempting to smother the burning light of her sword. She wielded it with one hand and yanked her Aurastone from its sheath, lashing out at the creature ambling toward her, snapping its jaw. She pierced its chest with her dagger, and the dark fae turned to dust, vanishing without a trace.

Her gut clenched. These were not wicked fae creatures under Parisa's rule. These were mortal souls. The lives of innocents. And she was *destroying* them. They would never know a life after this, there would be no eternal paradise awaiting them in Maghmell, no uncertainty of the in between in the Ether. There was nothing left for them. They would simply cease to exist.

All around her, the roar of the Furies clashed with the screams of their victims. Human screams. The sound of it was enough to splinter her heart. A smaller creature, with eyes of murky ink and rows of dagger-like tiny teeth, lunged for her throat. This one was a child. Maeve thrust her Aurastone directly into its heart, and a harrowing cry tore from her lips. Her vision swam and she blinked the tears away, letting them slide down her cheeks as she ducked low, avoiding a set of claws taking aim for her chest.

Flashes of silver stole across her vision. Bolts of violet unraveled like violent ribbons, extinguishing every dark fae in their wake. And still they continued to come. It was as though Fearghal had a never-ending supply of mortal captives in his arsenal. All around her, the fighting raged. She stabbed and parried, sliced and killed, and each life she took left a smear of remorse upon her heart.

"Fight me!" she screamed, knowing Fearghal could hear her. "Show yourself, you bastard!"

The horde of darkness pressed into them, cornering her, Tiernan, Saoirse, and even the Furies, into a wall. There was no way out.

Fearghal's heinous laughter caused the ceiling to shudder and the ground to quake. "Not until you kill every one of these precious mortals you so foolishly care for, Maeve."

Blinding rage pulsed through her. No more. She would endure no more. Her magic swam inside her, scraping and raking, frenzied and wild. When she released her wrath upon this place, the world would know her name.

"Back!" She stormed forward, shoving past Tiernan and Balor when they attempted to protect her, to shield her from the onslaught of dark fae. "Stand back!" she commanded, her voice laced with the promise of death.

Tiernan yanked Saoirse backward, dragging her out of the way. The Furies fell back behind Maeve.

"Goddess above," Maeve whispered into the fray, "forgive me."

Power filled her, overwhelmed her. She called to the shadows of darkness swirling around them, beckoned to them, twisted them until they took the shape of a thousand blades. The darkness belonged to her. She owned it. Controlled it. Magic funneled through her as she imbued the monster of night with its own life force. Tendrils of shade crawled along the walls and floors, slithering like venomous snakes ready to strike. The shadow blades she created positioned themselves like an army, each tip an extension of her hand, and the dark fae shrank back.

From behind her, Saoirse breathed, "Seven hells."

Maeve's blood thrummed. Magic throbbed. She raised her chin, ever defiant. "Attack."

At once, the darkness obeyed her command, piercing the dark fae in one vicious assault. Screams exploded, echoing up into the furthest reaches of the cavern. She took them all, she killed them all. In less time than it took to breathe, she vanquished a hundred lives, she devastated a hundred souls. A cloud of dust bloomed and the silence that followed left her skin pebbled in goosebumps.

She released her magic and her sword of sunlight burst brighter than ever, vanquishing the night.

The soft click of boots against stone drew her gaze up to the far end of the dungeon.

"Well done." Fearghal strolled forward, and Maeve's heart stilled inside the constricted wall of her chest.

His copper hair fell to his shoulders now, a stark contrast to the blackened veins running up and down his body. One of his horns was missing, she realized, the area on top of his head where it should've been was charred, like it had been burned off. Likely one of Parisa's punishments.

His eyes locked onto her and with each step he took, memories of the cell she'd been locked into deep beneath the underground of the Spring Court slammed into her mind. The metallic scent of her blood lingering in the air. The way his hot breath had coated her skin right before he sculpted her body with his blade dipped in nightshade. The way he smiled when his dagger scored under her breast and around her nipple.

Maeve's breath lodged somewhere deep inside her chest. She would not go back there; she would not return to that seventh circle of hell. He tried to break her once before, and he would not be given the same opportunity again.

Fearghal withdrew his blade, the same one he'd used to torture her. "I didn't think you had it in you, High Princess."

"That's High Queen to you," she corrected coolly, sheathing her Aurastone and twirling her sword of sunlight. Sparks flickered from its edge, skittering and bouncing off the stone walls surrounding them.

From her left, Dian stepped forward, his hollow face carved with malice.

"No," Maeve hissed and flung her arm out, halting him. "He's mine." She looked back at the Furies, at the trio who would not only kill Fearghal if she asked, but who would ensure he suffered a gruesome and painful end. "Only when my death is imminent, then you may intervene. But not a moment sooner."

They bowed, their fiery eyes never leaving the trooping fae who sauntered her direction.

"Don't forget, Your Grace," said Tethra. "Fearghal is a Puca."

A Puca, meaning he could shape shift at any moment, and she would have to be prepared. She nodded, lifting her sword, when Tiernan appeared by her side.

He grabbed her chin, and his twilight eyes reflected an emotion she'd never seen before.

"You were born to rule, it's in your heart." She faltered and his thumb grazed her bottom lip. "It's in your soul. And you show mercy to *no one.*"

Tiernan released her and she nodded sharply, indebted to this male who somehow saw the truth of her beneath all the layers of misdeeds and regret. This male who held her heart in the palm of his hand, willing it to beat. She sucked in a breath of foul air and whipped around to face Fearghal. She stalked toward him, predator to prey.

"Bedding the High King of Summer now, are we?" Fearghal drawled and his lascivious gaze raked her up and down.

She smiled cruelly. "Who I fuck is none of your concern."

"My, my. Such language." He planted a hand over his heart in feigned astonishment. "Though I wonder what Rowan would think about your current affair. That is, of course, if he was still alive."

Maeve ground her teeth together until her temples ached. She refused to falter, and she would not have Rowan used against her. "If you ever speak his name again, I'll cut you open from your throat to your cock, then hang you off the Cliffs of Morrigan by your intestines."

Fearghal's grin stretched across a row of sharp teeth. "I rather like you when you're feisty."

Maeve launched herself at him, and their swords met in a deafening crash of power. It was nothing more than a dance, just as he'd requested. Except this time, her partner was her enemy. She recalled all those grueling days spent on the training field with Casimir, all the positions he'd drilled into her, until her weapon was merely an extension of her body. She cut across the room like she walked on air, feigning and attacking, driving him back with each clang of their swords. But Fearghal was no fool. He was not some worthless soldier made to do Parisa's bidding. He was highly trained, and his skill matched her every move.

Her muscles burned from exertion. Her body ached and beads of sweat slid down her neck and back. Blood rushed through her veins, and her heart raced, emboldened by the surge of fury coursing through her.

She slammed into him again, her breath hitching, catching the gleam of nightshade on his blade. He laughed, shoving her back and swinging his sword down, barely missing her neck.

"You won't get away this time, Princess." He attacked again and she stumbled backward.

"Queen," she spat.

He swung once more and she ducked, the threat of his sword cutting through the air above her head. "When you're back in Spring's dungeon, and locked away with no one to save you, I will not be so kind. I will ruin your body in every way possible, and I will fuck you so hard, you'll beg for my blade instead."

Thunder cracked, ear-splitting, and Tiernan plunged into the fray, vehemence roiling around him like a vengeful storm.

"No!" Maeve spun on her heel to force him back, realizing her mistake all too late.

Fearghal kicked one leg out, sweeping her feet out from under her. She landed hard on the freezing ground and pain streaked up her spine, the ache deep in her bones. He hovered above her, plunging his sword downward, a feral smile stretched across his lips.

But his blade never met its mark.

Her bubble, her shimmering shield of protection, encased her. Saved her.

Anger boiled on his face, contorting his cruel features. "Cheater." He spewed and spittle clung to his chin.

"You've cheated your whole life, Fearghal." Maeve rolled away from him and popped up, gripping her sword with both hands. "And despite your best efforts, you're still just someone else's bitch."

Rage exploded from him in dense waves. His chest heaved, his breathing uneven. He was angry. Furious. Such a turbulent emotion only led to one thing.

Mistakes.

"How does it feel to be second best?" she taunted, circling around him, igniting the ill-tempered wrath building inside him. "How does it feel to know that Parisa values my brother more than she does you?"

"Shut your mouth, you bitch," he snarled and dove for her, tackling her to the ground. Her sword of sunlight slipped from her grip against the strength of the blow, clattering onto the stone floor. Maeve strained for it, reaching with her left hand, but the tips of her fingers barely grazed its hilt.

Fearghal laughed, but it was rough and cruel. He held her to the ground, snaring both of her arms and pinning them above her head with one hand. She caught the flicker of nightshade in the dim light as he pressed the flattened length of his blade beneath her chin, tilting her face up to him.

"Maeve..." Tiernan's panicked voice sounded in her mind.

She gritted her teeth. *"Not yet."*

"It will be such a *pleasure* when I carve you up again." Fearghal's sick threat loomed above her and his hideous grin widened. "Except this time, your scars won't be so..." He traced the tip of his cold dagger around one of her tattoos. "Pretty."

Maeve strained against him, sinking her teeth into her bottom lip. Fearghal tracked the movement with his glowing eyes.

Typical fucking male.

"Perhaps I shall invite the High King to watch when I take you," he murmured softly, bringing his grotesquely hot mouth by her ear. "Do you think he'd like that?"

Maeve laughed. Harsh. "Not a chance."

She jerked upward, slamming her forehead into the bridge of his nose. Blood sputtered and he swore, instantly covering his face with his hands. Maeve rammed her elbow into his throat, so he choked. Wheezed. Throwing him off her, she rolled away, snatching her sword of sunlight from off the ground. She clambered away, bracing herself for his attack, when a low growl tore from between his lips and the world shifted. A glamour. He was going to shape shift. No chance in hell.

Fearghal threw his arms out, preparing to morph into whatever animal he chose. Black mangy fur coated his skin, his eyes took on a hellish gleam. Right as his jaws snapped, lunging for her throat, Maeve heaved her sword and plunged it directly into his heart.

He screamed, a convoluted howl, then fell to his knees.

Maeve attacked, throwing herself on him and tackling him to the ground. Straddling him, she tossed her sword aside and pulled out her Aurastone, driving it into him again and again.

He thrashed. Jerked. Twitched. The pungent scent of blood filled her nostrils as it pooled around his lifeless body, staining the stone beneath him. But the screaming didn't stop. It continued until her throat was raw, until her tears dried to salt on her cheeks, until his chest was nothing but a pulpy mess of flesh beneath her revenge.

"Maeve."

Somewhere in the back of her mind, a soothing baritone whispered her name. But she was too far gone to stop. She wouldn't quit until there was nothing left. Until Fearghal was unrecognizable. Until she ended him completely.

"Enough, *astora*."

She gasped, her Aurastone still clutched in her hand, as two strong hands hauled her up and away from the lifeless body sprawled on the ground. The earth surrounding them quaked, crumbling from the cavernous ceiling above.

"Out!" Tiernan yelled. "Everyone out!"

Maeve slumped against the hardened wall of his chest, unable to stop the broken sob ripping from her heart as he carried her out of the darkness.

Chapter Thirty-Five

Maeve sat on the blackened earth with her back pressed firmly against Tiernan's chest, his arms locked tightly around her. His knees were propped up on either side of her while he rested against the crumbling remains of a building.

Her body had not yet stopped trembling.

Saoirse was crouched in front of her, wiping the splatters of Fearghal's blood from her face with a piece of fabric she'd torn from her blouse.

The Furies kept watch. Though sunken in and scarcely human, the look of awe and something that could've been mistaken for concern haunted the planes of their faces.

Tethra looked upon Maeve, then glanced over at his brothers. "Remind me to never piss her off."

His comment elicited no response from his queen.

She simply sat there, cradled in Tiernan's arms, unmoving. Her mind was numb, lost to the terrors of what she'd just done. Lost to the agony of her past, of all that was taken from her. Of all she'd destroyed.

Those mortals within the Scathing...in a matter of seconds, she'd erased their very souls from existence. Was that all she was now? Magic, and power, and death? Was this to be her entire existence? Just defeat the dark fae, kill Parisa, then become an empty husk of a soul with no purpose unless someone needed to be murdered?

She shuddered in Tiernan's hold. His arms enveloped her, holding her close. She was meant for more, destined for more. But this magic, this power she wielded, wasn't enough to heal the broken parts inside of her and she wondered if she would ever truly be whole again.

"You are not broken, astora." Tiernan's rumbling voice slid into her thoughts, and she welcomed him. *"You must first collect all the pieces of you—new and old. Shards of who you were, what you lost. Your childhood. Your humanity. Friends. Then focus on the fragments of who you are now, what you've gained. Magic. A family."* He bent down so his mouth lightly brushed the tip of her pointed ear. *"Someone who would destroy the world for you."*

Then he whispered, "You are not broken. You are the pieces of everything good and beautiful in this world. You've just yet to see it."

"Thank you." Maeve sighed. Somehow, he always knew exactly what to say. He always managed to make her feel worthy. To make her feel...loved.

The word played through her mind, tugged on her heart. He pressed a faint kiss to her temple and her soul settled.

Saoirse smoothed Maeve's hair back from her face and met her gaze. "What happened to you when you were taken back to Faeven?"

Maeve stiffened, her breath leaving her on a harsh exhale. Behind her, Tiernan rubbed his hand along her back in slow, comforting circles. He was her solace. Her peace. With his silent encouragement, Maeve told Saoirse everything. She told her of Casimir's betrayal, of how she was brought to Parisa's dungeon and tortured because she refused to comply, because she refused to be used as a weapon against the Four Courts.

"A weapon?" Her blue eyes widened. "Why would you be used as a weapon?"

"Because I'm the *anam ó Danua*. My mother was Fianna, the High Queen of Autumn. After Danua took the soul away from Parisa, she gifted it to Fianna instead. Upon discovering she was pregnant, Fianna fled to the human lands to save me from Carman's wrath." Maeve shifted, pulling her knees to her chest. "Casimir found me instead."

Saoirse blinked, pieces of the past slowly clicking into place like a puzzle. "But why? Why did Casimir bring you to Parisa instead of the Summer Court?"

Tiernan laughed but it was harsh. "Because he was a fool. He made the mistake of falling in love with Parisa long before she was something awful. Something wicked. In his desperation, he bound his soul to Carman, after the sorceress promised to help save Parisa from the corruption the greed of power bestowed upon her."

"The bastard." She scrubbed her hands over her face, smearing the grime plastered there. "But if Casimir brought Maeve to the Spring Court, then how did she escape? Who freed her?"

"In the end, it was Casimir who rescued me." Maeve looked to the sky, half expecting to see a drakon circling overhead. "I don't think he ever imagined Parisa would go so far as to have me brutalized by Fearghal. I think he lives with that regret."

Saoirse nodded toward Maeve. "The tattoos?"

"They cover my scars," she confirmed, and Saoirse's face blanched, then turned red with anger.

She dropped onto her knees, shaking her head, and squeezing her eyes shut. "And what of Rowan? What happened to him?"

Maeve ducked her head, fiddled with the hem of her leggings. "He sacrificed himself to save me."

"Seven hells, he didn't tell me." Saoirse murmured. Maeve looked up and the face of the silver-haired warrior almost fractured. "Merrick didn't tell me."

Maeve pressed her lips into a thin line, understanding. "He wouldn't have wanted you to worry."

Saoirse tilted her face up to the sky, to where the cloak of eternal gray had begun to fade, to where shreds of sunlight slipped through the mass of clouds. "I wish I'd known."

Behind her, Tiernan adjusted his hold, letting his hands coast up and down her arms. "It would've made no difference, only put another life at risk. And you, Saoirse Doran, are not immortal. If anything happened to you, Maeve would never forgive me."

"He's right." Maeve offered her friend the smallest of smiles. Then she eased up, her gaze trailing over the ground they sat upon.

The gaping chasm of the Scathing had closed and was nothing more than a barren landscape. The earth was still covered in decay and rot. It stretched for miles. To the port. To the Moors. With the Scathing gone, Kells was no longer threatened. It was just a wasteland.

She gestured vaguely to their desolate surroundings. "Why does Kells still look like this?"

Balor shifted forward, bending down to greet his queen at eye level. "Dark magic is not always easy to purge, Your Grace."

"He speaks the truth." Tiernan stood slowly, helping Maeve to her feet, keeping one arm firmly wrapped around her waist. "The goddess Danua is the only reason the Four Courts stand as they do today. She restored all of it, she poured her soul into Faeven."

"Her soul?" An idea took shape in the back of her mind. It was risky, given the weight of the unknown, but maybe there was a chance she could bring Kells back. She could save this place that had once been her home, restore the land where she grew up and maybe that would help mend the hole in her heart. "That's what I'll do. I can use the magic of Danua's soul, *my* soul, to revive Kells."

"Maeve," Saoirse began, a line forming across her brow.

Tiernan scowled down at her. "Absolutely not."

She whirled away from him. "Excuse me?"

He threw his hands up in innocence. "I only mean that you haven't extended yourself to such lengths before. There's no way of knowing how you'll respond or react. There's always a give and take with magic, my lady. That kind of power comes with a price."

"Then I'll pay it." Her chin jutted upward, to an angle of obstinance. "Whatever it is, I'll pay it." Her gaze slid to Saoirse and the vibrancy that shone so clearly shifted to something else entirely. Pain.

Saoirse stepped closer and took Maeve's hand. "Why?"

"Because..." When Maeve spoke, her voice cracked. "Because this used to be my home. Because it was vibrant and full of life. Despite everything, I loved it here. I grew up here. Pieces of me are here and because if I leave it looking like this, I'm not sure if I'd ever be able to forgive myself." She lifted her gaze to Saoirse. "And because I know you're not going to come back with us. Are you?"

The warrior ducked her head, her silver hair clinging to the sweat and filth on her face. She dragged her boot through the decrepit earth. "It's not that I don't want to, believe me I do, but—"

"But Kells is your home," Maeve finished for her, a sheen of tears in her eyes.

"Yes." Saoirse held her gaze. "And Faeven is yours."

"Yes. Faeven is mine. It's where I belong, and it calls to my soul. It's the part of me I never knew existed." Maeve threw her arms around Saoirse, locking her into a tight embrace. One tear slipped from the corner of her eye. "And besides, I'm a fucking fae now."

"Yeah, you are." Saoirse pulled back, cupping Maeve's cheeks with her hands. Her answering smile was lit from within. "Your soul is as brilliant as a thousand suns, Maeve."

"And you are a warrior with the heart of a poet, Saoirse." Her bottom lip trembled. "I don't want to be without you."

"You never will."

Saoirse released her and Maeve knelt on the ground. "Maeve, no—"

"Let me do this for you. For this land. For this place I once loved." Then softer, in her mind...*for myself.* She splayed her hands wide, pressing into the earth, and her gaze lifted to the Moors. To her haven. "Just promise me you'll build yourself a new castle."

Saoirse laughed, but her eyes were glassy with unshed tears. "I'll see what I can do."

Maeve closed her eyes and poured her magic into the earth. Power sifted and stirred around them, a well of love and creation. It ebbed and flowed like the tide, rising and falling, restoring life back to the world around them. The ground healed and blades of green grass burst through the surface. Flowers blossomed, trees bloomed as the decay and rot of the land vanished. Powerful waves of magic flowed around them, rebuilding the fallen city, saving it from its cursed state. The skies cleared, the sun kissed the Cliffs of Morrigan, and in the distance, even the Moors returned to their former glory. Everything was lush. Everything was beautiful. And a tiny shred of Maeve's heart healed.

The pulse of magic diminished, and Maeve swayed. Her stomach clenched, threatening to heave. Sweat prickled along her brow, and beads of it slid down her neck. Tiernan had been right, as usual, though she would never admit as much to him. Kells was draining her. She'd gone too far.

"Let go, Maeve," Tiernan commanded softly. "Let go."

She saw him dive for her, catching her up in his arms as she succumbed to oblivion.

"Fuck." Tiernan scooped Maeve into his arms, cradling her against him.

"Maeve!" Saoirse cried, grabbing her limp hand. "What happened? What's wrong with her?"

"She'll be fine, she just needs to rest. To sleep." Tiernan glanced down at her, unconscious in his arms. Though he knew she would recover without issue, it didn't make it any less unnerving to see her so vulnerable, so delicate. "She expended too much, if not all of her magic."

But in doing so, she brought Kells back to life. An astounding feat unto itself.

Saoirse gnawed on her bottom lip. "So, what now?"

"We wait for her to wake up." Tiernan glanced over at the Furies. They would need to get back to Faeven as soon as possible. It wouldn't be long before Parisa launched her attack on the Winter Court. "We must return to Niahvess. But it's not safe for me to *fade* with her in this condition."

"Why?"

"When a faerie *fades*, there's a rise in magic. Almost like the crushing swell of a wave. The amount of stress it puts on a body is intense, even for a fae who is fully conscious." Her brow furrowed at his explanation, so he tried again. "To *fade* with Maeve like this would pose a great risk to her health. It could take her even longer to recover."

"I see. So *fading* is out of the question." Saoirse shielded her eyes from the sunlight and looked up at the castle. "What about horseback?"

"A fine idea," Tiernan said with a nod, "but there's still the Eirelan Pass to consider."

"Aran, then?"

He glowered. "No."

Saoirse fisted her hands on her hips, and one eyebrow shot skyward. "Don't tell me you're still hung up on whatever decades old feud is going on between you two."

Anger simmered along his skin and the Furies took note, moving closer. Watching carefully. "His offense, the crime he committed against my family, is beyond forgivable."

"What'd he do?" Her flippancy was annoying. "Kill someone?"

Her words gutted him. "Yes, actually. My parents."

Saoirse paled. "I'm so sorry, my lord." She dropped her chin to her chest. "I didn't realize—"

"It's of no consequence now." He turned away from her.

Dian glided toward them. "That's not entirely true, Your Grace."

Tiernan drew himself up to his full height, clutching Maeve against him. "I beg your pardon?"

"Aran Ruhdneah, High Prince of the Autumn Court, did not

murder your parents." Dian's shadowy arms spread wide. "That was the work of the Puca. They are to blame."

"I know this," Tiernan spat out. "I was *there*."

He'd been beaten, carved up with blades of nightshade, and left for dead on the forest floor. Even in his subconscious, he'd heard his mother scream. He could still hear his father shouting his name. Days later, after he'd woken starving, brutalized, and half dead, he'd discovered his parents' bodies. Each of them had been bound to a tree, their flesh charred like they'd been burned alive. The pungent smell and their blackened flesh had haunted his dreams for more than a decade. It was not something he would soon forget.

There'd been no way to track down all the Puca responsible; trooping fae were notorious for vanishing without a trace.

Tiernan had been so consumed with grief, he'd gone after the one who'd been responsible for orchestrating the meeting in the first place.

Aran.

"The Autumn High Prince may not have been the one to place his hands upon my parents," Tiernan faced Dian, his blood boiling, "but he issued the order."

From beside him, Saoirse gasped, clamping one hand over her mouth.

"Are you certain?" Balor drifted toward him, the shadowy lines of his body shifting in the breeze. "Rumors circulating from the Dorai are that the Autumn High Prince is the most honorable among them."

"And the most loyal," Tethra added, moving closer.

Dian tilted his head, considering. "And the most trustworthy."

"Perhaps," Balor ventured, "there's another whose devious ways are more suited to the picture you paint."

Tiernan stilled.

Another more devious...

Garvan.

"Shit," Tiernan mumbled.

He hadn't considered Garvan before. During the Evernight War, Garvan had led the High Army of Kyol in a series of attacks against Carman. Shay had taken a unit of warriors to the north to help Ciara strengthen her borders while Aran remained behind to protect their citizens. Tiernan had assumed the letter had been from Aran since both Garvan and Shay were off fighting. But it was possible. All of it was possible. The message requesting a meeting could've been forged. The ambush easily could have been Garvan's idea the entire time. Even now, he was in Parisa's confidence, no one else. He was willing to hand over his own sister if it meant improving his standing and gaining more control.

But Aran hadn't refused the claims Tiernan made against him. At the same time, he never admitted to them either.

Damn it.

Overhead, the sun was gradually descending in the western sky. Before long, night would be upon them. He glanced down at Maeve, who was still asleep in his arms.

As if reading his thoughts, Saoirse stepped forward. "The Shores are a day-long trip from here."

Tiernan's brow arched. "At what speed?"

She smiled knowingly. "I'll get you a horse."

Minutes later, she reappeared with a stallion whose coat resembled the darkest night. Balor took Maeve from him, and he climbed into the saddle.

Saoirse gently tucked a lock of Maeve's hair behind her ear, then placed a kiss on her forehead.

"I'll see you again, Maeve." Her sapphire eyes locked onto Tiernan. "When she wakes, will you..."

He nodded sharply. "I'll tell her."

Then Balor lifted Maeve into his arms, helping to situate her in his lap so she could at least stay comfortable while she slept. Tiernan held her tightly and gripped the stallion's reins. He glanced over at Balor, Tethra, and Dian. "How fast can you move?"

"You set the speed, Your Grace." Tethra bowed. "I assure you we can keep up."

"Very well." Tiernan lifted one hand in a slight wave. "We'll see you, Saoirse Doran."

A sheen misted over the silver-haired warrior's eyes, and she waved in return. "Fair winds, my lord."

Without a backward glance, he steered the stallion away from Kells. They traveled through the Moors and the Fieann Forest swiftly. By the time they reached the Shores, the moon was high, the stars glittered like diamonds, and on the horizon, he caught sight of faintly glowing faerie light moving across the Eirelan Pass.

The *Amshir* approached.

Chapter Thirty-Six

Aran was coming.

Despite everything, relief settled into Tiernan's bones. Even if he and Aran were not exactly on speaking terms, Maeve needed a comfortable place to rest, and he knew for a fact the *Amshir* was well-equipped with all aspects of luxury, including a bed.

"Let me help you, Your Grace." Tethra reached up, and Tiernan transferred Maeve into his arms.

He dismounted and sent the steed back to Kells.

Tiernan looked around for some place where Maeve could sleep until Aran arrived. Unfortunately, the Shores were made up of sand, sea glass, and shells. He debated on whether to even try to create a makeshift bed for her when something in the water splashed just off the shoreline.

He froze, his gaze narrowing on the quiet, rippling waves. He scanned the dark waters, seeing nothing, but the Furies had heard it as well. Tethra moved backward with Maeve, while Balor and Dian drifted to the forefront, protecting him.

"What is it?" Balor asked, his voice a harsh whisper.

Tiernan shook his head. "I don't know. I don't see anything out of the ordinary."

Another splash. This one was closer than the last.

The Furies shifted, barricading Tethra and Maeve. Tiernan pulled one of his swords, stepping closer to the water's edge, the uneven shoreline crunching loudly beneath his boots. He peered out, eyes straining, when a glimpse of a shadow slithered in the moonlight. Sword raised, he took one more step, and it was then he noticed the glittering of iridescent scales. Merrow scales.

He lowered his weapon. "Queen Marella? What are you doing here?"

She stayed in the water, close enough that he could just make out the pearls encrusting her upper body. She angled her head by way of greeting and her ink-colored hair spilled down around her shoulders. "My lord, I must speak with you at once."

Tension coiled inside him like a vise. The merrow queen rarely sought him out and when she did, it was of great importance. "Is it Garvan? What has he done?"

He feared the worst for the merrows, especially since Maeve brought news of Garvan's heinous crimes against them.

"It's not, at least not yet." Her glassy eyes remained focused on him, never blinking. "The hunting of merrows has ceased for now, but I worry this is only because the High Prince is preoccupied with more nefarious plans."

"You mean regarding Parisa?" Tiernan glanced out to sea. The *Amshir* was still a ways offshore, but it would be here soon enough.

"I do," Marella confirmed. "Though the Spring bitch dares title herself a queen, she has no right to make such a claim."

"On that, we agree."

Marella sifted through the water, letting the small waves wash over the scales of her fins. "I came to speak with you on another matter. The Astralstone."

His hand subconsciously slid to his thigh, where he kept the dagger in question on him at all times. "What of it?"

Her onyx gaze landed on it as well, then returned to his face a second later. "I withheld information when I originally offered it to you, my lord."

Concern gnawed at him, and his brows lifted. It wasn't like the Queen of Ispomora to take him for a fool. "Is that so?"

"Yes, my lord, though it was not done with malicious intent. It was more a matter of...waiting for the most opportune moment." Her fingers, slightly webbed, flicked over the surface of the sea.

Tiernan sheathed his sword and crossed his arms. "Continue."

"The Aurastone and Astralstone were gifts to me and my sister, from the skies. Forged from stardust and sunlight, they both possess great power." When she spoke, she looked up to the night sky reigning above them. "But the twin daggers were never meant for us alone. They would claim their owners as was prophesied by my sister, Delphina."

She hesitated now, her voice dropping so low, he could scarcely hear her over the waves lapping against the shore. "The Aurastone chose Maeve, the Dawnbringer. The Astralstone, however, did not choose you."

Tiernan stiffened, his muscles tightening. The blow struck home. It was frustrating to think the Astralstone was not intended for him, to imagine he was not worthy. He knew the Furies watched, which did nothing but wound his pride even further.

"If not me, then who?" he ground out.

"The Nightweaver."

He recollected stories of the Nightweaver and the Dawnbringer from his childhood. The demigod and demigoddess of all realms, both creators and destroyers of worlds. One glowed with the dawn, while the other ruled with shadows. There was no doubt in his mind that Maeve was the Dawnbringer incarnate. He'd seen her wield the Aurastone with such caliber, it looked as though it had been *made* for her. Yet he rarely used the Astralstone. He kept it on his body, but he never withdrew it in battle. He reached for his swords every time he fought. As much as he was loath to admit it, he knew there must've been a reason the Astralstone did not call to him like the Aurastone did to Maeve.

He never expected it would be because the dagger hadn't chosen him as its owner.

"Queen Marella, are you saying the Astralstone is useless in my possession?" It wasn't like he needed it. He was well aware of the depth of his power and the strength of his magic. But the knowledge that he was not destined to be the Nightweaver bruised his ego.

On this, she held his gaze. "I am."

He considered this information. He would never willingly withhold something of greatness strictly out of arrogance. If finding the true Nightweaver meant that Faeven would once again thrive, then so be it. "Do you want it back?"

"Only if you offer it willingly, my lord."

The Astralstone had only fallen out of his possession once before, and he'd lost it for many years. Rowan had been the one to discover it during one of the many battles of the Evernight War. Tiernan had lost it then, as he'd once more found himself on the brink of death. The ground had been soaked with the blood of his enemies, with the blood of his allies. The skies had turned black, dark magic had permeated the air, and Rowan had run away.

The coward.

He bent down and unhooked the sheath on his thigh where the Astralstone was stored.

"Here." He handed it to the merrow queen. "Find the one worthy."

She dipped her head in acknowledgment. "You truly are a king of kings."

He offered her a friendly smile. "Take great care, Marella. War is coming."

She clutched the Astralstone to her chest. "I shall have my forces ready to aid you and all of Summer, should ever the need arise."

"The Summer Court appreciates your devotion." He bowed, then stepped back. The *Amshir* was fast approaching. "Fair winds."

"May the seas always be on your side." Queen Marella blinked once, then disappeared beneath the surface of the Eirelan Pass.

"Your Grace." Tethra floated close to him and offered Maeve. "I do not think the High Prince of Autumn would take too kindly in knowing his sister was being held by a Fury."

Tiernan took her in his arms. "Smart move."

The *Amshir* drifted closer and anchored just offshore, a svelte vessel of glossy wood and burnt orange banners bearing the image of a three-headed *trechen*. It didn't rely upon the wind or seas, instead it sailed with magic. Planks unfolded like a staircase from the side of the ship all the way to the stretch of beach where Tiernan and the Furies waited in the shadows of night. Aran remained on the deck, leaning out over the railing, looking rather smug, and more than a little pleased with himself.

"Imagine my surprise," he called out, "to find that the High King of Summer is in need of a favor."

Tiernan stepped into the glow emanating from the faerie light lanterns hanging from the ship's starboard side. "Aran."

"Maeve." Aran's face twisted. He was by Tiernan's side and on the shore in less time than it took to breathe. "What's happened?"

The Furies closed in, and the Autumn High Prince took an abrupt step back, his eyes widening in shock.

"She expended her magic; she only needs time to recover. I'll tell you everything." Tiernan nodded up at the *Amshir*. "Perhaps over a shot of whiskey or two?"

Aran offered him a threadbare smile. "I'm sure that can be arranged." His green eyes slid to the Furies. "Them as well?"

Tiernan blew out a breath. "Yes. The Furies answer to Maeve. They're under her command."

"Alright."

Unease dripped from his tone, but Tiernan supposed it couldn't be avoided. Bad blood still brewed between the Archfae of Faeven and the Furies. At some point, it would have to be confronted.

"Come aboard then, and I'll get you that whiskey." Aran turned, climbing the planks back to his ship. "You can start by telling me why my sister is unconscious."

MAEVE WOKE to the sound of boisterous laughter. It was jarring and she jolted upright. She hadn't heard anything like it in quite some time.

Squinting into the darkness, she let her eyes adjust to the soft amber glow of faerie light before taking in her surroundings. She was on a bed, of that much she could be sure, and there was something familiar about the gorgeous papering on the walls. It depicted fallen leaves flecked in gold. She inhaled deeply, breathing in the scent of spiced woods and crushed berries.

Aran.

She was onboard the *Amshir*.

Maeve scrubbed her hands over her face. The last thing she remembered was pouring her soul into Kells. A sharp twinge struck like a chord in her heart—she hadn't been able to say goodbye to Saoirse. She didn't know the next time she'd see her best friend, if she'd ever see her again at all. Maeve wished she could've witnessed the outcome of her magic; she would've loved to have seen Kells brought back to life. What she wouldn't give to stand on the Cliffs of Morrigan and overlook the city, or sneak into the Moors and swim in the hidden lake.

But all those dreams were lost to her now. If she was already on the *Amshir*, it meant they were sailing for the Summer Court. But Tiernan couldn't tolerate even being in the same room as Aran, so had he left her in Aran's care and returned to Summer without her? If that was the case, where were Balor, Tethra, and Dian? And who was laughing?

She climbed out of the bed and glanced down. She was in a crimson velvet nightgown. Her armor had been removed and cleaned and was lying neatly in a pile at the end of the bed. She held her arms out in front of her. From the looks of it, she'd been cleaned as well. She must have slept much longer than she thought.

Following the sound of the voices, Maeve climbed the steps to the small verandah on the second deck of the *Amshir*. The night was clear and lovely, the laughter only increasing. When she reached the final step, she stopped in her tracks. Seated at a table, taking shots, and laughing like they didn't have a care in the world, were Tiernan, Aran, and all three of the Furies.

Tiernan instantly spun around, sensing her, and when his eyes landed on her, his smile was so wide, so full of relief, it sent her own racing in return.

The other four males followed suit.

"Sister!" Aran shouted a little too loudly and waved like he was an ocean's distance away from her instead of only a few feet. His auburn hair swept over one side of his face, falling in a sharp angle, and he shoved it back.

"*Astora*." Tiernan slid his chair back and opened his arms. "Come sit with me."

The Furies at least had the decency to duck their heads and stand, each of them mumbling some semblance of a proper greeting.

"What is going on here?" she asked, worried she might've slept a little too hard and was lucid dreaming.

"Just catching up on the days of before." Aran rocked back in his chair and it bobbled. He grabbed the table, holding onto it for purchase, then grinned up at her. "Join us!"

She inched forward and took note of the empty bottles of alcohol on the table. The shot glasses. The half-eaten sandwiches and unidentifiable liquid that had been spilled on the wooden deck. "Are you drunk?"

Aran laughed. Balor, Tethra, and Dian refused to meet her gaze.

"Are *all* of you drunk?"

"That would appear to be the case, my lady." Tiernan flashed her a wolfish grin and heat pooled low in her belly. He crooked his finger, beckoning her to him.

"Careful there, Tier." Aran propped his elbows on the table and his smile vanished. "That's my sister you're attempting to seduce."

Maeve flushed, then quickly recovered.

"Tier?" she repeated. "Did you just call him *Tier?*"

Aran tapped the cleft in his chin, the one marked by a scar. "I did indeed."

"But I thought you two hated each other because of..." Because of what happened during the Evernight War, but she kept those thoughts to herself.

Tiernan tucked his hands behind his head and leaned back. "A misunderstanding."

"A misunderstanding?" Maeve blinked, dumbfounded. "Are you serious? You mean to tell me you banished my brother from his home and by default put Garvan in charge over a *misunderstanding?*"

"I think she's angry," Tethra whispered, though it wasn't really a whisper at all.

Tiernan stood and strolled over to her. "I intend to exonerate him at once." He cupped her cheek, kissed her lightly. "I'm glad you're well."

"Oh, no." She drew back and planted her hands against his chest. "You are not getting off the hook that easily, my lord."

"As it would happen," Tiernan continued, wrapping his arms around her in a poor attempt to derail her train of thought, "it was Garvan who forged the letter from Autumn with the intent to ambush me and my parents."

Maeve knew it. She knew Aran could never be responsible for such an atrocious plot. Her gaze landed on her brother. "Why?"

Aran blinked up at her. "Why what?"

"Why didn't you deny it when Tiernan accused you of plotting against his family?" she demanded, turning in Tiernan's arms. "Why didn't you prove your innocence?"

A look passed over his face, one she couldn't read. Shadows of the past darkened his emerald eyes. "Sometimes, little sister, we all do things we regret. Even if such actions are done out of love."

"You protected him?" The words fell from her lips in a harsh whisper.

"I did what I thought was right at the time." Aran lifted the nearly empty bottle of whiskey. "Unfortunately, it cost me more than I could ever imagine."

Beats of weighted silence passed between them. Even the Furies pretended to take more interest in their shadows and drinks, refusing to look at her.

Maeve bit her bottom lip. "So, you get to come home?"

Aran nodded, pouring himself another drink. "Yes."

"But Garvan will try and kill you."

"Let him try," he countered, his voice so cold it nearly burned her skin. He stared down into his drink, scowling.

"He wants power, Aran. The same as Parisa." Apprehension needled its way down her spine, and she shuddered, scrubbing her suddenly damp palms against the velvet of her nightgown. "It's too risky."

Tiernan pulled her into his side, his twilight eyes focused on the necklace she wore. His hand coasted lazily up and down her waist. Calming her. Soothing her.

"It's a risk I must take, dear sister." Aran looked at her from over the rim of his glass. "Our Court is failing because of his greed."

Our Court.

Her heart surged at the words.

"I've already agreed to help Aran take up his rightful position as heir, Maeve." Tiernan placed an absentminded kiss on top of her head.

Heir. He'd said heir. Which meant they both must believe Dorian was still alive.

She looked up at him. "When?"

"Once all this business with Parisa is settled. Once we win." The corners of Tiernan's mouth lifted in a smile. A promise. A vow. "Sooner if we can."

She rose and kissed the underside of his chin, then looked over at

Aran, who was watching them with brows raised. "Will you come stay with us in the Summer Court? Until then?"

Aran's gaze shifted between her and Tiernan, and uncertainty passed over his handsome features.

"Your presence in my Court would be most welcome, High Prince." Tiernan clasped Maeve's hand in his own, then lifted it to his mouth, placing a kiss on her knuckles. "And I have a feeling it would make someone we both care for extremely happy."

Aran downed the rest of his drink and his emerald green eyes, flecked with bursts of gold, focused on her. "Is that your wish?"

Maeve nodded furiously. "Yes. Yes, it is."

He stood, stretching, and laughed. "Then that's what I'll do."

A squeal pealed from her lips, and she launched herself at him. He caught her midair and swung her around, knocking over the empty bottles of alcohol. From somewhere behind her, she could've sworn she heard the Furies laugh. Aran twirled her around once more, and she glimpsed Tiernan standing there, with his hands shoved into his pockets. The beautiful smile he gave her left her heart bursting. For once, everything was right.

Aran was coming home.

Tiernan was fated to her, and even though he had never told her the words, she knew he loved her. Though worshiped her was likely a far better term.

In that moment, she relished the joy she'd longed for her entire life. She wouldn't think of what lingered on the horizon, just out of sight. She wouldn't dwell on the trepidation surrounding their future. Right now, on this night, she was happy.

But a small, quiet voice in the back of her mind softly reminded her of one thing.

The stars made no promises.

Chapter Thirty-Seven

Tiernan sat on the deck of the Amshir, sipping his glass of whiskey, watching Maeve converse with the Furies. Whatever story she was telling them must've been entertaining, because all three were captivated by her. He studied her while he tried to shove away the cloud of concern harboring in his thoughts. She shouldn't be awake, not yet. For her to expend that kind of power, to use that well of magic coursing through her to revive Kells, she should still be asleep. Any normal Archfae would need at least twelve hours to recover after such an occurrence, maybe even a full day or two. But Maeve had only slept a handful of hours. Barely four. Now her eyes were bright, and she was practically glowing while talking with the Furies.

It left him apprehensive, so an air of disquiet settled around him.

He sensed Aran approach before he saw him. The High Prince stood just within his line of sight, swirling the glass in his hand so the ice clinked and sloshed in what remained of the amber liquid. He knocked back the last of its contents, his gaze never leaving Maeve.

"She's fated to you."

It was a statement, not a question. Tiernan took another slow pull of his whiskey. "She is."

Aran glanced down at the empty glass, nodding slowly.

The alcohol burned down the back of Tiernan's throat. He wasn't afraid of the High Prince of Autumn. In fact, he knew he could challenge him, and they'd be squarely matched. But he had been hoping to avoid this conversation.

Aran ran his thumb along his chin, mulling the information over in his mind. "I suppose I don't need to tell you that if you hurt her, if you give her cause to shed a single tear, that I will hunt you down and kill you from the inside out."

"I assumed as much." The corner of Tiernan's mouth ticked up in a knowing smile. "Shay, too, has already made his sentiments on the matter quite clear."

"Has he?" Aran turned toward him then and distress harbored in the lines of his face. "How can you be sure he means her no harm?"

"I've seen the way he looks at her, Aran. The bond between siblings is strong, you know this as much as I do. He treasures her and wishes to spend more time with her." Tiernan finished off his drink. "He even gifted her your mother's wardrobe."

A flicker of emotion flashed in Aran's eyes. "He did?"

Tiernan nodded, stretching out his legs and crossing his ankles over one another. "Shay would lay down his life if it meant saving hers. Of that I have no doubt."

"Well, then." Aran clamped his shoulder with one hand. "That makes three of us."

Maeve looked over at them then, and the look on her face was enough to make Tiernan's heart stop in his chest. Ribbons of silver moonlight cascaded around her, washing her in an ethereal glow worthy of a goddess. Her smile was so pure, her eyes so bright with delight, that if he hadn't done so already, he would've fallen in love with her all over again.

Aran spoke, tugging him out of his entranced state. "I'm going to turn in for the night. I already know I'll regret my indulgence in the morning."

Tiernan laughed, briefly wishing Deirdre was there with them. She made an excellent cup of tea to cure such agony.

Aran set his empty glass down, lightly tapping his fingers against its rim. "Might I leave you with one more word of caution?"

"I wouldn't expect anything less."

The High Prince's smile faded. "Whatever you do, don't fuck up."

Then he strolled away, taking the stairs down to the first level of the ship to go sleep off his drunken state.

Tiernan let his gaze return to Maeve, whose eyes had grown sleepy, and she disguised a yawn with the back of her hand. To the Furies' credit, each of them stood and bade her a good night before silently retreating to other parts of the Amshir. He wasn't entirely sure they even needed sleep, but they'd been smart enough to realize their queen was exhausted.

He rose from his seat and went to her, taking her hand and easing her into a standing position. "You need rest, *astora*."

She rolled her neck from side to side, letting her gaze drift skyward where the blue of night was fading and giving way to the gold of sunrise. "I think I'll stay up."

His brow furrowed. "What for?"

"There's something I want to see." Maeve led him from the verandah to the first level of the ship and together they walked toward the stern, the horizon of sky and sea meeting and stretching out like a canvas of blended watercolors.

The world glimmered, coating them in magic.

They'd crossed into the boundaries of Faeven.

THE FURIES NEVER SLEPT.

Maeve supposed they didn't need to, not when she could hear the low rumbling of their voices from the port side of the Amshir. But right now, she didn't need sleep either, not when the sun would make its ascent at any moment and light the skies on fire.

She took Tiernan's hand, guiding him around the back of the ship. Already, the eastern sky was aglow with the first rays of the morning. Soon, it would be just as she remembered from her first crossing of the Eirelan Pass.

"What are we doing?" He leaned against the railing and toyed with one of her curls, tugging it gently only to let it bounce free.

"Watching the sunrise." She shifted into him, and his arm slid around her waist, pulling her close.

Seconds floated through the space between them, slow and languid. When the sun finally graced the horizon, the cresting waves sparkled like diamonds and golden beams burst through the lazy stretch of early morning clouds, illuminating them with radiance so they seemed to glow from within. It stole the breath from her lungs, and she swiped the unbidden tear that slid down her cheek.

It was as beautiful as ever. Just like when Rowan had shown her the first time.

"Sun and sky." Tiernan's voice was filled with awe, and his grip on her tightened while he drank in the beauty of the world before them.

"Yes." Maeve wrapped herself in his embrace. "Sun and sky."

Chapter Thirty-Eight

Tiernan, Maeve, and Aran *faded* into the main courtyard of the palace with the Furies right there with them. Somehow, the otherworldly beings seemed to defy all magical laws. They moved with unrivaled speed, despite not being able to *fade* or fly. They required no sleep and didn't appear to need food either, though they made short work of four bottles of whiskey the night before.

Ceridwen, Lir, Merrick, and Brynn were waiting for them.

It wasn't exactly the homecoming he expected, but his friends had a right to be wary. The Furies had been an intimidating trio when they were flesh and bone. Now that they were nothing more than shadow and distorted bodily figures, they were far more frightening. To make matters worse, and slightly more uncomfortable, Merrick was sending the Autumn High Prince a death glare.

Merrick rocked back on his heels, crossing his arms. "I have a feeling we've missed something."

"Aran will be staying with us for the foreseeable future." Tiernan addressed all of them, ensuring he met each of their dubious looks with a leveled stare. "Until we can overthrow Garvan from the Autumn Court."

"And what of them?" Lir nodded toward the Furies, who'd slowly gathered around Maeve.

"They will remain as well." Tiernan gestured vaguely behind him. Lir and Merrick shared a look.

"I know what you're thinking," Maeve began, "and I know you have cause for concern."

Merrick's fingers tapped restlessly against the hilt of his sword. "Bit of an understatement, my lady."

She gave him a soft smile. "The Furies answer to me. They will fight with me, and they will fight for us. They came to our aid in Kells when we were attacked by a group of rogue soldiers. Their loyalty is unwavering, and we can use all the help we can get."

Lir stepped toward her and draped one arm around her shoulders. "How do you fare, little bird?"

"Well enough, commander." She patted his hand. "Well enough."

Ceridwen shifted around from behind Merrick, coming to stand in front of them. She smoothed the front of her pale blue silk gown. "We've received another influx of Spring refugees. They arrived a day after you left."

"How many?" Tiernan asked.

"Thirty-two." She gestured vaguely to the gates beyond. "Brynn and I set them up at the camp with the others. They have everything they need, including clothing, food, and shelter."

Maeve reached out and clasped Ceridwen's hands. "I appreciate you doing that. For them and for me."

Her ruby lips lifted. "Of course. I'm happy to help."

"My lord, I have my report if you're ready to hear it." Merrick came up beside him and handed him some scrolls of parchment bound with the Summer Court's crest.

"I am." He would read the contents thoroughly later tonight. "Continue."

"The Spring Court is in shambles, just as we suspected. Parisa's army is massive but aside from the dark fae she's collecting, I couldn't find any signs of advanced weaponry. The dark fae venom Garvan used against Maeve hasn't appeared to be forged into any other blades, but that doesn't mean it won't be used in other ways." Merrick ran a hand through his pink hair. "All in all, we should be able to take them out. Nothing shy of a short day's work."

Tiernan laughed. If only. "I don't think it will be quite that simple, Mer."

He shrugged and a cocky grin spread across his face. "Worth a shot."

Tiernan's gaze slid to his twin. "Has there been any word from Shay?"

At the mention of his younger brother, Aran's brows rose. "Shay? What does he have to do with any of this?"

"Shay has agreed to supply us with information in exchange for protection." Tiernan turned to face Aran; he would have to tread carefully here. The relationship between the Autumn Court and Summer Court had been unstable for years and bringing to light that Shay willingly sided with Summer could raise Aran's guard. Especially since everything Shay was doing for them was blatant betrayal and grounds for treason. "He's been shut out of Garvan's negotiations with Parisa and has chosen to no longer sit idly by while his Court deteriorates around him."

He took note of the way Aran's eyes darkened. Of the way his brows were lined with apprehension. "My brother is no fool, my lord."

Brynn snorted. "Which one?"

Aran's face reflected no humor. "Neither of them."

Tiernan coughed, clearing the growing tension. They already had to fight one war, they didn't need another one at home. "Anything else to report?"

Lir and Merrick turned to Brynn.

"Brynn?" He faced his healer. "What is it?"

She pulled a thin crystal object from her pocket. It was made of rose quartz and the tip was fashioned of rainbow moonstone. The tube was slender, expertly crafted so that the end of it took the shape of a whorl.

"I've been working with some of the healers in the city to try and create a surplus of this siphoning tool we used on the wound that almost left Maeve incapacitated."

That was what they used to pull the dark magic from her? It resembled an ornament of some kind. Something a child would hang upon an evergreen during Yuletide. It looked too delicate to be a healing instrument.

She held it out to him, and he carefully lifted it to the light, inspecting it. The crystal was cool in his hands, smooth and polished.

"This looks promising."

"Indeed, my lord." Brynn gnawed on her bottom lip, her eyes shifting from brown to sympathetic gold. "But there's one problem."

"What's that?"

"We've not been able to find anything else like it." Dismay leadened her voice. "Anywhere."

"That's because it's not from here." Aran held out his hand. "Might I see it?"

Tiernan handed it over, and the High Prince examined it, running his finger along the rose quartz and tracing the whorl.

"This was not designed in Faeven. If you look just here," he held it out for all of them to see, "the letters B and A are engraved in gold on the bottom. This particular bauble comes from a little shop called Belladonna's Atelier."

"Belladonna's?" Maeve edged closer, curious. She peered down at the instrument, and he could almost hear her thoughts working. Somehow, she was not as surprised by this news as Tiernan would've expected. "This is the same shop where you bought the marble you showed me. You've seen it on your travels, haven't you?"

Aran nodded, returning the instrument to Brynn. "I have. Belladonna has a certain...talent for the arts. She often works with crystals and glass, as well as many other media."

Brynn slipped it back into her pocket. "Can we get more of them?"

"Well," Aran drew the word out and ran his thumb over the scar that trailed from his jaw to his chin. "That depends."

"On?" Brynn prompted, glowering.

"On how many you need," he answered with a smirk. "And how soon you need them."

"As many as this Belladonna you speak of is willing to spare. Garvan attacked Maeve with a small blade, my lord. It was insignificant in size, but it was laced with dark magic." She cut him down with a glare, her gaze narrowing. "He paralyzed her mid-air."

Aran's brows lifted in shock. "He what? How is that possible?"

"That's what we're trying to figure out. And the only thing that saved her from losing control of her body completely was that crystal healing tool, whatever it is." She crossed her arms, seemingly pleased by his bewilderment. "So, let me ask you again, High Prince. Can we get more of them?"

"It can be done." Aran glanced over at Tiernan, already knowing what he would ask. "I can retrieve more of these if they're required but doing so will take time. I'll have to travel across the Gaelsong Sea and back again. There's no telling how long it will take, or if she'll even be willing to construct more of them."

"I'll send you with enough gold she won't be able to refuse you." He looked to the eastern sky, to where thin shreds of clouds stretched over brilliant blue, to the realms beyond. "How soon can you leave?"

From beside him, Maeve started. She'd only just got her brother back, and Tiernan knew she didn't want him to leave again. But if this crystal healing tool was the only way to cure the venom and if Aran was the only one who could retrieve them, he would be forced to ask the favor.

Aran smiled, but it did not reach his eyes. Instead, his gaze fell to his sister. "I can leave at once, if the urgency of the matter demands it."

Tiernan stilled. "I'm afraid it does."

Maeve turned away from him then, letting her hair fall into her face, blocking his view. She wrapped her arms around herself and refused to meet his eye. He hated to disappoint her, but surely she knew these healing instruments were important. They would need more of them, especially if the dark magic Garvan used against her was plentiful. If it could be imbued onto a tiny blade, then it could be used on anything. Swords. Daggers. Arrows. They would need to be prepared. He would talk to her about it later tonight, when they were alone. Explain that sending Aran off on this errand was necessary to ensure Faeven survived.

"I'm sorry," Tiernan spoke softly into her mind. *"He'll return soon. I promise."*

Maeve's sea-swept eyes found his and the smile she offered him nearly broke his heart. *"I know."*

He grabbed her hand, intertwining her fingers with his own.

Aran swept into a low bow. "Then I shall sail immediately."

"If there's nothing else," Tiernan gestured toward the corridor that would lead to the balcony where they usually dined, "I suggest we all—"

He was interrupted by shouts and thundering footsteps racing down the stone walkway.

One of Merrick's scouts rounded the corner at a full sprint. Grime and filth covered his cobalt and gold leathers. His face was stained with dirt, and sweat poured from his temples, streaking through the muck down his cheeks. Though his chest heaved in ragged breaths, he stood at attention.

Merrick stormed forward but Tiernan was faster.

"Report," he demanded.

The fae scout bowed and wiped the sweat from his brow. "Movement to the northwest, Your Grace. Something's happened. All was quiet for the past four days but now, Parisa...she's slaughtering everyone in her wake and trekking toward the borders of the Winter Court."

"Fuck." He pinched the bridge of his nose. This was the last thing they needed but they were ready. The Summer Court was always ready.

Lir stood, stoic as ever, and asked, "What exactly happened in Kells?"

Tiernan moved closer to Maeve, gently placing his hand on the small of her back. "Maeve destroyed the Scathing."

She lifted her chin. "And I killed Fearghal."

"Butchered, more like." This from Balor, who'd been so quiet Tiernan had nearly forgotten he and the other two Furies were still there.

"Wrecked," Tethra agreed, flashing a smile gruesome enough to make even the most seasoned warrior cringe.

Dian shifted forward, his ember-lit eyes burning bright. "She slaughtered him."

"Sun and sky. That'll do it." Merrick rocked back onto his heels and grinned, dimples winking. "No wonder Parisa's so pissed. I'd be mad too if my fuck buddy was killed."

"Mer," Brynn groaned, rolling her eyes to the heavens. "Now is not the time."

He spread his arms wide in a poor attempt to look innocent. "Look, all I'm saying is—"

"You don't have a fuck buddy." Ceridwen's voice was as frosty as the northern mountains of Ashdara. She folded her arms, a storm brewing in her eyes.

Merrick paled, and Tiernan's brow arched in question. Maeve watched the exchange with wide, curious eyes.

But his twin spun away from the hunter on one heel, cutting him off. Her lips were pulled into a thin line and her fingers were coiled into fists at her side. He didn't think he'd ever seen her quite so pissed. She huffed, annoyed. "Tiernan, we're awaiting your orders."

Orders. He would be the one to decide whether he kept everyone he loved safe, or whether he sent them into harm's way. But they would not go alone. He would be right there beside them. Beside all of them. Duty to his Court came first, above all else.

"Ready our forces." He flexed his arms, adjusted the rolled sleeves of his shirt, and cocked a cruel half smile. "Parisa has left us no choice but to intercept and attack."

Maeve stood in Tiernan's room, watching him on the balcony. He braced himself against the railing and stared out at Niahvess, at the Floating City of the Summer Court, as the rush of dusk overtook the sky. He fiddled with the ring he always wore on his pinky, twisting it back and forth, never actually taking it off.

She knew he was lost in his thoughts, so she said nothing when Deirdre shuffled into the room, carrying piles of fresh clothing and clean armor. She glanced once at her High King and placed the stack of laundry on the end of the bed.

"Thank you, Deirdre." Maeve smiled, but she knew it did nothing to ease the older woman's heart.

"Of course, dear heart." Deirdre patted her softly on the cheek and a sheen of tears coated her eyes. "Just promise me you'll be careful out there. Dark magic is not the sort of thing to be trifled with."

"I promise."

Deirdre nodded and slipped away without saying another word.

Maeve went to Tiernan then, rising up on her toes to drape her arms around his neck and pull him close. He nuzzled the area between her jaw and shoulder, one of her most sensitive spots. The summer evening wrapped around them like a velvet cloak, comforting, while delicious goosebumps pebbled over her skin.

"What's on your mind, my lord?"

"Many things," he murmured, kissing her temple, then cheek. His hands cupped her bottom, dragging her hips forward so she could feel the proof of his arousal pressing into her. "Mostly you."

"Obviously." She smiled, intending for it to be a lighthearted jab, but Tiernan's arms moved, coming around her back instead. He held her so close, their noses almost touched.

"I meant it in earnest, Maeve." His eyes were reflecting pools of cobalt and violet, threaded with golden sunlight. In them, she saw the fervent extent of his love for her. "What happened in Kells with Fearghal, I never want to see you like that again."

"What, full of rage and hellbent on vengeance?" The memory of what she'd done, of how viciously she'd stolen a life, wasn't something she would soon forget.

"No." Tiernan captured her face, running his thumbs lightly back and forth against her cheekbones. "Your face was a mask of emptiness. Your eyes were devoid of all emotion. I never want to see you so lost. So forlorn. Your glow, the very essence of you...it was gone. I worried I would never see it again."

"I appreciate your concern for me." She let her hands skate down to his arms and she gave them a reaffirming squeeze. Rising on her toes once more, she kissed him, allowing her lips to melt against his. He held her firmly, tightly, like he never wanted to let her go. She broke the kiss, meeting his heated gaze. "I promise I'm okay."

Then she slid out of his arms and padded across the balcony toward her bedroom.

"Where do you think you're going?" he called out, and the sound of his voice rumbled around her, causing a shiver of desire to bloom.

"I'm gross." She spun, taking slow steps backward. "I need a shower."

"Use the one in my room instead."

"Is that an invitation, my lord?"

One dark brow arched before he said, "I'm fairly certain you know it's a command."

Maeve laughed. "Still trying to boss me around?"

"Don't act like you don't like it." His voice was a dark whisper, a promise in her thoughts. She turned around, sauntered into his bedroom, intentionally letting her hips sway, enticing him to join her.

But despite undressing slowly and keeping a careful eye on the door, the minutes ticked by, and she found herself alone in the shower, with the hot water pouring over her in places she didn't even know ached. Her back. Her arms and shoulders. Her calves and thighs. Gradually, the tension fled her body, her muscles softened, and she let her eyes drift close, content to let the strain and suffering she kept locked inside wash away.

She scrubbed her body, then shampooed and conditioned her hair so her curls soaked up every drop of moisture. Just as she was getting ready to shut off the water, Tiernan walked in.

Through a curtain of steam, he removed his clothing methodically, casually dropping each article on the counter. The more of his perfect body he revealed, the more Maeve's stomach clenched in anticipation. Her nipples hardened and currents of hot desire coursed through her. The stream of water, once a relief, was now a powerful stimulant. It set her aflame with need. Every part of her— her breasts, her abdomen, the apex of her thighs—throbbed.

Tiernan inhaled sharply.

"Your scent," he growled, opening the door and stepping inside the shower to join her, "is provoking me to do a number of unsavory things to you."

"Is that a fact?" she asked, drinking him in.

She'd seen him naked before, but this moment, this time, was different. Rivulets of water sluiced down his golden chest, following the swirl of tattoos that covered his solid body. They clung to his abs and arms, following the dip of his hips to where his cock was bulging and ready to take her. Maeve had never been more jealous of water before in her life.

He shifted behind her, tilting his head back, letting the shower soak him thoroughly. He ran his hands through his midnight hair, shoving it back from his face. Maeve had never seen a god before, but she imagined they paled in comparison to the High King of Summer. He was chiseled, sculpted by the fates like some kind of deity. Glorious. Exquisite. Striking.

He looked down at her, the corner of his mouth curving. "You flatter me, *astora*."

"Listening to my thoughts again, are you, my lord?" She grabbed a bar of soap and started lathering it between her hands.

He chuckled softly and the sound of it reverberated in her soul. "It's difficult not to when you're looking at me like that."

"Like what?" Her teeth sank into her bottom lip, and he tracked the movement, his gaze darkening to a late summer storm.

"Like you can't wait to have me inside you. Like you need me to live. To breathe." He moved closer but she put her hands up, stopping him.

"Shower first," she murmured. "Play later."

Then she was washing him, running her hands over every inch of his hardened body, covering him in silky suds. She started with his shoulders, rubbing his arms and ribs, massaging his back, stomach, and thighs. When he groaned in relief, her blood simmered, catching fire. Staring up at him, she gripped his cock with one hand, jerking him in her slippery grasp.

He slammed his hands against the tile behind her, barricading her next to the wall. His forehead rested against hers.

"Is there something you want, my lady?" he ground out.

"I want whatever you're willing to give me." She spoke the words against his lips, where they hovered barely a breath away from hers.

"Everything," he growled, rinsing off the soap. "I will give you anything you ask of me."

One second, she was on the ground and in the next, her legs were locked around his waist, and she was anchored against the wall.

Tiernan slammed into her, and she cried out, holding onto him to keep from falling. With every thrust, he stretched her wider to accommodate his size, driving himself deeper until she could take every inch of him.

"So tight," he muttered, kissing her while his tongue slid over hers. "Always so fucking tight for me."

"Maybe you're just too big."

383

"Gods," he groaned, gripping her ass so hard she knew she'd bear the mark of his fingers before they were done.

Over and over, he pumped himself inside her. Magic simmered along their skin, heating them until the water turned to smoke and steam. Energy crackled in the air above them, sparked with shards of violet and gold. Their matching Strands reached for one another, binding them, dragging them further to a point of no return.

Until a resounding knock on the bathroom door jolted them back to reality.

"What is it?" Tiernan shouted, his voice taut with rage that would cause even the most valiant of fae to cower.

He stilled and Maeve whimpered.

"We're ready to go, *moh Rí*." Merrick's voice sounded from the other side of the door, his tone mocking. "Come whenever you're ready."

The insinuation wasn't lost on either of them, and Tiernan clamped one hand over Maeve's mouth as he rammed himself inside her. She clenched around him, urging him on. Her nails dug into his shoulders as she held tight. He smothered her pants and cries with his palm, then grinned. Bending his head down, he sucked her breast into his hot mouth. Maeve bucked against his hold, but he held firm, his tongue swirling around her nipple as he fucked her harder. She swore his cock grew then, emboldened by the fact that Merrick was just outside, knowing exactly what he did to her.

"I'll come when I'm damn good and ready," Tiernan barked, and the only response was Merrick's wild laughter.

"When this is over," Tiernan whispered, sliding out of her only to shove himself into her again. "I'm going to spend every waking hour fucking you." He repeated the movement. "From sunrise." Then again. "To sunset."

He buried his thick cock in her once more, filling her to the hilt, and she shuddered around him as the orgasm shredded them both. She collapsed onto him, her body spent, her heart longing to hear all the words she worried he would never say.

Chapter Thirty-Nine

They traveled for three days through parts of Faeven Maeve had never seen before, finally reaching the outskirts of the Winter Court.

At her back was the half of the Summer Legion, along with the Furies, and before her was a wondrous landscape of frost-covered beauty. Breathtaking yet treacherous. Thick snow covered the ground and towering evergreens stood watch overhead, their rich decadent branches swooping low and decorated with glimmering icicles. Snowflakes fell around them, each one intricate in design like patterned lace. Furry white foxes with crystal blue eyes bounded past the hooves of her horse and a snowy white owl dove from the trees on the hunt for its next meal.

It was cold here, but not bitter like the winters in Kells. Still, she was grateful for the gloves and fur cloak to keep her warm. Even the air here was different. Magical. It smelled of spruce, peppermint, and something warm. Everywhere she looked, the world seemed to sparkle like it was frozen in an eternal celebration of Yuletide.

In the distance, she could make out the mountains of the Crown City of Ashdara that carved the horizon with their rugged peaks.

Silver flowers with blood red centers bloomed from a bush nearby, and she bent down to see if they too, would smell as lovely as the rest of Winter.

"Don't be fooled by its beauty, my lady." Lir rode up beside her, blocking the tempting blossoms from her view. He dusted a small accumulation of snow from his cloak. "The Winter Court is known for disguising its lethality behind its allure."

"He's right." Merrick brought his horse up alongside them and nodded toward the bush. "Those are *cohlah* blooms. One sniff, no matter how slight, will put you into a deep sleep."

Maeve smirked. "I'll keep that in mind in case your sister ever decides to make amends and send me flowers."

Merrick's laughter rang out and he flashed her a winning smile. "How did we ever survive without you? I don't think I've laughed so often in years."

The sentiment warmed her heart.

"Keep a steady eye," Tiernan called from the front, piercing both his commander and hunter with one look. He raised one hand, halting everyone behind him.

Brynn rose from her saddle, scanning the skies and the forest. She gave her mare a gentle pat on the neck. "If the scout's coordinates were correct, we should've intercepted them by now."

Maeve peered over the pristine scenery before her. Surely a swarm of dark fae would stand out against a backdrop of winter white.

From beside her, Merrick hopped off his horse and paced the outer perimeter of the forest, snow crunching beneath his boots. He inhaled deeply, a line furrowing across his brow. "This isn't right. There's no sign of them, at least not for miles."

Just then, Maeve witnessed the world shimmer before her eyes. Glamour.

"There!" she cried, pointing directly in front of them, to where magic shifted and the untouched snow upon the ground started to swirl.

Except it wasn't the dark fae. Or Parisa. Instead, Queen Ciara, Malachy, and a few other Winter warriors *faded* into view.

"Mer! What a pleasant surprise!" The High Queen's eyes glinted when she looked upon her brother. She smoothed the front of her silver gown, adjusting the cloak of fur that fell to her feet. Her gaze landed on Maeve, and her berry lips curled in disgust before she finally sauntered toward Tiernan, flashing him a sultry smile. "My lord, it's not like you to show up unannounced."

Tiernan climbed off of his horse and strode toward her. Maeve debated on dismounting as well, but Lir caught the reins of her horse in one hand, sending her a look of warning.

"Not yet," he whispered.

"We received word that Parisa intended to attack Winter." Tiernan bowed before the High Queen and she dipped into a curtsy, never taking her eyes off him. "Her army of dark fae was spotted west of here with plans to ambush you."

Ciara remained unaffected. She didn't even look surprised. "What utter nonsense. Parisa wouldn't dare attack the Winter Legion."

Merrick walked over, adjusting his gloves. "I assure you, dear sister, she would."

Ciara's gaze shifted from her brother to the force of warriors standing behind them. Her lips pressed into a thin line. "I am not blind, Tiernan Velless. I have scouts along the entire margin of Winter's borders. If Parisa even so much as took one step in my direction, I would know. I don't need you or my baby brother looking out for me. I'm quite capable of ruling my Court on my own."

"She plans to take over, Ciara." Tiernan folded his arms, towering above the female. "She wants to—"

"Do not take me for a fool," Ciara interjected, her eyes flaring with indignation. "I know she intends to divide us so that she may sit back and watch our collapse."

Tiernan fell silent. Uncomfortable tension burgeoned between the Archfae, and he shifted his weight, the freshly fallen snow crunching beneath his boots. "Then something is wrong. We were told of movement coming this way. I only meant to offer my assistance."

The High Queen of Winter spread her arms wide and glanced around them. "If they were here, they're gone now. Perhaps your informant has chosen to fight on the wrong side."

Thunder rumbled in the distance and the branches of the evergreens shook, the icicles clanging together like chimes. "You speak of treason."

"I speak of possibility." She grinned, insolent and haughty. "Surely not even you can believe every soul within your Court would choose to grovel at your feet." Her icy gaze landed on Maeve. "Though I do suppose some may choose to suck your cock instead."

It happened so fast, Maeve's lungs seized.

From beside her, Lir vaulted off his horse, transforming mid-air. His warrior-like body morphed into that of a monstrous wolf. His silver and black coat glinted in the overcast sunlight as his thick fur stood on end. Baring his fangs with jaws snapping, a guttural, menacing growl tore from his throat as he charged the Winter Queen.

Maeve sat in her saddle, gaping at the fae commander, at the male sworn to protect her with his life. She had no idea he was a shifter. He never mentioned it. *No one* ever mentioned it.

Tiernan stormed forward, capturing Ciara by her neck, saving her from Lir's attack. He hefted her into the air so her feet dangled like a puppet. She didn't fight. She didn't claw. She just smiled. At once, swords were drawn, each blade pointed to a member of the opposing Court.

"Maeve is the Dawnbringer." When Tiernan spoke, the ground trembled in fear. "She is the High Princess of Autumn. The High Queen of the Furies as well as the Spring fae who swore a vow of allegiance to her. She bears my Strand, and she is *mine*." Thunder exploded across the sky, causing even the mountains to quake. "If you ever disrespect her again, I will ensure your blood stains your Court red."

"My lord." Brynn had two daggers drawn, each of them aimed for the heart of two Winter warriors. "We have bigger battles to fight than those that stem from the High Queen's petty jealousy."

"It isn't jealousy, Brynn Banlisch." Laughter squeezed from Ciara, strangled and choking. "If the High Princess wants my seconds, she can have them."

Her face turned a hideous shade of reddish-purple and she gasped, her legs flailing in the air.

"Tiernan, let her go," Maeve pleaded. As much as she despised Ciara, she was still an ally. A bitch, but an ally. "She isn't worth it."

He squeezed once more, then dropped her, the mark of his hand branding her frail neck. "Next time, there will be no warning."

Lir growled, shifting back into his faerie form, and Maeve blinked, amazed he could do it so quickly.

"Your Grace!"

Tiernan whipped around at the use of his formal title. From across one of the snow-covered hills, a Summer fae was urging his horse at a full gallop, so fast the wind seemed to carry them.

"Your Grace!" The Summer fae jumped off his horse and fell to the ground.

Merrick was by him in an instant, hauling him to his feet.

"Report," Tiernan demanded.

"Attack, my lord." His chest heaved. "Niahvess has come under attack."

"What?" An emotion Maeve had never witnessed before clouded his eyes.

"It's High Princess Ceridwen." The Summer warrior's chest rose and fell in rapid breaths.

Tiernan paled.

Merrick gripped the fae, forcing him to face him. "What happened to her?"

"She's gone, my lord." His gaze darted back and forth between Merrick and Tiernan. "She's been taken by Garvan. To Autumn."

The storm came down upon them. Violet lightning slashed across the slate gray skies, thunder crashed, and the icicles fell from the trees like swords. Bitter gusts of wind ripped across the frozen landscape, kicking up snow so that it swirled around them violently, as though they were caught in a tormented snow globe.

Ciara rushed forward, her once calculating eyes now lit with panic.

"Go," she urged. "Go now, Tiernan. I'll ensure your army returns home."

Tiernan nodded once.

Lir ran to Maeve, plucking her off the horse like she was nothing more than a fallen feather.

"Back to Niahvess," Tiernan commanded. "The Furies, too. At once."

In less time than it took for Maeve to catch her breath, they *faded*.

CHAOS STORMED the outside of the Summer palace.

It was shrouded in smoke and debris. The dense scent of fading magic lingered in the air. Stifling. Blood smeared the ground, mingling with dirt and sand. Everywhere Maeve looked, fae warriors ran, their footfalls pounding with determination. Voices rang out from everywhere, bellowing orders. Some of the warriors moved more slowly, their injuries hampering their movements while others were dragged to safer locations, removed from the remnants of battle.

Lir's hand locked around Maeve's arm, his grip firm and his sword drawn. His silver gaze darkened, sweeping over the area surrounding them, seeking any potential threat.

"Search the grounds!" Tiernan shouted.

Merrick took off in one direction, yelling for his scouts to follow.

Brynn had vanished completely. Tiernan whipped around and faced Lir. Maeve saw it then. All traces of the male she loved were gone. He was a High King. An Archfae. He was ready to destroy the realms.

"Do not, under any circumstances, leave Maeve's side."

He didn't so much as look at her. He simply *faded* without another word.

Maeve gaped at the spot where Tiernan had been standing only seconds before. "He's not seriously expecting me to stand here and do nothing."

"It was a surprise attack, my lady." Lir maintained his effortlessly calm demeanor, but his hold on her arm didn't lessen. "We need to eliminate every threat."

"Lir," she pleaded. "I can fight just like the rest of you. I trained for battle since I was a child. I took out the Hagla, defeated Fearghal and the Scathing. I'm a warrior, damn it."

She could do more than stand by like some helpless princess—she was a fucking fae. She was never meant to be shuffled away to a safe space, to be guarded and protected like her life was somehow more valuable than those around her. Here was where she belonged, amidst the madness, just like the rest of them.

"I know." But the look Lir gave her was that of a male torn between duty and knowing the worth of the female who stood in front of him.

It was infuriating.

Frustrated, she turned and faced the Furies. "Balor, Tethra, and Dian." They bowed at her command. "Secure the palace and the city. If you find any enemies hiding within the Summer Court, destroy them."

Balor nodded swiftly. "Yes, Your Grace."

They started to move away, but she had to add one more thing. "Oh, and boys?"

The Furies faced her at once.

"Try not to terrify the innocent."

391

Their smiles, no matter how threatening, exhibited a glimpse of humor. Then they were gone, doing her bidding without question.

"Lir," she huffed, "what else can I do?"

But he wasn't looking at her. His gaze was trained beyond her and the expression he wore coasted prickles of alarm along her skin. It resembled...regret? Remorse? She couldn't be sure.

"Lir? What is it?" She attempted to follow his line of sight, but he captured her other arm and hauled her back around, making her face him, refusing to let her go.

He swallowed. "I beg you not to look, my lady."

She stared up at him, into silver eyes that mirrored molten steel. If he didn't want her to look upon a dead body, she could understand that, but it wasn't as though she was absolved from witnessing death. She'd seen her fair share. Many moons over. But this was different. His jaw was clenched tightly, his face somber. Whatever was behind her, it would do more than make her stomach turn.

She asked a more pointed question, her gut clenching. "Lir, who is it?"

He didn't answer her. He looked over her head, unwilling to make eye contact.

An unwanted wave of hysteria bubbled up inside her. Something was wrong. He never acted like this. Her heart rate spiked, and she gulped down air, tasting nothing but smoke and death. "Lir, tell me at once."

Still he remained silent, his grip on her never wavering.

"Lir, we are beyond this!" How many times had she fought to get him to speak to her, to open up to her, even in the most trivial of ways? "If you trust me, if you have an ounce of respect for me, then I beg you to tell me now. Please."

His eyes flashed and he dropped his hands, releasing her.

She whipped around, confused at first, because she couldn't pinpoint who or what had consumed him. She glimpsed Brynn kneeling by a body, crimson pooling around them both, staining the stone and her leggings. Except...that particular body was familiar to her.

Golden hair and clothing in jewel-toned hues. The colors of Autumn.

"Shay?" Maeve stumbled forward, tripping over herself before bursting into a full sprint. "Shay!"

Her heart caught in the back of her throat at the sight of him.

He was sprawled on the ground, his skin leached of all color. The length between the rise and fall of his chest was too long. He was dying. And to Maeve's utter horror, she could see why. He'd been gutted. Wholly. His abdomen shredded, his insides exposed to the elements.

Icy panic slammed into her. She couldn't think. She couldn't breathe. Her heart raced and her magic surged, imploding inside of her. Fear raked its claws down her back, ripping her to pieces. Grief consumed her, all-encompassing.

She clamped her hand over her mouth, swallowing down the rise of hot bile. "Oh, gods."

"I'm so sorry, my lady!" Brynn's voice broke, shattering her. She glanced up, tears streaking down her cheeks, her hands covered in Shay's blood. "I don't...I don't know what to do! I can't save him!"

"Shay," Maeve breathed, dropping onto the ground next to him. She ignored the way his blood seemed to stick to her leathers, and she bent down, smoothing his hair back from his clammy forehead.

"I can do it." She croaked the words out. "You're going to be alright. Just stay with me, Shay. Stay with me."

"Maeve." His voice reminded her of gravel.

"Don't...don't talk. I'm here." Tears burned her vision, and she stared down at the mess of his body. Her magic billowed. "I'm going to save you, okay?"

He smiled, but it was a ghost of its usual beauty. His lips were dry, cracked and peeling.

"He knew." Shay tried to speak again, his words garbled. He stole a breath and the sucking sound of it made a knot of acid roil in

Maeve's stomach. "Garvan knew I was against him. He used...used me to get to you."

Maeve shook her head. "He didn't though, see? He didn't get me. I'm right here."

Carefully, she placed her hands upon his heinous injuries and tried not to retch.

"Yes. But he has Ceridwen. He wants to trade...a sister." He coughed and Maeve winced against the jerking motion that pressed his insides into her blood-soaked palms. "For a sister."

Maeve was breaking. She tried to focus on what he was saying, but the power inside her was churning, begging for release. It roiled and flared, a storm all its own. After one shaky breath, she poured her magic into him. It rose up, vast and pulsing, so that Shay's entire body seemed to glow. She urged more, called to it, pulled it from that well deep inside. Her body trembled, drawing on the power radiating from her. The air pulsed yet nothing happened. The swell of magic simply hovered over him, as though searching for a way to mend and heal, to try to save what was going to be lost, but there was nothing to be done. Her magic wasn't enough this time.

The fates were cruel.

His cold hand covered hers. "It's too late for me, Maeve."

"No, no, it's not." Her words were rushed, spilling from her. "I can save you. I know I can."

Maeve would not let him die. She'd lost so much already. Gods, she'd lost everything. Her heart—she could feel it breaking. All those old wounds were rushing to the surface. All the heartache, the trauma, the suffering. She'd failed so many. She could not fail her brother, too.

Again, he coughed. Blood trickled from the corner of his mouth.

She was losing time.

"My lady." Lir's voice sounded from somewhere above her, and the warmth from his hand spread along her shoulder. "Nothing can be done. This is beyond...beyond even magic."

She shook her head, refusing to believe it. No. Her magic was *power*. Her magic was the life source, the soul of a fucking goddess. She had to save him. Darkness swirled inside her—her past come to life. All the things she sheltered and shoved away. She swallowed as Shay's eyes closed. Maeve captured his cheeks with her bloody hands. She rubbed her thumbs back and forth, streaking blood across his pallid skin, willing the life back into his eyes.

"Don't die on me!" she screamed. "Don't you dare die on me!"

His eyes, those beautiful eyes that were such an exact match to her own, squinted open. He gasped.

"I'm sorry, Maeve. I'm sorry I can't stay and..." Shay's chest rumbled, wheezed, as he struggled to breathe. "And get to know you."

"You can," she whispered. "You will."

Her hands, coated in his blood, hovered over him, trembling. Before her, he blurred. Proof of her tears. If her power couldn't keep him alive, then perhaps it could ease some of his pain. The glow of her magic wrapped around him like ribbons of gossamer silk, and though his heart continued to beat far too slowly, the sibling bond between them suddenly frayed. Like it was unraveling...about to snap.

Terror gripped her.

His throat worked as he tried to speak again and Maeve pressed her own lips together, willing him not to speak. "Don't."

"You look like her...you know," he rasped. "Our mother. You h-have her eyes."

Maeve's heart contorted, like it was wrenched from inside her chest. Her shoulders shuddered and she hastily swiped away her tears. "They're your eyes, too."

His smile was brief, then it faltered.

"No. Shay, please," she begged. Lir was right. There was nothing she could do. She was helpless. "Please."

"Believe me." He reached up and ran one finger along her cheek. She held his hand to her, warm life against the cold of death. "If things had been different...I would have loved you...from the moment you took your first breath."

The hand she kept pressed to her fell limp and Shay's eyes drifted close for the last time. It was as though a piece of her heart had been carved out. The pain sliced through her, hot and fast, severing the sibling bond, cutting it in half.

"Shay!" Maeve shrieked. She didn't care if her wailing wouldn't bring him back. It was all she had, it was all she could do. "*Shay!*"

Lir knelt beside her. "Let him go, little bird. You have to let him go."

"I—I can't." Her watery gaze met his. "I can't do it by myself."

He nodded, lips pressing into a thin line. Then he slowly slid Shay's lifeless hand from her grasp, laying it across his heart.

Tears ravaged her and the air simply wouldn't come. Erratic, choking sobs escaped from her, and her chest heaved and ached. Her head fell back, the agony of losing Shay too much to bear. She was broken. Useless. What good was the soul of a goddess, what good was being the life source of magic, if she couldn't save the lives of those she cared for the most?

"I couldn't save him." The words trembled as they fell from her lips. Brynn knelt and took Maeve's shuddering body into her arms. "I tried, but I couldn't. I failed him. Just like I failed all the others. They're all dead because of me."

"No." Lir's firm voice cut through her cries. "They are dead because of Parisa. Do not carry the burden of blame with you, my lady. You have to release this or it will torment you for the remainder of your days."

She looked at him then, at the fae warrior who was always a symbol of strength, and she collapsed. "I don't know how."

"Maeve!"

She barely had time to glance over her shoulder before Tiernan was there, scooping her into his arms and cradling her against him.

"*It's going to be okay, astora.*" The deep timbre of his voice was a balm to her shattered soul. "*I've got you...I've got you.*"

But Maeve felt nothing. Because she was no one.

Chapter Forty

Tiernan had never seen Maeve full of so much despair.

She sobbed in his arms as he carried her into his bedroom. Her tears were silent, except for when she struggled to get air. Then her breathing would hitch, her eyes would go wide, and her shoulders would tremble as she continued to cry. She was breaking. She was falling apart in his arms, and he wasn't sure if he would be enough to put her back together.

Maeve stood motionless while he slowly undressed her, while he removed the leathers and leggings soaked in Shay's blood. In her brother's blood. Carefully, he lifted the hem of her blouse, and she raised her arms, letting him tug it over her head. But her gaze wasn't on him. She was looking past him, lost to her own torments. The necklace he gave her overwhelmed him with a swell of emotion. Regret. Grief. Sorrow. Agony.

Her feelings destroyed him.

He would have to hurry if he wanted to bring her back.

Tiernan stalked into the bathroom and turned on the bath. Once the temperature was hot enough, he added some soothing rose oil and some bubbles. While the tub filled, he returned to the bedroom and took Maeve by the hand.

"Come along, *astora*." He traced little circles over the back of her hand. "Let's get you cleaned up."

She didn't move. Her gaze, desolate and empty, flicked to him.

"Okay." He scooped her into his arms, grateful when she didn't fight him, when she didn't tense or stiffen. He nudged open the bathroom door with the toe of his boot, stepped inside, then gently lowered her into the steaming tub of silky bubbles.

Maeve sat there and curled her knees into her chest, resting her cheek upon her knee so her hair tumbled around her. Red lined her eyes, and her lids were swollen, surrounded by thick, damp lashes.

If she wouldn't speak freely to him, then he would have to extend his hand first to bring her back. Tiernan started by trickling warm water over her skin, then doing the one thing he knew would reach her.

He sang.

"In the before, there was a goddess of lore
Whose soul was resplendent and pure
But her heart, it would ache and often times break
Till she thought it more than she could ever endure.

Though radiant as the sun, she saw herself undone
Tormented by her past, the terror and the strife
But she will rise and burn bright, far brighter than sunlight
For she is passion, eternal love, this queen of life."

Maeve's watery gaze met his. "Tiernan."

The pain in her voice nearly broke him. Then she shattered. She cried out his name, over and over, her body convulsing, shaking from the agony of her grief. He climbed in the tub with her, fully clothed, and pulled her trembling form into his arms. She collapsed against him. Her head fell against his shoulder as she wept, releasing everything she'd fought to ignore. Every loss. Every death. Every shred of torment. She released all of it, and Tiernan swore his own heart broke. For his Strand burned hot, reaching for the other half of his soul that was lost in a well of sorrow.

MAEVE HAD FINALLY BROKEN.

When Shay died, her heart splintered. She crumbled, she crashed, unable to spare herself from the impact. She shattered; the fragments of her soul lay all around her like shards of a smashed prism. Incandescent. Reflective. Capable of casting thousands of rainbows. But useless if not fully whole.

In Tiernan's arms, she let the darkness take her. In his arms, she let herself grieve.

She mourned all that had been taken from her. Kells, the land she once sought to rule, was no longer her home. She cried for her mortal heart, for the pieces of her humanity, the shredded scraps she clung to for fear that if she let go, she'd lose herself completely. She thought of Casimir and remembered that even though his betrayal cut far deeper than she could ever have imagined, he still came back for her. He took her from that dungeon beneath the palace in the Spring Court. Another stab of grief pierced her, and tremors overtook her as her mind drifted to Rowan. So often, his memory would haunt her dreams. She lost track of the number of moons when her nightmares crawled back to terrorize her and forced her to relive the rain of swords all over again. He'd protected her. Saved her. Died for her.

She'd never been given the chance to say goodbye.

Tiernan held her tighter, crushed her naked body against him. His clothing was soaked from the water in the tub and bubbles clung to his arms, but he didn't let go. He would never let her go.

His song, it spoke to the very essence of her life. Overcome with shadows and suffering, Tiernan had stepped into the brilliance of what was left of her heart, offering his own to help hers mend.

So she took it. She let him pull her, bring her back, and in doing so, she faced all that she'd fought to ignore. It wasn't just Shay's death that ruined her. It was all of them. The tragic deaths of the mortals trapped within the Scathing, the ones Fearghal glamoured into dark fae. The guards in the Moors she used to fight alongside while training with Casimir. It was Rowan, with his lavender eyes and knowing smirk. It was even Garvan, how she focused on him to distract herself from losing the only family she'd ever known. And Shay...when the familial bond between them snapped and severed, it was as though the hand of death had reached inside and ripped her heart from her chest.

She never wanted to experience that ever again.

But she would...when the god of death came for Tiernan.

Another choking sob escaped her, and Tiernan murmured soothing phrases to her in Old Laic. His left hand was wrapped around her middle, and he captured her cheek with his right, tilting her face to him.

"Talk to me, *astora*."

Maeve bit her lip. "I think I'd prefer it if you just read my thoughts."

The barest of smiles. "There's no easy way out of this. You know it. I know it."

Another wave of heartache slammed into her. Tears fell hot and fast down her cheeks. She couldn't stop them. She couldn't stop anything.

"I thought my magic would be enough, but it's not. I thought it would help fix all these broken pieces of me, but it can't. I tried so hard to ignore everything, all I've been through. All I've suffered. I thought my power would help ease the hurt. But it doesn't. And it won't. Not ever. Will it?"

"No, Maeve. Magic is not a bandage to heal the wounds on our hearts."

She looked up at Tiernan then. His words were so much like her own, and he would know. He'd made a deal for more power to avenge those he loved to heal his own heart, and it hadn't been enough. But he was proof of overcoming the torment of the past.

He was right. Magic couldn't heal the wounds on the inside. Power did nothing to soothe one's suffering. Bandages didn't last forever and yet he'd persevered. He was steadfast and sure. Confident. And Maeve knew he would always be there for her. He would catch her when she fell. When she couldn't carry the weight of the world anymore, she knew he would pick her up. Lift her up.

There was no doubt in her mind that the memories of his past continued to cause him pain, but he'd managed to survive. He'd found his place in this world and for the first time in a long time, Maeve realized she'd found her place as well.

With him. Beside him. Always.

Her fingers curled around the necklace she'd forged from sunlight, the one in the shape of mountains and the rising sun— Summer's crest. Tiernan's Court. Her home.

She swallowed, forcing down the knot of emotion threatening to choke her. "Tiernan?"

His twilight gaze landed on her and held. His thumb brushed away a fallen tear. "Yes, *astora?*"

A quaking breath left her in a rush. "Tiernan, I love you."

For a moment, he didn't move. The look on his face was unreadable. His eyes were swirling with emotion, but he shuttered it away quickly. Then he bent down toward her, so his lips were barely a breath away from her own. "I love you too, Maeve."

Their matching Strands glowed bright, crimson and gold. The mating bond between them sealed for eternity.

Chapter Forty-One

"There has to be another way."

Tiernan looked around the table at the solemn faces surrounding him. To his right, Maeve sat quietly, her eyes slightly red and puffy from all the tears she'd cried. Lir stood behind her, one hand placed protectively on her shoulder. Merrick was stewing in his own anger, his face the epitome of rage. And Brynn kept her head ducked down, unable to meet anyone's gaze.

Garvan had learned Shay was supplying information to the Summer Court, and he used that knowledge to get to Maeve. Multiple sources confirmed they could hear Shay's screams coming from outside the palace walls. Ceridwen rounded up a group of Summer warriors and when they went to investigate, they were overwhelmed by Autumn soldiers. They stormed the grounds, stole Ceridwen, and left Shay to die. Maeve's sphere of protection held, but the assault took place outside of its boundaries, and no one was able to stop it.

Now it seemed, Garvan wanted a trade.

A sister for a sister.

Maeve eased back in her chair, withdrawn. She rubbed her hands over her face, shoving her hair back. "Garvan and Parisa will stop at nothing until they have me in their clutches."

Tension wound its way through Tiernan's body, and he looked over at her, covering her hand with his own. "What would you have me do?"

She lifted one shoulder, then let it fall, docile. "Give me up."

"Never." The words left him in a harsh breath.

"What other choice do you have?" Her eyes were pleading. "How many more lives will be lost until we give her what she wants?"

"Maeve," he began, but she lifted one hand, silencing him.

"No." She pressed her lips together, intertwining their fingers. "Look around you, my lord. They may not say it directly, but everyone here at the table knows this is entirely my fault."

"Bullshit, my lady." Merrick's words were laced with venom. "This war with Parisa started before you were even born."

"Merrick is right." Brynn's eyes shifted from warm brown to near black. "We would never give you up to that monster of a bitch."

"But we have to get Ceridwen back," Maeve argued, determination filling the smooth planes of her face.

Tiernan nodded. "And we will. But not at the cost of you."

Silence fell between them. Maeve was willing to give herself up in exchange for Ceridwen, and as much as he longed to have his twin returned to the Summer Court, he couldn't bring himself to let Maeve walk into danger unless he had a foolproof way to get her out. But as of now, no one could think of any alternative means. All of which brought him back to his original point.

There had to be another way.

Merrick leaned forward. His brow was furrowed in thought, his gaze contemplative. "I think I have an idea."

"Does it involve handing Maeve over to Garvan?" Brynn asked, inspecting the dagger she held in her hands.

"Yes." He lifted one finger as her gaze shot to him, a silent plea for her to hold her fire. "And no."

At that, Tiernan sat up, interest in his hunter's scheme taking root. "What do you mean?"

"I mean, if we can get Maeve into the Autumn Court in exchange for Ceridwen," he paused, the idea taking form in his mind, "then I think I know a way we can also get her out."

Lir's hand fell away from Maeve's shoulder. "How do you figure?"

"Garvan isn't stupid. If he's holding Ceridwen hostage, then he's got the entire palace warded. He'll be expecting us to attack him, not agreeing to the trade." Merrick spread his hands on the table and started drawing up invisible outlines with his fingers. "Kyol's palace is built into the side of a mountain. I've been there numerous times, and I know for a fact there's a balcony on every level. The palace is designed to be impenetrable from above and below, mostly in part due to the—"

"Waterfalls," Lir finished for him, slowly nodding.

Brynn flicked her dagger between her fingers, agitated. "You're seriously implying she should jump to her death?"

"No, of course not." Merrick's bright blue gaze landed on Maeve. "I'm implying she should jump to her freedom."

Brynn's scowl only deepened. "Mer, that's a suicide mission. You have no way of knowing if the palace in Kyol is still intact. For all we know, Garvan could've changed everything. Reinforced it somehow. I mean, it's been years since you've been to the Autumn Court."

His answering smile was calculating. "Has it though?"

Brynn struggled to control the grin tugging at the corner of her mouth. "Bastard."

"Hunter," he corrected smoothly.

"They'll catch her." Lir's cool voice filled the space, chilling the air. "Assuming she survives the fall, she'll be target practice for Autumn's archers if she tries to fly."

"She won't be flying." Merrick raked a hand through his hot pink hair. "She'll be swimming."

Brynn shifted in her seat, her eyes switching colors so rapidly,

Tiernan could barely keep up. "Even still. Lir is right. Whether she's in the air or in the water, she'll be caught."

Merrick clicked his tongue. "Only if she resurfaces."

Maeve's head snapped up and her gaze landed on him. "The merrows."

He nodded once. "Exactly."

Tiernan sat back in his seat, impressed. It could work. He had to admit, the plan was slightly reckless and there was no guarantee of Maeve's safety, but it was a start. The waterfalls running on both sides of Kyol's palace flowed into the Black Lake, and from there, it emptied into the Gaelsong Sea. Maeve had survived when the merrows caught her by surprise and took her to the depths of Ispomora below the Lismore Marin; and that was a saltwater sea, not a small, winding river. Not only that, but Queen Marella had promised to offer the Summer Court support if they needed it, and right now, her assistance could be the determining factor between losing his sister or his *sirra* forever.

It was precarious, and though he knew she would agree, there was something else there. Her necklace alerted him to it...to the hesitation she was feeling.

Brynn gnawed on her bottom lip, her apprehension clearly visible. "Do we really think this can work?"

"It's a risk." Tiernan strummed his fingers idly on the table. There would always be an element of risk. "But it's the best we've come up with so far."

"Agreed." Merrick crossed his arms, awaiting Maeve's decision. "It could be our one shot to get both High Princesses back."

"What about you, little bird?" Lir dropped into the chair across from Maeve, tracking her every movement with his silver eyes. "Are you up for it?"

"Yes." She swallowed. "I can do it."

But...but there was something she wasn't saying. Something she wasn't telling them.

"I've been to Ispomora before, so I'm not worried about that." Her brow was pinched when she focused on Merrick. "You said every level of Kyol's palace has a balcony overlooking the falls?"

He nodded sharply. "Right."

"Okay," she drew the word out. "So, all I have to do is make it to a balcony and jump?"

"Exactly." A shadow fell across his face, and he reached out to her, gently patting her hand. "I know it's not the best idea, my lady."

She bristled. "I'll make it happen."

"When you get to the railing, don't hesitate. Don't look back. Don't waste a single second, okay?" Merrick had never been so somber. "Just jump."

Maeve glanced down at her lap and ran her teeth along her bottom lip. She fiddled with the hem of her oversized blouse, smoothing away imaginary wrinkles. Her thoughts were a whirlwind. Panicked. All she seemed to focus on was the water and its current. If it was cold. If it was dark.

Ah.

Tiernan finally understood. This was where her uncertainty stemmed from. It came from her memories of Kells, the cage, and when Carman nearly drowned her out of spite. She was struggling to find her strength, to convince herself she could go through with it. The jump from one of the balconies, from any of them, would be no small feat. It would be like reliving her fall from the Cliffs of Morrigan all over again, the one he'd witnessed in her nightmares. If her terror resurfaced, she could panic. She could drown. She could die.

Lir inched forward, his exterior calm, but he read her like one of the many pages in her books. "There's a waterfall on each side of Kyol's palace, supplied by a river of water that flows south from an inlet off the coast. The palace is built into the side of a mountain, and the water pools at the base, much like a moat. The water you will be jumping into is frigid. It will steal your breath. From what I've gathered," he said, with a fleeting look to Tiernan, "you've been in the Black Lake before."

The understated slight was not overlooked.

In Tiernan's defense, when he'd tossed Maeve into the lake to cure her of the *spraedagh* she'd inhaled, he didn't think she would drown. She knew how to swim, but her terror had been too great.

"But it is also extremely dark. You won't be able to see anything, you will be relying completely upon the merrows to guide you." Lir trailed his finger across the table in front of her. "It feeds into the Black Lake and that's where we will be waiting for you. The current is fairly strong through the river section, but once the merrows have you, they will be the ones to bring you to safety."

Maeve nodded, processing. "When should I jump?"

"As soon as the opportunity arises," Tiernan answered, not allowing anyone the chance to contradict him. "We don't know how long Garvan will wait before summoning Parisa, if he waits at all."

"Alright." Maeve continued to fidget with her blouse, twisting the fabric around her finger, then loosening it altogether. "And how will the merrows know when I've jumped?"

"They'll be on a constant rotation until you do." Merrick glanced at Tiernan for confirmation. "We'll have two of them waiting for you, and a third will be the messenger to alert us. They'll be there for you as soon as you hit the water."

Maeve blew out a breath, a rush of calm radiating from her. "Okay."

"So." Merrick propped his elbows up on the table, clasping his hands together. His hot pink hair fell into his face. "Are we doing this thing?"

"Yes." Maeve's chin lifted and she was the epitome of resolution. "Let's get Ceridwen back."

Tiernan stood and everyone followed suit. "Send word to Queen Marella of our plan. We need to have her forces in position before Maeve even steps foot into the Autumn Court."

Brynn sheathed her dagger. "And Garvan?"

"Name the time and place to our benefit." Thunder echoed in the distance, and he welcomed its threat. The promise of his own destruction. "If he wants Maeve so badly, he will do as we demand."

GARVAN WASTED no time in honoring Tiernan's request.

Maeve saw his written response and agreement to meet less than twelve hours after they devised their strategy to get Ceridwen back to the Summer Court and hand her over to Autumn.

They would all meet on the border of Summer and Autumn tomorrow at dusk. There would be no magic. No fighting. Already the ground was being charmed to create a non-binding faerie ring. It would be a neutral zone, one where neither party held the upper hand. And when Ceridwen was brought forward, if she had been harmed in any way, then it would be considered an act of war.

Tiernan had chosen dusk because it offered Maeve the cover of nightfall to make her escape. Already, the merrows were below the falls, waiting for her. Everything was in place, all the pieces of their scheme set. It was only a matter of well-timed movements. It would be a game of strategy and precision, one she could not afford to lose.

The Furies, however, were none too pleased by Merrick's grand plan. They didn't want Maeve out of their sight, and it was only when she commanded them to remain behind that they agreed, but their reluctance was bitter. It was necessary. Balor, Tethra, and Dian were extremely powerful. They were dangerous. They were a threat. A weapon Maeve planned to release upon Parisa at the right moment, and not a second sooner.

After tomorrow, Maeve would be in the Autumn Court.

And there was only one way to escape.

Chapter Forty-Two

T he next evening, Maeve found herself on the edge of two
worlds.

At the base of the mountains dividing the Summer and
Autumn Courts was a well-worn footpath. It was there the two
Courts collided. Skinny trees with white trunks and leaves of gold-
enrod and ginger reached for the lush green ferns that sprouted up
from the earth. The air was cool, an intoxicating mix of florals and
spice. Caught between the pull of two seasons, it was the last breath
of Summer and the first life of Autumn. An eternal equinox.

Twilight hues of indigo and lavender stretched across the sky like
watercolors paints, blending into the drifting clouds, absorbing the
clash of golden sunlight. The stars looked down upon them, watching, waiting to see who would be first to step into the faerie ring made
of crushed leaves and rose petals.

Tiernan explained there were strict rules to follow when an
exchange of such caliber was to be made—only two from each side
would enter the ring. Maeve and Ceridwen would pass one another,
but no words were allowed to be spoken between them. If anyone

caused a disturbance, if anyone attempted to alter the arrangement or intervene, blood would be spilled.

Maeve hadn't thought it was such a terrible thing.

She would love to be the one to make Garvan bleed.

To her left stood Tiernan and Merrick. To her right, Lir and Brynn. Opposite her, on the other side of the faerie ring were Garvan and Ceridwen, Aeralie—the fae she met during the Autumn Ceilie—and four other Autumn soldiers she didn't recognize.

Garvan spoke first. "Hello, sister. So good to see you again."

She stared him down, saying nothing.

Tiernan's voice instantly filled her mind. *"Don't provoke him, astora."*

"But it's so much fun."

His rumbling laughter echoed through her thoughts. She locked her spine into place, schooling her features. "Garvan," she said coolly.

"Let's get this over with, High Prince." Tiernan spat out her brother's title in disgust.

Garvan smiled but it was forced. Unnatural. He gestured in Maeve's direction. "This should be a quick exchange. A sister for a sister."

Merrick rocked back onto his heels, shoving his hands into his pockets. He flashed Garvan a ruthless smile. "I hear Parisa's a bit pissy now that her favorite toy is dead."

Her brother's hands curled into white-knuckled fists. "She is the Dark Queen, and you will address her as such."

Merrick scoffed. "Not a chance."

Garvan glowered and jerked his head toward Aeralie. "Make the exchange."

Aeralie gently nudged Ceridwen, and they moved forward together. Lir took Maeve's upper arm, guiding her so they stepped over the leaves and petals and into the faerie ring. The air inside the ring was strange. It was dense, powerful, yet not magical, as though time moved slower, and in this space, they were untouchable. Her movements were intentional and precise. Every noise was amplified.

The sound of falling leaves. The crunch of the earth beneath her boots. The breeze whispering through the trees, spreading rumors of what they would witness this night.

Ceridwen was graceful, a High Princess in every right. Pride glowed from inside her effervescent beauty, but a silent tear slid down her cheek as they drew closer. Aeralie, on the other hand, was not the same as before. The lightness that once surrounded her was gone. Her features were stern, her lips pressed into a thin, hard line, and Maeve wondered if she perhaps mourned Shay. If maybe there was a division within the Autumn Court, if maybe it was an essential piece of information she could use to her advantage.

"*I can hear you plotting, astora.*" Tiernan once again slid into her thoughts. "*I know you're curious and want to learn all you can to help, but this is not a spy mission. We need you back here as soon as possible.*"

Maeve kept her face impassive. "*We?*"

"*I need you.*" His voice was firmer now, more ominous like that of an approaching storm. "*And I swear to the gods, if our plan fails, I will come for you. I will destroy everything and everyone in my path until you're returned to me.*"

An unbidden sigh escaped her, and mist swirled at her feet. "*You'd destroy the realm for me?*"

"*And then I'd sit back and watch while you build a new one made of dreams.*" His murmur of a vow sank deep into her soul. "*I love you.*"

Maeve bit back a smile. "*I love you, too.*"

Ceridwen passed her, and Maeve kept her hands by her side as she walked. The tips of their fingers just barely grazed one another and then there was nothing. Aeralie led her out of the faerie ring and Maeve turned just in time to see Lir repeat the motion with Ceridwen.

It was done.

The trade was made. She was in Autumn now and on her own. But the Autumn Court was *hers*. It was her breath, her life, her soul.

It *knew* her. Its lifeblood was the beating of her heart. Its magic was alive inside of her.

Maeve would survive this, and she would not become Parisa's pet. She would escape not only for herself, but for the future of the Four Courts. For the Spring fae who'd been abused, for the merrows who'd been butchered. For Rowan and Shay. For them all. And she would not stop. She would never stop. She already killed Carman. She demolished the Hagla and destroyed Fearghal.

Garvan would be next.

Tiernan stood there, helpless to do anything but watch as Garvan and his crew *faded* away with Maeve.

Ceridwen rushed forward, throwing her arms around him, but Tiernan found himself unable to look away from the spot where Maeve had been standing only moments before. His twin eased back, and her wide-eyed gaze searched his face.

"You shouldn't have traded her to him. Not for me. I would've managed on my own. Despite popular belief, I'm not entirely incapable of defending myself."

Something in his chest tightened.

"I know that," Tiernan ground out, staring at the faerie ring as the rose petals and fallen leaves fluttered away on the breeze. Like nothing had happened. Like his mate hadn't just vanished before his eyes. "We have a plan."

"It better be a damn good one." Ceridwen crossed her arms and a thin line furrowed across her brow. She turned then, facing the border of the Autumn Court. "Giving Maeve up..." She shook her head, her plaited blonde hair shimmering in the fading sunlight. "I don't have a good feeling about this, Tiernan."

"I swear," Lir cracked his knuckles, then popped his neck, "if we don't get her back—"

"We will." Tiernan refused to think of any alternate possibility.

They'd get her back. *He* would bring her back himself, and if it meant summoning the Furies and catapulting Faeven into the chaos of darkness, then so be it.

Brynn admired the honed tip of her dagger, turning it so it reflected the last shreds of sunlight dwindling from the sky. Then she used it to file one of her nails. "If he so much as lays one finger on her, if one fucking hair on Maeve's head is out of place—"

"He wouldn't dare," Merrick countered.

"But Parisa would."

Tiernan cut his hunter down with a look, but Merrick didn't blanch or falter. He kept his face impassive, firmly believing that his plan to bring Maeve back would work. Tiernan wanted to have faith in him, but the truth was already out there. Parisa *would* hurt Maeve. She'd already done so once before. Images of Lir carrying Maeve, bleeding and nearly broken, stole through his memory. The way Fearghal had carved her body with his blade caused Tiernan's blood to burn and his temper to rage. Parisa would attempt to break Maeve again, wholly this time. She would stop at nothing to bend Maeve to her will.

"You shouldn't have done it." Ceridwen's lips pressed into a thin line, and she tucked an errant strand of hair behind her ear. "You shouldn't have given her up for me."

"Don't worry, High Princess." Merrick grinned, but it didn't quite reach his eyes. "It's just as the High King said, we have a plan."

Ceridwen twisted the bangles hanging from her wrist. Around and around. Her eyes, the same swirl of deep blue and purple like his own, flicked between each of them...disbelieving.

"She's going to get out of there." Tiernan rarely heard his twin's thoughts, as she was so often calm-natured and content. But now they roiled, bouncing around through every worst-case scenario imaginable. His skin crawled, knowing his sister was capable of even thinking such things. "I promise she'll escape. And when she does, we'll be waiting for her."

She spun on him, and her face was a mask, calm before the storm.

"And what if Garvan throws her into the dungeon? He locked me in a bedroom worthy of my station, but it was charmed. My magic was dampened, just out of my reach. I couldn't access anything, Tiernan. His wards are strong, they always have been, and there's no telling where in that damned palace he'll put Maeve."

"She'll get out," Tiernan reiterated, grinding the words out. "She is not weak. She's the fucking Dawnbringer, Cer."

"But you sent her into the lion's den, Tiernan!" Ceridwen's cheeks flushed with vexation and her slender fingers clenched into fists. "She walked right into enemy territory. You sent her in there to fight her way out against dark magic with no means of self-defense, no weapon. No anything!"

Merrick slung an arm around Ceridwen's shoulders, and this time when he smiled, his dimples winked into play. "Who said she doesn't have a weapon?"

Chapter Forty-Three

G arvan *faded* Maeve onto one of the many balconies.

To say Kyol's palace was spectacular was an understatement. Coiling spires of obsidian speared upward, the peak of each one crowned with a magnificent bronze leaf. Pointed archways surrounded by carvings of trees and all the phases of the moon revealed a maze of vaulted corridors. Decadent stained-glass windows were illuminated from within by faerie light, reflecting a world washed in jewel-toned hues. Buttresses rose from each balcony, slanting to support the level above her, like the wings of a dragon.

It was positively breathtaking, and were it not for the rushing sound of the waterfalls on either side of the palace, Maeve could've sworn she heard music playing. A whisper of old, from a time long before.

Standing there, with the Autumn Court at her back and the legacy of her parents before her, she could almost picture it. She could envision the lavish parties, the extravagant celebrations, the moon shining down upon the glittering harvest Court. If she closed her eyes, she could see *them*. Dorian and Fianna. Hand in hand. Twirling across a ballroom. Devoted to one another. Full of passion and affection for one another and their children. They weren't her memories though, merely fragments she longed to put together to recreate the life she never had... the one that had been stolen from her. But she didn't need false memories to know the High King and High Queen of Autumn were infatuated with one another. Rowan had told her as much, once upon a time.

The balcony Maeve stood upon soared above the crashing falls below. And the water, where she prayed the merrows waited for her, was *very* far down indeed. Merrick had failed to mention exactly how far she would have to fall once she jumped. She wrapped her arms around herself to keep from shaking and looked up. Rugged mountains surrounded the palace, protruding across the horizon like slashes of slate, their shadows outlined against the night sky.

Garvan watched her, his mouth curling into one of those oddly unnatural smiles.

Maeve called to her magic, to the fire and smoke, to the soul of the goddess, but the response was faint. Like her power was smothered. She could feel it inside of her, but it was fuzzy, simmering just out of reach. Charmed, exactly like Brynn had thought. Garvan had the entire palace warded against the use of magic. Damn him.

Her nails bit into the leather of her armor. Her stomach twisted into knots, but she blew out a low, calming breath. Despite forcing herself to maintain a false sense of composure, her blood boiled. She wanted to murder Garvan for what he did to Shay, for the way he brutalized him. She would have his head on a stake and set fire to his body before she ever allowed him to harm another.

"You're awfully quiet, dear sister." Garvan tilted his head, analyzing her. "Nothing to say?"

She didn't fear Garvan. She would never fear Autumn. Maeve narrowed her gaze and said, "Not to you."

He shrugged, dismissive. "Probably for the best. I bet that mouth of yours gets you into plenty of trouble."

"So I've been told."

He smiled, but even that was scornful. "This way."

Two guards flanked Maeve, each of them with their swords drawn. The blades glinted in the faint light, but nightshade did not coat them. It was something else...something familiar, she just couldn't put her finger on what. A magic of some kind. She could attack them now. She was certain she could take them all. But she was outnumbered and only had her Aurastone to defend herself. Not impossible. But not a risk she was certain she wanted to take, at least not yet.

One guard flicked his sword, urging her to walk. Left with no choice, Maeve followed Garvan down a dimly lit hall. Their footfalls echoed off the vast and sloping ceiling, and their shadows crawled along the stone wall. She hadn't expected to be placed in the guest quarters by any means, but she had hoped to avoid another stay in a dungeon.

"This would've been easier, you know," Garvan said over his shoulder, "if you hadn't put up such a fight the first time Parisa caught you."

"She didn't catch me," Maeve fired back, taking careful note of how Garvan addressed Parisa by her given name instead of her fabricated title.

He stilled, turning to face her. "What?"

"Parisa didn't catch me the first time." She kept her voice level, her breathing even. "Casimir Vawda turned me over to her. Apparently, she can't do anything on her own." She gestured vaguely toward him. "I mean, look at you."

Maeve expected a flash of anger or annoyance, but Garvan's expression remained unreadable, and when the faerie light flickered over his face, his eyes lacked any real emotion.

"Yes, well. We all do as we must."

He continued down the hall and she fell into step just behind him, trying to memorize every turn, trying to discern any landmarks so when the time came, she could find her way out. She would attempt to distract while she noted her surroundings.

417

"So, you're telling me you had no other choice than to work for someone who wants to see Faeven destroyed?"

"She doesn't want to destroy Faeven, Maeve." He suffered her a sigh, looking down at her like she was merely a child who didn't yet understand the ways of the world. "She wants to unite it under one ruler...her."

Exasperation thrummed through her blood. Was her brother really so foolish? "So you willingly bowed down before a former Archfae with no power and no magic?"

Garvan's gaze cut to her, his emerald green eyes igniting. "I bow before *no one*."

Maeve's brow arched.

Interesting.

"We are equals." But his voice had lost some of its conviction.

"No." Maeve jabbed her finger into his chest, shocked when none of the guards made a move to detain her. "*You* are a High Prince of the Autumn Court. *She* is nothing. She's the one relying on outsourced dark magic to seize control because she abused the power bestowed upon her. And the gods saw fit to punish her for it. You, Garvan, are *not* her equal."

She didn't care if she was playing into his ego, if her attempt to bolster his confidence caused her insides to flinch. If she could just get him to see reason, if she could get through to him somehow, then maybe...maybe she could convince him to abandon Parisa. She could never forgive him for his crimes, especially not the death of Shay, but she could at least prevent him from doing more damage. From hurting more people. From ending more lives.

His mood shifted, and his eyes cleared. Something in his expression changed, and for a second, he looked almost pleasant. Kind. Like she imagined he would have been before Parisa. Before Carman. Before the Evernight War. Before their mother died.

"You know I'm right." She glanced cautiously at the guards who stood back, pretending not to listen. Then softer, "Everyone here knows I'm right."

"So what if you are?" He countered, throwing his arms out to his sides. "What's done is done."

"And what exactly has been done?" Maeve demanded. "What did you do? What did you give her?"

His jaw clenched and shadows fell across his face.

"Tell me. Tell me now." She searched his face, desperate to get through to him. If she could break him down a little further. "Whatever it is, I can help you fix it."

"No one can help me."

"Garvan," she pleaded, "you can trust me. You can help us stop her. Help us end her. Whatever Parisa holds over your head, whatever bargain you made with her, is of no consequence once she's dead. I'll forgive you for—"

He barked out a harsh laugh, his lips curling into a sneer. "You? Forgive *me*?"

Maeve stiffened and tried not to wince. She'd been so close but had taken their conversation too far.

"The deal I made with her is none of your concern." Garvan spun on his heel and stalked off.

The guards gently urged her to follow so she did, staying a few paces back as Garvan led them deeper into the mountain, further away from the waterfall. The corridors blended together like a winding maze, a labyrinth of damp stone and feeble light. Worry niggled at the back of her mind. The deeper into the mountain they ventured, the more difficult it would be for her to find her way out. For her to make it to one of the balconies. Alarm crawled along her spine like dozens of tiny spiders, but she shivered, forcing her trepidation to the back of her mind. She would find a way out, no matter what.

The air was cooler here. It smelled of ancient earth and despair. She counted at least eight posted guards, not including the ones walking alongside her. Even if she managed to escape from wherever Garvan was taking her, it wouldn't be easy. Her glamoured Aurastone was safely tucked into the sheath strapped to her thigh, and she would be forced to use it to get back to the Summer Court. Innocent lives would be lost unless she convinced them to side with her instead.

The thought, though hopeful, was terribly unlikely.

Garvan stopped before a massive door hinged with a metal lock and swung it open. He stepped back, allowing her entry. "Your quarters, my lady."

It was a small room, not quite a dungeon, but not exactly a proper bedroom. The bed was plain, nothing more than a mattress sitting on top of a wooden platform. A wash basin was positioned in the corner with a small toilet next to it. And there were no windows.

"And how long will I have to stay here?" Maeve asked, rubbing her hands along her arms to ward off the lingering chill.

His shoulders rose and fell, carelessly. "Could be an hour. A day or two. Weeks. Maybe a month. I suppose it depends on her mood."

Just then, another Autumn fae appeared in the doorway.

One she recognized.

Aeralie stood there with a blanket in her arms. She bowed toward Garvan and strode forward, her movements stiff.

"Here's a blanket, my lady." Her voice was rough. Aggressive. Maeve drew back, away from the unexpected outburst. "I doubt it's what you're used to in the Summer Court. But if you don't move around too much, the fabric won't scratch your skin and you might stay warm."

Aeralie thrust it into Maeve's arms and then she did the unthinkable.

She winked.

"Try not to fret too much, dear sister." Garvan exited the room, followed by Aeralie and the two other guards. "I know Parisa can't wait to get her hands on you."

Maeve allowed him to have the last words, and she feigned panic, ensuring he caught sight of her horrified expression as he pulled the door shut and locked it.

She waited, counting to twenty slowly, then she searched for a way out. But there was nothing. The lock on the door was solid and unless she had a way to destroy the toilet or wash basin and crawl through drainage pipes and waste, escape was impossible. She dropped onto the bed and tried not to give into the rising sensation of despair.

There had to be a way.

Maeve glanced down at the blanket in her lap.

The wink.

Keeping a steady eye on the door, Maeve unfurled the blanket. There, tucked into the folds of the rough-hewn fabric, was a gold key.

Just big enough for a lock.

MAEVE'S BREATH hitched and her gaze snapped up to the door once again, terrified Garvan would return and discover someone had aided her. But no one opened the door. No one came barging in, threatening her life. It was the same eerie silence as before.

Aeralie had given her a key, she'd given her a way out. But the dark halls were long and winding. Maeve had a general idea of how to get back to the balcony, but there'd been so many corners and turns, she wasn't even sure if she could find her way back. She'd wished Merrick had given her a map.

A map.

Aran. Aran had a plethora of maps. She squeezed her eyes shut, trying to remember every detail of his map-making room aboard the Amshir. He had hundreds of maps, certainly one of them would've been of his palace, of his home. Perhaps she'd seen it once or twice. But even if she had, she'd been far too distracted by all the other far-off places he'd been. Her memory came up empty.

Damn it.

She knew she was deep into the mountain and that the palace was built into the face. When she arrived, the sun's dying rays were at her back, which meant the palace itself faced west. If she wanted to reach the balcony, then west was the direction to go, which seemed easy enough except for the ridiculous amount of turns it took to bring her here. She would have to be stealthy and silent, listening only for the sound of rushing water to guide her.

Maeve stood. She had a key, so she had a way out. She could do this. Every minute she spent debating on what to do next was a minute of darkness lost. Carefully, unwilling to even breathe, Maeve slid the key into the lock and slowly twisted it.

All she could do was pray to the heavens that no one was standing on the other side.

Chapter Forty-Four

Tiernan spoke to no one. He saw no one.

He sat upon his throne in silence, waiting for something, for anything, for any news at all. Moonlight washed the outdoor ballroom in a haze of silver, but the grounds were oddly quiet. The breeze did not whisper through the palms. Even the call of the sea was too soft to hear. It was as though the Summer Court knew Maeve was gone, and it too, held its very breath. Watching. Waiting.

In the stillness, alone with his thoughts, he knew what needed to be done. It was something he should've done moons ago and he wouldn't allow another second to go to waste.

The moment Maeve returned from the Autumn Court, he would make her his queen. He would place her upon her throne of dreams, right where she belonged. Beside him. With him. Forever.

Gods and vows be damned.

Chapter Forty-Five

The lock opened soundlessly, but Maeve didn't dare move. She didn't even breathe. She just stood there, frozen, waiting in the quiet for sounds and voices.

She'd counted eight guards in this hall alone. Gods save her if she had to take so many lives.

She slipped into the corridor, giving her eyes a moment to adjust to the faint light. It wasn't much, but it was just enough. Garvan must have thought her painfully weak to not even consider charming the door or warding it to prevent her from escaping. Holding her breath, she called to her magic again; it was nothing more than a dull thrum. A faint beat of existence.

Frustrated that her visibility was so poor, she began trekking forward to the western side of the palace. One foot after the other, every step featherlight, every breath measured. Slow. Steady. Straining, she desperately tried to listen for the sound of rushing water to guide her. She clung to the shadows, melting into them, using them to her advantage. She was only a few paces away from her room when she heard the distinctive thud of boots heading her way.

Shit.

There was nowhere to hide.

She crouched low, pressing herself into the cold stone as the footsteps drew nearer. Even with the weak light, she could just make out the outline of a male fae in scarlet leather armor. If he discovered her room empty, he'd sound the alarm.

He huffed out a breath as he stalked past her, muttering to himself, then pounded against the door to her room with his meaty fist. "Dinner!" He unhooked one of the keys dangling from his belt and slid it into the lock.

Maeve knew what would come next.

The door swung open, and she leapt up, rushing him from behind.

The guard whipped around, eyes wide and mouth open, right as she plunged her Aurastone into his chest.

She yanked it out, hating the sound of the blade sliding against flesh. Crimson soaked his leathers, looking almost black in the faint light. He crumpled, the weight of his large body nearly crushing her, but she hooked her arms under his and dragged him into the room. Maeve panted, heaving his lifeless body onto the bed. She snatched the blanket Aeralie had given her and draped it over his body. Already so much time had passed, and she was right back where she started. Locking the door behind her and refusing to look back, she set off down the hall again, forcing herself to move faster.

One.

She would keep count of all the lives she took that night.

Picking up her pace, she caught sight of another guard coming her way, likely to see what was taking the other one so long. She slid closer to the ground, Aurastone poised to strike. He strode by and she lunged, coiling one hand into his hair, yanking his head back, and slitting his throat. He gurgled and choked, causing Maeve to cringe. She sucked in a breath, hating herself. Just like with the first guard, she took the brunt of his dead weight and gradually lowered him to the ground to make the drop as soundless as possible.

Two.

Her heart raced, frantic with the pulse of distress and regret.

She continued down the corridor and came upon another guard. He was lounging against the wall, his silhouette illuminated by the only burning sconce in the hall. Faerie light washed over him in an amber glow, and he looked to be reading a thin piece of parchment. Maeve didn't even hesitate. She sprinted forward, piercing him with her Aurastone, ramming it right into his heart. He went down quickly, and the parchment he held fluttered to the ground in a slow, swirling movement.

Only when it landed did Maeve realize it wasn't a letter at all.

It was a small, intricate painting on gossamer paper. The image depicted was one of the faerie she just killed, as well as a female with striking eyes. In her arms was a tiny infant.

Maeve's heart wrenched inside her chest. Disgrace coated her skin, leaving her palms clammy and damp.

He was a father. He had a wife and a child.

And she'd murdered him without a second thought. She'd stolen away his life. Taken it without thinking about what he left behind. What any of them left behind.

Unbidden, tears sprung to her eyes.

Three.

Shame coursed through her. She forced her gaze away from the intimate painting, from the sweet, small family she'd ripped apart. Her mortal heart seized. She forced herself to keep going even though her chest ached. She couldn't stop.

If she quit now, if she turned back, if she caved to the dark thoughts crowding her mind, then Faeven would fall. The dark fae would overrun the Four Courts and they would all eventually succumb to Parisa's rule. History would repeat itself like it had done when Carman invaded, and Maeve couldn't allow that to happen. She would protect the innocent, she would protect her Court. She would defend those she loved, and she would defend her throne. Faeven was her home now, and she would fight for it to the death.

She was Archfae. The Dawnbringer. The soul of the goddess Danua ran through her blood.

But she was more than all those titles.

Maeve was a *warrior*. It didn't matter if she'd been broken. It didn't matter if the only life she'd ever known had been ripped away from her, if she'd been forced into a world she'd been born to hate. She would take every hard day, every obstacle, every trial, and conquer them all. Because she would never back down. She would never quit.

I'm a fucking fae and I fear nothing.

Tightening her grip on the Aurastone, she pushed on toward the direction she hoped would lead to her freedom. Her breathing was ragged now, labored as the pressure of what she'd done sat heavy upon her heart. Rounding a corner, she struggled to focus, to keep herself detached from the situation at hand. But she couldn't shake her last kill from replaying over and over in her mind. The way the little painting haphazardly floated to the ground was a memory she couldn't quit. These were her citizens as well. Her guards. Even if they weren't quick to admit it. She was the High Princess of Autumn...and she was committing treachery.

Panicked thoughts muddled her mind, and she wished Ceridwen was there to fill her with calm and purpose, to ease the burden overwhelming her. Distracted, she didn't even see the guard approach her until it was too late.

He lurched forward, sword drawn, and Maeve dropped low, rolling away from him. She popped back up to his right.

"You're making a mistake!" he shouted, and Maeve winced, all remaining opportunities to be discreet vanishing at the sound of his booming voice.

"No," she countered, ducking out of the way once more, "you are."

He swung again and she blocked his sword with her dagger, the clash and clang of blade against blade reverberating up her arm. He was a beast of a male. Burly and brutal, and he bore down upon her with the strength of a mountain. Maeve's knees began to buckle. Sweat slid down her neck and back, and her hair clung to her face. Her arms ached, the pain from holding him off becoming too much, but she didn't surrender. She couldn't. Jaw clenched, she planted one foot against the wall behind her and shoved herself into him.

Maeve attempted to sidestep out of his reach, but despite his size, he was faster than she anticipated. He reached out, capturing her in one fell swoop, bear-hugging her against his chest. With her arms pinned to her sides and her feet dangling off the floor, she squirmed and kicked in a pathetic effort to break his hold on her.

He squeezed even tighter until she thought her lungs would crack.

"Be still," he demanded.

"That's the thing," she spat. "I hate being told what to do."

Maeve snapped her head back, hearing the satisfying crunch of a broken nose. Pain burst up the back of her skull and down her neck, but she ignored it. He grunted and muttered a vulgar swear, then stumbled backward, loosening his grip on her just enough for her to twist free from him. Arcing the Aurastone back, she jammed it directly into his jugular.

Bright red blood squirted, splattering all over her chest and face. It was warm. Fresh. Her stomach recoiled and bile scalded the back of her throat. His hands clawed at his neck, at the gushing wound she inflicted. Maeve pulled the dagger out, striking him in the heart next, praying to whatever god would heed her to make his death as swift as possible.

The guard toppled to the ground in a bloody heap.

So much for being stealthy and silent.

She expelled a breath, closing her eyes for a brief second, and whispered, "Four."

Maeve opened her eyes, regained her composure, then turned and came face to face with a female guard who aimed a sword at her heart.

Neither of them moved. Neither of them spoke. They simply

stared at one another in pained silence.

The female flicked her wrist so her sword glinted in the low light. "You're Fianna's."

"Yes," Maeve croaked. Her mouth was dry, like she'd been forced to swallow wads of parchment. "I am."

"Do you have a plan?" Her velvety voice was laced with spite. "Or are you just going to run around and kill all of your soldiers while you try and find a way out?"

Her muscles drew taut, and she lifted her chin, refusing to cower beneath the fae's indignation. "I didn't think any of you would fight for me."

"Did you bother to ask?" she sneered. "Or are you nothing more than a cold-blooded killer like your brother, Garvan?"

Anger ripped through her, hot and stifling. "I am nothing like him."

The female lowered her sword, motioning to the body of the dead guard lying between them. "The trail of death you leave in your wake says otherwise."

Guilt ravaged her, ripped her from the inside out. How careless she'd been, how foolishly self-righteous. The implication was there; those Autumn soldiers she killed would've fought for her if only she'd asked. She could've spared them, saved them. What had she done? The image of the male soldier and his family glared in the forefront of her mind and a strangled sob caught in the back of her throat.

"I wasn't thinking." Maeve shook her head, heart hammering. Gods, perhaps she was just as awful as Garvan. Like calls to like. Would it not be the same for a brother and sister? "Forgive me," she croaked.

"Your plan, Your Highness?" the female asked, never wavering. She offered Maeve no sympathy for her actions or choices.

She looked past the female guard, stealing a hasty glance down the rest of the corridor. "I'm going to jump."

Her eyes widened in disbelief. "Off the balcony?"

"Um...yes."

"You don't sound so sure."

She would admit the fault in her plan now, because if this one fae was willing to help her, then she would take what she could get. "I don't know where it is."

The female fae pointed. "Straight down this hall. Make your second right, you can't miss it."

"I—" Maeve opened her mouth to speak but words failed her.

"Go." The guard tossed an anxious glance behind them. "Go now."

Maeve ran.

MAEVE DIDN'T ENCOUNTER another Autumn soldier as she sprinted down the corridor, but guilt gnawed at her gut. The female guard had been right. She was a cold-blooded killer, the same as Garvan. Never once did she stop to consider that one of them would let her go, or maybe even help her escape. No. She assumed death had to be the only way and she'd wielded her Aurastone brutally. Without consequence. Without consideration for the lives she was taking.

Angry shouts echoed from somewhere behind her and Maeve pushed herself faster, her legs firing. She bolted around the second corner, just as the female had instructed, and already she could hear the noisy cascade of the waterfall beckoning to her. A sudden burst of energy crackled in the air around her, sparking violently like a force field of some kind. She stumbled against it, into it. The world shifted, but it wasn't a glamour. It was something else entirely. A ward, maybe. She couldn't be sure, but right now, there was no time to think. No time to question.

The soft glow of moonlight spilled into the hall in a flood of silver. Maeve bolted toward it, then came to a sliding halt.

It was a balcony all right, but she'd have to find a way to climb it without impaling herself on one of the many stakes vaulting up from the railing. They rose in varying height and formed two complete rows with a long rod anchoring the top to the bottom. She darted over to the edge, wrapping her fingers around the slick metal and looked down.

Nausea roiled inside her, and she backed away.

Fade. The thought flared inside her like a burst of lightning. Her magic was faint, barely a glimmer inside her, but she would try anything if it meant she didn't have to jump from that godsforsaken balcony. She didn't want to fall into the darkened depths of the waterfall waiting to swallow her whole. She was too afraid to care if the merrows were down there, swimming, waiting for her. Too weak. Once again, her past was going to become her downfall.

Her magic flared and she thought of Summer. Of Tiernan's bed, not her own. Of the way the warm breeze brushed across her skin like a lover's caress. Of plumeria, sandalwood, and palm trees. She held her breath and...nothing.

Nothing happened.

Her magic was blocked. Barricaded. She reached out again, calling to it, entreating a response, but it flowed through and around her. That must've been what she felt during that intense burst of energy. The palace had been charmed, likely Garvan's doing. Merrick knew Maeve would have to jump. There was no other way.

Stepping forward, she peered over again and clamped down on the swell of panic. She was *so* high up. Flashbacks of the cage dangling over the Cliffs of Morrigan assaulted her mind. The creaking of the branches, and the sting of the salty air. The angry waves. The rugged cliffs. The terrifying moment when she thought for certain she would drown.

Maeve shook her head.

No.

She was past that. Beyond it. She'd overcome that fear of the water, that fear of imminent death. Gods be damned though, if she survived this, she would throttle Merrick for this absolutely absurd idea.

Sheathing her Aurastone, she grabbed the stakes and attempted to hoist herself up. She planted one foot on the crossbar, but the poles were coated in a faint sheen of mist from the falls. They were damp and slippery, and she couldn't maintain her balance. Her grip slid and the dagger-like tip of one stake cut across her palm.

"Sun and sky." Blood coated her hand, and she scrubbed it off onto her leggings. Pain rippled through her and a second later, the burning sensation took over as her body tried to heal the wound.

"And just where do you think you're going?" Garvan's cruel voice sounded from behind her.

Maeve whipped around to face him and paled. All the blood drained from her face when she caught sight of what he held in one hand.

It was the decapitated head of the female guard who'd helped her. His fingers were curled into her chestnut brown hair.

Maeve's stomach revolted, but she clamped down on the urge to vomit.

"Pity. She was one of the prettier ones." He tossed the head to the side, and it rolled across the stone balcony, the long brown tresses wrapped and tangled in blood. "Though I always suspected she sided with Shay on things."

At the mention of her brother's name, Maeve's skin caught fire with rage. "You'll pay for what you did to him."

Garvan's upper lip curled in disgust. "He died a traitor's death."

"As will you." Maeve's fingers tightened around the bar until her knuckles turned white. "Not only as a traitor to your Court, but as a traitor to all of Faeven."

His laughter was despondent, like his soul had been lost long ago.

Four more guards came rushing out of the corridor. One gaped in horror at the head by his feet, the other three zeroed in on her.

Garvan flicked his hand in her direction, flippant. "Get her down."

Two of them started forward and Maeve pulled herself up onto the railing. "Touch me and I'll ensure you're skinned alive just like the merrows your precious prince has murdered."

The guards stopped in their tracks and shared a look of disdain. Of remorse. The female Autumn guard had been right, they *could* be swayed. They would fight for her instead. All she had to do was ask.

Garvan spun on them, furious. "You do not obey *her*! You obey *me*!"

The guards glanced between her and her brother, hesitating, torn between duty to their High Prince and trusting the one they knew to be their High Princess.

Maeve inched herself higher. She was at the ledge, teetering between two stakes. All she had to do was jump. Mist cooled her cheeks and froze her fingers, but she held on, refusing to let go. "Perhaps they no longer wish to follow the demands of a monster."

He rushed her then and tried to pry her off the railing. Maeve kicked her foot out, but he dodged it and reached for her arm, wrenching it away from the railing.

Maeve screamed as the tip of one of the stakes skewered her arm. Glancing down, she realized the spear had driven straight through. Blood soaked through her blouse and coated her leathers. Spasms of pain ricocheted up and down her arm, her bicep throbbed, and her knees weakened. He stumbled back, gaping at her. Sucking in a deep breath, she did the only thing she could do.

She jerked her arm upward, yanking it clean off the stake.

It was then, when her piercing cry of agony filled the air and warm blood gushed from her arm, that the Autumn guards attacked their High Prince. Maybe they hated Garvan that much. Or perhaps their loyalty and love for Fianna had never wavered. Or maybe... maybe they believed in Maeve and her cause to save the Four Courts, to protect Faeven from Parisa's wrath. Whatever their motives, they showed no mercy as they brought her brother to his knees. They were on him faster than she could blink, tearing him away from the railing, tackling him to the slick ground. Two of them held him down while he thrashed, shouting obscenities, while the third twisted his arms behind his back, locking his hands and feet into manacles.

It was a valiant attempt. But Garvan was Archfae and those cuffs would not hold him for long.

As if sensing her train of thought, one of the guards carefully approached her. "They're iron, my lady."

Iron.

She thought the metal had some sort of adverse effect on fae. It muted their magic, dulled it, drained it. She was certain she'd read about it somewhere before, in one of her many books. A wave of dizziness swept over her and the Autumn guards standing before her blinked in and out of her vision. She was losing too much blood. If she didn't hurry, she'd be unconscious before she hit the water.

"She'll find you!" Garvan shouted, even as another guard pinned him to the ground, smashing the side of his face into the damp stone. "Not a day will pass where she won't be hunting you down!"

"Maybe so," Maeve muttered, clutching her arm to her chest. "But not today."

Her balance wavered and wobbled, and she almost lost her grip.

"High Princess, wait!" One of the guards bolted toward her. He raised his arms, offering to help her down. "You're injured!"

She shook her head and nearly blacked out. The one bar she held onto was ice in her hand. Numbness was taking over and slowly her fingers uncurled from around it. "Your rightful heir will return."

"But you are—"

"Dorian lives," she cut him off before he could ask her the one thing she wouldn't be able to give them. She couldn't be their High Queen. Her heart belonged to another. Her soul was bound to another. And if she ever took a throne, it would be next to him, and him alone. "Aran...Aran is Autumn's true heir."

She cast one more look over the edge and her knees buckled.

Gods damn. The water was so far away. She shifted, preparing to jump, and her hand, the only lifeline to the railing, finally lost its grip. Maeve blinked and toppled toward the falls.

"Princess!"

But the Autumn soldier couldn't save her. No one could save her. She was falling. Falling. Her consciousness was slipping. Down into the abyss she went, plunging into the cold depths of the falls. The shock of its freezing temperature jolted her body, and she convulsed against it. Darkness surrounded her. Empty and eternal.

Her mind cried out to him. For him.

"Tiernan!"

Maeve couldn't see anything. She couldn't feel anything. And then, there was nothing at all.

Chapter Forty-Six

His name exploded through his thoughts, and Tiernan was on his feet. He'd heard her. He'd heard her in his mind. It must be through the bond, through the Strand binding them to one another. He'd never been able to hear the thoughts of anyone from such a distance before. Except for Maeve. She'd called out to him and there was nothing he could do. Panic cut through him, sharp enough to carve out his heart.

Something must have gone wrong.

His power surged, his magic raged. The destruction inside him started rising, clawing, begging for release. If Garvan touched her, harmed her in any way, he would walk through every circle of hell to bring her back.

With every passing second, the darkness within him billowed, threatening to overcome and overtake. He wanted to rage. To wreck and ruin. He wanted to annihilate everything in his path.

Without warning, Merrick burst through the double doors of the ballroom and skidded to a stop in front of him. His chest heaved. His blue eyes were bright.

Tiernan held his breath and time evaporated.

"They've got her." The words spilled from him.

Tiernan silently thanked whatever gods might still bestow him any favors.

"Come on, my lord." Merrick nodded toward the door. "Let's go get our queen."

Chapter Forty-Seven

Maeve was drowning.

Consciousness barreled into her, startling her into a state of hysteria. Bone-chilling water engulfed her, her lungs seized, and with one arm she fought her way to the surface. Until a hand that felt like cool silk curled around her wrist, tugging her back down.

She kicked, flailing, until she saw a pair of wide-set eyes gazing back at her. They were murky green, glossy, and belonged to a merrow with skin the color of moss. The scales along his tail glinted like shards of sea glass and he wore a necklace of brown shells.

He pulled her close, his gaze flicking to the wound on her arm, before he whispered, "Be still, High Princess." His voice crashed over her like ocean waves. Then his mouth was on hers, frigid and slick, filling her with oxygen, helping her breathe. He pulled away. "You are safe with us."

Another merrow swam up, moving through the water with a slow, methodical elegance. She watched Maeve, unblinking. Studied her. Her tail, however, wasn't covered in scales like the other merrows she'd seen. It was wrapped in kelp and each long, individual piece was fastened with a shiny black pearl. Like a bandage. Awareness coated Maeve's already cold skin until fresh goosebump pebbled all over her. The merrow had been skinned. Garvan had removed her scales and sold them for gold.

With one hand she reached up, the skin between her fingers slightly webbed, and placed her palm to Maeve's cheek. "Dawnbringer."

Maeve nodded, unsure if she could speak for fear the brackish water would pour into her mouth.

"Good." The female merrow smiled, revealing small, pointy teeth. She exchanged a look with the male, and he swam closer, locking his arm tightly around Maeve's waist. "Do not fight the current."

Without warning, the merrows started to swim. The male kept his arm firmly wrapped around Maeve, and she coiled into him, bracing her injured arm between them both as the water flowed over and around them.

The wide expanse of water narrowed into a channel, racing over a riverbed of smooth stones and silt. Again, her lungs felt tight, and she stiffened in the merrow's arms. She squirmed, unable to catch her breath as they passed through the river. The merrow pressed his mouth to hers once more and she inhaled, greedily sucking in the oxygen he offered her. He anchored Maeve to his chest as the current quickened, winding through small rapids, and she squinted into the darkness. Cold bit through her skin, down to her bones until her fingers and toes were numb. It was just as Lir had said. The merrow slowed, holding her well below the surface, as Maeve struggled to see through the water that was as dark as night.

The Black Lake.

"Almost there, High Princess," he murmured.

Suddenly, they stopped swimming, and the female held up one hand. "Keep the High Princess below the water and out of sight." Her tail swished as she drifted away from them. "I will ensure it is safe first and that the High King of Summer is ready to retrieve her."

Tiernan.

Maeve's heart soared at the mere mention of his title.

A moment later, the female returned. "It is safe. We will bring her to him now."

At once, they surged upward and broke through the surface.

She gasped, sputtering and coughing as the merrow lifted her onto a bank of dry land. Collapsing onto the bank, Autumn welcomed her. She toppled onto the ground, her cheek pressed firmly into the damp earth while leaves swirled around her, while the cool breeze sifted over her. Water dripped from her hair. Her skin was like ice. She could barely move, barely breathe. And gods, her arm *hurt*.

Behind her, the merrow boosted her onto the shore of the Black Lake. She shivered, teeth chattering, and gradually dragged herself forward with her good arm, pulling herself out of the water.

"There she is!" Lir bellowed.

"Thank you," Maeve choked out, easing herself into a sitting position as the merrow slunk back into the water, his glassy eyes focused on her. "I owe you a life debt."

He shook his head, his long black hair flowing around him like ink. "The debt was paid when the Aurastone chose you."

She opened her mouth to object, but he dove back into the water, the female following swiftly behind him. Then they vanished, as though they'd never been there at all. She looked up to see Tiernan running toward her. He slid onto his knees, capturing her face, his hands warm against her chilled skin.

"*Astora.*" He lifted her gently, helping her to stand, enveloping her into him. Magic fell around her shoulders like a blanket. The lovely scent of orange blossom and cedarwood perfumed the air as he dried her clothing, her hair, her skin. Then his gaze landed on her arm, on the hole that had not yet fully healed. Blood continued to seep from the wound. A storm brewed in his eyes. "What happened?"

"Garvan tried to pull me off the railing during my escape." She bit her lip, wincing as Lir held out his hand, a silent demand. "I was skewered in the process."

"Fucking bastard," Lir muttered. Lines furrowed across his brow. He looked pained. Troubled. "Let me see, little bird."

She held out her arm for him to inspect it.

"I should've been there." His tone was razor sharp. "This never would have happened if I had been there to protect you."

Guilt. It was guilt that hammered his features into stone.

She offered him a small smile. "Just promise me you'll be there next time to ensure it doesn't happen again."

The corner of his mouth ticked up. Just barely.

Brynn marched over, curls bouncing, with Ceridwen on her heels. She lightly ran her fingers over the wound and heat poured into Maeve's skin. She almost sighed.

"What did you do? Impale yourself?"

"More or less. There were stakes positioned along the railing." Maeve hissed as the heat intensified and the wound sealed itself, closing completely. "The mist from the waterfall made all the bars slippery. I'm surprised it wasn't worse to be honest."

"Stakes?" Ceridwen's gaze snapped to Merrick. "You failed to mention that."

He winced and ducked his head, pink bleeding into his cheeks. "A mistake."

Thunder cracked and Merrick straightened, his head snapping up to face his High King. "And one that I won't make again, my lord."

"See that you don't," Tiernan rumbled. "Are you alright, Maeve? Are you hurt anywhere else?"

Her heart hurt, but she kept that much to herself. Though judging by the way Tiernan's brow shot up in response, he'd obviously heard her thoughts.

Brynn continued to heal Maeve's arm, her magic flowing through her until the pain dissipated. "It might leave a scar."

Maeve glanced up at Tiernan, and the corner of his lip curved into his signature half smile.

"Nothing I can't fix." He nodded toward the group. "A moment, please."

They exchanged looks but headed to the forest's edge without question.

Tiernan took her hands in his and held them clasped against the hard wall of his chest. "Tell me what's bothering you. Why does your heart hurt?"

So, he had heard her thoughts.

"I took five innocent lives tonight." She dropped her head, images of the painting of the Autumn soldier with his little family flashing through her mind and she bit her lip to keep from crying.

"They would've stopped you from escaping, Maeve." He released her hands and tilted her chin up with one finger. "You did what any of us would've done."

His words didn't ease the self-condemnation building inside her. "I'm not so sure."

"What do you mean?"

"There was a female soldier. She came upon me right as I killed the fourth guard. She called me a cold-blooded killer and said I was no different than Garvan." Even as she said it, traitorous tears slid down her cheeks.

Tiernan wiped them away with his thumbs, softly caressing the skin just beneath her eyes. "She doesn't know your heart."

"She didn't need to, but she helped me escape." Maeve blinked, a poor attempt to will the tears away. "She implied that every soldier I killed would've helped me, if only I had asked. She wasn't loyal to Garvan. I don't think any of them were."

His arms came around her then, embracing her and she welcomed his strength, burying her face in his chest. "There's no way she would know such a thing. And it's impossible for you to have known either."

"Perhaps." Maeve peered up at him. Moonlight poured over them, dousing half of his face in shadows. "But I didn't ask them, did

I? I just killed them without another thought. It never even occurred to me they might be on our side."

"You can't take the blame for this." Tiernan's hand fell to her shoulders and he held firm. "You were in survival mode. Had you stopped to ask each one of them whose side they were on, you would've lost time to escape. And what if one of them was against you?"

He made a valid point, but the Autumn guard's words echoed in her ears.

The trail of death you leave in your wake says otherwise.

A shallow breath escaped her, and she resigned herself to her actions. She would do better. She refused to be anything like Garvan.

"And what of Garvan?" Tiernan asked coolly.

"He took the head of the female who aided me." Just speaking the words out loud was enough to make her stomach clench.

"That fucking prick." Wrath lined the features of Tiernan's handsome face. "There is no worse way for a fae to die."

Maeve didn't want to think of all the other ways a fae could be killed. So many of them were long and torturous. So many of them were gruesome in nature. She tucked her damp hair behind her ear and looked up at him. "He won't be going anywhere any time soon. His own guards shackled him in iron."

"Iron," Tiernan repeated, slightly stunned.

Now that Maeve was more level-headed and could think clearly, she recalled that iron in any form was extremely harmful to the fae. In a few books, she'd read stories about fae bound in iron cuffs, their magic muted beyond reach, completely inaccessible. The metal made them lethargic, disoriented, almost like they were drugged. It wasn't the worst situation a fae could suffer, but for Garvan, it still seemed too kind.

"We must recover Dorian, if he's still alive, or return Aran to Kyol at once." Tiernan's arm fell around her shoulder. "Autumn is not a Court that should be without a sovereign for long."

"Aran has already set sail." Maeve bit her bottom lip and her gaze slid east, in the direction of her brother. "I know Dorian is out there; we just have to find him. The only real question is how?"

As though in answer, a breeze billowed through the Autumn woods. It whispered through the stiff branches and falling leaves like a song, beckoning her. There was a tug, a gentle pull on her heartstrings. Her blood hummed in response. The trees shifted and swayed, as though the entire Court took a breath and released it on a sigh. Magic permeated the air, ripe with the scent of spice and woodsmoke. Swirling leaves of soft gold and burgundy fell around them, a kaleidoscope of colors. The forest yawned open, revealing a small fox.

Maeve's chest tightened. Squeezed.

The fox trod toward them, then paused as a crimson mist engulfed him.

Lir bolted to Maeve's side, his sword drawn. She flung her arm out to halt him. "No, wait."

The mist amplified, churning, and a figure stepped from the shadows. Early morning sunlight glinted off shoulder-length blond hair threaded with strands of deep auburn. He wore dark brown pants with a shirt the color of rubies. He brushed away some debris from his fur cloak, striding out into the open. Wings of crimson and ivory exploded from his back, stretching and beating as the breeze sifted through the feathers. His face was all hard, chiseled planes, and there was a cleft in his chin. Just like Aran. Power radiated from him. Glowing. Radiant. A crown of golden leaves sat upon his head.

Dorian Ruhdneah, High King of the Autumn Court, had returned.

Ceridwen and Brynn dropped into a curtsy. Merrick and Lir bowed, each of them murmuring, "Your Grace."

Emerald green eyes locked onto her, and the High King spread his arms wide.

"*Alanuhv.*"

His voice was rough and gravelly, but he spoke Old Laic and her mind quickly translated the meaning. *My child.*

Maeve's breath hitched. A bond blossomed in her heart, connecting her to him. To her father. To her blood. "Papa."

She darted across the space between them, catapulting herself into his waiting arms. He lifted her off her feet like she was lighter than air, crushing her to him. He was pure strength, the very essence of Autumn, and when he finally set her back down, the torrent of emotion inside her slid unbidden tears down her cheeks.

"It *was* you," she sniffled.

"Maeve." The rich timbre of her father's voice floated over her. He eased her back and gently tucked a loose strand of hair behind her ear. He slowly hooked one finger under her chin, willing her to look up at him. His callused fingers wiped away her tears. "You have your mother's eyes." She grinned up at him. "But you have my smile."

Dorian pulled her close to him again, and in his embrace, another piece of Maeve's heart healed. After another moment, he finally released her.

"Your Grace." Tiernan stepped forward, inclining in head. "Welcome home."

When Dorian smiled, the entire world ignited. Maeve could easily see why her mother fell in love with him. He clasped Tiernan's hand. "It's been some time, has it not?"

The corner of Tiernan's mouth ticked up. "Indeed."

"I'm sure we have much to catch up on, just as I know you likely have many questions." His gaze skimmed the woods, the Black Lake. "Allow me to answer what I can."

Then he told them a story. "Losing Fianna left me devastated. I searched for her everywhere to no avail, until the mating bond between us was severed, silenced by her death. But by then it was too late. Garvan had already fallen to Parisa's corruption and in doing so, he'd spelled me, making it impossible to shift back to my fae form."

Dorian paused, blowing out a low breath. "I'd been trapped in the body of a fox for years, unable to escape the prison of my own magic. Gradually it became increasingly difficult to remember I'd ever been anything else. My mind slowly slipped into madness. The

445

longer I remained a fox, the more I took on animalistic traits." He looked at Maeve. "Until the night I found you by the Black Lake."

Her heart lurched, aching to hear whatever he was going to say next.

"I saw you and mistook you for Fianna. I thought she'd returned to me." He shook his head and his eyes darkened. Pain etched its way into his hardened features. "But you, my daughter, you reminded me of all I was...in you, I saw myself. I saw your mother. I saw our Court."

Maeve reached out, took his hand, and squeezed. "I'm glad you're back."

"As am I."

Tiernan's hand slid to the small of Maeve's back.

Dorian tracked the movement, one brow arched in question. "Taking her away from me already, are you?" There was a hint of amusement in his tone.

Tiernan's grin widened. "Only if she'll have me."

Maeve's Strand, her mating bond to the High King of Summer, warmed, and Tiernan dropped onto his knees before her.

Maeve's piercing eyes widened, but Tiernan captured her hands, clasping them in between his own. With the sun at his back, he spoke to her, and only to her.

"Maeve Ruhdneah, High Princess of Autumn, High Queen of the Furies and Spring Fae...Dawnbringer." He swallowed. Fuck, he didn't think he'd be this nervous. He supposed much of it had to do with the fact that her father was watching his every move, eyes as keen as a fox. "From the moment I first laid eyes on you, I knew you were mine, and that my soul would never search for another."

A sheen of tears sparkled in her eyes, and he hated he was making her cry. Even if it was to give her the whole of his heart.

Tiernan pressed a kiss to both her hands.

"You eclipse the moon and shatter the stars. You are the object of my every desire. You are dreams and eternal promises." He bowed his head before her. "I will only ever kneel before you."

Maeve sucked in a breath.

"Are you asking me to marry you?" Her voice pitched. Whether she was on the verge of complete happiness or total hysteria, he couldn't be sure.

"I'm asking you to be my wife. My queen." He slid the ring he always wore off his pinky finger. The one with the vibrant bluish-purple stone set inside a golden sun. He slid it over her ring finger and held it there. "This belonged to my mother. She told me once before she died that whoever wore it would be the one to bring me to my knees."

"Yes." Maeve's head bobbed once and then she launched herself into his waiting arms. He caught her up before they both toppled to the ground, then spun her around twice before setting her back on the ground. She threw her arms around his neck and whispered, "My soul is yours, Tiernan. Always."

He captured her tear-stained cheeks, kissing her full and lush lips that tasted lightly of salt and deeply of warmth and spice. He ran one palm down her soft curls, tucking them back from her face, then he broke the kiss. Just barely. His mouth hovered over hers when he said, "You are mine."

Then he was kissing her again, dipping her back, sliding his hand down her thigh and lifting her leg to his waist.

"Alright." Merrick cleared his throat. "Let's get back to Summer before the two of you start trying to extend the Velless bloodline right in front of us."

"Mer," Brynn scolded and thumped him on the back of his head.

"What?" He threw his hands out to both sides. "We were *all* thinking it."

Dorian cleared his throat, and Merrick's face turned scarlet. He shoved his hands into his pockets and ducked his head. "I beg your pardon, my lord."

The High King of Autumn chuckled. "You're forgiven...this time."

Maeve, however, was flushing beautifully.

"He's only teasing," Tiernan soothed, placing a kiss on her forehead, then whispered, "We've got all the time in the world for that."

Her gaze lifted to his, and all the embarrassment vanished from her face. "When I do bear our children, they will be born into a world of peace." She turned then, looking out over the Black Lake, across the vast expanse of the Autumn Court. "Not one on the brink of war."

"As you wish, *astora*." Tiernan pressed a kiss to the inside of her palm, mindfully taking note of the fact that Maeve had said *when* and not *if*. But the possibility of a family was a discussion for another time. A time when war wasn't looming on the horizon. A time when he didn't have to worry about the lives of those he loved.

Clouds rolled in above them and the temperature dropped, instantly cooling the air. But it wasn't his storm.

The sound of slow and steady clapping caused his stomach to drop. The icy touch of dread ran its frozen fingers down his spine.

"How romantic." An airy, feminine voice slithered out from the edge of the forest.

Tiernan drew his sword, blocking Maeve with his body, right as Parisa stepped out from the shadowed woods.

There was no time to react.

The dark fae attacked.

Chapter Forty-Eight

The dark fae overwhelmed them.

Creatures with gaping jaws and spiders crawling out of their eyes and mouths lumbered out from the dark folds of the forest. Beings of shadow and death with spindly arms and claws for fingers staggered toward them in a wave of terror. The stench of decay clogged the air, smothering them, making it almost impossible to breathe. It was a mob, a monstrous wall of darkness barreling toward the cliffs, shrouding out the sun, leaving them in a void of darkness and chaos.

Maeve pulled her Aurastone and began cutting them down.

"Aim for the throat!" Maeve shouted, remembering how much more difficult these dark fae were to kill than those poor mortals Fearghal had glamoured. She plunged her dagger into a fae whose eyes were empty pits of black and whose body resembled a mass of limbs all stitched together with vines. It turned to dust a moment later.

Brynn darted off to her left, slashing and slicing, wielding her sword and dagger with on point accuracy. Each strike was a direct hit and the fae dropped to the ground. Lir and Merrick worked as a unit, twisting and dodging, attacking and fighting. Lir's curved blades arced through the air like streaks of lightning.

Bolts of violet exploded from Tiernan, shattering across the space, eliminating an entire swarm of dark fae in one fell swoop. Power erupted from her father as he stormed into the fray, unleashing the wrath of death and decay. Maeve's magic swirled and she released the fire building inside her, decimating another group of dark fae aiming straight for Ceridwen.

Maeve's heart lurched.

Like her, Ceridwen only had daggers to defend herself. She tossed all five of them, one right after the other, and their silver blades glinted through the overcast sky, piercing her opponents. More dark fae poured from the line of the forest, ambling toward her.

"Ceridwen!" Maeve sprinted toward the High Princess, obliterating any fae that tried to stop her. But Ceridwen wasn't nearly as vulnerable as she seemed.

She raised her arms, palms out. Her golden blonde hair came unraveled from its plaits, swirling and snapping in the breeze. An ethereal glow of golden mist surrounded her, and her eyes turned white. The dark fae rushing upon her froze in their tracks, shrieking, covering their ears. They cowered before her, whining and whimpering, thrashing like they were being tortured from the inside out. Magic pulsed and swelled, sending the dark fae scattering in every direction.

Maeve stumbled to a stop, staring. She had no idea what Ceridwen was doing, but then the High Princess was running, leaping over the fallen bodies, and plucking out each of her daggers.

"Maeve!" Tiernan hauled her to his side, just missing the claws of a dark fae.

She blinked, drawing back. Raising her Aurastone high, she slashed it down across the creature's throat. It howled once before turning to dust.

Tiernan captured her chin, sending violet bursts out around them. He smiled. "It's not like you to be so distracted, *moh Rienna*."

Her blood stirred. *My queen.*

"Apologies, *moh Rí.*" The smile he sent her weakened her knees. "But were you aware your sister has some type of feral magic inside her?"

He laughed and it rumbled like thunder. "She does indeed. She doesn't talk about it much."

Maeve snorted. "I can see why."

He dropped low and she flipped over his back, jumping up on the other side of him. She took down two more fae, shooting projectiles of fire from the tips of her fingers as Tiernan destroyed another with his sword.

From somewhere in the distance, Parisa cackled.

"Fucking bitch," Maeve muttered, taking inventory of their surroundings.

Dark fae were everywhere. It seemed like whenever one died, another took its place. She thought they were doing well, but the fae continued to come at them, driving them backward, closer to the edge of the cliffs. They needed to *fade*; it would be their only means of escape, but they couldn't get a clear chance if they weren't ever able to catch a breath from the constant onslaught of fae attacking them.

Lir ran up, sweat pouring down him and soaking his clothing. Blood drenched his shoulder and the fabric of his shirt stuck to his skin. "There's too many, my lord."

"I don't know how much more we can take." Brynn hobbled closer, swiping at a dark fae in her path. Her leg was injured and she winced, sending a desperate glance to the mountains dividing Summer from Autumn.

"Tier, we have to do something." Maeve yanked Brynn behind her, slashing through the throats of two dark fae at once. They evaporated, but more poured out from the forest line. "We can't keep fighting them off like this, we'll exhaust ourselves. The more we kill, the more she sends."

"I know," he grunted, dodging the attack of one with spiders crawling out of its eyes. His blade swept up and he struck down two more.

One with horns and bulging veins swiped at Maeve, knocking her to the ground. Air wheezed from her lungs, and she gasped, rolling out of its reach as Tiernan drove his sword through the base of the fae's neck. It crumpled, gurgling, spurting black blood everywhere. Maeve recoiled from the revolting creature. Tiernan reached down, grabbed her hand, and hauled her back to her feet.

"Maeve." His voice was cold. Deadly. "Make your bubble."

"What?" She searched his face, trying to understand his intent.

"Just do it, *astora*. Do not ask questions." His magic exploded above them, violent and devastating. "Make the damn bubble. Surround everyone but me."

"Now is not the time for heroics, High King," Dorian called out as dark fae fell violently at his feet, thrashing and gurgling, their bodies rotting from the inside out.

"My father is right." She plunged her Aurastone into another fae, tearing her blade up its sternum until it turned to dust. "I will do no such thing. We fight together."

Tiernan grabbed her waist, drawing her into him. She breathed in the scent of him, but it was tainted by the metallic stench of blood. His eyes were a storm, brewing and fierce.

"There is no other way."

She grabbed a fistful of his shirt, the ring he gave her flashing like lightning. "I would rather die alongside you than live a lifetime without you."

The corner of his mouth quirked. "Stubborn."

"Arrogant," she tossed back.

He laughed and his gaze darkened. She watched as he summoned his magic, demanding it. The powerful storm shook the ground, and the wind lashed out at all of them. The dense scent of orange blossom and cedarwood permeated the air as his power sank into the mind of every dark fae, of every nightmarish creature. He called to the chaos, to the destruction he kept locked away in the darkest part of his soul. Maeve stood there, awestruck, as he took control, as he poisoned the minds of the dark fae, as he turned them against each other. His magic spiraled, raw and relentless, amplifying the turmoil. The dark fae clashed, attacking one another, decimating their own ranks.

"No!" Parisa shrieked, running out from the protection of the forest. Her face was pale and gaunt, leached of all color. A crown of spindles and onyx sat atop her head and her short brown hair, once angled and sharp, was thin and graying. She wore a gown of all black; the lace cut across her emaciated shoulders like a spider's web and hung loose around her withering body. But dangling from her neck, flickering like green fire, was a stone—one that was painfully familiar.

A *virdis lepatite.*

The same one Carman used to wear, the one that granted the power of dark sorcery.

Shit.

"It's too much!" Ceridwen's voice pitched with hysteria, and she grabbed Maeve's arm. Her panicked gaze focused on her twin. On Tiernan. "He'll die if he continues this madness!"

Maeve whirled around to face him, and shock reverberated through her. He was pale. So pale. Death-like. His brow was slick with sweat and tremors wrecked his body.

"Enough!" Maeve cried, throwing her arms around his neck and hauling him to her. He convulsed in her arms, and apprehension seized her. Her heart skittered at the sight of him. He looked so vulnerable, so weak. "Tiernan, stop! Stop it, right now!"

He swayed, and his eyes turned so dark they were nearly black. Her fingers dug into his biceps, holding him upright.

"Enough," she murmured again, before her lips crashed against his.

There was no response from him at first, like kissing stone. Cold and rough. She lightly ran her tongue along the seam of his lips and then he opened for her, their mouths meshing like every touch, every taste would be their last.

His magic ebbed, and slowly Maeve drew back to look up into his eyes.

The storm had calmed. The destruction eased.

Tiernan jerked backward as some invisible force dragged him away. His eyes were wide, and his mouth fell open while shadowy tendrils wrapped around him, smothering him. Suffocating him. His body contorted, pinned in place by dark magic.

"Tiernan!" His name wrenched from Maeve's throat as his pain reverberated through her. His agony carved itself into her heart, it stole the light of her soul. "No! Let him go!"

Parisa cackled, her eyes wild with vengeance. Malice swarmed her. Dark magic rolled off her in choking waves. "Stupid girl! Did you honestly think you could best me? That I wouldn't win?"

Maeve ignored her. She wouldn't let her take him, not like this. Without warning, the world shimmered.

"You see, Maeve, darling," Parisa hissed, the veins on her neck bulging, "You took Casimir from me. You took Fearghal from me. And you cost me Garvan. So, it's only fair that I return the favor."

Lir shifted then, fur and fangs appearing as he took his full wolf form. His growl stood the hairs on Maeve's neck on end, but she was faster. The retribution she sought blinded her with rage. She was the sun and the storm. The reckoning and the wrath.

Flipping her Aurastone high in the air, she caught it by the hilt and hurled it at Parisa. It stuck in her face, just below her left eye. The female shrieked, her frail body thrashing and flailing. Maeve sprinted forward. She did not relent. She did not release. Grabbing the Aurastone, she yanked it upward, screaming and releasing all her fury. Until she gouged out Parisa's left eye. Her skin boiled and blood sprayed out from the wound like a fountain, splattering all over like acidic rain.

Maeve ripped the dagger out, and Parisa stumbled backward, howling. She would die first before she let Parisa take him from her.

Tiernan slid into her mind, his voice strangled. *"Be brave, astora."*

She blinked up at him, shaken. "What?"

But he was no longer looking at her. His face was stone, his brows furrowed.

"Call in your favor!" he shouted, and Maeve's blood turned to ice.

"No!" Ceridwen cried. "No, Tiernan, don't say it!"

Determination lined his handsome face as he lifted his voice to the heavens and beyond. "I summon you now, Aed, god of death! Call in your bargain!"

"*No!*" Maeve screamed.

The ground beneath them shuddered and trembled, quaking in fear.

"Tiernan," Maeve whispered, her breath fanning out before her, as she clung to the steady beating of his pulse, of the bond between them.

The trees recoiled. The seas churned. Ominous and foreboding shadows emerged, engulfing them in a swath of darkness.

Lir, Merrick, and Brynn ducked their heads. Dorian stood motionless, his gaze latched onto the emerging pitch of night. Ceridwen, eyes bloodshot, lowered her gaze to the blood-stained ground. But Maeve looked up, refusing to shrink away from the immensely powerful magic that brought all life to a standstill.

The god of death had arrived.

Chapter Forty-Nine

Aed, the god of death, stood before Maeve.

She'd never seen a god before, never even imagined what one might look like. But he was terrifyingly beautiful. So painfully lovely, it almost hurt her to look upon him. A cape of darkness flowed around him, revealing a broad chest and sinewy muscle, like he'd been carved from granite. His jaw was chiseled, his cheekbones high and prominent. His flesh, nearly the same color as her own, was flawless. Silver hair fell to his shoulders, though small strands were braided and twisted back from his face, the tips of them black. Kohl lined his illustrious eyes, a cool slate gray.

He strolled toward them, confident in his every step, and no one dared to move or even breathe in his presence. Cold air sank deep into Maeve's bones and a breeze sifted around her, carrying the scent of him. Tempting, forbidden fruit. Wintry, frosty nights. And something dangerous she couldn't quite place.

"Hello again, Parisa." Aed's sharp voice cut through the deafening silence.

The fae in question paled. Black blood oozed from what remained in the space where her eye had once been, but Maeve knew her pallor had nothing to do with the wound and everything to do with the god standing before her. Parisa's sullied magic swelled with panic, then receded. Her shadowed bindings released Tiernan, and he fell to the ground as she *faded*, leaving nothing in her wake but the remains of overwhelming fear.

Tiernan was on his feet in a second, his wings unfurling as he flew to Maeve's side, shielding her.

Maeve stepped out from behind his barricade, ready to defend the ones she loved. Ready to defend all of them. "You can't have him."

"I haven't come for him." Aed arched one dark brow and held out his hand to her. "I've come to retrieve what is owed to me."

Fisting her hands on her hips, she glared up at him. "And what exactly is owed to you, Aed, god of death?"

His answering smile sent chills straight to her heart. "You, Dawn-bringer."

"Excuse me?" She balked and stared down at his proffered hand. From beside her, Tiernan stiffened. He hauled her against him, locking his arm around her waist. His gaze darkened, then narrowed, leveling the god of death.

"No. She is not part of our deal." Tiernan's voice lowered, all menace and fury. "In exchange for the power of destruction, you said you would take everything from *me*. My magic. My power. My life."

"No," Aed responded, his tone dismissive. He sighed, annoyed. "Perhaps you should've been more careful when agreeing to our terms."

Tiernan's muscles went taut and Maeve curled into him as fresh panic crawled up her spine.

"Our bargain was that on a day of my choosing, I would take everything from you." The god of death had the audacity to roll his eyes. "But since you so graciously demanded my presence, I've come to collect Maeve." He smiled and it was terrifying. "Your *everything*."

Oh gods.

Dorian sucked in a breath. "No."

"Come along, Your Highness." Aed stretched out his hand once more, his patience thinning. "I don't care to stay outside of my realm for longer than necessary."

Tiernan pulled her into a fierce embrace. He cupped both of her cheeks, kissing her until her body trembled. His lips were soft, and she committed the feel of them against her own to her memory. He was everything she ever wanted in this life and the next. He was the beating of her heart. The depth of her entire soul.

"And you are mine," he whispered into her mind, shuffling her behind him. He picked up his swords from off the ground, twirling them so the pointed blades were aimed at the god.

"I will fight for her."

"You dare go back on your word to a *god?*" Aed spoke and the whole of the Autumn Court cowered in fear. "I just saved you from Parisa and already you wish to meet death again so quickly?"

Tiernan straightened, sword raised. "If it means sparing her from you...then yes."

"She's our queen." This from Merrick. He had his blade drawn, ready to face down the god of death. "You can't have her."

Lir stepped up to one side of him, armed with both of his curved swords. Brynn appeared on the other with Maeve, her spine locked into place, her jaw set in fierce determination. Ceridwen stood at the ready, her fingers flickering over the hilt of each dagger strapped to her waist. Even Dorian came forward, his face a mask save for his eyes. They reflected the depths of war.

Alarm flared to life inside of Maeve. This was her family, and they were prepared to die for her.

She would take her own life before she let any of them fall for her.

Tiernan's magic amplified, and she darted out from his hold. "No!"

But the god of death simply smiled. "Fools."

Power blasted through them, a wave so immense it vibrated through her, all the way to her soul. Darkness engulfed them in a throng of shadows, the air bitter and cold, intensified by the god's wrath. The might of his power carved its way inside her, and the ghost of an icy hand took hold of the magic in her blood, gripping it, crushing it. Pain exploded from her heart, splintering through her body like shards of frozen glass.

Maeve shuddered and screamed. Her lungs seized. From somewhere off to her right, she heard Tiernan groan in agony. All around her, sounds of anguish pierced her ears. Aed was going to rip their power from them, just as he'd done to Parisa.

Her magic churned, panicked and frenzied. Harrowing agony tore through her, clutching her, strangling her. She couldn't move, she couldn't breathe. Dropping onto her hands and knees, she crawled through the frozen blades of grass. They pierced her palms like dozens of tiny daggers. The god's power wrenched inside her—her back bowed and her head snapped back. He tugged again and she lurched forward, her arms giving out from under her. The side of her face smacked into the hard earth and black stars danced across her vision. She caved, clinging to the shreds of her magic as it twisted and yanked, ruining her.

Maeve gasped and reached for her sword of sunlight. Called to it. Begged it to answer her plea.

The brilliance of the dawn exploded in her hand.

Her sword had answered her call.

She curled her fist around its hilt and its burning blade shone brighter than ever. Her magic siphoned and she pulled it back, drawing it inside her, wielding it against the god of death. His power raged, scouring her, but she pushed through the fire and flame to where the magic of a goddess's soul lashed out in vengeance. Steam erupted from her as she struggled to her feet, as the breath of life and the touch of death warred inside her. Gathering what remained of her weakened strength, she heaved the sword of sunlight high above her head and sent it down in a slashing arc, cleaving through the shadows.

I fear nothing.

Aed's power shuddered. Shivered.

"Call it back!" she screamed, repeating the motion, and driving the darkness back, away from those she loved. "Call it back, *now!*"

Again, the might of his force wavered.

"Withdraw now and let them live, Aed!" Maeve continued to cut through the shadows, her magic an endless well, a never-ending source of power. She reached out with one hand, capturing the shadows that swarmed her, bending them to her will. "For if you do not, I will invoke the soul of the goddess Danua herself, and I swear I will destroy you. I will vanquish you from every realm, and you will never know another whose wrath is more unforgiving than mine."

A gust of wind slammed into her, stealing her breath, and then everything fell silent.

The darkness ebbed. The shadows vanished. And the god of death stood before her.

He glowered down at her and clicked his tongue. "Threatening a god now, are you?"

"Not a threat." She met the cruelty of his stare head on and glared up at him, her chin raised, her spine a rod of steel. "A promise."

They stood like that, inches from one another, neither refusing to back down.

"It's me you want, not them. I was the deal." She glanced over her shoulder to where Tiernan, Ceridwen, Lir, Merrick, Brynn, and her father were all sprawled on the ground, pinned in place by Aed's vengeance. "Let them live and I'll go with you to the Ether."

His eyes turned to molten silver, the power in them swirling. "The High King retracted his vow."

The ground shuddered again, but she held firm.

"No." Maeve smiled, baring her teeth. "He merely considered it. You, however, attacked first."

Aed's mouth opened to argue then snapped shut.

She arched one brow, daring him to contradict her.

His massive frame straightened, and he offered her his hand. If she refused him, he would simply take her. "It's time, Your Highness."

"*This is not goodbye, astora.*" Tiernan's roughened voice filtered through her thoughts. "*You are mine. I will destroy every realm and burn down this damned world if I must, until you're in my arms again.*"

She looked over at him, memorized his twilight eyes, committing every feature of him to her memory. "*I love you.*"

"Release them Aed, god of death." She flicked her sword of sunlight and didn't miss the way he hissed. "Now."

There was no time to say goodbye. As promised, she placed her hand in his and Aed led her away from them. From her family. She thought she heard Ceridwen cry out. Desperate for a final look back, she turned, taking in their faces one last time. But they were blurred from her tears and before she could blink them away, she was smothered by a shadow of darkness and cold.

ETHER WAS nothing like she imagined.

The world of the in between, as so many often called it, was not rife with wandering souls and wails of despair. It was a glorious city in another realm, an alternate place of existence. There were cobblestone streets and brick buildings with shops and restaurants. Darkened woods lined the city, and in the distance stood a glittering palace of obsidian, presumably the House of Death. Mountains of silver cut across the horizon, their peaks already frosted with snow. The skies were overcast and the air was cool against her skin, like the breeze of Autumn. Beings, both mortal and fae alike, were everywhere, carrying on as though they continued to live. A few glanced their way, though many averted their gazes, not wanting to draw the god of death's eye or meet his steely gaze for too long.

"Welcome to Ether, my lady." Aed's gaze slid to the ring on her finger. "Or should I say, High Queen."

Maeve stiffened and her thumb slid over the band on her ring finger. "Am I dead?"

He laughed, shaking his head. "You are not."

She stared up at him. Except for when he tried to rip her magic from inside her, Aed was far from a raging deity. He wore slim pants and a collared shirt, bracelets of silver hung from both of his wrists, and he almost looked normal. Save for the silver mist that seemed to haunt his eyes. He was actually rather...casual. Understated. Composed.

It set her nerves on edge.

He strolled along one of the cobblestone streets, and she followed closely behind, until he looked back at her, arching one brow in question.

"Do you need something?"

"I..." She stumbled, almost bumping into him. "I mean, you brought me here."

"And?" He smiled and she shrank inside herself.

"I assume you want something from me?"

His booming laughter echoed through the bustling street, and everyone turned to stare. Maeve ducked her head to hide her embarrassment. Her skin heated and a blush colored her cheeks.

"Darling," he cooed, coming closer. "I have no need of your entertainment. Though you are radiant, I prefer my pleasures a bit...*darker*." His smile would've brought any soul to their knees. "If you know what I mean."

"I...of course." Maeve fumbled over her words, realizing how stupid she must've sounded.

But Aed ignored her foolishness and spread his arms wide. "This is the Ether. Roam where you please. I will warn you not to venture too far into the forest. The souls there are not always so kind. And so long as you stay away from Diamarvh, you'll be fine."

Diamarvh. She'd never heard of it.

"That's it?" she asked, daring to look up at him.

He smiled again, except this time it was otherworldly and stole the air straight out of her lungs. "That's it."

Maeve glanced around the city, then sheathed her sword of sunlight. "But what am I supposed to do here?"

"There's plenty to do. Go paint. Go read one of those books you're so fond of." He gestured vaguely to a vast row of buildings stacked one next to the other. "Go knit."

Maeve reared back, affronted. "Knit?"

"Apologies, Your Grace." He shrugged, nonchalant. "I was merely tossing out ideas."

"Can I train?" Maeve countered.

"If you so wish." He dipped his head. "My training grounds are at your disposal."

"Is there a library here?" Maeve asked, knowing that she would need to collect and understand as much information as possible while she was in the Ether. Especially if she wanted to find a way out.

"There is." He nodded toward a side street where vines bursting with deep red blossoms crawled up the sides of two stone buildings. "Straight down there, the third building on the right. If you like, there's an empty apartment above the library for you to make your own, so you can have access to books anytime you please."

"An apartment?" Maeve couldn't believe the god of death would be so kind without expecting something in return.

His gaze narrowed. "Would you prefer to find your own living arrangements?"

"Of course not, I just—"

"You're Archfae." He bent down even closer, overwhelming her. "I'm not a total monster."

She crossed her arms, protecting herself. "You ripped Parisa's magic from her and tried to do the same to me and mine."

"Ah, right. I did do that, didn't I?" He sounded entirely too pleased with himself. "Well, she deserved it."

Maeve wasn't sure what to say to that, so she remained quiet instead.

With a flourish, Aed handed her a pair of leather leggings, a thick sweater, and fur-lined boots. "Take these until you can commission something else of your choosing."

She glanced down and winced. Her clothing was nearly shredded, and she was covered in blood. Even if she wasn't dead, she certainly looked like it. "I don't have any money."

"Just put it on my tab."

She blinked.

"You're my guest, High Queen. Not a prisoner. If you're in want of anything, you need only ask." Again, he nodded toward the side street. "Clean yourself up and make yourself at home. I have a feeling you'll find what you're looking for in my library."

Then he vanished without another word, and Maeve was left standing on the street with a pile of clothing at her feet.

What in the everlasting fuck was going on here?

She hastily gathered up the clothing and made her way down the cobblestone path. She found the library easily enough. It was an older building of crumbling beige stone. Navy blue paint peeled from the shutters and when she stepped inside, the door groaned open, announcing her arrival.

But no one came to greet her.

She wasn't even sure anyone was there at all.

The library was a towering masterpiece of shelves and books. Rolling ladders were perched on the tallest section, making everything easy to reach. Granted, she had wings, so she shouldn't really care, but it made her heart skip a beat. Plush, brown leather chairs were situated near a roaring hearth, and faerie light illuminated the room, casting the space in a soft amber-hued glow. There were couches for lounging and reading, a massive window to watch the world pass by, and tables piled with books, jars of fountain pens, and blank parchment.

It looked more like someone's personal study, and for a moment, Maeve felt like she'd stepped back in time. Like she was standing in a personal room belonging to someone else, instead of a public space.

In the center was a spiraling staircase with a gilded railing and obsidian steps leading to a small balcony and what she assumed was the apartment upstairs.

Dumping the clothing on one of the leather chairs, Maeve sank into the other next to the hearth. She didn't care if she was in armor and leggings that were frayed, torn, and splattered with blood.

What in the seven hells was she going to do?

Her chest ached and the Strand binding her to Tiernan warmed. She pressed her hand over it, desperate to feel him. To hear him. Silencing all other thoughts, she closed her eyes.

"Tiernan."

For a moment there was nothing and then, *"I'm here, astora."*

Relief filled her, and an emotion she couldn't quite define seized her, left her trembling. She clutched her necklace and sent him all her emotions. Grief. Yearning. Love.

His rumbling voice slid into her mind through their bond. *"I'll get you back. I swear it."*

She gasped, longing for the one thing she couldn't have...him. *"I know."*

"I love you, Maeve."

"I love you, too."

Maeve sniffed, hastily wiping away a fallen tear. There would be no time to cry here. No time to panic. She had to find a way out of this place and back to Faeven. Parisa was still out there and if anything, Maeve had done nothing but piss her off even more. She had to get back. Tiernan needed her. The Four Courts needed her. With all the books in this library, certainly there had to be something useful, some bit of knowledge she could use to her advantage. But if not, she feared her only path of escape was through Aed.

A deal with the god of death would be a steep price, and Maeve could only hope she'd be able to pay it.

On the table beside her was a pile of books with well-read bindings and loose gold stitching. She picked up the one on top and flipped it open, skimming the contents. She froze, unable to believe what she was reading.

Diamarvh: The realm of the eternal warriors.

The one place the god of death had warned her away from was the home of the Wild Hunt. The home of the eternal warriors. The ones she intended to beseech in her efforts to rid the realms of Parisa.

Perhaps this library would prove beneficial after all.

Maeve settled in, preparing to read as much as she could, when a distinctive tinkling sound filled her ears. She looked up, confused. Her gaze shifted to the window, and she sat back, surprised to see tiny droplets of water cascading down the glass.

Rain.

Did it really rain in the Ether?

It had been so long since she'd seen or heard rain, she'd almost forgotten what it sounded like. The last time she could recall was when she was in Kells, hanging in a cage jutting out over the Cliffs of Morrigan.

Maeve shuddered, but her body didn't relax. Instead, tension crawled up her spine and a trigger of awareness prickled over her flesh. She was being watched.

Pretending to flip a page, she casually slid her Aurastone from its sheath. She turned another page; the sensation lingered. Her grip tightened around the hilt of the dagger, ready to fight. She didn't know the rules of Ether, but surely Aed would see fit to forgive her if she acted out of self-defense. Wandering souls or not, she would not hesitate to vanquish them if they attacked. Sucking in a breath, she jumped up from the chair, spinning, sending the book tumbling onto the floor.

Maeve's breath caught in her lungs, held tight. Her heart stopped beating completely. The weight of a gaze fell upon her from the shadows and a low baritone wrapped around her like midnight velvet.

"Hey, Princess."

Starysa

The *Amshir* glided through deep navy waters, maneuvering its sleek, curving frame around other ships twice its size, before docking in the dazzling harbor in the Ladova Bay. Aran Ruhdneah stood on the bow, taking in the glamorous port city. Late afternoon sunlight spilled over twisting spires that rose up from buildings, casting long, spindly shadows. Row after row of ivory stone townhouses and shops were crammed together on the cobblestone streets, their rustic red roofs sweeping upward in sharp angles. A gilded palace stood watch, overlooking the expanse of a place that was once foreign to him. Starysa, the capital of Prava, was the home of Oldrich Skye, ruler of the Imperial Korvny Fae. The Golden City, as it was coined, was also one of the last remaining cities in existence where mortals and immortals lived semi-peacefully.

This city, this realm, was nothing like home. It was a far cry from the magical ports of Faeven. Whereas the Four Courts were captured in a world of eternal seasons and lush landscapes, Prava was decadent, bursting with things Aran only thought he'd ever see in his dreams.

Being a Dorai once had its perks.

Aran glanced over at the fae standing beside him. Treasa's copper hair was pulled back into a low bun at the nape of her neck. She was lovely, with an angular jaw and high cheekbones. Tiny wisps of hair floated around her face on the breeze as she drank in the scene before them. She'd worked for him for a few months now, living onboard the *Amshir*, and their relationship was one of progressive friendship more than anything else. Some years ago, she'd been a member of the Autumn Court, pursued at least once by almost every male. Until Garvan came into power. Once the High Prince learned she fancied Shay, Garvan had taken to making her life a living hell. Aran found her standing upon the edge of the mountain cliffs overlooking the Gaelsong Sea, contemplating taking her own life.

He'd offered her safety and a new place to call home instead.

"I've never seen anything like it." The words slipped from between her lips on a breath.

"And you won't." Wooden planks unfolded from the *Amshir* toward the docks and he stepped onto them, inhaling the salty scent of the sea. "Not anywhere else in the world."

The port was fairly busy with crews unloading wares. The breath of autumn slowly approaching and the air already held a distinctive chill. It wouldn't be long before the sun sank into the horizon behind him. It had been some time since he'd visited Starysa, but if he kept a quick pace through the maze-like streets, he should be able to make it to Belladonna's before she closed up her shop for the evening.

"Don't wander too far from the ship, Treasa." Though Starysa was welcoming, not everyone was so kind.

She nodded, taking a few steps back, closer to safety.

"I won't be long." With that, Aran stepped onto the dock, and headed into the city.

Rolling, uneven cobblestone streets stretched out before him, each one bursting with ivory buildings and charming arched entrances. Dozens of windows decorated the stone fronts, outfitted with scrolling bronze balconies, and pots of summer's last flowers. Music poured from one of the local cafes, mingling with the sounds of passing conversation. Delicious scents of meat stew, freshly baked bread, and mouthwatering pastries surrounded him, causing his stomach to rumble.

He rounded a corner, tucking his hands into his pockets, marveling at how much Starysa had grown since the first time he visited. Usually he liked to stay in town for a few weeks and patron his favorite places—a few night clubs, the early morning market, and the opera house. But he was on a strict errand this trip and was anxious to return to Faeven. Especially since he'd finally be able to return home. To Autumn.

His fingers curled around the crystal device in his pocket. The rose quartz was cool to the touch against his skin. The thought that this mechanism had been used to extract some venomous dark magic was still unbelievable. He had no idea how Brynn discovered such a tool in Niahvess, or whether it was pure luck, but it had saved Maeve's life.

There was a sharp twist inside his gut. An uneasy sensation he couldn't quite place. It was harrowing and left him wondering if something more sinister was at work. Goosebumps pebbled across his skin, but he blamed it on the shadows of the setting sun cloaking the street.

Aran glanced up and Belladonna's Atelier came into view.

It was a quaint little shop with a white canopy and sun-catchers hanging in every window. The front display was filled with all of her creations. Everything from mirrors and baubles to jewelry and sculptures. All of them were handcrafted by her and her peculiar type of magic.

He strolled in and the little bell above the door tinkled, announcing his arrival. Immediately he was assaulted by the smell of jasmine oil, neroli, and sandalwood. It was a scent he recognized well.

"Can I help—"

His head snapped in the direction of the feminine voice.

There stood Belladonna, just a few feet away from him. As lovely and deadly as ever. He knew, because she stabbed him once.

While Starysa had changed, Belladonna had not. Her silvery blonde hair fell over one shoulder in a braid, twined with black silk ribbon. Icy blue eyes lined heavily with kohl stared back at him. She wore a skirt of burgundy that hit at the middle of her thighs and a cream-colored sweater fell off one shoulder, displaying her lightly tanned flesh. Silver bangles jingled from both of her wrists and three necklaces draped from her slender throat in varying lengths. She cocked her hip to one side.

"Aran." She crossed her arms and leveled him with a steely look. "It's been a long time."

"Too long, if you ask me."

Her deep red lips quirked. "I didn't."

He bit down on a grin. She was just as sarcastic as the last time he saw her. She was one of the only ones who could get away with speaking to him so brazenly. It was a quality of hers he'd come to admire.

There was a time when his travels as a Dorai took him to other continents but he never stayed for longer than a week. It didn't help that the company of a particular witch made him less inclined to set sail.

Images of her silky moonlit hair spilling across his pillows slammed into him and he pushed the memories of their time together out of his mind.

"What brings you back to Prava?" Belladonna fiddled with a fallen strand of hair that swept over her forehead, carefully tucking it behind her ear. Silver wolves with sapphires for eyes dangled from her lobes.

He held her gaze, keeping his face impassive. "I find myself in need of your assistance."

Her brows lifted and a taunting smile tugged at the corner of her mouth. "I told you last time, you're going to have to find someone else to warm your bed while you're in town. My hands are full."

At one time, her hands had indeed been full. Full of him. He remembered it clearly. The way she moved above and below him.

The way her soft palms coasted over him, like she was memorizing every inch of his skin. Those little sighs she would make whenever he'd trail a path of kisses between the valley of her breasts were a sound he would never forget.

He snuffed the fire of that particular memory out.

"Not that kind of help, Bella." Aran kept his voice low and took a step toward her. She took one step back. "This involves my sister."

"Your...your sister?" Her pale blue eyes widened with curiosity. "You never mentioned a sister."

He shifted, letting his shoulders rise and fall. "Up until recently, I was unaware she existed."

"Oh." Something flickered across her face. An emotion he couldn't place. "What is it you need help with?"

Aran pulled the siphoning device from his pocket and held it out to her. "I need more of these."

She reached out, taking it from him. Her fingers roved over the swirled rose quartz, tracing the delicate lines all the way to the rainbow moonstone tip. "I haven't seen this in years. Not since..."

The unsaid words seemed to die away.

"Not since when?" Aran prodded, noticing the way a slight frown furrowed across her brow. A hollowed out sadness stole the light from her eyes.

"Not since my mother died."

"I'm sorry." It was a gutting pain he understood all too well. The grief of losing his mother was familiar, the devastating loss was something he'd never quite been able to move past. Guilt cloaked him. He shouldn't have brought up such an unpleasant memory.

"You couldn't have known." Her gaze drifted to the wall of jewelry and other trinkets beside them. "It was years ago."

"How many?"

She looked at him and her voice was eerily quiet when she said, "Two hundred and three."

He quickly did the math in his head and locked his jaw to keep his mouth from falling open. "Your mother died during The Harvesting?"

It was a dark time that predated the Evernight War, when witches were rounded up, enslaved, and used for their magical abilities. He had no idea witches could age so...gracefully. "How old are you?"

"Aran." She clutched one hand to her chest in feigned shock. "That's an incredibly rude question to ask a lady."

"Apologies, Bella." He offered her his best smile. "I meant no offense."

She answered him with a smirk of her own and it left him wondering if she was older than she let on.

She lifted the gemstone tool so it caught the light, twinkling in her hand like a star. "Do you know what this is?"

"A device of some kind, used to withdraw magic." How though, he wasn't entirely sure.

"Venomous magic," Belladonna confirmed.

"So I've heard."

She arched a brow in question. "You've had to use it?"

"Not me, personally. But a very talented healer." He would be in Brynn's debt eternally, whether she knew it or not. "My sister was attacked and the blade used against her was laced with venom meant to leave her incapacitated. This tool saved her life."

Belladonna nodded. "She's one of the fortunate ones. Others have not been so lucky."

A wave of unease settled over Aran's shoulders and his spine tensed, locking into place like lead. "This has happened recently?"

She moved closer and the tempting scent of her filled him. "There's rumors the gods of old have returned." She stole a glance to the door then back to him, and she dropped her voice to a whisper. "It's happening again."

Now Aran bent down, closing the distance between them. "You mean the disappearances?"

"Yes." She was almost breathless.

In all the histories of the realm, there had only ever been one time he could recall when immortal souls started disappearing, and it happened when the Ancient Ones sought vengeance against those who had grown too independent.

He watched her, his gaze betraying him when it dipped down to her mouth. He swallowed. Hard. "I see."

Belladonna looked down at the siphoning device cradled in her palm. "How many do you need?"

Aran found himself grateful for the distraction. He couldn't allow his mind to wander into dangerous territory, and anything regarding Belladonna was dangerous. "As many as you can spare."

She pressed her lips together. "Are things in Faeven as horrible as I imagine?"

He considered the Four Courts. He'd been a Dorai for so long, all he heard about his homeland were stories told from the outside. There was no way to discern an embellished truth from a fabricated lie. Often he overheard tales on a street corner, or if he was passing through some insignificant port city. The rumors drifted past him on the seas, but they were as wild as the wind. Impossible to collect and tricky to navigate.

"Things are...strained." It was as much truth as he could give her. Dread coiled its vise-like fingers around his throat and though he tried, he couldn't seem to shake its chilling grip.

"I see." She blew out a breath. "And how soon?"

"The end of the week."

"That's a large ask, my lord." Belladonna studied him, a ghost of a smile playing along her mouth. "Your trust in my abilities is flattering."

"I trust you not to fail me." Aran pulled the bag of gold coins given to him from Tiernan from his cloak and handed it to her. "This should cover it."

"Yes." She blinked at the large sum weighing down her hand. "I suppose so."

Aran inclined his head, knowing it was time to take his leave. "I'll see you at week's end."

Another flicker of emotion splintered her lovely features. Though this one resembled hurt more than anything else. "Okay. Week's end it is."

With that, he turned on his heel and left Belladonna's Atelier, forcing himself not to glance back at the woman whose wintry eyes were tracking his every movement. The bell jingled at his departure and he headed down the cobblestone street, back to the docks.

At some point during their relationship, he'd wanted more. A life with her. A future. But she was a witch and he was fae—it would never work. Their worlds, their lives even, were simply too different.

He was trying to think of a way to distract himself from thinking about Belladonna, when a wall of apprehension stopped him in his tracks. Anguish tore through him, caused his chest to ache and burn like he was on fire. Tiny beads of sweat formed on his forehead and the hairs along the back of his neck prickled. For a fleeting moment, he worried Belladonna had cursed him, or spelled him somehow.

But no. She would never.

Stab him, yes. Curse him? Not in this lifetime or the next.

Another wrenching ache seized him and he nearly doubled over. The sun was already well into its western descent, and so he ducked into an alley to avoid being stalked by any meandering street urchins who might see him as easy prey.

Backed against a cold stone wall, he ripped open his shirt and glanced down. There was nothing. No mark or cut. No redness or swelling. Not even a Strand.

What the hell was happening?

The agony swelled. It felt like...death.

His breath caught in his lungs. His heart squeezed, the torment almost too much to bear.

"No." The harsh whisper of his voice scraped against his ears.

He clutched his chest as a wave of terror drowned him. Sweat soaked his clothing so the fabric clung to his skin. Terror twisted its way through him, ensnaring him with its sharpened talons. Panic bubbled up in the back of his throat, but there was no one there to witness his raw, pained agony.

Aran slumped against the stone wall of the shadowed side street while life in Starysa carried on around him, as the bond tying him to his youngest brother Shay pulled taut.

Then snapped completely.

Acknowledgments

All good things to those who wait.

If you read that in the voice of Mother Gothel from Tangled, then we're already best friends. But in all seriousness, this book took an effort of patience. Which I will be the first to admit, is not one of my finer virtues. Even though the past year was filled with learning curves, major life lessons, and a few tears, I'm so pleased with the story Throne of Dreams has become.

First and foremost, I want to thank my alpha reader, Whitney, for being there for every up and down of this story. Your energy and excitement kept me going. To my wonderful beta readers—Chelsea, Angie, Kristin, Joelle, Nicole, Rietta, and Becca—thank you so much for your comments and gentle criticisms...and for not making me cry. To my lovely editor, Emily Michel, for making Throne of Dreams shine in the best way possible. And to Elayna Maratta, my darling. Your skills just continue to bloom and grow. Thank you for the gorgeous daggers featured on the hardcover of Throne of Dreams. I can't wait to keep working with you!

I should probably thank my publisher, but alas, that's me. So, job well done. To Bree, my forever Hype Girl, and all the wonderful ladies who make up the Hype Girl crew.

Rietta, thank you for being there every step of the way. Thank you for helping me through every up and down of this crazy journey.

Nicole, thank you for listening to everything. The random thoughts. The crazy snaps. All of the what ifs...Throne of Dreams wouldn't be what it is without you. Emilia, thank you for talking shop with me, giving me the greatest kind of tough love, and for helping me figure out how to wrench out my readers' hearts in the best way possible.

To Momma Chaos and my found family—you helped me survive. In more ways than one.

For my adoring patrons, Joella, Kellie, and Alex, thank you for your constant support.

For my parents and family, who've cheered me on from the sidelines. Thank you for always being there for me. Nate, thank you for being my constant anchor and for keeping me grounded whenever my head is in the clouds. To my girls, Lobug and Breezy, thank you for being willing to survive off of mac and cheese and chicken nuggets while I was on deadline.

And lastly, to my readers. I wrote this story for you. I hope it inspires you to draw, paint, create, and never give up on your dreams.

About the Author

Hillary Raymer is a fantasy romance author. She's a wanderer, a storyteller, and the founder of BohoSoul Press.

Hillary has always been a dreamer, and lucky for her, she turned those dreams into stories. She has an unfinished Bachelor's Degree in English because she ran off and married a Marine halfway through college. She has an affinity toward plants, loves the mountains, and enjoys scoping out metaphysical markets for crystals. Wanderlust comes to her naturally, and she's doing her best to instill the same wild and free values in her daughters. When not writing, Hillary can be found attempting to do yoga, buying more makeup she doesn't need, or discovering small businesses on Etsy.